John Selby Watson

The Life of Richard Porson

Professor of Greek in the University of Cambridge from 1792 to 1808

John Selby Watson

The Life of Richard Porson
Professor of Greek in the University of Cambridge from 1792 to 1808

ISBN/EAN: 9783337729561

Printed in Europe, USA, Canada, Australia, Japan

Cover: Foto ©Raphael Reischuk / pixelio.de

More available books at **www.hansebooks.com**

THE LIFE

OF

RICHARD PORSON, M.A.

SOR OF GREEK IN THE UNIVERSITY OF CAMBRIDGE

FROM 1792 TO 1808

BY THE

REV. JOHN SELBY WATSON, M.A., M.R.S.L.

Fluctibus è mediis terras dabit ille magistro,
Et dabit astra rati ; cùmque æthera Jupiter umbrâ
Perdiderit, solus transibit nubila Lynceus   *Valerius Flaccus*

LONDON

LONGMAN, GREEN, LONGMAN, AND ROBERTS

1861

PREFACE.

It may seem strange that so eminent a scholar and critic as Richard Porson, a man whom not only his countrymen, but the whole learned world, acknowledge to have been at the head of his department in literature, should have been honoured with no complete biography. Various notices of him were published about the time of his death, and anecdotes and short accounts of him have occasionally appeared since, but no full history of his life has ever been offered to the public.

The object contemplated by the writer of the following pages has been to throw into some kind of order the several particulars concerning Porson which have hitherto been suffered, for the most part, to lie scattered and unconnected, and to combine with them any additional information regarding him that might be discoverable. With this view no available source of intelligence has been neglected. The Porson manuscripts at Cambridge have been carefully consulted, and several letters extracted from them which have never before been published. Applications, also, for information, have been made to Porson's surviving connexions, and to all from whom it seemed likely that it might be obtained.

From Mr. Siday Hawes, Porson's only surviving nephew, I have received several acceptable communications, containing replies to every point on which I have desired to be instructed.

The kindness of the Archdeacon of Colchester, Dr. Charles Parr Burney, the son of Porson's intimate friend, has enabled me to give, from his father's papers, a nearly complete list of the subscribers to the fund for Porson's annuity, and has supplied me with some letters and anecdotes relating to the learned professor.

To the Rev. H. R. Luard, Fellow of Trinity College, Cambridge, author of a memoir of Porson in the "Cambridge Essays" for 1857, who has collected numerous documents, in print and manuscript, concerning Porson, and who has arranged, with praiseworthy care and judgment, the great scholar's manuscripts in Trinity College Library, my sincere thanks are due for many obliging answers to inquiries, and for permission to inspect his Porsonian treasures, especially a body of manuscript memoranda of Mr. Edmund Henry Barker, not included in the assemblage of heterogeneous fragments called "Barker's Literary Anecdotes." To Barker, it may be observed, every one who writes of Porson must be in some degree indebted, for though he had little judgment to combine or arrange, he had great industry in collecting and laying up stores by which others might profit.

The facilities afforded me by the Rev. J. Glover, the Librarian of Trinity College, Cambridge, in consulting the manuscripts under his charge, deserve my best acknowledgments.

To the gentlemen whose names are subjoined, also, I desire to offer my thanks for obliging communications or references regarding the subject of my biography: The Rev. Joseph Thackeray, Rector of Coltishall and Horstead, Norfolk; the Rev. J. W. Flavell, Rector of Ridlington and East Ruston, Norfolk; the Rev J. C. Wright, Vicar of Bacton, Norfolk; the Rev. John Gunn, Rector of Irstead, Norfolk; the Rev. Edward Hibgame, Vicar of Fordham, Cambridge; T. L'Estrange Ewen, Esq., Dedham, Essex; the Rev. R. B. P. Kidd, Vicar of Potter Heigham, Norfolk; the Rev. P. C. Kidd, Vicar of Skipton, Yorkshire; the Rev. C. W. Whiter, Rector of Clown, Derbyshire; the Rev. T. J. Blofeld, Vicar of Hoveton, Norfolk; Robert Postle, Esq., Kimberley Terrace, Yarmouth.

My information concerning the authorship of Gregory Blunt's Letters, I owe to James Yates, Esq., Lauderdale House, Highgate.

Dates, in the following narrative, are carefully given, as well as references to authorities wherever they appeared necessary; and nothing is stated, whether authorities are given or not, for which the author did not consider that he had sufficient warrant.

The life of such a scholar could hardly be written without exhibiting in its pages some portions of Latin and Greek; but moderation, in this respect, has been studied; and it is hoped that the book is of such a nature on the whole as to be no unacceptable offering to the literary world in general.

The notice of the Travisian controversy may appear somewhat long; but many readers might justly complain if, in the life of the great champion in the contest, they were to find no satisfactory account of the dispute. For the episode on Ireland's Shakspearian forgeries some apology is offered at the part where it is introduced.

The plural *we*, which is used in some passages, might seem to indicate that there are more authors of the work than one; but it is to be understood that for all faults in the narration I only am responsible.

J. S. W.

STOCKWELL :
April, 1861.

CONTENTS.

CHAP. XVII.

CHAP. XVIII.

CHAP. XIX.

CHAP. XX.

CHAP. XXI.

CHAP. XXII.

CHAP. XXIII.

CHAP. XXIV.

APPENDIX.

LIST OF ILLUSTRATIONS.

ERRATA.

THE LIFE

OF

RICHARD PORSON.

CHAPTER I.

REMARKS ON BIOGRAPHY. — ITS ATTRACTIONS. — CONSIDERATIONS ON IN-
TELLECTUAL EXCELLENCE. — BIRTH OF PORSON. — CHARACTER OF HIS
PARENTS. — HIS EDUCATION BY HIS FATHER, AND AT A VILLAGE
SCHOOL. — HIS MANIFESTATIONS OF TALENT, AND FONDNESS FOR
READING. — SPECIMEN OF HIS EARLY ATTEMPTS IN POETRY. — HIS
ABILITIES BECOME KNOWN TO MR. HEWITT AND MR. NORRIS. — HE IS
SENT TO CAMBRIDGE TO BE EXAMINED BY THE GREEK PROFESSOR AND
OTHERS. — THEIR REPORT OF HIM. — MR. NORRIS RESOLVES TO RAISE
A FUND FOR HIS EDUCATION. — IT IS PROPOSED TO PLACE HIM AT
THE CHARTERHOUSE, BUT HE IS EVENTUALLY SENT TO ETON.

THE charms of fiction are much less forcible than those
of truth. Histories of imaginary personages, however
strikingly represented, are much less interesting than
those of eminent characters that really existed. The
man who read Robinson Crusoe as a true tale found
much fewer attractions in it when he was told that it
was an invention.

The desire to know how our fellow-creatures, especially the most distinguished of them, have lived, is
the cause that biography gains so much attention.

B

Whoever relates the life, or any considerable portion of the life, of any remarkable person, has the satisfaction of expecting that his narrative, unless given in an absolutely repulsive style, will attract some share of regard.

But the pleasure which the biographer thus derives from his occupation is often somewhat diminished by the consciousness that, to satisfy those who seek his pages, he must tell the whole truth concerning the person of whom he writes, and that much of the truth cannot always be told without reluctance. No human character is perfect; and those who speak of the best of men have frequently to notice in them errors and deficiencies which they cannot but lament. Yet, unless the biographer offers a mere apology for a life, or produces a simple éloge after the fashion of the French, he must tell alike the evil and the good, and must adhere to the maxim, *ne quid falsi dicere audeat, ne quid veri non audeat;* he must, while he asserts nothing that is false, admit everything that is true; he must set forth whatever tends justly and fully to characterise the subject of his narrative.

The higher that subject rises in intellectual excellence, or in any particular department of it, the greater will sometimes be the failings or irregularities that the writer of his life will have to disclose. "Nature, apparently," said Styan Thirlby, as we are told by Mr. Nichols, in his "Literary Anecdotes," "intended a kind of parity among her sons; but sometimes she deviates a little from her general purpose, and sends into the world a man of powers superior to the rest, of quicker intuition and wider comprehension; this man has all other men for his enemies, and would not be suffered to live his natural time, but that his excellences are balanced by his failings. He that by intellectual exaltation thus towers above his contemporaries, is drunken, or lazy, or capricious; or, by some defect or other, is hindered from exerting his sovereignty of mind; he is thus kept upon the level, and thus preserved from the destruction which would be the natural consequence of universal hatred."

Whether the mass of mankind would ever rise to destroy a fellow-creature possessed of unrivalled intellectual powers, may be doubted; for it might be expected that such a being would act so as to secure the approbation and esteem of at least a majority of those around him; but it is certain that men distinguished by eminent mental abilities are often drawn down, whether by the influence of others, or by their own imprudence and misconduct, to a condition far below that of many others who are too much their inferiors in mind to be able even to estimate their merits. It is not necessary to recur to the lives of Edmund Smith, or Samuel Boyse, or Edgar Poe, for examples of such degradation; for almost every man, whether high or low, whether of little education or of much, has seen something of the kind among his own connexions or acquaintance. Those who contemplate the lives and fortunes of mankind, too often, as they increase their knowledge, increase their sorrow. If they discover great merits in eminent characters, they find them, perhaps, the more they search, obscured by such defects as they could at one time have scarcely imagined. They find gold, but gold mingled with clay.

It might seem, indeed, that superior qualities of any kind are often bestowed upon their possessors only to their harm.   Intellectual greatness is envied ; the possessors of it are frequently denied, or unwillingly allowed, any other merit ; and the virtues of independence of spirit, integrity, and honourable ambition, appear, in many cases, to obstruct the worldly progress of those who possess them in a high degree, while those who have but a small, or inconsiderable portion of them, make their way easily in the world, and rise unimpeded to offices of profit and distinction.   Even if we look only to peace and quiet of life, it might seem that the less highly endowed have the advantage. It might seem that honour, with its frequent attendant disquiet, is ill gained by the sacrifice of tranquillity and ease.   It might seem that those who are content to pursue the humble path of life, who feel and acknowledge the inferiority of their mental endowments, who seek no high position, and court no public applause, but who are satisfied to float along the stream of existence without trouble or exertion, pass their days far more happily than those who are incited from within to pursue honour and renown.   It might be questioned whether he who remarked the antipathy of *quick bosoms to quiet*, had, in reality, more enjoyment of his existence than the tradesman who passes his forty or fifty years in sluggish quietude, who has no higher ambition than to pay his way, and who seeks no greater gratification than that of eating and drinking, or the leisure of a few days, which he knows not how to turn to account.   If it be said that the higher mind has the advantage in variety of thought, and frequently of action, it may be questioned whether the course of life which resembles the smoothly-flowing river, is not preferable to that which may be compared to the swiftly-rushing flood, agitated and broken with rocks, trunks of trees, and other obstacles.

The man whose life we propose to relate was eminently distinguished for tenacity of memory, quickness of perspicacity, and accuracy of judgment; and we shall see how much these qualities appear to have contributed to his comfort.

RICHARD PORSON was born at the village of East Ruston, near North Walsham, in Norfolk, on Christmas Day 1759. His father, Huggin Porson, was a weaver, and clerk of the parish. Anne, his mother, was the daughter of Thomas Palmer, a shoemaker, of the neighbouring parish of Bacton. He was the second of a family of four, the others being a sister, the eldest, and two brothers, all possessed of considerable ability. Neither of his parents had had any education, beyond what might be gained at a village school; but his father was a man of great sense and strong memory, and appears to have attained a considerable knowledge of arithmetic, for he taught his son, while he was yet a child, to work sums in the common rules of arithmetic by memory only; and before he was nine years old enabled him, with the aid of an old book on arithmetic, to extract the cube root in that way. Being of a steady and sedate character, he bred up all his children in habits of frugality and order. His mother had a taste, limited as was her education, for poetry, and was familiar with the plays of Shakspeare, of which she could repeat many of the more popular and striking passages; an accomplishment which she had gained by having had access to the library of the vicar, Mr. Hewitt, where she had been at service. He surprised her, one day, reading Congreve's "Mourning Bride," and finding, on questioning her, that she understood what she read, kindly gave her permission to read any book in his library. She is also said to have been of a gay and lively temper, such as cheered and relieved the gravity and seriousness of her husband. Porson himself always spoke highly of her.

His father taught him to write at the same time that he taught him to read. He traced the form of a letter with chalk on a board, or with a stick in sand, and the child was made at once to remember the figure, and to imitate it. Thus he was enabled to form letters almost as soon as he could speak, and grew so fond of the occupation, that he was ready to cover every surface within his reach with characters, which he delineated with great neatness and accuracy.*

He was not, however, confined till the age of nine to his father's tuition, for he was sent when he was but six years old to the village school of Bacton, kept by a man named Woodrow, who had also an appointment under the Excise Office, and who may consequently be supposed to have been a fair arithmetician. Woodrow used to speak with admiration of the proofs of ability which Porson's childhood manifested. Porson is said to have remained, however, only three or four months with this teacher, as, being but weak and tender, he suffered greatly from the rudeness of the bigger boys.

* Gent. Mag. Oct. 1808.

His health had been affected at the age of four by the hooping-cough, and he is said to have been, even from infancy, a bad sleeper.

Whatever he did, even as a child, he appears to have been anxious to do well. His mother often employed him in spinning, and he would always produce, from the same quantity of wool, more yarn, and of a better quality, than his sister or his brothers. While he was spinning, he kept a book open before him, in which he read, as well as he could, during his occupation.

In his ninth year he was put to another school, in the adjoining parish of Happisburgh, of a rather better character, the master of which, Mr. Summers, was able to ground him in Latin. When Porson first went to this place of instruction, he wrote with a pen but imperfectly; but in three months he became the best writer in the school, and in six months is said to have known as much of arithmetic as his master. He very early fixed his thoughts on the structure of language, and when he had once learned the English grammar he was never known to make a grammatical error; nor did he ever seem to forget what he had once read. His love of algebra he caught from a book on the science at his father's; and he was greatly attracted by logarithms. In studying Euclid with Mr. Summers, he did not proceed with the same deliberation as his schoolfellows, but everything seemed to come into his mind by intuition. "On his daily return to school," said Mr. Summers, "it was evident that he had been thinking, when he was not asleep, of his studies; for he generally came armed with some algebraic or mathematical problem solved in his own way:" a process which he adopted, to Mr. Summers's admiration, with the forty-seventh proposition of Euclid's first book. "His temper," Mr. Summers used to say, "was quiet .and sedate; he was reckoned unsocial among his school-fellows, because out of school hours he preferred his book to joining with them in their play;" though he is reported to have excelled at marbles and trap-ball.*

His father still contributed to his improvement as much as he could; he obliged him to repeat at home every evening all the English lessons that he had learned at school during the day, requiring him to say them, not in a lax and desultory manner, but with the same exactness and in the same order as they had been learned. The boy profited wonderfully under this discipline, and while the tenacity of his memory was increased, began to show great force and comprehension of intellect, and an extraordinary inclination for reading all kinds of books.† But to gratify this propensity he had to borrow from the neighbours, for his father's shelf contained but very few volumes, the chief of which were Jewell's " Apology," Greenwood's " England," some books of arithmetic, eight or ten volumes of the " Universal Magazine," and an odd volume of " Chambers's Cyclopædia."‡

It was not to be expected that the clerk would notice such remarkable abilities in his son without

---

* Letter of The Rev. W. Gunn to Dawson Turner; Barker's Parriana, vol. ii. p. 734.

† Gent. Mag. Oct. 1808.

‡ Rev. H. R. Luard, Cambridge Essays, 1857.

speaking of him to the clergyman. The Rev. Charles Hewitt, curate of the united parishes of Bacton and East Ruston, being a man of much kindness, and being engaged in educating his own family, offered, on finding that the father had made no exaggerated representation of the boy's capacity, to take him under his care, and to give him instruction gratuitously with his own sons. This offer the clerk was but too happy to accept, and accordingly, after young Porson had been with Mr. Summers three years, he came under the tuition of Mr. Hewitt, by whom he was instructed, to some considerable extent, in Latin, and with whom he continued also about three years. As Mr. Hewitt's residence was four miles from East Ruston, the boy used to trudge thither every Monday morning, with a stock of some kind of humble provision for the week, which he spent at the vicarage, and returned to his father's on Saturday afternoon.

He seems to have shown some inclination to composition at this period, but not much. "Proofs of a serious turn of thought in his early years are still extant," says Mr. Kidd; "they are in the shape of hymns and grave reflections, but in no respect remarkable except in tracing out the adorable nature of the First Cause."

We have made inquiry for some of these pieces, and have been presented by Mr. Siday Hawes, the son of Porson's sister, now residing at Hayes, near Horsham, with the only copy in his possession, written when Porson was about twelve years old. The handwriting is beautiful as copper-plate.

On a Moonlight Night.

Who can the beauties of the night describe,
When the bright moon, and all the starry tribe,
Emit their splendor, and, when day is gone.
Those brilliant orbs succeed it one by one ?
Who can consider this but for an hour,
And not b' astonish'd at th' Almighty pow'r ?
With how much regularity they're made,
And with such beauty as will never fade !
Then cease, proud man, thy own vain works to prize ;
Consider what is placed in the skies :
If thou thy study unto this should'st turn,
A lesson of humility thou'dst learn.

R. Porson excogitavit, Anno Domini Jes. 1771.

These lines, proceeding from a boy of that age, of no great reading, indicate some, if not very much, power of thought, and certainly show an ear for the Popian couplet.

At nine years of age he had written some verses on the loss of the Peggy, a seventy-four gun ship, lost off Happisburgh in 1768. When Mr. Hewitt gave him a fable of Phædrus to translate into prose, he would sometimes, in preference, turn it into verse.

Mr. Hewitt seems to have had many good qualifications for the office of an instructor. He succeeded in educating, on an income, from three small charges, not exceeding two hundred pounds a year, five sons for the university, four of whom became fellows of their respective colleges, and the fifth was expected to obtain a fellowship, but died soon after he had taken his degree.* To effect so much with such small means, it

---

* Letter of The Rev. W. Gunn to Dawson Turner; Barker's Parriana, vol. ii. p. 736.

may well be supposed that Mr. Hewitt was very economical, and it is yet related, among the people of that neighbourhood, that he has been seen roasting a turnip, like Curius Dentatus, for his supper, and rocking a cradle and reading a book at the same time.

Being desirous to advance young Porson in life, Mr. Hewitt spoke of him in high terms to Mr. Norris, a wealthy and benevolent gentleman of Witton Park, in an adjoining parish, who afterwards founded the Norrisian Professorship of Divinity at Cambridge. Mr. Norris expressed his willingness to assist the boy, if his abilities should be found correspondent to Mr. Hewitt's representations, and requested a friend of his, the Rev. Thomas Carthew, incumbent of Woodbridge in Suffolk, to examine him. Mr. Carthew, not being a regularly bred scholar, as he was some years a solicitor before he took orders, declined to undertake the responsibility of pronouncing on Porson's merits, but being acquainted with the Rev. James Lambert, who had been recently appointed Greek professor at Cambridge, asked him to make a thorough investigation of the boy's qualifications. Lambert assented, with conditional offers of further service, and Carthew, in acknowledgment, wrote him a very sensible letter, which well deserves to be made public.

Woodbridge, Feb. 26th, 1773.

"Dear Sir,

"Your interesting yourself so kindly on behalf of the poor lad whose genius you heard me commend, is not only an act of benevolence towards him, but also a very obliging civility to me, and as such I shall ever acknowledge it.

"Immediately on the receipt of your letter I wrote to the lad's friends, and last night I received an answer from my friend Mr. Norris, wherein he expresses his sense of the generosity of your conduct, and directs me to inform you that, after full consideration, he has judged it expedient to send the boy immediately to Cambridge, in order that his abilities may be put to the test *by the Professor himself*, for, he observes, that these luminaries, like the phenomena in the sky, very often shine only just long enough to excite attention and surprise, and then drop at once into obscurity. If, on examination, his genius shall be found by you to be answerable to those high presages which the partiality of his present instructor has conceived of him, so as to be worthy of a successful recommendation to the Charterhouse, Mr. Norris will be responsible for his expenses there; but if you should think his talents have been overrated, which is not improbable, as his poverty and mean birth may have encouraged a favourable prejudice, Mr. Norris *will then direct his kindness towards him on a more humble plan, and more suitable to his rank.*

"I apprehend the lad will be with you nearly as soon as this letter.

"I am, dear Sir, with all possible esteem and respect,
"Your most obedient servant,
"THOMAS CARTHEW."

P.S. "You will find the lad rather an unwinning cub than otherwise, but you will, I doubt not, make allowance for the awkwardness of his manners."

About the same time Mr. Hewitt wrote to Lambert, relating what Porson had read with him while under his tuition.

"SIR,
        *   *   *   *   *

"As I have had the orderly and good boy under my care for almost two years, I think it proper to tell you how he has been employed during that time. He had read some of Corderius' 'Colloquies' when he first came, and having two little boys of my own who were reading Erasmus, I put him to them, the greatest part of whose ' Colloquies ' they read together, and translated into English, *which last task the boy performed in about half the time they could.* I ordered him to lay by his Erasmus, and endeavour to turn his English into Latin, which he did so accurately that he varied but little from his author either in order or words. He is now doing the same by Cæsar's ' Commentaries.' When he first began Ovid, I expected some little trouble in teaching him to scan, but, to my great surprise, found none, and I do not remember that he ever read six lines false as to quantity through his whole ' Metamorphoses.' He has read all Terence, the ' Eclogues,' and ' Georgics ' of Virgil, and is got into the ' Æneid.'

"Perhaps you may wonder that I have said nothing of Greek hitherto, but my method (perhaps a wrong one) is to have lads pretty well versed in Latin first, and, as my own boys are by no means equal to him, I was obliged to defer it the longer. I have not time to attend to the boy by himself, otherwise I doubt not but he might have made a considerable progress in that language. *What I do for him is gratis,* otherwise I should think myself guilty of injustice. They are now getting the Greek verbs, and will begin the Greek Testament shortly. This boy and one of my own generally employ an hour or two every day in mathematics, in which science Porson had made such proficiency before he came to me as to be able to solve questions out of the ' Ladies' Diary,' to the great astonishment of a very able mathematician in these parts. To say anything more about the lad is needless, as you will try him yourself, and I heartily wish you may find him worthy of your recommendation, and your success herein will be a great pleasure and satisfaction to,

"Sir, your most obedient and very humble servant,
"T. HEWITT,
"Of Bacton, near North Walsham, Norfolk."

Before this letter was written, a translation of a stanza of Beattie's " Minstrel," done by Porson, had been sent to Lambert, as an indication of what might be expected from him with further cultivation.

Lambert, being unwilling to take the whole weight of the affair on himself, called to his assistance Mr. Postlethwaite and Mr. Collier, head tutors of Trinity College, and Mr. Attwood, assistant tutor, esteemed an eminent mathematician. Each of these three gentlemen testified strongly to Porson's abilities, and Lambert transmitted their reports, through Mr. Carthew, to Mr. Norris. The whole account of the circumstances attendant on this examination of Porson, is recorded in a paper in Lambert's handwriting, preserved, with Hewitt and Carthew's letters, in the library of Trinity College, Cambridge. The paper was written to confute a notion of Beloe's, that Porson's journey to Cambridge at this time, though often mentioned by his family, had in reality never taken place, as it was utterly improbable that a mere boy would be sent to be examined by a Greek professor. Lambert concludes the document thus: "Porson returned home; but how long he remained under Mr. Hewitt's charge, by what means his patronage became afterwards so extensive, or in what manner he accumulated that stupendous mass of knowledge in a language of which in the beginning of 1773 he was only studying the verbs, I cannot say." Lambert ceased to reside in college soon after, and heard nothing more of Porson till he had grown up and become distinguished.

He continued under Mr. Hewitt's tuition for something more than another year, during which time he seems to have advanced into Livy, Cicero, and Horace, and to have read some portion of Homer.

It being determined to send him to the Charterhouse, Lambert kindly introduced him to the Marquis
of Granby, who was then an undergraduate of the
college, and who immediately wrote to the Duke of
Rutland and the Earl of Mansfield, to engage their interest for him at that seminary, of which they were
governors. But their nominations for the next vacancy
had been long pre-engaged, and some other plan of
education was to be sought for him.

Mr. Norris still held to his resolution of serving him,
and determined on raising a fund, by contributing
largely himself, and by procuring such subscriptions
as he could, for educating him at a first-rate school, and
for afterwards maintaining him at the University. This
scheme succeeded beyond Mr. Norris's expectations, for
many persons of eminence interested themselves about
a youth of such ability, and gave liberal donations.
Among the contributors were Bishop Bagot, another
bishop whose name is now unknown, Sir George Baker,
Dr. Poynter, Dr. Hammond, a prebendary of Norwich,
and Mrs. Mary Turner, a grand-daughter of Sir George
Turner, and relative of Mr. Norris. This lady took a
great liking to Porson, paid him constant attention, and
gave him permission, when he should return from
school for the holidays, to pass them at her house.

The treasurer of the fund was Sir George Baker,
then president of the College of Physicians, and eminently distinguished for his learning and classical taste.
It was perhaps by his recommendation that the school
chosen for Porson was that of Eton, at which he was
entered in the month of August 1774, when he was in
his fifteenth year.

CHAP. II.

OF Porson's career at Eton we have no detailed account, but we may gather some information about it from the various notices of him. Two sources from which we learn something of it are Beloe's "Sexagenarian," and a paper in the "Gentleman's Magazine" for October 1808. "In that great seminary," says the writer in the Magazine, " he almost from the commencement of his career displayed such a superiority of intellect, such facility of acquirement, such quickness of perception, and such a talent of bringing forward to his purpose all that he had ever read, that the upper boys took him into their society, and promoted the cultivation of his mind by their lessons, as well, probably, as imposing upon him the performance of their own exercises. He was courted by them as the never-failing resource in every difficulty; and in all the playful excursions of the imagination, in their frolics as well as in their serious tasks, Porson was their constant adviser and support. He used to dwell on this lively part of his youth with peculiar complacency; and we have heard him repeat a drama which he wrote for exhibition in their long chamber, and other compositions, both of seriousness and drollery, with a zest that the recollection of his enjoyment at the time never failed to revive in him."

Beloe says that he wrote two dramatic pieces, and acted in them himself; but that nothing more is remembered of them than that the one, which was entitled "Out of the Frying-pan into the Fire," was more ingenious and elaborate than the other, which was founded on some petty affair that occurred in the school. In other respects Beloe's account differs from that of the other writer. Many of Porson's schoolfellows at Eton, he observes, were living at the time that "The Sexagenarian" was written, who all declare, without variation, that when Porson went to Eton he was not particularly distinguished above other boys either for knowledge or disposition to acquire it.

Dr. Goodall, when Provost of Eton, being called upon, after Porson's death, to give evidence on the state of education in the country, before a Committee of the House of Commons, and being asked, among other questions, "if he was acquainted with what had happened to the late Professor Porson, to prevent his election to King's College," made the following statement:—

"'Every account that I have read about him, in relation to that circumstance, is incorrect. When he came to the school he was placed rather higher, by the reputation of his abilities, than perhaps he ought to have been in consequence of his actual attainments. With respect to prosody, he knew but little; and as to Greek he had made comparatively but little progress when he came to Eton. The very ingenious and learned editor of one account of him has been misinformed in most particulars; and many of the incidents which he relates, I can venture from my own knowledge to assert, are distorted or exaggerated. Even Porson's compositions, at an early period, though eminently correct, fell far short of excellence; still we all looked up to him in consequence of his great abilities and variety of information, though much of that information was confined to the knowledge of his schoolfellows, and could not easily fall under the notice of his instructors. He always undervalued school exercises, and generally wrote his exercises fair at once, without study. I should be sorry to detract from the merit of an individual whom I loved, esteemed, and admired; but I speak of him when he had only given the promise of his future excellence; and, in point of school exercises, I think he was very inferior to more than one of his contemporaries: I would name the present Marquis Wellesley as infinitely superior to him in composition.'

" On being asked whether he wrote the same beautiful hand as he did afterwards, Dr. Goodall replied he did, nor was there any doubt of his general scholarship.

" To a question whether he made great progress during the time he was at Eton, or after he left, Dr. Goodall said he was advanced as far as he could be with propriety, but there were certainly some there who would not have been afraid to challenge Porson as a schoolboy, though they would have shunned all idea of competition with him at Cambridge. The first book that Porson ever studied, as he often told me, was ' Chambers's Cyclopædia; ' he read the whole of that dictionary through, and in a great degree made himself master of the algebraic part of that work entirely by the force of his understanding.

" Dr. Goodall was then asked if he considered there was any ground for complaint on the part of Porson in not having been sent to Cambridge; to which he answered, ' No; he was placed as high in the school as he well could be: as a proof, however, of his merits, when he left Eton contributions were readily supplied by Etonians in aid of Sir George Baker's proposal to secure the funds for his maintenance at the University.' "

Another account says that Dr. Goodall remarked that Porson, as a boy, showed but little taste in his compositions, and was fond of mixing, especially in his verses, Greek with Latin, as "*Ingemuere* πόθοι."

According to the "Short Account of Porson," he himself used to say that he added little to his acquirements at Eton except facility in Latin versification, as he had read with Mr. Hewitt, before he went thither, almost all that was required from him in the school, and had learned many portions of Horace, Virgil, Homer, Cicero, and Livy, by heart. He was unwilling to own that he was, on the whole, greatly indebted to Eton, but he must, as the writer remarks, have been "much obliged to the collision of a public school for the rapidity with which he increased his knowledge, and the correction of himself by the mistakes of others. *Magnos enim viros non schola, sed contubernium facit.*"

Mr. Kidd says that Porson, when he entered Eton, was "wholly ignorant of quantity;" and that "after he had toiled up the arduous path to literary eminence, he was often twitted by his quondam schoolfellows with those violations of quantity which are common in first attempts at Latin verse." " Our Greek Professor," he adds, "always felt sore upon this point. One of his best friends and greatest admirers has preserved a copy of verses, which indeed evince the rapid progress of his mind, but would not do honour to his memory."

That he could repeat by heart almost all the books read at Eton, before he became an Etonian, he himself told Mr. Maltby, and said that almost the only thing he recollected with pleasure during his Eton course was the rat-hunting with which the boys amused themselves in the Long Hall.

He continued, however, to be fond of reading. Jonathan Raine, a brother of Dr. Matthew Raine, Porson's firm friend throughout life, was one of his school-fellows at Eton, and was possessed of a Shakspeare which Porson, having none of his own, was ever eager to borrow. When Raine, who kept it locked up, was reluctant to lend it, Porson would take his knife out of his pocket, and say, " Come now, give us your key, or I shall pick the lock."

One remarkable instance which he gave of the power of his memory at Eton is recorded. He was going up one day with the rest of his form, to say a lesson in Horace, but, not being able to find his book at the time, took one which was thrust into his hand by another boy. He was called upon to construe, and went on with great accuracy, but the master observed that he did not seem to be looking on that part of the page in which the lesson was. He therefore took the book from his hand to examine it, and found it to be an English translation of Ovid's Metamorphoses. Porson was good-humouredly desired to continue his construing, and finished the lesson · without erring in a single word.

He was so disinclined to composition when he was at Eton, that he would, to save himself the trouble of writing an exercise, borrow that of any other boy, and transcribe it with all its faults. Yet he was ready to assist others with advice, and to correct their errors.*

Mr. Barker tells a story of Porson's boyhood, for the

* Kidd, Tracts, p. lxix.

truth of which he must himself be left responsible.
When Colonel Disney was a Westminster boy, he was
in the habit of meeting Porson at his master's house.
When they were alone together in the evening, Porson
asked Disney if he knew his way to the ale-cellar.
Disney replied that he did, but that he was engaged in
doing his Greek verses. "Never mind," said Porson;
"I will look to them; take the largest jug you can find,
and fill it with beer." This Disney did, and on his return found his Greek verses finished. This occurred
more than once, and Disney was always on such occasions at the head of his class. He told Porson not to
let the handwriting be too good.* How Porson found
opportunities of being with Disney at Westminster when
it was not vacation time, is not explained.

There was a boy named Murphitt at Eton, of a
somewhat ungainly figure, with whom he used to spar.
He observed that Murphitt need never be in want of a
corkscrew, as he had only to swallow a tenpenny nail,
and the sinuosities of his frame, as it passed through,
would twist it into an excellent shape for a cork-
extractor.† Murphitt was afterwards vicar of Kendal.

His propensity to satirical composition began to
show itself at Eton. One of his schoolfellows was
Charles Simeon, whom he afterwards called a "coxcomb in religion," but who was then a coxcomb in dress.
Porson, disliking his vanity and conceit, wrote some
verses addressed "to the ugliest boy in Dr. Davies's
dominions," and threw them over a wall where they

---

* Barker's Lit. Anecd. vol. ii. p. 17.
† Ib. vol. i. pp. 23, 189.

were sure to be found. A good-natured friend soon
handed them to Simeon, who was much stung by them,
and used every possible means to discover the author,
examining the handwriting of all the boys in his form,
and soliciting the assistance of the monitors; but his
efforts were fruitless, for Porson had written them with
his left hand, so as to defy detection.*

When he had been about three years at Eton, his
patron, Mr. Norris, died; and Porson is said to have
shown much concern at his loss. The suddenness of
his death, it is supposed, prevented Mr. Norris from
making any provision for him. But Sir George Baker
still determined to protect him; he received him into
his house in the following vacation; he continued
to collect sums, whether as subscriptions or donations,
for his maintenance, and at last secured enough to
purchase for him an annuity of eighty pounds a year,
for a few years, in the short annuities, an income
which was sufficient to enable him to remain at Eton.
Mrs. Mary Townshend and Lady Middleton are mentioned as two of the contributors to Sir George Baker's
fund.

About the time of Mr. Norris's death, Porson's life
appears to have been in danger from the formation of
an imposthume on the lungs, and though his lungs were
relieved by a copious discharge, yet he recovered his
strength but slowly, and is considered to have escaped
from consumption only to be troubled, during much of
his life, with asthma.†

* Barker's Parriana, vol. ii. p. 700.
† Monthly Magazine, Nov. 1808.

The drama which he wrote at Eton, entitled " Out of the Frying-pan into the Fire," is preserved in the library of Trinity College, Cambridge, to which it was presented in 1850 by Bishop Maltby, into whose hands it had passed.   We have perused it, and found it, as might be expected, but a schoolboy performance ; but, as the youthful production of one afterwards so famous, the reader may not be displeased if we. give a short notice of it.   It is in three acts, and may be called an opera, for it consists chiefly of songs.   The subject is the old story of Friar Bacon's attempt to build a wall of brass round Britain to defend it from its enemies.   But, in Porson's play, the business is taken, we know not why, out of the hands of Friar Bacon, and put into those of Doctor Faustus.   Lucifer and Satan, also, two of the characters, are made distinct personages.   The *dramatis personæ*, and the names of the boys who acted them, are these :

Dr. FAUSTUS	Mr. Stephenson.
SATAN, ⎫ two devils, familiars ⎰	Mr. Chafie.
LUCIFER, ⎭ of Dr. Faustus ⎱	Mr. Goodall.
VULCAN, a god turned smith .	Mr. Moore.
PUNCH, servant to Dr. Faustus .	The Author.
JOAN, his wife . . .	Mrs. Smith, the real wife of Hob Smith.

The piece opens thus :—

SCENE,—*A garden.*

Dr. FAUSTUS *discovered.*

INCANTATION.

Now pale Cynthia's borrowed light
Faintly gilds the glimpse of night,
And the hour-announcing clock
Twelve times sounds with iron stroke.

> Now the ghosts with sullen stalk
> Round the dreary churchyard walk,
> Till the harbinger of day
> Chases them from earth away.
> I alone, while others sleep,
> Watchful to this garden creep,
> And, to conjure up my slave,
> Thus in air my rod I wave.
> Twice I turn to th' eastern sky ;
> Twice the western world I spy ;
> Twice the south whence Auster blows ;
> Twice the north which Sol ne'er knows.
> Next, these flowers of deadly juice,
> Which my fertile lands produce,
> On the ground, in order meet,
> Thus I strew beneath my feet.

He then invokes " Satan, and Lucifer his partner," to assist him in building a brazen wall " round Britannia's chosen land." The two immediately appear in thunder and lightning, and " dance the hay," to the tune of " Deil tak' the wars," to which Faustus sings a song. They then " dance again," while Faustus sings another song, to the air of " Fill your glasses, banish grief," as follows :

> Wheresoe'er materials lie,
>   On the earth or in the sea,
> Or i' th' middle air or sky,
>   You must seek them out for me.
> To the furthest regions haste
> Ere a single hour be past ;
> Haste and quickly bring whate'er
> Will be necessary here.

Satan replies,

> Whatever you think, Dr. Faustus, expedient,
> To fetch or to carry you'll find me obedient ;
> Pray tell your intent, and if I do but swerve in't,
> As you will you shall punish your most humble servant.

Lucifer expresses himself to the same effect. Satan then proposes to call in Vulcan, to make " a head all of brass," which may give directions how to build the brazen wall; telling Faustus,

> As soon as it speaks, which it will when you roast it,
> With questions in plenty at pleasure accost it.

But he cautions him to be careful of making any mistake. Satan and Lucifer then depart to find Vulcan, who comes in by chance, while Dr. Faustus is waiting for him, singing,

> Whoe'er wants to buy, to my office repair,
> And I'll furnish you quickly with all kinds of ware,
> Whether hammer, or chisel, or gimlet, or axe,
> Or tenpenny nails, or the smallest of tacks.

The Doctor signifying his wish to have the head, Vulcan promises to make it in an hour and a quarter, and takes his leave. Faustus sends his servant Punch to fetch the head, and, as he is not over expeditious in going, threatens to whip him, and sings,

> If a servant you have, he's the plague of your life,
> For with him you've nought but contention and strife;
> Of the orders you give him he's never observant:
> Oh! what a plague is an impudent servant,
>   Vexing, perplexing,
>   Staying, delaying,—
> Oh! what a plague is an impudent servant!

This Punch parodies thus:

> If a master you have, he's the plague of your life,
> For with him you have nought but contention and strife;
> Go as fast as you can, he would have you go faster:
> Oh! what a plague is a whimsical master,
>   Ordering and bothering,
>   Stripping and whipping,—
> Oh! what a plague is a whimsical master!

Thus ends the first Act.

In the second Act Joan enters, singing. Vulcan comes to her with the head of brass, and Joan observes,

I think that it looks rather frightful and horrid :
What hideous eyes, what a terrible forehead !

Punch joins them, and the whole act is composed of their talk and songs.

The third Act discovers Punch and Joan sitting half asleep, with bottle and tumblers beside them, and the head in a huge frying-pan on the fire ; Dr. Faustus having charged them to watch the roasting of it, and to let him know when it should speak. They talk and sing, and the head says, " Time is," of which they take no notice ; soon after the head says, " Time was," and, in a little while, exclaims, " Time is gone," and falls into the fire and bursts. In comes Faustus to ask if it has not spoken. Seeing it broken, he laments, and upbraids Punch and his wife for their carelessness, who endeavour to excuse themselves, but are at last driven off by Satan and Lucifer to Tartarus. Faustus mourns, in a parody on Wolsey's speech, that " his shoot has been nipp'd when he thought his greatness was a ripening," but adds that, though Britain must still continue open to our foes, yet

——Still beneath our arms the foe shall fall,
And England's valour be its brazen wall.

Three copies of school-Latin verses, written by Porson when he was at Eton, are in the library of Trinity College, having been presented to it in 1851 by T. L'Estrange Ewen, Esq., of Dedham, Essex. One is in iambic verse, a translation of a passage of Pope's

" Essay on Criticism," extending to thirty-three lines ; another consists of thirty-six hexameters from " The Dying Indian," in Dodsley's Collection ; and the third of thirty hexameters and pentameters on the Progress of Pastoral Poetry.   We have extracted a few lines from the first as a specimen :

> Natura solers ipsa legibus suis
> Sese coercet, ut tenetur ordine
> A se reperto, se regens, Licentia.
> Sedem superbo Græcia in cacumine
> Sibi vindicat, natosque demonstrans suos
> Queis laureorum palma cingit tempora,
> Nos et decora tendere ad certamina
> Jubet triumphi, nos et æquali gradu
> Hortatur exercere munus ingenî.

Pope's lines are,

> " Nature, like liberty, is but restrain'd
> By the same laws which first herself ordain'd.
> Hear how learn'd Greece her useful rules indites,
> When to repress, and when indulge our flights ;
> High on Parnassus' top her sons she show'd,
> And pointed out those arduous paths they trod ;
> Held from afar aloft, th' immortal prize,
> And urged the rest by equal steps to rise."

To turn " liberty " into *licentia*, and to make licence *se coercere et regere ordine a se reperto*, is extremely boyish.   But there are some good lines here and there. They are written in a small neat hand, on both sides of the paper, and "Porson" is carefully printed in italics at the top, on the left hand.

His mind was first inclined to critical researches, as he himself used to relate, by reading Toup's " Longinus," with a copy of which he was presented by Dr. Davies as a reward for a good exercise. Some time afterwards he read Bentley on Phalaris, and Dawes's "Miscellanea Critica," and these writers he used to call his great masters in the art of criticism.

For Bentley he preserved through life an unbounded veneration. He calls his work on Phalaris, *immortalis illa de Phalaridis Epistolis Dissertatio*, and omitted no opportunity of praising him. When, in after life, he had made many emendations in Aristophanes, and Bentley's copy of that poet was shown him, containing a number of his corrections in the margin, he is said to have shed tears of joy at finding a large portion of Bentley's conjectures exactly coincide with his own.[*] He once spoke to some scholars at the Gray's Inn Coffee-House, on Bentley's literary character, with such warmth of eulogy that a North Briton, who was present, asked him if Bentley was not a *Scotchman.* "No," replied Porson, "Bentley was a *Greek* scholar."[†] This story is told in more ways than one, but Porson's stress must have been upon the word "*Greek.*"

Bentley was, indeed, a mighty man in the province of literature to which he devoted himself. Notwithstanding all the *slashing with his desperate hook*, he still showed himself, except in his attempts on Milton and in some of his later pamphlets, a sound and perspicacious critic. Pope would have gained himself more credit by praising than by satirising him. He is said to have been in doubt, when he was writing the

---

[*] Rev. H. R. Luard, Cambridge Essays, 1857.
[†] Kidd, Tracts, p. lxxxviii.; Barker's Lit. An. vol. ii. p. 10.

"Dunciad," whether he should extol or depreciate Handel, till some musician, whose opinion he asked, assured him that Handel was a great man. It may well be wished that some scholar had had the power to give him a similar impression of Bentley.

CHAP. III.

PORSON was too old when he went to Eton, as may
have been inferred from Dr. Goodall's evidence before
the House of Commons, to have any chance of going to
Cambridge as a King's scholar. After having remained
at Eton four years, he was entered at Trinity College
in October 1778, when he was nearly eighteen years
of age.

Concerning his course of life as an undergraduate at
Cambridge, little is told. He was at first, however, so
much influenced by the *genius loci* that he applied himself to mathematics, but soon relinquished the study
for others more agreeable to his inclination. His reading would appear to have been very miscellaneous.
Whether the perusal of Chambers's Dictionary, of which
Dr. Goodall spoke, and which is also mentioned by
Beloe, took place before he went to .Cambridge, or
afterwards, is uncertain ; but it would seem more probable that the achievement was performed at Cambridge. He was said by his old master, Mr. Summers,

to have been well-conducted, and to have incurred no punishment, during the whole of his undergraduate-ship.*

He impressed the scholars of the University with strong notions of his aptitude for attaining distinction in classical pursuits.

Two emendations which he made about two years after he entered Cambridge, his earliest attempts of the kind on record, deserve to be noticed. In the first Idyl of Theocritus, ver. 66, we still read,

Πᾶ πόκ' ἄρ' ἦσθ' ὅκα Δάφνις ἐτάκετο ;

Porson altered it to·

Πᾶ τόκ' ἄρ' ἦσθ' —— ;

In Virgil, Æn. iii. 702, the common reading is

Immanisque Gela, fluvii cognomine dicta,

for which Porson proposed to read

Immanisque Gela, fluvio cognomine dicta,

which Kidd calls an admirable emendation, and which, though it may at first startle a young reader, is supported by Æn. vi. 38, *gaudet cognomine terrâ.* These criticisms of Porson were communicated to Kidd by Dr. Goodall.

One fellow-collegian with whom he was very intimate was Walter Whiter, afterwards rector of Hardingham, and well known to classical scholars. He would go into Whiter's rooms, open whatever book Whiter would allow him to take, and, with any pen

* Notes and Queries, 1st series, vol. iii. p. 28.

that he could find on the table, write notes on the margin in the neatest of hands. Mr. Whiter's nephew possesses a copy of Athenæus that belonged to his uncle, in which are many annotations written by Porson with the greatest distinctness, though the paper is porous.

He was elected scholar of his College in 1780, and gained the Craven University Scholarship, without difficulty, in December 1781. A translation of an epitaph into Greek iambics, which he performed at the examination for the Craven scholarship, is preserved. It is said to have been completed in less than an hour, with the help only of Morell's Thesaurus, according to Dr. Thomas Young, but, according to others, without any help from books at all. Who was the author of the English lines is not known. The Reverend William Collier, Senior Fellow of Trinity College, set the verses, and told Mr. Kidd that he took them from a magazine of the day. Kidd says that he searched most of the magazines for them, but to no purpose; and Porson himself expressed a suspicion that they were Mr. Collier's own.

> " Stranger, whoe'er thou art that view'st this tomb,
> Know that here lies, in the cold arms of death,
> The young Alexis. Gentle was his soul
> As softest music ; to the charms of love
> Not cold, nor to the social charities
> Of mild humanity. In yonder grove
> He woo'd the willing muse. Simplicity
> Stood by and smiled. Here every night they come,
> And, with the virtues and the graces, tune
> The note of woe, weeping their favourite
> Slain in his bloom, in the fair prime of life.
> " Would he had lived ! "   Alas ! in vain that wish
> Escapes thee. Never, stranger, shalt thou see
> The youth. He's dead. The virtuous soonest die."

Ω ΞΕΙΝΕ, τουτον ὁστις εισορᾳς ταφον,
Ισθ' ὡς ὁδ' ενδον σωμ' Αλεξιδος νεον
(Ψυχρον παραγκαλισμα ταρταρου) στεγει
Μολπης γλυκυτατης αἱμυλωτερου φρενας·
Ουδ' ἡν αθαλπτος Κυπριδος τερπνῳ βελει,
Ουδ' αὖ παρωσε τον φιλανθρωπον τροπον,
Αρθμον θ' ἑταιρων· ἀλλ' εκειν' αλσος κατα
Ἑκουσαν εζητησε Μουσαν· Χρηστοτης τ'
Εγελα παραστᾶσ'· αἱν ἑκαστης ενθαδε
Νυκτος παρουσαιν, αἱ ' ρεται τε και καλαι
Χαριτες συνωμιλησαν· ειτα τον φιλον
Ποθουσ' εραστην δυσθροῳ μελωδιᾳ,
Ὁν ἀρτι θαλλοντ' ηρινῳ καιρῳ βιου
Εδρεψατ' Αιδης. ΕΙΘ' ΕΤ' ΕΝ ΖΩΟΙΣΙΝ ΗΝ.
Ευχη ματην ἀρ', ω Ξεν', ἡδε το στομα
Πεφευγεν· ου γαρ μηποτ' εισοψει νεον·
Τεθνηχ' ὁ δη—ταχιστα πασχουσ' οἱ 'γαθοι.

We give them without accents, just as they are printed by Mr. Kidd, but the last line, as Dr. Young has observed, should undoubtedly be written

Τεθνηχ· ὁ δη ταχιστα πασχουσ' οἱ 'γαθοι.

In the first line he uses unjustifiably the Ionic form ξεῖνος. The ninth line shows that he had either not then discovered what he afterwards called *the pause*, or disregarded it. Young remarked that there are some inaccuracies in the use of the tenses, but there seems to be nothing in this respect that is indefensible. When the iambics were shown, several years afterwards, to Parr, he said, "You do not, Mr. Porson, consider these as faultless?" Porson answered, evasively, that for every single fault that Parr could point out, he himself would find seven.

He took his degree in 1782 as third *senior optime*, the number of wranglers being eighteen. Soon afterwards he obtained the first Chancellor's medal, Sparke, subsequently Bishop of Ely, being awarded the second. On the first of October, in the same year, he was elected to a fellowship in his College, being chosen, in violation of the custom then prevailing, while he was still a junior bachelor, a relaxation being made in his favour on account of his eminent abilities.* Since 1677, when Newton was elected fellow, junior bachelors had not been allowed, with three exceptions, to be candidates for fellowships till 1818, when Connop Thirlwall was chosen; the three exceptions being Richard Bentley, the son of the critic; 'Rogerson Cotter, and Thomas Robinson, the author of "Female Scripture Characters."† At present, and since 1830, all bachelors without distinction are admitted to the fellowship examinations. The emolument of Porson's fellowship did not exceed 100*l.* per annum.

At what time of his life he first began to pay those ardent devotions to Bacchus for which he was afterwards so remarkable, is not, we believe, stated in print. He probably first indulged in them, like Addison, as a *lene tormentum ingenio*, a pleasant excitement to his faculties, and was unable to restrain himself from frequent repetitions of the gratification. Indeed, when a remark was once made to him, in a subsequent period of his life, by a gentleman at a dinner party, as they were sitting over their wine, and as Porson was beginning to talk, that he had been " exceedingly shy during dinner," he rejoined, with an arch look, that

---

* Monthly Magazine, Nov. 1808.

† Monk's Bentley, vol. ii. p. 348. Rev. H. R. Luard, Cambr. Essays, 1857.

"Addison had never been himself till the second
bottle."*   The writer in the " Gentleman's Magazine,"
whom we have already cited, suggests that he may
have found wine or spirits a relief to his asthma, and
that this may have been the origin of his attachment to
the cups which, unlike Bishop Berkeley's tar-water,
cheer, but inebriate.

Mr. William Maltby, who, being Porson's intimate
friend, has bespattered him with ungracious anecdote
more than any other person that has written of him,
relates that " during the earlier part of his career, he
accepted the situation of tutor to a young gentleman in
the Isle of Wight, but was soon forced to relinquish the
office, from having been found drunk in a ditch or a
turnip-field."†   Mr. Maltby, before publishing this,
should have considered whether there was a time at
which it could have occurred. *Ponendæque domo quæ-
rendå est area primum.*   It did not happen before
Porson went to Eton, and from Eton he went directly
to Cambridge, where he seems to have resided pretty
constantly till he got his fellowship in his twenty-third
year ; after which event it surely did not take place.
He might indeed have entered into a short engagement
of the kind during one of the vacations, but, if he did,
it is strange that there is no allusion to it in any other
writer of him.   Mr. Siday Hawes, Porson's nephew, has
expressed to us a firm belief that Porson never was
a private tutor, nor ever in the Isle of Wight.   The
interval between his election to his fellowship and the

* Stephens's Memoirs of Horne Tooke, vol. ii. p. 315.
† Rogers's Table Talk, " Porsoniana," p. 300.

time when he took his M.A. degree in 1785, he seems to have "assiduously employed," according to Mr. Kidd, "in highly useful but ungainful pursuits. It was a season which he recollected with pleasure, and would, at times, fondly wish to live over again *Pieriosque dies et amantes carmina noctes.*"

As he became distinguished, his company was much sought, especially by the young men of his college. But he did not conduct himself in such a way, in the convivial hours which he spent among them, as to secure from them much personal deference, however they might admire the powers of his mind. Familiarity seems to have produced its proverbial effect in his case as in others. In his disputes with the young fellows he was fond of threatening to punish their insolence by splitting their heads with the poker. One evening an undergraduate distinguished for pugilism, with whom he had a dispute, seeing Porson catch hold of the poker, seized the tongs, observing that he could play at that game as well as Porson. Porson, looking in his face, said in a sneering tone, "If I should crack your skull, I believe I should find it empty." "And if I should crack yours," replied the other, "I believe I should find it full of maggots." This was a retort such as Porson liked, and he immediately laid down the poker with a smile, and repeated a chapter of "Roderick Random" suitable to the occasion. The author of the "Short Account of Porson" says that this cured him of using the poker; but he is mistaken, for we shall find him brandishing it again hereafter.

Sir Egerton Brydges*, who was at Cambridge at this

* Autobiography, vol. i. p. 58.

time, speaks of Porson's roughness, and thought him vain and arrogant; but Sir Egerton admits that he was in his company only once or twice, and he assuredly never penetrated Porson's husk.

In 1782 he made some proposals to republish Budæus's "Commentaries on the Greek Language," with notes; a book which, as Kidd thinks, would have been better for our public schools than Vigerus. But the design was never·executed.

In March 1783 he appears to have first published an essay in criticism, a review of the first volume of Schutz's Æschylus, in "Maty's Review;" a publication which was started the year before by Maty, a fellow of Trinity, Porson's senior by a few years, and which Porson continued to support till it fell to the ground in 1787. The paper occupies only a few pages. Porson's propensity to sarcastic remark is just shown in it. Speaking of Schutz having separated two *excursus* on the "Septem contra Thebas" from the main body of his commentary, he says that he is at a loss to know why he has done so, for "they would have been as easily read, or turned over without reading, if they had been inserted in their proper order."

About this period, having read with great pleasure Ruhnken's preface to the second volume of Hesychius, and his historical disquisition on the Greek orators, he wrote to Ruhnken, saying that he was contemplating an edition of Æschylus, and requesting to be favoured with any fragments of that author that had occurred to Ruhnken in his body of inedited Lexicons and Grammarians; a source from which Brunck had drawn many valuable glosses for his·"Lexicon Sophocleum."

That Ruhnken might not be ignorant of his qualifications for editing Æschylus, he sent him specimens of two or three emendations. Ruhnken was pleased with the letter, and after showing it to Wyttenbach, who was much struck with the ability that it displayed, sent him a reply addressed " Viro præstantissimo Ricardo Porsono," and consisting of eight leaves of foolscap crowded with fragments of Æschylus extracted from the treasures of his library. This manuscript afterwards perished by fire.

At this time Porson's attention was closely fixed upon Æschylus ; and Maty, doubtless with Porson's permission, announced in his " Review " for March and October, 1783, that " a scholar of Cambridge was preparing a new edition of Stanley's Æschylus, to which he proposed to add his own notes, and would be glad of any communications on the subject either from Englishmen or foreigners." It happened at the same time, too, that the Syndics of the University Press had in contemplation à reprint of Stanley's edition, with additional notes from his manuscripts, of which he had left eight large folio volumes. Porson, being consulted about the publication, offered to undertake the editorship of it, if he were allowed to conduct it according to his own notions of an editor's duty. But on being told that he must preserve Stanley's text unaltered, and must admit all Pauw's annotations, however valueless, he declined to execute the work on those conditions. In one of his conferences with the Syndics, he urged upon them the necessity of obtaining the various readings of the Medicean manuscript at Florence, which Professor Salvini had inspected for Dr. Askew, and offered to undertake a journey thither for the purpose of collating it, at an expense to the University not greater than that for which the task could have been performed by a person on the spot; but the proposal was rejected, and one of the Syndics, speaking strongly against it, asked why Mr. Porson could not *collect* his manuscripts at home? The name of this learned objector has not been recorded, but Kidd seems to have known who he was, for he calls him "a grave man, and most wonderful scholar, then perching on the pinnacle of power;" and another of the opposers he designates as "a genuine critic, well known in the *Primrose Path* as well as in the *Fosse* and the *Watling Street*." Porson afterwards alluded to this display of ignorance in a note to his "Letters to Travis:" "I have heard of a learned Doctor in our University who confounded the *collection* with the *collation* of manuscripts."*

This repulse is said to have dispirited Porson so much as to have had an ill effect on his whole critical career. Had he been now fairly started with Æschylus, he might, on its completion, have been animated by success to proceed to other works, and have accomplished those great undertakings which men who could fairly estimate his powers expected from him. But this discouragement seems to have weakened his exertions, to have turned his thoughts from great enterprises, and to have caused him to waste much time in comparatively trifling occupations.

The only excuse to be made for the Syndics is that

---

* Letters to Travis, p. 57; Kidd, Tracts, p. xxxvi.

Porson was then untried as an editor, and that his success may have seemed doubtful. But they ought to have had Greek learning enough among them to know the value of Stanley's text, and to suppose that a man who had given such proofs of scholarship as Porson, was likely to do it little harm by a few alterations, in which his own reputation would be concerned.

Some verses, which have been much circulated, have given rise to the belief that Porson actually visited the continent : —

> " I went to Strasburg, where I got drunk
> With that most learn'd professor Brunck :
> I went to Wortz, where I got more drunken
> With that more learn'd professor Ruhnken."

By whom these verses were written is not certainly known, but it is believed among scholars that they came from Porson himself, who, for the sake of the rhymes, described, as having really occurred, that which he thought might have occurred if he had met with those continental professors.

CHAP. IV.

IN the same year, 1783, Porson wrote another article
for "Maty's Review," a critique on Brunck's Aristophanes. It contains great commendations of Brunck
as an editor, and some very acute emendations of passages that had perplexed or escaped Brunck. Some
introductory remarks on the writings and character of
Aristophanes, setting forth his principal merits and defects, are well worthy of extraction : —

"Before I give an account of the editor's merits, it may
not be improper to say a word of the excellences and defects
of the author; especially as some modern critics have thought
proper, not only to greet him with the title of a scurrilous
and indecent buffoon, but to wonder how such monstrous
farces could be endured by the chaste ears of an Attic
audience. That many should have been greatly exasperated
with Aristophanes for publicly exhibiting Socrates on the
stage, and making him speak and act in a manner most
inconsistent with his known character, is not surprising; but
as the accusation urged by some against the poet, of being
instrumental to Socrates's death, has been substantially refuted by many critics, so the present editor has very judiciously observed, with regard to the other part of the charge,
that Socrates is not so much the object of ridicule in the

comedy of the 'Clouds' as the philosophers in general, who, of whatever benefit the lessons and example of Socrates himself might be to the state, were, from their idle lives, their minute, ridiculous, and sometimes impious disquisitions, highly prejudicial to their disciples, and, by consequence, to the public. If, says Mr. Brunck, Aristophanes had really in the smallest degree contributed to the death of Socrates, it is not credible that Plato would have introduced them in his 'Symposium,' sitting together at the same table; it is not credible that he would have been so great an admirer of him as to write an epigram in his praise, containing a most extravagant compliment. *Missa igitur hœc faciamus.* Of the indecency which abounds in Aristophanes, unjustifiable as it certainly is, it may, however, be observed that different ages differ extremely in their ideas of this offence. Among the ancients plain speaking was the fashion; nor was the ceremonious delicacy introduced which has taught men to abuse each other with the utmost politeness, and express the most indecent ideas in the most modest language. The ancients had little of this. They were accustomed to call a spade a spade; to give everything its proper name. There is another sort of indecency, which is infinitely more dangerous; which corrupts the heart without offending the ear. I believe there is no man of sound judgment who would not rather let his son read Aristophanes than Congreve or Vanbrugh. In all Aristophanes's indecency there is nothing that can allure, but much that must deter. He never dresses up the most detestable vices in an amiable light, but generally, by describing them in their native colours, makes the reader disgusted with them. His abuse of the most eminent citizens may be accounted for upon similar principles. Besides, in a republic, freedom of speech was deemed an essential privilege of a citizen. Demosthenes treats his adversaries with such language as would, in our days, be accounted scurrilous enough; but it passed in those days without any notice or reprehension. The world is since greatly altered for the better. We have, indeed, retained the matter, but judiciously altered the manner.

" In the management of his plots too, it must be owned, Aristophanes is sometimes faulty. It ought, however, to be observed that his contemporary comic poets did not pique themselves upon the artful management of the plot. Aristophanes has, therefore, the usual failing of dramatic writers, to introduce speeches, and even scenes, not much conducing to the business of the drama. But if the only use of the plot be, as the great Bayes has decided, to bring in good things, our poet will stand totally clear on this head of the charge, and the ' Knights ' may be mentioned as an honourable exception even to this censure, as the design of the play, to expose Cleon, and to turn him out of his place, is admirably supported from beginning to end.

" To sum up Aristophanes's character : if we consider his just and severe ridicule of the Athenian foibles ; his detestation of the expensive and ruinous war in which Greece was engaged ; his pointed invectives against the factious and interested demagogues, by whom the populace was deluded, ' who bawl'd for freedom in their senseless mood ; ' his contempt of the useless and frivolous inquiries of the sophists ; his wit and versatility of style ; the astonishing playfulness, originality, and fertility of his imagination ; the great harmony of versification whenever the subject required it, and his most refined elegance of language, — in spite of Dr. Beattie's dictum, we shall look over his blemishes, and allow that, with all his faults, he might be a very good citizen, and was certainly an excellent poet."

Brunck excuses himself for having left some faulty readings in the text " on account of the great hurry," he says, " in which he was obliged to write his notes." " I am aware," he observes, " *partem haud minimam istarum fabularum à me descriptam iterum fuisse, dum in Museo meo vel ludebat filius meus, quo animum meum nihil magis advertit oblectatque, vel confabulabantur boni quidam viri, qui quot fere diebus horisque matu-*

tinis ad me visere solent."   Upon this Porson exclaims,
" *Tantamne rem tam negligenter?*   I think in such a
case I should have sent Master Brunck out of the
room.   Pugh! says Mr. Brunck (or, I suppose, would
say, if he read Shakspeare), ' He talks to me that never
had a son.'   But, to be serious, what right has any man
to publish a work of this kind in a hurry?   Mr.
Brunck, I believe, is not in that unfortunate situation
which some learned men have experienced, to be obliged to publish as fast as the avarice or tyranny of
booksellers required."

This article, though of considerable length, was
written in one night and part of the following day.*

In 1784 he reviewed, in the same publication, an
edition of Hermesianax, an elegiac poet of whom only
fragments remain, by the Rev. Stephen Weston, Fellow
of Exeter College, Oxford.   He gives Mr. Weston
some praise and not much blame, except for his Latin
metrical version, which, he says, one so little able to
rival Grotius should not have attempted.   Whether
the review led to any personal communication between
Porson and Mr. Weston, I do not know; but Mr.
Weston is generally thought to have written the "Short
Account of Mr. Richard Porson," published by Bald-
win in 1808, soon after Porson's death; a meagre pamphlet, filled with matters which the writer might have
learned without ever having seen Porson.   This production was re-issued in 1814, with an addition, of a
similar character, called " Τεμάχη, or Scraps from Porson's Rich Feast," which there seems to be better

---

* Kidd, Tracts, p. xxxix.

ground for attributing to Weston. Kidd was told that the "Short Account" had proceeded from a dignitary of the church.*

Shortly after, in the same Review, appeared a brief notice of George Isaac Huntingford's "Apology for his Monostrophics." It is well known that Huntingford published, when he had just ceased to be an undergraduate, a volume of Greek verses under the title of "Monostrophica," in which Dr. Charles Burney, in the pages of the "Monthly Review," exposed several metrical errors, one of which was the shortening of the first syllable of κῦδος. In reply to Burney's strictures Huntingford printed his "Apology for the Monostrophics published in 1782," to which he had the hardihood to add "A Second Collection of Mono-strophics." In this "Apology" he tries to defend his use of κῦδος, which Dawes, as Burney had observed, had pronounced to have the first syllable always long, by the authority of two Greek epigrammatists in the Anthologia, who had shortened the second syllable in Θουκυδίδης, saying, "the mere *ipse dixit* of the pedantic Dawes must give place to two poetical authorities." Porson was enraged at this contemptuous mention of Dawes, whom he held in high esteem, and resolved not to spare Mr. Huntingford, whose second "Monostrophics" he perceived to be as vulnerable as his first. He makes Mr. Huntingford a present of a third example of Θουκυδίδης from the same source, and then says : —

"But wherever the word κῦδος, or its derivatives, occur in ancient Greek poetry (and they occur very frequently),

* Kidd, Tracts, p. lxvi.

they have the υ invariably long. In what licences three epigrammatists, who wrote long after the purity and perfection of the Greek language was entirely lost, may indulge themselves, is of no consequence ; and as for Thomas Scholasticus, his taste may be guessed from his joining Thucydides and Demosthenes in the same encomium with Aristides, a decision almost as judicious as would be that critic's who should rank Valckenaer and Dawes in the same class with Barnes and Pauw," (as Huntingford had done in the preface to his " Apology.") " If Mr. Huntingford believes," continues Porson, " that every licence which the later epigrammatists take may be allowed in a modern poet, he will find it difficult to commit any errors in quantity, as there is scarcely a violation of metre which may not be defended by the example of one or other of these poetasters. When an imitator of the ancients unites in his own compositions all the different dialects and metres which the Greek language admitted through the space of a thousand years, it is not easy to decide what system of prosody or style he may have formed. for his own use. What would Mr. Huntingford think of a foreigner who, by way of writing English *monostrophics*, should studiously collect and mingle the phraseology, diction, and prosody of Chaucer, Shakspeare, Milton, and Pope, *et tum mirificè speraret se esse locutum ?* In my judgment, therefore, Dawes's observation has not been materially hurt by what Mr. Huntingford has advanced. Dawes does not say that there is no example to be found of the licence that Mr. Huntingford defends, but that whoever takes such a licence is ignorant of quantity ; as ignorant, I may add, as he would be who should make ἐπαραι (New Monostroph. p. 20) an anapæst, γυπων (p. 30), or ψυχος (p. 36) an iambus, or εἰ συ (p. 38) a spondee. Part of Mr. Huntingford's civility to Dawes has been already quoted. The paragraph concludes with saying that ' he is positive, hasty, and wrong, in more passages than in one.' Without entering on a long defence of Dawes, I shall venture to urge one plea in his favour. He wrote, in his youth, some Greek verses full of mistakes in syntax and dialect, *though faultless, I believe,* in point of metre. But afterwards, becoming sensible of his error, he quitted what he esteemed so idle and unprofitable a study, and chose rather to read good Greek than to write bad. An example of candour and prudence well worthy to be imitated ! "

"If the character of Dawes as a critic," says Mr. Kidd *, " had been treated with due respect, this article would not have been thought of." "Porson," he adds, "considered the making of Greek verses as wholesome exercise ; it requires extensive reading and a retentive memory, and produces a facility in the application of those nice discriminations of style adopted by the Homeric, tragic, and comic poets, which have been pointed out by master-artists ;" but he " did not encourage the publication of such attempts ;" since " all that is good in the modern composition of ancient Greek is good for nothing ; for, unless such composition be a cento, it can never certainly be correct : and if it be a cento, where is its value ?"

For modern Latin verses, too, as well as Greek, Porson, according to Mr. Maltby, always expressed contempt. When the first portion of the "Musæ Etonenses" was published, he exclaimed that it was " trash, fit only to be put behind the fire."† In passing this judgment he regarded it with the eye of a utilitarian, as adding nothing to the stock of human knowledge, but presenting only well-known thoughts in varieties of old phraseology.

In 1785, nothing is recorded as having proceeded from his pen but the following *jeu d'esprit* on an

* Tracts, p. xli.
† Rogers's Table Talk, " Porsoniana," p. 236.

animal that was attracting much attention at the time.

This gentleman, professing himself to be extremely learned, will have no objection to find his merits set forth in a Greek quotation :—

Πρηὺς ὅδ' εἰσιδέειν καὶ μείλιχος, οὐδέ τι χοίροις
"Αλλοισι προσέοικε· νόος δὲ οἱ ἠΰτε φωτὸς
Αἴσιμος ἀμφιθέει, μούνης δ' ἐπιδεύεται αὐδῆς,

which, no manner of doubt, he will immediately translate for the benefit of the dilettanti who visit him.

But, as the pig's Greek might possibly want rubbing up, from his having kept company so long with ladies, Porson gives in a note the following translation, which he attributes to the *chien savant :*

A gentle pig this same, a pig of parts,
And learn'd as F.R.S. or graduate in arts ;
His ancestors, 'tis true, could only squeak,
But this has been at school, and in a month will speak.

" The well-earned admiration this pig meets with from a sensible and discerning public," proceeds Porson, " puts one in mind of a pleasant story told by Lucian at the beginning of the first Prometheus. One of the Ptolemies was, it seems, very desirous of gratifying the Egyptians with the sight of something new ; for this purpose he introduced into the public games he was exhibiting, a black camel from Bactria, splendidly caparisoned, and a man half black and half white ; but, far from giving the monsters the applause they deserved, the Egyptians, who, as our sneering author says, were a people who did not like things because they were *new* and *uncommon,* but rather delighted in *fitness* and *propriety,* were frightened at the camel, and fairly hissed the man. The consequence of this uncourteous reception was, that the camel (who was a camel of spirit, and very worthy to wear a bridle from the stable of Cambyses, as we are told she did) died of grief. The man's fate was, if possible, harder; for he was given to an opera singer, who had sung well at a great supper, at which Theocritus and the members of the tragic Pleiades were present."

In 1786, he published, in "Maty's Review," some letters of Le Clerc and Bentley, transcribed from the manuscripts in the library of Dr. Askew. He appended a few notes.

In the same year, to oblige Nicholson the Cambridge bookseller, he added some notes to an edition of Hutchinson's Xenophon's Anabasis, which was then about to be published. In a short note prefixed, he tells the reader that whoever will consult the manuscripts and old editions, may find plenty of various readings to improve the text of Hutchinson, who consulted but one manuscript, and that not of the highest character. What has since been done in this way by Kühner leaves little to be desired.

In 1787 appeared Sir John Hawkins's "Life of Johnson;" and Porson, disgusted with the tone of vanity and pretension pervading the book, addressed to the "Gentleman's Magazine," in August and the two following months of that year, three epistles of ironical panegyric on it, in which he exposes, with great truth and pleasantry, Sir John's blunders, ignorance, and folly. These letters are, indeed, the finest specimens of Porson's satirical humour that ever appeared. He commences thus:

" MR. URBAN,
        " Have you read that divine book, the 'Life of Samuel Johnson, LL.D., by Sir John Hawkins Knt.' ? Have

you done anything but read it since it was first published?
For my own part, I scruple not to declare that I could not
rest till I had read it quite through, notes, digressions, index
and all; then I could not rest till I had gone over it a second
time. I begin to think that increase of appetite grows by
what it feeds on; for I have been reading it ever since. I
am now in the midst of the sixteenth perusal; and still I
discover new beauties. I can think of nothing else; I can
talk of nothing else. In short, *my mind is become tumid,
and longs to be delivered of those many and great concep-
tions* with which it has laboured since I have been through
a course of this most perfect *exemplar* of biography. The
compass of learning, the extent and accuracy of information,
the judicious criticisms, the moral reflections, the various
opinions, legal and political, to say nothing of that excess of
candour and charity that breathe throughout the work, make
together such a collection of sweets that the sense aches at
them. To crown all, *the language is refined to a degree of
immaculate purity, and displays the whole force of turgid
eloquence.* Johnson, to be sure, was thought to have a
knack at life-writing; but who, in his senses, would compare
him to our Knight? Sir Thomas Urquhart, in the account
of Crichton (which the Knight has given us, p. 304, because
it is so intimately connected with Johnson's life) *honder-
sponders* it pretty well; but even he must yield the palm.

> Read Hawkins once, and you can read no more,
> For all books else appear so mean, so poor,
> Johnson's a dunce; but still persist to read,
> And Hawkins will be all the books you need.

*   *   *   *   *

" Of the Knight's learning, which some profane critics have
been hardy enough to question, no Zoilus will dare to doubt
in future, when he learns from the 'Life of Johnson,' p. 4,
that *struma* signifies *the king's evil;* and, from a long Latin
note, that other people have been afflicted with it besides
the doctor. But the passages quoted from Latin authors
are numerous, though, it must be owned, very happily

applied; p. 19, from Erasmus's 'Colloquies,' to prove that
dutiful children wait upon their parents; p. 312, from Arch-
bishop Peccham; p. 347, a new quotation from Ovid; p. 470,
we are informed, to our unspeakable comfort, that to *appose*
means to *put questions;* and this is cleared up beyond a
doubt by seven lines from Ingulphus. . . . . Besides
these damning proofs, the work abounds in such flowers as
these: *Temp. Car. I. Temp. Car. II. Dictamen. Verbatim et literatim. Sui generis. Notanda. Vide supra in
Not. Ex relatione* Peter Flood. *Exemplars. Quoad* the
person. *Evidentia rei. Ex cathedrâ.* Testamentary dispositions *in extremis. Inops consilii.* I should be glad,
after this, to see the wretch that will dispute Sir John's
Latin. As for his Greek, the proofs are not indeed so many,
but equally strong;

> And when one's proofs are aptly chosen,
> Three are as valid as three dozen.

p. 318, 562, *myops,* or near-sighted persons. Seized with a
paralysis; p. 461, Νὺξ γὰρ ἔρχεται. The meaning is, says Sir
John, *for the night cometh.* And so it is, Mr. Urban."

Hawkins gives a description of a watch which Johnson bought for seventeen guineas. Porson affects to
find the history of the watch broken off abruptly, and
to have accidentally picked up a leaf which appears to
have originally filled the chasm of which every reader
must be sensible.

Fragment.

. . . . "And here, touching this watch, already by me
mentioned, I insert a notable instance of the craft and selfish-
ness of the Doctor's negro servant. A few days after that
whereon Dr. Johnson died, this artful fellow came to me, and
surrendered the watch, saying, at the same time, that his
master had delivered it to him a day or two before his de-
mise, with such demeanour and gestures, that he did verily

believe that it was his intention that he, namely Frank, should keep the same. Myself knowing that no sort of credit was due to a black domestic and favourite servant, and withal considering that the wearing thereof would be more proper for myself, and that I had got nothing by my trust of executor save sundry old books, and coach hire for journeys during the discharge of the said office; and further reflecting on what I have occasion elsewhere to mention, *viz.*, that since the abolishing general warrants, *temp. Geo. III.*, no good articles in this branch can be had any longer in England, I took the watch from him, intending to have it appraised by my own jeweller, a very honest and expert artificer, and, in so doing, to have bought it as cheap as I could for myself, let it cost what it would. Upon my signifying this my intention to Frank, the impudent negro said, 'he plainly saw there was no good intended for him,' and in anger left me. He then posted to my colleagues, the other executors; and there being in the people of this country a general propensity to humanity, notwithstanding all my exertions to counteract the same both in writing and otherwise,—this being the case, I say, he had found means to prepossess them so entirely in his favour, that they snubbed me, and insisted with me that I should make restitution. Finally, though perhaps I should not have been amenable to any known judicature by keeping the watch, I consented, being compelled thereto, to let this worthless fellow retain that testimony of his master's ill-directed benevolence *in extremis.*" . .

This is an excellent imitation, with scarcely a tinge of caricature, of Sir John's style. But all the three letters are equally effective throughout. They were written at the house of Dr. Burney of Greenwich, with whom he had now become acquainted.

On the publications of Boswell, Mrs. Thrale, and Sir John Hawkins, concerning Johnson, Porson wrote these lines:

Lexiphanem fatis functum, quà femina, quà vir
   Certant indignis dedecorare modis :
Hic quantum in Scotos fuerit testatus amorem
   Enarrat, fatuos vendidit illa sales.
Fabellas, Eques, ede tuas, seu musice mavis,
   Si famæ Herois vis superesse nihil.

Thus Englished, as we believe, by Beloe :

At Johnson's death both sexes join
His character to undermine,
Proclaim his courtesy to Scots,
And print his stupid anecdotes.
'Tis now thy turn, musician knight :
Publish, and damn his fame outright.*

In January 1789, he published a notice in the
"Monthly Review" of the Rev. J. Robertson's "Dissertation on the Parian Chronicle," defending it against
the suspicions which Robertson expressed of its authenticity.   He observes that though Mr. Robertson appears at first in the modest character of a doubter, he
at length assumes too much of the dogmatist, and that
the marble may very well be allowed to be genuine
till arguments more probable than his are brought
against it.   He, however, praises Mr. Robertson's taste,
learning, and candour, and says that his book may be
read with much pleasure even by those who are adverse
to his notions.

In 1789, Professor Heyne, who was making preparations for his edition of Homer, wrote to Cambridge
for the loan of such of Bentley's papers as contained
remarks on Homer.   When the authorities came to
take this request into consideration, they felt desirous to

---

* Sexagenarian, vol. ii. p. 306.

know, before they granted it, whether Porson was disposed to make use of the papers, and commissioned Professor Hailstone, it appears, to ascertain Porson's inclinations regarding the matter. Porson replied to Hailstone thus:

Eton, Nov. 1789.

" DEAR HAILSTONE,

    " I have received yours, and, after desiring you to thank the Seniors for the honour they have done me, shall answer you with all possible conciseness, that I have no design of making any use of Bentley's papers respecting Homer, and that, generally speaking, I think there will be no harm in letting Professor Heyne have a copy of his notes and emendations; for that, I should imagine, to be more proper than to let the manuscript travel so far. But there is another question which perhaps ought to be asked, whether these notes, as being hasty and negligent, written principally for private use, &c. &c., always answer to the known character of their author, and whether for that reason they ought to be published at all? I must confess myself unable to solve this question, having only had a cursory and superficial view of the papers, though I recollect approving very much of some things in them. But as I make no doubt that there are many of less or no value, if it should be thought advisable to grant the Professor's request, it ought perhaps to be made a condition that he should preserve and publish nothing of Bentley's but what was agreeable to his known abilities and worthy of his acumen. And this irresolute resolution is all that I am able to resolve upon at present.

" R. PORSON."

CHAP. V.

PORSON'S fellowship was held under the obligation of resigning it at the end of ten years, unless he should enter into Orders. He in consequence devoted himself, according to his biographer in the "Gentleman's Magazine," to a large course of theological reading, that he might ascertain whether he could, with satisfaction to himself, subscribe to the Articles of the Church. He did not come to a determination on the subject, we are told, without many painful days and months of study. "His heart and mind," says the writer, "were deeply penetrated by the purest sentiments of religion; and it was a memorable and most estimable feature of his character, that in no moment the most unguarded, in that ardour of discussion which alone drew him into indulgence, was he ever known to utter a single expression of discontent at the Establishment, of derision at those who thought differently from himself, much less of profanation or impiety." But the result of his reading was, that he resolved not to go into the Church. He therefore, " as early as 1788, made up his mind to surrender his fellowship, though, with an enfeebled constitution, he had nothing to depend upon but acquirements that are very unprofitable to their owner."

In speaking to Mr. Maltby of his theological studies, "I found," said he, "that I should require about fifty years' reading to make myself thoroughly acquainted with divinity,—to satisfy my mind on all points,—and therefore I gave it up. There are fellows who go into a pulpit assuming everything, and knowing nothing; but I would not do so." * If Porson had entered a pulpit, his audience would at least have heard from him sense of some kind, not visionary conceitedness, such as proceeded from his schoolfellow, Simeon. But how, if he had taken charge of a parish, he would have been regarded by his parishioners, may be doubtful, for, as the shepherd told Don Quixote, "that clergyman must be over and above good, who obliges his parishioners to speak well of him, especially in country towns."

But to resign a Trinity fellowship, from difficulties as to creed, at a time when most of the clergy had laxer notions in regard to doctrines than they appear to have at present, and had certainly less show of strictness in their lives, manifested great conscientiousness and honesty.

Among the volumes with which he met in the course of his theological reading was that of Archdeacon

* Rogers's Table Talk, "Porsoniana," p. 309.

Travis's "Letters to Gibbon" on the disputed text of
1 ,John v. 7 ; a work which he determined to assail.
The genuineness of this text had ceased to be maintained among scholars, except by a very few; and
Gibbon had observed, in a note on the third volume of
his "History," that "the three witnesses have been
established in our Greek Testaments by the prudence
of Erasmus, the honest bigotry of the Complutensian
editors, the typographical fraud or error of Robert
Stephens in the placing a crotchet, and the deliberate
falsehood or strange misrepresentation of Theodore
Beza." This dictum of Gibbon Mr. Travis took upon
himself to overthrow, and in consequence addressed to
the historian those five Letters which appear to the
unexamining reader to present many satisfactory arguments, but which, when subjected to the critical perspicuity of a Porson, are found to contain little of
solidity beneath their speciousness.

Porson's strictures appeared in the form of Letters in
the "Gentleman's Magazine," in 1788 and 1789, and
the whole was published in a volume by Egerton,
whom Beloe calls "the black-letter bookseller," in 1790.

It is not our purpose to weary our readers with a
recapitulation of all the arguments that have been
made on every point in this controversy, but it is
hardly fitting to write a Life of Porson without attempting to show what he had to overthrow in the
contest, and how he made his attacks.

Before entering upon the summary that follows, it
will be better for the reader to peruse the beginning of
the fifth chapter of St. John's first epistle, with the
omission of the seventh verse and the words " in earth "

in the eighth, and he will see that the sense and scope
of the passage are quite complete without those insertions. The question respecting their genuineness is
merely a question of criticism; the Christian religion
will stand equally sure, whatever be the opinion of
Christians concerning them.

Erasmus, in 1516, published the "Editio Princeps"
of the Greek Testament from Greek manuscripts. But
as the five Greek manuscripts which he consulted did
not contain 1 John v. 7, he omitted the verse. For this
omission he was attacked by the Papists, and afterwards by some of the Protestants, who supposed that,
as it was in their Latin copies, it was also in the Greek.
He was importuned to insert it in the second edition,
which appeared in 1519, but refused: "I give you,"
said he, "a Greek Testament; I cannot print the First
Epistle of Saint John differently from what I find it in
the Greek; but if you, on examining your manuscripts,
show me one that has the verse, I will insert it." The
advocates of the verse sought for a long time in vain;
but at length it was announced that a manuscript containing it had been found in England. A transcript of
it having been forwarded to him, he adhered to his
word, and inserted it, though with a remark that he
suspected interpolation from the Latin, in his third
edition in 1522. Where this manuscript was, the
researches of later days were long unable to discover,
but it was at last found, after a "profound sleep," as
Porson says, "of two centuries," in the library of
Trinity College, Dublin.

In the same year, 1522, though bearing the date of
1514, was published the Complutensian edition of the

Greek Testament, in which the verse was given. Stunica, or Astuniga, a learned Spaniard, one of the Complutensian editors, fell into controversy with Erasmus about his suspicions, which he still continued to express, of the genuineness of the verse, and Erasmus said, as he had said before, " Produce your manuscripts containing it;" but the Complutensian editors could not allege that it was in any of their manuscripts, and could indeed offer nothing in its support but the Latin Vulgate and the tradition of the Church.

In this dispute, Luther, with many other promoters of the Reformation, took the side of Erasmus. Luther, in his translation of the New Testament, omitted the verse ; and in his preface to the last edition, published in 1546, earnestly desired that no alterations should be made in his version. His request, however, has not been regarded, for in the German Bibles of the present day, the text of which is still called Luther's, the verse appears in exactly the same form as in our English Bibles.

Colinæus, in his edition of 1534, omitted the verse, on the authority of manuscripts.

In 1546, 1549, and 1550, Robert Stephens published three editions of the Greek Testament, the text of which was formed, as he represents, from a collation of sixteen exemplaria ; the first being the edition of Complutum, which, he says, as its text was settled by the most ancient manuscripts, may well be allowed the authority of a manuscript; the second, a very old manuscript in Italy, which had been collated for him by some friends ; eight others, which he had borrowed from the French king's library ; and the remaining six, *quæ undique corrogare licuit*, such as he could anywhere procure. In the last edition, which is of a larger form than either of the two preceding, he noted deficiencies in manuscripts by an obelus and a semicircle, the obelus being prefixed, and the semicircle subjoined, to any word or passage that is wanting in any manuscript or manuscripts of which the designation is given in the margin. In the seventh verse of the fifth chapter of St. John's first epistle, the words ἐν τῷ οὐρανῷ were thus marked as absent from seven manuscripts, giving the reader to understand that the rest of the verse was found entire in those and all the other manuscripts.

This seems to have been understood by Beza, who, in a note on the verse in his edition of the Greek Testament published in 1556, says that it appears the verse ought to be retained, because of its satisfactory correspondence with the eighth verse. "It is not indeed acknowledged," he observes, "by the Syriac version, or by the old Latin interpreter, or by Nazianzen in his fifth oration on Theology, or by Athanasius, or by Didymus, or by Chrysostom, or by Hilarius, or by Cyril, or by Augustin, or by Bede; but it was recognised by St. Jerome, and by Erasmus from a British manuscript, and it is found in the Complutensian edition and in some of the old copies (*libris*) of Stephens." "Not that all copies represent it alike," he adds, "for the British manuscript reads πατήρ, λόγος, καὶ πνεῦμα, without any articles. But in our copies the articles are inserted; (*In nostris verò leguntur articuli;*) and the epithet *holy* is added to the word *spirit*, to distinguish it from the *spirit* mentioned in the following verse, the spirit which is on earth." What copies those were that he called "*ours*," the reader is

left in doubt; Travis says that they were Stephens's
manuscripts, which he had lent to Beza; but, if they
were, they were not in Beza's possession, or at least all of
them, when he published his Greek Testament, for Stephens had sent back, as early as 1552*, the eight manuscripts which he had borrowed from the King's Library.

In 1670 Christopher Sandius, a Socinian of Prussia,
published a denial of the genuineness of the verse; and
soon afterwards M. Simon, in his "Critical History of
the New Testament," took the same side. About the
year 1700, Sir Isaac Newton wrote a dissertation on the
verse, "in which," says Porson, "he collected, arranged,
and strengthened Simon's arguments, and gave a clear,
exact, and comprehensive view of the whole question.
This dissertation, which was not published till 1754,
and then imperfectly, has been lately restored," he adds,
"by Dr. Horsley in the last edition of Newton's works
from an original manuscript." Sir Isaac's disquisition,
indeed, for lucidity and calm strength of argument,
deserves the highest praise that can be bestowed upon it.

Next appeared Mill's edition of the Greek Testament,
who, after producing far more evidence against the
verse than in its favour, chose nevertheless to patronise
it. About the same time appeared a dissertation from
Abbé L. Roger, Dean of Bourges, who maintained the
authenticity of the verse, but acknowledged, with M.
Simon, that the semicircle in Stephens's edition, which
follows ἐν τῷ οὐρανῷ in the seventh verse, ought to have
been placed after ἐν τῇ γῇ in the eighth.

Next came upon the stage Emlyn, an English dissen-
ter, author of a "Full Enquiry," unfavourable to the

verse, and Martin, pastor of the French church at the Hague, who maintained its genuineness against Emlyn. Emlyn published an "Answer" and a "Reply," but Martin retorted with reiterated assertions that Stephens's semicircle was in the right place, since Stephens was a printer of such accuracy, that he could neither have committed himself, nor have allowed any of his subordinates to commit, a single error in a work of such importance.

In 1734 appeared the edition of Bengelius, who, in his note on the verse, admits that it is found in no genuine manuscript, and supposes that the Complutensian editors took it from the Latin version. Yet he does not admit that the verse is spurious, but conceives, on what ground it is difficult to discover, that the Fathers of the Church thought the verse of so sublime and mysterious a character as to require to be withdrawn, by the *secret discipline* of the Church, from the copies of the Scriptures in public use, and that thus it was gradually lost.

Wetstein and Griesbach, in their editions, gave summaries of the arguments on both sides; and Griesbach was decidedly adverse to the genuineness of the verse. On the whole the opinions against it greatly predominated, when Gibbon was considered to have expressed, in a few words, the judgment of the learned on the subject, in the passage which we have quoted.

" I had read," says Porson, "though without examining every minute particle of their reasoning, Mill, Wetstein, and Newton, and I was fully satisfied of the spuriousness of the verse from my general recollection of their arguments. But I must thus far confess my obligations to Mr. Travis, that

the appearance of his book induced me to reconsider the
subject with a little more attention.   In the course of this
inquiry, I found such astonishing instances of error, such
intrepid assertions contrary to fact, that I almost doubted
whether I were awake while I read them.   But at last I discovered that Mr. Travis was a stranger to all criticism, sacred
and profane; and that he had read scarcely anything even on
the subject of the contested verse, except Martin's publications.   This discovery opened my eyes, and made me see why
Mr. Travis was, as Professor Michaelis rightly says, *half a
century behindhand in his information.*"

Mr. Travis took Martin for his guide. He first
mentions many writers, of greater or less authority,
posterior to the fifth century, that cite or allude to the
verse, as Thomas Aquinas, Duns Scotus, Euthymius
Zygabenus in his "Panoplia Dogmatica," Walafrid
Strabo in his "Glossa Ordinaria," and others whom it
is superfluous to name. He notices also that as early
as A. D. 484, the assembly of African bishops, convened
at Carthage by the Vandal King Hunneric, who was an
Arian, but who professed to offer his opponents an
opportunity of defending their tenets, alleged it in a
written vindication of their belief; and that the re-
visers of the Bible under the commission of Charlemagne, the chief of whom was Alcuin, exhibited it in
their text. But his chief allegations in support of its
authenticity are that it is contained in the old Italic
version, or *Itala vetus*, and in that of St. Jerome,
published at the beginning of the fifth century; that
there is an allusion to it in St. Jerome's Prologue to
the Seven Canonical Epistles; that it is cited still
earlier, by Cyprian and Tertullian; and that it was
found in seven Greek manuscripts collected by Lauren-

tius Valla, who flourished about a hundred years before Erasmus.

Let us consider first Mr. Travis's assertion that the verse is contained in the old Italian version. This is an affirmation without proof ; for Mr. Travis admits, as he must necessarily admit, that there is not a single manuscript of the old Italian version known to be extant. " Why, then," says Porson *, " must this version be pressed into the service ? Because it is cited by the writers who lived before Jerome. This version, therefore, ultimately resolves itself into the authority of those writers." And among those writers the only ones that are cited in its favour are Tertullian and Cyprian.

To what do Tertullian's words amount ? They are these : " *He* (the Paraclete) *shall take* (says the Son) *of mine* (John xvi. 14), as I myself of the Father's. Thus the connexion of the Father in the Son, and of the Son in the Paraclete, makes three [Persons] cohering one with the other, which three are one [being, *unum*], and one [person, *unus*], as it is written, *I and my Father are one* (John x. 30)."†

" As often as I read this sentence," adds Porson, " so often am I astonished that the words *tres unum sunt* should ever be urged as a quotation. On the contrary, it appears to me demonstrable, that, instead of being a quotation, they are the words of Tertullian himself, and expressly distinguished from the words of Scripture. Tertullian does not declare them to be a quotation. . . . If the three heavenly witnesses were in his copy of the New Testament, why does he never appeal to them in the rest of this treatise, particularly in his twenty-second chapter, where he insists, at length,

* Porson, Letters, p. 137. † Ibid., p. 240.

on the expression *Ego et Pater unum sumus*, which he quotes five times in the whole book? . . . If Tertullian had two texts before him, one asserting the unity of two of the divine persons, the other the unity of all the three, he must have been strangely forgetful, or something worse, to reason so much upon his weaker authority, and so little upon his stronger."*

We then come to Cyprian. We find that he is represented by Mr. Travis as alluding to the verse in two of his writings, his treatise *De Unitate Ecclesiæ*, and his Epistle to Jubaianus. It will be necessary to give the passages from each in full, for they are so similar, as to any deduction that can be formed from them, that, as Porson says, if Cyprian does not appear to quote 1 John v. 7, in one of them, neither will he appear to have quoted him in the other.

"Dicit Dominus, *Ego et Pater unum sumus*. Et iterum de Patre et Filio et Spiritu Sancto scriptum est, *Et hi tres unum sunt*. Et quisquam credit hanc unitatem de divinâ firmitate venientem, sacramentis cœlestibus cohærentem, scindi in ecclesiâ posse, et voluntatum collidentium divortio separari? Hanc unitatem qui non tenet, Dei legem non tenet; non tenet Patris et Filii fidem; et veritatem non tenet ad salutem."—*Cyprianus de Unitate Ecclesiæ*, (edit. Oxon.) p. 109.

"Si peccatorum remissam consecutus est, et templum Dei factus est, quæso cujus Dei? Si *Creatoris*, non potuit qui in eum non credidit; si *Christi*, nec hujus fieri potest templum, qui negat Deum Christum; si *Spiritûs Sancti*, cùm *tres unum sunt*, quomodo Spiritus Sanctus placatus esse ei potest, qui aut Patris aut Filii inimicus est?"—*Cyprian. Epist. ad Jubaianum*, lxxiii. p. 203.

"I allow," says Porson, "that by saying of the Father, Son, and Holy Ghost, it is written, *And these* (or *the*) *three*

---

* Porson, Letters, pp. 240—242.

are one, Cyprian affirms the words which follow 'it is written' to be extant in Scripture. But, he asks, if the entire seventh verse existed in Cyprian's copy as we have it at present, why would he not quote it?"

The old Italic version, therefore, being found destitute of support from Tertullian and Cyprian, to whom Mr. Travis trusted to uphold it, we proceed to consider what dependance is to be placed on that of St. Jerome, commonly called the Vulgate, which is supposed to be a recension of the old Italic version, and in which, as we have it at present, the text of the Three Heavenly Witnesses is found. "In examining the manuscripts of this recension, we have to ascertain," observes Porson, "whether it appears scrupulously to follow the Greek, especially in guarding against interpolations ; whether all the manuscripts of it agree in retaining 1 John v. 7 ; whether all that exhibit the seventh and eighth verses exhibit them in the same condition, without any important alterations, omissions, or additions; and whether the oldest and best manuscripts have the verse from the hand of the first writer without erasure, interlineations, or marginal insertions ; for, unless these questions be answered in the affirmative, the main prop of the verse is but 'in a lame and tottering condition.'" "But whoever has inquired," he adds, "with the least share of diligence, into the state of the Latin manuscripts, knows that *not one* of these questions can be answered in the affirmative."

Porson then remarks on the variations in fifty manuscripts which he had the patience, he says, to consult, thirty-two of which omit the final clause of the eighth verse, one omits the final clause of the seventh, nine

change the order of the verses, and almost all exhibit
redundancies, deficiencies, or *consarcinations*, such as
prove that there could have been no common standard
of certainty as to that part of the Epistle.

But there was a revision of the Vulgate, as has been
already observed, at the command of Charlemagne, and
under the direction of Alcuin, in whose *Correctorium*,
the result of the united labours of the commission, presented to Charlemagne, " the Testimony of the Three
Heavenly Witnesses," says Mr. Travis, " is read without
the smallest impeachment of its authenticity." This
Correctorium, he adds, " was extant at Rome in the
time of Baronius," who calls it " a treasure of inestimable value." Mr. Travis also supposes that Alcuin
and his assistants would not have attempted to settle
the text without referring to Greek manuscripts, the
oldest that they could procure, some of which, *in
all probability*, would be as old as the days of the
apostles.

" But," retorts Porson, " you cannot prove that Alcuin
ever saw a Greek manuscript, much less that he collated
any for the use of his edition. The knowledge of Greek
was so scarce a commodity in those days that the contrary
supposition, which is expressly affirmed by Vallarsius, in
Bianchini's ' Vindiciæ Veteris Vulgatæ,' p. 328, is much the
more probable of the two. It was labour and honour enough
for Alcuin to collate the copies of the Vulgate. . . . But you
will be delighted, Sir, I doubt not, to hear that this treasure
of inestimable value is still in being. Bianchini has given a
specimen of the character in his ' Evangeliarium Quadruplex,'
from which it appears, as far as I can judge, to be less
ancient than he would make it."

Porson intimates that this copy of the *Correctorium*

may not have been Alcuin's, or written in his age, but a subsequent transcript.

" In these matters," however, he proceeds, " most editors are naturally apt to be a little partial. When you say that 1 John v. 7 is found in this famous manuscript *without the smallest impeachment of its authenticity,* what do you mean by *the smallest impeachment?* Would you have the writer of the manuscript inform his readers, by a marginal note, that he had inserted a spurious verse in his edition? An editor would hardly be mad enough to become such a *felo de se.*

"But I shall advance one step farther, and maintain that this manuscript, upon which so much stress is laid, is at least as much against the verse as in its favour. For how is the verse read in the manuscript? Not in the text, but in the margin, are added these words: Sicut *tres sunt qui testimonium dant in cœlo, Pater, Verbum, et Spiritus Sanctus, et tres unum sunt.* The text has only these words, *quoniam tres sunt qui testimonium dant, spiritus, aqua, et sanguis, et tres unum sunt.* Between *sunt* and *qui* the same hand has interlined *in terrâ.* (Vitali in Bianchini Evang. Quadr. Part I. p. 567.) Now, Sir, this is so far from being a small impeachment of your favourite verse, that it is a direct and violent attack upon it; for it plainly says that the Latin manuscripts varied; and it more than hints that the older surviving manuscripts were without the addition of the heavenly witnesses. If, then, this manuscript was only a copy of Alcuin's autograph, Alcuin might be unacquainted with this verse, though without its aid he believed the doctrine which it is supposed to contain, as appears from his treatise on the Trinity."*

Thus we see that there is little support for this verse in Jerome's Vulgate. But there remains to be examined what is called Jerome's Prologue to the Canonical Epistles. "At the request or command of Pope Damasus,"

---

* Porson, Letters, p. 145, *seqq.*

says Porson, "Jerome revised the Latin translation, and corrected it upon the faith of the Greek manuscripts. Did he therefore replace the three heavenly witnesses at this revision or not? If he did, why did he not *then* write his preface to inform the world of his recovered reading? But, after Damasus was dead, Eustochium, it seems, a young lady, at once devout, handsome, and learned, requests him once more to revise the Catholic Epistles, and correct them from the Greek. Jerome undertakes the task, and, having completed it, advertises her, in this Prologue, that other inaccurate translators had omitted the testimony of the three heavenly witnesses, the strongest proof of the Catholic faith. Such a story as this carries its own condemnation upon its forehead. It has therefore been given up by most of the defenders of the verse; by Mill, by Abbé Roger, by Maffei, Vallarsius, Vitali, Twells, Bengelius." Porson then proceeds to observe that in many manuscripts of Jerome his name is not prefixed to the Prologue; that he himself collated thirty-four which omit the name, and six which omit the Prologue altogether; that he found, indeed, among all that he consulted, only eight that at once retained the Prologue and attributed it to Jerome; and that consequently the Prologue, " by being often absent, and often anonymous, betrays marks of a late birth and dishonourable extraction." "The style alone," too, he adds, "would determine it not to be Jerome's," for " Jerome's language is always spirited and perspicuous, while the Prologue is written in a barbarous and uncouth jargon." Nor is the reasoning and connexion less unlike the manner of Jerome. " The author does not positively assert that he has restored the verse upon the authority of Greek manuscripts, but, in order to possess the reader with that belief, envelopes his meaning in a cloud of words. . . . If Jerome himself had told us such a piece of news as is hinted in the Prologue, he would have spoken out and told it plainly, whether it were true or false. If it were true, an affected obscurity would be as needless as it was contrary to his manner. If it were false, he would have affirmed it no less boldly, and called God to witness no less solemnly, than when he attested the miracle of his being whipped by angels for reading profane authors."

Jerome's Prologue being thus set aside, we have now only to glance at one other alleged authority, the manuscripts of Valla. Mr. Travis positively asserted that 1 John v. 7 " was found in all Valla's manuscripts, and was commented upon by him." The whole of Valla's words on the first fifteen verses of the chapter are, "*Et hi tres unum sunt. Græcè est, Et hi tres in unum sunt, εἰς τὸ ἕν εἰσι.*" * These words Mr. Travis wished to represent as a comment on the seventh verse, but Porson asserts that the seventh verse is not thus read in any manuscript, and that the note must consequently be on the eighth verse ; as was indeed acknowledged by Martin, who " only argues that Valla had the seventh verse in his Greek copies, because Valla is quite silent."†
If Valla, asks Porson, had seven manuscripts containing the verse, how is it that none of these manuscripts have appeared since Valla's time ? " All the rest of the Greek manuscripts, which, if I have counted right,

---

* Porson, p. 25 ; Vindication of Porson, p. 109.
† Porson, Letters, p. 27.

amount to ninety-seven ancient and modern, oriental and occidental, good, bad, and indifferent, do with one consent wholly omit the seventh verse, and the words ἐν τῇ γῇ of the eighth. " You have said, I know," continues Porson, addressing Mr. Travis, " that the words ἐν τῇ γῇ seem to have been omitted in a few copies only ; but this is a little pious fraud, which is very excusable when it tends to promote the cause of truth and the glory of God. If you think this charge of fraud too severe, I shall be very happy to seize the slightest probabilities that may acquit you of so odious an imputation, and shall acquiesce in the milder accusation of shameful and enormous ignorance. But be this assertion of yours owing to fraud or to ignorance, I defy you to specify a single Greek manuscript that omits the seventh verse, and retains these words [ἐν τῇ γῇ]."* The truth is, that no Greek manuscript has been found containing the seventh verse, except a Berlin forgery, and the *codex Britannicus* which came to light in the time of Erasmus, and which is the same that is now called *codex Dubliniensis*. This manuscript, in Porson's opinion, " was probably written about the year 1520, and interpolated in this place for the purpose of deceiving Erasmus. This hypothesis," he continues, " will explain how it so suddenly appeared when it was wanted, and how it disappeared as suddenly after having achieved the glorious exploit for which it was destined."† Similar opinions regarding the manuscript had been expressed by Michaelis, Griesbach, Wetstein, Marsh, Mill, and Bengelius. Dr. Adam Clarke, however, who

* Porson, Letters, p. 26.   † Ibid. p. 117.

examined the Dublin manuscript, thinks that it is as old as the thirteenth century*, and, if so, it was not, as he observes, written with an intention to deceive; certainly not to deceive Erasmus. But is not a manuscript, which differs in this passage from other manuscripts, greatly to be suspected? If corrupted, may not the corruption have been made to seem older than it really was?

As to the versions of the New Testament, Porson employs two letters in showing that there is no authority for the genuineness of the verse in the Syriac, Coptic, Arabic, Æthiopic, Armenian, or Slavonic versions.

The last letter mentions the host of Greek and Latin writers who might have quoted the verse if it had been in their copies of St. John's Epistle, but in whose works it is not found.

Porson's judgment, therefore, is, that " the only genuine words of 1 John v. 7, 8, are these; Ὅτι τρεῖς εἰσιν οἱ μαρτυροῦντες, τὸ πνεῦμα, καὶ τὸ ὕδωρ, καὶ τὸ αἷμα, καὶ οἱ τρεῖς εἰς τὸ ἕν εἰσι. This is the reading," he states, " of all the Greek manuscripts, above a hundred and ten; of near thirty of the oldest Latin; of the two Syriac versions; of the Coptic, Arabic, Æthiopic and Slavonic."

As to the introduction of the spurious words into the text, Porson supposes that Tertullian, in imitation of the phrase, *I and my Father are one*, had said of the three Persons of the Trinity, *which Three are One*; that Cyprian, adopting this application of the words from Tertullian, said boldly, *of the Father, Son, and Holy Ghost, it is written, And these Three are One*; that in the

---

* Vindication of Porson, pp. 8, 9.

course of two centuries, when this interpretation had been expressly maintained by Augustin and others, a marginal note of this sort, *Sicut tres sunt qui testimonium dant in Cœlo, Pater,* &c., crept into the text of a few copies; that such a copy was used by the author of the Confession which Victor, the historian of the Council convened by Hunneric, has preserved; and that such another was used by the historian of the books *de Trinitate.**

The origin of the text is also attributed to Augustin by a writer in the " Quarterly Review " for December 1825 : †

" Augustin, who died about the year 430, had taught the African church with an authority only inferior to that of the Apostles, that the Homoüsian doctrine of the Trinity was contained in the words of St. John : *Tres sunt qui testimonium dant, spiritus, et aqua, et sanguis; et hi tres unum sunt.* It is not improbable that, as a security for the faith, this dogma of the great teacher was recorded in the margins of the Latin manuscripts of the New Testament; and thus it may have glided into the text. At all events these African bishops, or the compiler of the Confession, discovered what had escaped all the acuteness and all the researches of preceding times. To silence their opponents at once; to render their opinions clearer than the day, as they expressed it, they adduced as the words of St. John, *the disputed verse.* Perhaps this was not so bold a measure as it may at first sight appear; the judges of the correctness of the quotation were a set of fierce and intolerant barbarians, so ignorant that in all probability not an individual among them understood a word of Greek ; and few perhaps could read a Latin manuscript. *Nescio Latine,* said the patriarch Cyrila himself; an assertion which, although not literally true, is a sufficient indication that neither he nor his assessors were great clerks.

* Porson, Letters, p. 339.   † Vol. xxxiii. p. 84.

"Et ut adhuc luce clarius unius Divinitatis esse cum Patria et Filio, Spiritum sanctum doceamus, Joannis Evangelistæ testimonio comprobatur; ait namque, *Tres sunt qui testimonium perhibent in cœlo, Pater, Verbum, et Spiritus Sanctus; et hi tres unum sunt.* Such is the passage in the African Confession, as it appears in the printed editions of Victor Vitensis. It is easy to conceive the mode in which these words may have been derived into the text from Augustine's interpretation of the eighth verse; it is *not* easy to conceive that they could have existed, as Scripture, *unquoted,* till the close of the fifth century, and then be, all at once, advanced as an argument to make everything *luce clarius.* Perhaps it may be objected that Augustine enumerates *Pater,* Filius, *et Spiritus* Sanctus, as the witnesses, while the Confession mentions *Pater,* Verbum, *et Spiritus Sanctus.* This apparent discrepancy may be removed. There are in the Colbertine Library, at Paris, three manuscripts of Victor Vitensis, which Mr. Butler, whose attention has been drawn to the controversy, caused to be examined. A manuscript of the thirteenth century reads *Verbum* in this place, and a manuscript of the fifteenth century reads *Filius.* The oldest of the three, a manuscript of the tenth century, reads *Filius,* with this note in the margin, *In Epistolâ Beati Joannis ita legendum.* It is probable, therefore, that *Filius* is the true reading in the Confession, that is, the original reading, and that *Verbum* was an after thought. That word would appear to render the passage peculiarly St. John's; he being the only apostle who has written distinctly of the *Logos.* Moreover there is an expression in Augustine, which might suggest the substitution of *Verbum* for *Filius.* To show that by *the Blood* we are to understand *the Son,* he observes, *Nomine autem sanguinis Filium significatum accipiamus; quia* Verbum *caro factum est.* On the whole, therefore, it is probable that the verse originated in the interpretation of St. Augustine. It seems to have existed for some time on the margins of the Latin copies, in a kind of intermediate state, as something better than a mere dictum of Augustine, and yet not absolutely Scripture itself. By degrees it was received into the text, where it appears in by far the greater number of Latin manuscripts now in our hands. When, to use Newton's expression, 'the ignorant ages came on,' all further inquiry was at an end, and when the verse was fairly established in the text, it gained the protection of the Romish church ; and thus, at the period of the Reformation, few doubts were entertained on the subject. Such, in brief, is its history from the Council of Hanneric to the time of Erasmus."

Porson's conclusion of his Letters is this :

" In short, if this verse be really genuine, notwithstanding its absence from all the visible Greek manuscripts except two ; " [that of Dublin, and the forged one found at Berlin ;] " one of which awkwardly translates the verse from the Latin, and the other transcribes it from a printed book; " [the Berlin manuscript coincides exactly with the Complutensian edition ;] " notwithstanding its absence from all the versions except the Vulgate, even from many of the best and oldest manuscripts of the Vulgate ; notwithstanding the deep and dead silence of all the Greek writers down to the thirteenth, and of most of the Latins down to the middle of the eighth century ; if, in spite of all these objections, it be still genuine, no part of Scripture whatsoever can be proved either spurious or genuine ; and Satan has been permitted for many centuries miraculously to banish the finest passage in the New Testament," as Martin calls it, " from the eyes and memories of almost all the Christian authors, translators, and transcribers."

" At last, Sir, I see land. I have so clearly explained my sentiments concerning the authority of the disputed verse, and the merits of your book, in the progress of these Letters, that it will be needless to add anything upon either of these topics. As I was persuaded that Mr. Gibbon would never condescend to answer you, I have been bold enough to trouble you with my objections to your facts and arguments. The proofs of the spuriousness of 1 John v. 7, that I have enumerated, are, in my opinion, more than sufficient to convince any reasonable man. But whatever success I may have had in the main question, there is another point which I have proved to demonstration, that Mr. Travis is radically ignorant of the subject which he has undertaken to demonstrate. You may therefore reply, Sir, or not, as shall seem good to you. If you think proper not to expose yourself again, which, to speak as a friend, I should think your wisest plan, I shall attribute your silence to a consciousness of your own weakness. You will call it contempt of your adversary, and I cannot deny the retaliation to be fair enough, considering with how small respect I have treated an author, who *has vindicated the authenticity of that important passage* (1 John v. 7) *in a superior way, so as to leave no room for future doubt or cavil.*" [These words are from a pamphlet called "An Apology for the Liturgy and Clergy of the Church of England."] "But if you reply, I shall not think myself bound to continue the debate, unless both your matter and style much excel your letters to Mr. Gibbon, and still more that *crambe recocta* which you called a defence of Stephens and Beza," published in the "Gentleman's Magazine," for March, 1790. "Such replies will carry their own refutation with them to all readers that are not eaten up with prejudice ; and others it would be folly to expect to satisfy. I shall therefore be perfectly silent, unless you can disprove the charges that I have brought against you, of ignorance and misrepresentation. In case of conviction, I dare not promise to retract publicly (for I know how frail are the vows of authors and lovers), but I promise to try. If you confess the charges, and yet maintain that the errors you have committed are venial and consistent with a knowledge of the subject, I shall excuse myself from the controversy, and consider you as degraded from that rank of literature which entitles one writer to challenge another."

What is most displeasing in these Letters is the excessive virulence of their style. There appears in page after page too much railing at Mr. Travis's ignorance and presumption. The epistles would have been infinitely more agreeable to the reader if Porson had treated Travis as he treated Sir John Hawkins, or as Bentley treated Boyle, exhibiting the ease and good humour with which a higher mind can expose the folly and weakness of a lower; an exercise of which the finest specimen in our language is Johnson's critique on Jonas Hanway's "Eight Days' Journey." As it is, the Letters were not improperly said, by Dr. Rennell, to be "such a book as the devil would write, if he could hold a pen."*

* Rogers's Table Talk, "Porsoniana," p. 307.

CHAP. VI.

TRAVIS'S attack upon Gibbon has been characterised as
violent.   But it is mildness itself when compared with
Porson's attack upon Travis.   He said that, *facit indig-
natio versum,* he was stimulated by indignation to over-
come his dislike of writing, and that " he could not
treat the subject in any other manner if he treated it
at all.   To peruse such a mass of sophistry," he observed, " and to write remarks upon it, without sometimes giving way to laughter, and sometimes to indignation, was, to me at least, impossible.   .   .   .   I am
persuaded that every attentive reader, who believes me
right in the statement of my facts, and the tenor of my
argument, will allow that even harsher expressions
would in such a case be justified.   Besides, I confess
I never much admired that mock politeness which
expresses a strong charge in a long-winded periphrasis
of half a dozen lines, when the complete sense might
be conveyed in as many words." †

---

* Letters to Travis, Preface, p. xxii.

"The Travisian examination," wrote Burney to Parr, "is most excellent, and shows the clear acuteness of Porson's mind in as strong a point of view as it exhibits his wit and severity. But I feel little inclination to mercy, when ignorance, aided by a desire of misrepresentation, is chastised." *

"Travis," said Parr, "was a superficial and arrogant declaimer ; and his letters to Gibbon brought down upon him the just and heavy displeasure of an assailant equally irresistible for his wit, his reasoning, and his erudition,—I mean, the immortal Richard Porson."†

One peculiarity in the style of these Letters is the vein of irony and banter which everywhere pervades them ; the effect of which is such that readers, unless they be thoroughly acquainted with the point under consideration, are often in danger of being puzzled to know whether Porson is in jest or in earnest. Even Dr. Turton, afterwards his vindicator, who understood him in general well enough, is utterly mystified and deluded by the phrases which he uses concerning Gregory of Nazianzum. He speaks of himself as "having been *always extremely fond of Gregory*,"‡ and being desirous "to bring off," on one occasion, "his *favourite Gregory* with the least possible loss of honour ;"§ expressions which led Dr. Turton, and many others, seriously to believe that Porson had the highest esteem and liking for Gregory. But the truth is, that all these remarks are merely sarcastic allusions to a story which, as Mr. Kidd says ‖, was well known to every

---

* Parr's Works, vol. vii. p. 409.
† Bibliotheca Parriana, p. 601.   ‡ Letters, p. 223.
§ Ib. p. 272.   ‖ Tracts, p. lv.

member of Cambridge University. What the story
was, Mr. Kidd does not tell us; but Barker* learned
from Parr that it was a story about Bishop Watson.
The Bishop, while he was divinity professor, happened,
as he was taking a ride a few days before he had to
deliver a Latin oration to the University, to meet with
a learned friend, who began to talk to him on the
subject of his intended speech, and told him that there
was a notable passage in Gregory Nazianzen, which he
might introduce with effect. " Is there ? " said Watson.
" But I never read a page of him." " Well," said the
other, " I will send you the volume with the passage
marked in it." This promise was performed, and
the professor, having got the passage by heart, pronounced it *ore rotundo* in his oration, adding *Hæc ex
Gregorio illo Nazianzeno, quem semper in deliciis
habui.* Parr used to repeat this anecdote as an instance of *charlatanerie* in one whom he pronounced a
man of some ability, but of little learning. Watson's
religious sincerity, it may be observed, has, notwithstanding his "Apology," come to be pretty generally
disbelieved. Southey said his conversation was such
as to prove that " the articles of his faith were not all
to be found among the nine and thirty, nor all the
nine and thirty to be found among his ; " † and still
stronger testimony to the nature of his belief may be
seen in De Quincey's " Selections, Grave and Gay."‡
The Bishop seems, according to these authorities, to
have grown weary of professing the faith of which the
profession had made him a bishop.

* Barker's Parriana, vol. ii. p. 713.
† Letters by Warter, vol. i. p. 391.   ‡ Vol. ii. p. 215.

Another peculiarity in the style of the Letters is the constant introduction of phrases from eminent English authors, but especially from Shakspeare, with whom he gave his readers credit for being as intimate as himself. As he remembered so much of what he read, other men's expressions were perpetually rising in his mind, and he could draw language from the pages of others more readily than from his own thought. Kidd has given references to several of his allusions, but many of them still remain to be detected.

The publication of the book brought upon him a great pecuniary loss. Mrs. Turner, who had so liberally subscribed to the fund for sending him to college, and who had still continued his friend, being a lady of very pious disposition, was extremely desirous that he should take orders, and was greatly distressed when she heard of his decision rather to resign his fellowship than to subscribe to the Thirty-nine Articles; but when the "Letters to Travis" appeared, she was entirely alienated from him, for she thought that he had treated a dignitary of the church with too little reverence, and her attorney, through whose hands her money passed, and who found his letters to Porson sometimes slighted*, represented the work to her, officiously if not malignantly, as a fierce assault upon Christianity, and as intended to shake the foundations of all evangelical religion. Possessed with these notions, of which she was unable to see the falsehood, Mrs. Turner was induced to alter her will, in which

* Sexagenarian, vol. i. p. 222.

G

she had assigned Porson a large sum of money, and to bequeath him a legacy of only thirty pounds.*

Porson is said, however, to have always expressed himself favourable to the doctrines of the Church of England. "When a friend in the course of conversation," says a writer in the Quarterly Review, "asked him what he thought of the evidence afforded by the New Testament in favour of the Socinian doctrines, his answer was short and decisive: 'If the New Testament is to determine the question, and words have any meaning, the Socinians are wrong.'" †

After Porson's death, some publications in defence of Mr. Travis, and intended to invalidate what Porson had established, appeared from the pen of Dr. Burgess, Bishop of Salisbury, under the titles of "A Vindication of 1 John v. 7," and "A Letter to the Clergy of the Diocese of St. David's," in which the Bishop insinuated that Porson's sagacity of conjecture on the text of Greek poets, and on Greek metres and idioms, were of little use on the subject of *The Three Heavenly Witnesses,* and that he had brought no objection to the passage which had not been previously noticed by Newton, Whiston, Evelyn, or Benson. But the merit of Porson, when fairly stated, was that he triumphantly established all the objections to the text, whether those of others or his own, by exact critical research, and sound argument based upon it. His memory found an able defender in Dr. Turton, the present Bishop of Ely, who published, in 1827, an octavo volume entitled, "A Vin-

* Sexagenarian, vol. i. p. 210.
† Quart. Rev. vol. xxxiii. p. 99.

dication of the Literary Character of the late Professor Porson from the Animadversions of Dr. Burgess, Lord Bishop of Salisbury, by Crito Cantabrigiensis," with the motto, from the Ajax of Sophocles,

$$\text{———}ἄνδρα \; δ', \; οὐ \; δίκαιον, \; εἰ \; θάνοι,$$
$$Βλάπτειν \; τὸν \; ἔσθλον, \; οὐδ' \; ἐὰν \; μισῶν \; κυρῇς.$$

In this publication Dr. Turton exposes much unjust treatment of Porson's arguments, in Dr. Burgess's paragraphs, by misrepresentation or imperfect or unfair quotation. Passages taken from the pages of Porson are brought together or separated to suit Burgess's purpose, and words or sentences are omitted that are necessary to show Porson's sense. How well qualified Mr. Travis was to defend the Three Heavenly Witnesses, and how deserving of defence from Bishop Burgess, is shown by Dr. Turton by one ludicrous example : " To the phrase ὅτι ὑμεῖς οἱ ἀκολουθήσαντές μοι, ἐν τῇ παλιγγενεσίᾳ (Matthew xix. 28), Robert Stephens annexed this note in the margin: πρὸ τοῦ, ἐν τῇ παλιγγενεσίᾳ, διαστολὴν ἔχουσι τὸ γ. δ. ε. ζ. ιϛ. And Mr. Travis positively understood Stephens to affirm that these manuscripts presented the words διαστολὴν ἔχουσι as part of the text!"* This blunder did not escape the eye of Porson, though he has not noticed it in print ; for he mentions it in a letter to Mr. J. Pope, preserved among his manuscripts in the library of Trinity College, Cambridge.

Another absurdity may be worth notice. Martin, in defending the spurious text, had, in speaking of St.

* Travis's Letters to Gibbon, p. 225, 3rd ed. Vindication of Porson, p. 338.

Mark's Gospel in the Dublin manuscript, mistaken the date of the Gospel for the date of the manuscript itself, and had thus, as Wetstein expresses it, turned years into centuries, and St. Mark into a transcriber; a blunder which Travis, in his first edition, faithfully copied. Becoming aware of his error, however, he expunged Martin's words in his second edition, and said, in a note, that he had omitted them because they *may be applied* to the time when the Gospel was originally written; a kind of half-retractation which showed at once his want of candour and his want of perspicacity; for, if he pretended to the name of critic, he ought, especially when admonished, to have been able to see, and willing to acknowledge, that Martin's words could refer to no other time.

Porson sold the book to Egerton for thirty pounds, and told Dr. Maltby that he was glad to find that he had lost sixteen by the publication of it.* Why he was glad at Egerton's loss, I do not know. Perhaps he thought that the bookseller had made but a mean offer. He also told Dr. Maltby that he was occupied two years in the composition of the Letters; that he once thought of writing an appendix to them; but that, on the whole, he looked back with regret on the time which he had devoted to the study of theology. According to Kidd †, he wrote seven of the Letters to Travis at Eton, in a fortnight, from memoranda, when he was on a visit to Dr. Goodall.

In the preface appeared the famous character of Gibbon's History and its style; a passage which, though

* Barker's Literary Anecdotes, vol. ii. p. 32.
† Tracts, p. lvi.

it has been reprinted more than once, may very well be transcribed again.

" An impartial judge, I think, must allow that Mr. Gibbon's History is one of the ablest performances of its kind that has ever appeared. · His industry is indefatigable; his accuracy scrupulous; his reading, which indeed is sometimes ostentatiously displayed, immense; his attention always awake; his memory retentive; his style emphatic and expressive; his periods harmonious. His reflections are often just and profound; he pleads eloquently for the rights of mankind, and the duty of toleration; nor does his humanity ever slumber except when women are ravished*, or the Christians persecuted.†

" Though his style is in general correct and elegant, he sometimes *draws out the thread of his verbosity finer than the staple of his argument.*‡ In endeavouring to avoid vulgar terms he too frequently dignifies trifles, and clothes common thoughts in a splendid dress that would be rich enough for the noblest ideas. In short, we are too often reminded of that *great man,* Mr. Prig, *the auctioneer, whose manner was so inimitably fine that he had as much to say upon a ribbon as a Raphael.*§

" Sometimes, in his anxiety to vary his phrase, he becomes obscure; and, instead of calling his personages by their names, defines them by their birth, alliance, office, or other circumstances of their history. Thus an honest gentleman is often described by a circumlocution, lest the same word should be twice repeated in the same page. Sometimes epithets are added which the tenor of the sentence renders unnecessary. Sometimes, in his attempts at elegance, he loses sight of English, and sometimes of sense.

" A less pardonable fault is the rage for indecency which pervades the whole work, but especially the last volumes. And, to the honour of his consistency, this is the same man who is so prudish that he dares not call Belisarius a cuckold,

---

* Chap. lvii. note 54.   † See the whole of chap. xvi.
‡ Love's Labour Lost.   § Foote's " Minor." ·

because it is too bad a word for a *decent* historian to use. If the history were anonymous, I should guess that these disgraceful obscenities were written by some *débauché,* who, having from age, or accident, or excess, survived the practice of lust, still indulged himself in the luxury of speculation; and *exposed the impotent imbecility, after he had lost the vigour of the passions.**

" But these few faults make no considerable abatement in my general esteem. Notwithstanding all its particular defects, I greatly admire the whole; as I should admire a beautiful face in the author, though it were tarnished with a few freckles; or as I should admire an elegant person and address, though they were blemished with a little affectation."

Notwithstanding the severity of this critique, Gibbon spoke highly of the " Letters." He said, in his usual studied style, that he considered them " as the most acute and accurate piece of criticism since the days of Bentley. Mr. Porson's strictures are founded in argument, enriched with learning, and enlivened with wit; and his adversary neither deserves nor finds any quarter at his hands."† With these sentiments, he sought an interview with Porson, which was brought about, according to Beloe, by means of Peter Elmsley. " Porson," says Mr. Maltby ‡, "called upon the great historian, who received him with all kindness and respect. In the course of conversation, Gibbon said,

" ' Mr. Porson, I feel truly indebted to you for the Letters to Travis, though I must think that occasionally, while praising me, you have mingled a little acid with the sweet. If ever you should take the trouble to read my History over again, I should be much obliged and

---

* Junius.   † Gibbon's Miscell. vol. i. p. 159.
         ‡ Rogers's Table-Talk, " Porsoniana," p. 306.

honoured by any remarks which might suggest themselves to you.' Porson was highly flattered by Gibbon's
having requested this interview, and loved to talk of it.
He thought the *Decline and Fall* beyond all comparison
the greatest literary production of the eighteenth
century, and was in the habit of repeating long
passages from it.   Yet I have heard him say that there
could not be a better exercise for a school-boy than to
turn a page of it into *English.*"   No intimacy or correspondence appears to have resulted from the interview.
Porson, as Beloe observes, was little disposed to pay
court even to the highest: and Gibbon, who then stood
high in literary fame, made no further advances to
Porson.

Porson complained, too, that Gibbon was not so
ready as he ought to have been to take advantage of
suggestions that were made for giving correctness to his
pages. " A candid acknowledgment of error," says he*,
" does not seem to be Mr. Gibbon's shining virtue.   He
promised, if I understood him rightly, that in a future
edition he would expunge the words *of Armenia,* or
make an equivalent alteration.†   A new edition has
appeared; but I have looked in vain to find a correction
of the passage.   I am almost persuaded that the
misrepresentation of Gennadius was not wilful, but that
Mr. Gibbon, transcribing the Greek from the margin
of Petavius, wrote by mistake αἰδοῦμαι for αἰδοῦνται.
This error has now been so long published that it is
scarcely possible to suppose him ignorant of the charge.

* Preface to Letters to Travis, p. xxxi.
† Gibbon's Vindication, p. 75. History, chap. xv. near note 178.

He has had an opportunity of confessing and correcting the mistake.   Yet still it keeps its place in the octavo edition."

Charles Fox used to remark, that Gibbon had quoted many books as authorities, of which he had read only the preface.   One instance of this which he produced was a note in which " Gibbon had quoted a passage as being in the *third* book of a writer, whose work is divided into *two* books only.   Gibbon was led into this error," he said, " by the translator of the preface of the book quoted, who, in transcribing the passage, had made the same mistake."*

* Kidd's Tracts, p. xlvi.

CHAP. VII.

PORSON'S NOTES ON TOUP'S EMENDATIONS OF SUIDAS. — HIS PREFACE
TO THAT PUBLICATION, SHOWING THE NATURE OF HIS CRITICISM. —
PORSON WITH PARR AT HATTON.—INSULTED BY MRS. PARR.—PORSON'S
RESIGNATION OF HIS FELLOWSHIP. — HIS DIALOGUE WITH POSTLE-
THWAITE, THE MASTER OF TRINITY COLLEGE.—HIS WANT OF MONEY,
AND RESOLUTE FRUGALITY. — A SUBSCRIPTION TO PURCHASE AN
ANNUITY FOR HIM.—PARTICULARS RESPECTING IT.—A LIST OF SOME
OF THE SUBSCRIBERS.

IN 1790 appeared from the Oxford press a reprint of
Toup's *Emendationes in Suidam*, a republication which
had been commenced or projected in 1787, when
Porson had offered to append to it some short annotations of his own. The proposal being accepted, he
introduced them with a preface, which tells us his
reasons, not only for the purport of these animadversions,
but for the nature of his criticism in general. The
notes, which first gave the world full demonstration of
Porson's perspicacity in the elegant niceties of the
Greek language, and his intimate knowledge of the
dramatic poets and their metres, would have been
included by Kidd among his " Tracts and Criticisms,"
but that the sale of the Toup would probably thus
have been injured. The preface, which throws so
much light on Porson's critical character and notions,
we subjoin in an English dress.

"Having lately heard that Toup's 'Emendations to Suidas' would shortly issue from the Oxford press, I took the liberty of acquainting the learned gentlemen, who had undertaken the charge of editing them, that I had read that excellent work with some considerable attention, and would make them a present of some annotations, which I had written here and there on the margin, if they should think them worthy of appearing as an appendix to Toup's volumes. These annotations, gentle reader, are in consequence set before you; and, whatever may be thought of them, it is my earnest wish, not to say hope, that the perusal of them may not be altogether unprofitable to you.

"But there are two points on which I much desire to ask your indulgence. The one is, my assumption of the character of a censor, and my practice of blaming Toup oftener than praising him; the other, my frequent reference to books in which Toup's emendations have been anticipated.

"As to the first point, I have but spoken as I thought, and as I felt obliged to speak; for I have not written with juvenile presumption, nor with the view of gaining praise by detracting from greater men than myself; but, to say the truth, I have never admired the practice of those critics who exclaim *pulchre, bene, rectè*, 'excellent, just, incontrovertible,' at every second or third word. Had I not, indeed, had the highest respect for Toup's abilities and learning, I should never have offered these observations, such as they are, on his writings. But I consider it to be the part of an editor or commentator to correct the errors and supply the deficiencies of his author. I have hardly ever, therefore, expressed mere assent to Toup's remarks, except when it seemed possible to support them by new arguments, or when they seemed to have been unreasonably assailed by other critics.

"As to the second point, I trust that no one will do me such injustice as to think that whenever I notice Toup's agreement with other writers, I wish to fix on him, even in the slightest degree, a suspicion of plagiarism. When I see that two writers express the same thought, I do not consequently suppose that one must of necessity have borrowed from the other, but that the two, considering the subject rightly and reasonably, and influenced by the force of truth, have been led to the same conclusion; for *all of us,* says Bentley, *make many remarks without being aware that they have been already made by others** ; an observation of which I request I may have the benefit, if I shall be found to have said, in these annotations, anything that has been said before.

"London, July 1, 1787."

The winter of 1790-1, Porson spent with Dr. Parr at Hatton, and his habits and mode of life are thus described by Dr. Johnstone, who was there some weeks with him.

" Mr. Richard Porson remained at Hatton in the winter, 1790–1, collecting materials for future works, and enriching his mind with the stores of Parr's library, and of his conversation.   He rose late, seldom walked out, and was employed in the library till dinner, reading and taking notes from books, but chiefly the latter.   His notes were made in a small distinct text, of the most exquisitely neat writing I have ever beheld.   He was very silent, and, except to Parr, whom he often consulted, and to whose opinions he seemed to defer, he seldom spoke a word.   His manners in a morning, indeed, were rather sullen, and his countenance gloomy. After dinner he began to relax, but was always under restraint with Parr and the ladies.

" At night, when he could collect the young men of the family together, and especially if Parr was absent from home, he was in his glory.   The charms of his society were then irresistible.   Many a midnight hour did I spend with him, listening with delight while he poured out torrents of various literature, the best sentences of the best writers, and sometimes the ludicrous beyond the gay ; pages of Barrow, whole letters of Richardson, whole scenes of Foote ; favourite pieces

* Emendat. in Cic. Tusc. Quæst. iv. 21.

from the periodical press, and, among them, I have heard recited the ' Orgies of Bacchus.'

" His abode in the house became at last so tiresome to Mrs. Parr, that she insulted him in a manner which I shall not record. From this time the visits of Porson were not repeated at Hatton ; and though there was no open breach of friendship on his part, there was no continuance of kindness, notwithstanding Dr. Parr's strenuous endeavours to secure his comforts and independence."*

As Dr. Johnstone does not choose to describe Mrs. Parr's insult, we may suppose that it was of a very gross character. She may indeed have fancied that she had reason for offering such an insult. But there are women who imagine that they may say, without censure, the most disagreeable things to any man, however great or good, of whom they conceive a dislike, or wish to be rid. As they are safe from personal chastisement, they venture to utter all the bitterness that may arise in their minds. Nothing is more disgraceful to the female sex than these cowardly attacks on men, often of great ability and merit, whom they know to be restrained by good sense, and gentlemanly forbearance towards the sex, from retaliation. No man can know, who has not experienced, how much mischief may be produced by the impertinent intrusions of a wife between her husband and his friends. Mrs. Parr was a woman of violent and overbearing temper, presumptuous and inconsiderate, and having little respect or kindness for any human being.

Mr. Maltby believed that Porson's offence was, in the words of Horace, *Comminxit lectum potus*, and that

* Parr's Works, vol. i. p. 379.

Mrs. Parr, in consequence, made some allusion in his hearing to the duties of college scouts.*

As Porson had resolved on not entering into orders, it became necessary for him, in June 1791, to resign his fellowship. The Master of Trinity College, at that time, was Dr. Postlethwaite, probably the same gentleman that had assisted Lambert in examining him. Postlethwaite, from some cause, was now ill disposed towards him, and used his influence, it appears, to prevent him from being elected to a lay fellowship, which he wished to secure for John Heys, his nephew.† At this manifestation of injustice Porson was highly indignant, and spoke of it with no small asperity.

Postlethwaite having occasion to come to London this year, to attend the examinations at Westminster School, Porson called upon him; and the following dialogue, which Mr. Maltby took down from Porson's dictation, was held between them:—*Porson.* "I am come, Sir, to inform you that my fellowship will become vacant in a few weeks, in order that you may appoint my successor."—*Postlethwaite.* "But, Mr. Porson, you do not mean to leave us?"—*Porson.* "It is not I who leave you, but you who dismiss me. You have done me every injury in your power. But I am not come to explain or expostulate."—*Postlethwaite.* "I did not know, Mr. Porson, that you were so resolved."—*Porson.* "You could not conceive, Sir, that I should have applied for a lay fellowship to the detriment of some more scrupulous man, if it had been my intention to take orders."‡

* Barker's Lit. Anecdotes, vol. ii. p. 14.
† Parr's Works, vol. vii. p. 414.
‡ Rogers's Table-Talk, "Porsoniana," p. 312.

It has been supposed that the words, " in order that you may appoint my successor," could not have been used by Porson. If they were used, they must have been uttered sarcastically, in allusion to the appointment of Heys by Postlethwaite's means.

A letter from Postlethwaite to Porson, apologising for giving the lay fellowship to another, had contained a recommendation that he should take orders ; an admonition which Porson, perhaps not unjustly, considered as an insult.* Kidd said that Postlethwaite's object was to compel Porson to enter the Church, thinking that he would be compliant enough to do so rather than resign his fellowship, if a lay fellowship were refused him.†

According to Beloe, Porson spent with him the evening of the day on which his fellowship expired, when he expressed great anguish, even to shedding tears, at the gloom of his prospects, and the difficulty of deciding how he should shape his course of life. According to Kidd, though the occasion was " heart-rending," he observed, with his usual good humour (for nothing could depress him), that he found himself a gentleman in London with sixpence in his pocket.

This, after a while, must have become literally true, for he lived, he said, at this period of his life for six weeks on a guinea, which, at sixpence a day, would leave him with sixpence only on the last day. He used to dine on milk, or bread and cheese and porter.‡ Other accounts say that he lived only three weeks on

* Sexagenarian, vol. i. p. 215.
† Barker's Lit. Anecdotes, vol. ii. p. 9.   ‡ Ibid. p. 11.

the guinea. But he told his nephew, Mr. Hawes, that he lived at least a month on the sum, taking only two extremely frugal meals in the twenty-four hours.

During this period of forced economy he would sometimes walk, as he was possessed of great bodily strength, the whole distance between Cambridge and London in a day.

About this time a subscription was proposed, by certain scholars and literary men, to purchase an annuity for Porson. Among the chief promoters of the scheme were Dr. Raine of the Charter House, and the Rev. J. Cleaver Banks, both of whom thought, with many others, that Porson justly conceived himself ill-treated by Postlethwaite. The project will be understood from the following letter from Cleaver Banks to Dr. Burney, dated June 17th, 1792 ; a letter which has never before appeared in print :

"DEAR SIR,

"I am exceedingly glad to hear that our plan goes on so prosperously, and should feel inexpressible pleasure if I could flatter myself that my exertions might promote the success of our cause beyond the contribution of a very few friends added to my own.

"I explained to Raine my reasons for a particular discrimination in the applications I should make; which chiefly arose from my desire of secrecy, my dread of a repulse, and my knowledge of our worthy friend's delicacy. I have consequently hitherto been scrupulous in my choice of confidants, and have only written to Mr. Harper of Brazennose, and mentioned four other names; from whom I have no apprehension of a repulse. At the same time I told him that if he should happen to know any other men who were likely to contribute, or would at least keep the matter to themselves, he might apply; but enjoined the strictest privacy. I shall

write by this post to Dr. Routh, and shall be very cautious in
any future application, unless you should think such nicety
unnecessary; of which I should be glad to be informed either
by letter or by personal intercourse. I wish you could
contrive to meet us at Charter House Square on Tuesday
se'nnight. If you can, I will trouble you to acquaint me
without delay. In the meantime if you can suggest to me
any way by which I may render myself serviceable, you may
command my warmest zeal and attention. Raine likewise
knows my reasons for withholding the matter from my relations. They are numerous, and would, I dare say, have
seconded such a plan for the benefit of any friend to the
establishment; but in this instance I cordially lament that
their religion has restrained their benevolence. I wish I had
an opportunity of communicating to you more fully the circumstances which have led me to this opinion. At present
I must content myself with what I have already said, by
assuring you that

　　　　"I am your faithful and sincere humble servant,
　　　　　　　"JOHN CLEAVER BANKS."

In the same month Raine wrote thus to Parr:

"You will be at no loss to see the immediate propriety of
the subscribers being as few in number as possible. . . . But
we do not mean to limit ourselves in the subscription for
which we apply precisely to ten guineas. Our wish is to see
how much may be raised by this mode of procedure, and only
to have recourse to less sums when we find it necessary. An
obvious caution, therefore, presents itself to those who interest themselves in the business; and that is, not to apply to
such persons as it may be a matter of consequence to whether
they give ten guineas or five, but wait till the necessity of the
case makes it expedient to accept such donations. Our
subscription is at present in a very flourishing state, and,
with your exertions, now amounts to nearly, if not quite, a
thousand pounds. Do not therefore, my good Sir, despair of
our efforts, and let us not value our friend's necessity too
cheap yet, for every additional name, you know, adds to the

obligation, and multiplies the difficulty which you suggest. Besides, no man ought to have it to say that he conferred a favour on R. P. which cost him less than ten guineas. I am still, therefore, of opinion that we should adhere, for the present, to ten, and that the well-wishers of the cause should be desired, *for the present*, to suspend such applications as only give hopes of five, or, in short, of any sum less than ten. You may be assured that we feel much obliged by your strenuous endeavours and services in the cause. Mr. Windham has already been a liberal contributor, and I hope that his great neighbour, Mr. Coke, will not be less so. By no means apply to the Master of St. John's, nor to the Master of Trinity, directly or indirectly; for it was stated to P. that this subscription was a tribute of literary men to literature, which had been deserted by the university, or rather its own college. And it would not, I think, be proper to lay him under obligation to the man by whom he conceives himself, and justly conceives himself, to have been injured. It is our wish to keep this matter off paper as much as possible, for fear of a Lord Orford or a babbling Boswell, who should hereafter, on finding a record of the circumstances, think it fit and charitable to intimate it to the world. Names also should be kept as much as possible out of sight for two reasons; first, that the donor may have the merit of a purely gratuitous act of munificence, and, secondly, that P. may not know to whom he is obliged.

"And here I am led to reply to an objection of yours to our keeping the names from P. If the subscribers are previously told that their names are not to be mentioned, they must necessarily take for granted, supposing them to fall into company or connection with P., that he is totally ignorant of his obligation to them; and, therefore, any offence arising from his singularities is not aggravated by the reflection of being committed against a benefactor, as he does not know the person to be his benefactor. If ever he knows of any individual's kindness to him, it must be from the individual himself, and the bare mention of the circumstance from such an one at once cancels the obligation. Supposing

H

that P. should, on seeing the list of subscribers, find names
to which he would not, in his own person, have owed
obligations, with what vexation must he reflect that the
officiousness of his friends had subjected him to the bounty
of one to whom he would on no account have been obliged!
I cannot readily estimate the extent of his mortification.
Pol me occidistis amici, might he exclaim, and I should dread
the idea of realising the quotation. · Whatever may be his
peculiarities, the relative situation of the parties will be the
same as if no favour had been conferred, P. being kept ignorant; and the party conferring the favour can expect no
sacrifice of feeling, when he knows that P. is not conscious of
having been obliged. Weighing, then, the ill-consequence
to himself of communicating the names to P. against the
accidental inconvenience that may arrive from the display of
his singularities before or towards any of his benefactors, I
find the former to preponderate excessively in my mind; for
I should be sorry to see the expansive force of his understanding weakened by the heavy load which would be laid
upon it by being presented with a long list of subscribers."

To these observations he adds the following, two
days afterwards, in a letter to the same correspondent :—

" Thus far had I written on Saturday, under the expectation
of seeing Dr. Burney to dinner, who was called another way;
for which I should not have forgiven him, had he not informed me that it was *the cause* which he found himself
likely to support by accepting another invitation. The subscription still thrives; we are 1100*l*. strong, and to-morrow I
have the promise of 45*l*. more, so that I adhere to my first
opinion, and I doubt not but that this statement will make a
convert of you."

Cleaver Banks, in a letter to Parr, says that, being at
Windsor, he took occasion to call on Dr. Goodall, and
learned from him that Porson had many zealous friends
at Eton, " who," he states, " are warmly disposed to
countenance our plan with all its imperfections.

Goodall," he adds, "as well as many other of his acquaintance, seemed to think we had been too indiscriminate in our applications, which should have been regulated by the known dispositions and wishes of the object and friends of this contribution."*

"Many thanks are due to you," he says, in the same letter, "for your unremitting zeal in the cause of our worthy friend, which I am persuaded no one has more at heart than yourself. We have received the most encouraging professions from all quarters; and, I believe, if we were to count up the sums already secured, they would exceed 1500*l*. When they verge upon 2000*l*. we shall stop."

By the kindness of a learned friend, I have been furnished with the following list of subscribers to the fund, from a manuscript in the hand of Dr. Raine. Notwithstanding what Raine says about "a Lord Orford or a babbling Boswell," it is thought not improper, after such a lapse of time, to publish it; for why should not the names of those who were thus liberal receive public honour?

	£	s.	d.		£	s.	d.
R. Griffiths	25	0	0	G. Nicol	25	0	0
Sir John H. Aubyn	10	0	0	R. Brocklesby	10	10	0
J. Horne Tooke	10	10	0	J. Cleaver Banks	50	0	0
B. Langton	10	10	0	C. S. Foss	10	10	0
W. Parsons	10	10	0	R. Carr	25	0	0
M. Raine	50	0	0	G. Tierney	25	0	0
J. Perry	25	0	0	T. Thompson	100	0	0
J. Gray	25	0	0	S. Parr	15	0	0
G. T. Huntingford	10	10	0	Archd. Pott	10	10	0
Wm. Gillies	25	0	0	Rev. — Gray	10	10	0
S. Berdmore	10	10	0	— Mellish	10	10	0
C. Burney	50	0	0	W. Seward	10	10	0

* Parr's Works, vol. i. p. 381.

	£	s.	d.		£	s.	d.
Earl Spencer . .	25	0	0	Jacob Bryant . .	10	0	0
Rt. Hon. W. Windham	25	0	0	Provost of Eton .	26	5	0
S. Whitebread, Jun.	50	0	0	— Lutmore . .	20	0	0
W. H. Lambton .	50	0	0	— Hinde . .	20	0	0
B. Barnard . .	10	10	0	— Johnson . .	10	10	0
J. Atherton . .	10	10	0	John Bellamy . .	10	10	0
R. Spencer . .	10	10	0	Earl Fitzwilliam .	105	0	0
T. Burgess . .	50	0	0	S. Shore . . .	20	0	0
— Dewes . .	10	10	0	Thos. Rogers .	10	10	0
— Wills . . .	10	10	0	P. Benfield . .	10	10	0
Rev. Dr. Routh .	10	10	0	G. Rowes . .	10	10	0
Sir J. Dundas . .	50	0	0	A. Pigott . .	10	10	0
L. Dundas . .	50	0	0	T. H. Stone . .	10	10	0
— Goodall . .	50	0	0	R. Wingfield . .	25	0	0
H. Dampier . .	25	0	0	— Dodd . . .	10	10	0
Rev. J. Smith . .	10	10	0	Dr. Vincent . .	10	10	0
Wm. Bosville . .	10	10	0	Wm. Morgan . .	10	10	0
Bishop of Cork .	10	10	0	S. Sharpe . .	10	10	0
Robt. Adair . .	10	10	0	Thos. W. Coke .	50	0	0
C. Cracherode . .				Rev. R. King . .	10	10	0

To these were afterwards added,

	£	s.	d.		£	s.	d.
Friends of Mr. Dampier . . .	42	0	0	Lord Ferrers . .	10	10	0
Mr. Hawksworth .	50	0	0	Dr. Barrington, Bp. of Durham . .	50	0	0
Mr. Wentworth .	50	0	0	Mr. J. Hayes . .	10	0	0

These sums amount in all to 1,660*l.* 5*s.* But other contributions, of which the donors are not known, appear to have raised the whole subscription to nearly the sum mentioned by Banks.

The amount of the annuity secured for Porson was about 100*l.* a year.* Dr. Burney, writing to Parr on the 15th of December in this year, alludes to the affair as " a gloriously terminated undertaking."†

---

* Encyclop. Brit.; art. "Porson."
† Parr's Works, vol. vii. p. 413.

In what mode, or with what ceremony, the contribution was offered to Porson is nowhere mentioned; but he consented to accept it, only on condition that he should receive but the interest of the sum during his life, and that the principal, being placed in the hands of trustees, should be returned to the contributors at his death.

It is said that this subscription would have been unnecessary, but for the somewhat sudden death of Tyrwhitt, in 1786, who, with that generosity for which he was distinguished no less than for his learning and understanding, had promised to make an ample provision for Porson.* Such an act would not have been surprising in one who was always doing good, and who gave away in one year, in charitable donations, not less than two thousand pounds.

---

* Rev. H. R. Luard, Cambridge Essays, 1857.

CHAP. VIII.

PORSON A CANDIDATE FOR THE GREEK PROFESSORSHIP.—HIS LETTER TO
POSTLETHWAITE ON THE OCCASION. — IS ELECTED. — HIS INAUGURAL
LECTURE ON EURIPIDES.—IS GRATIFIED BY THE DISTINCTION OF THE
APPOINTMENT. — INTENDS TO READ LECTURES, BUT FINDS NO EN-
COURAGEMENT FROM THE UNIVERSITY AUTHORITIES.

IT was on the 21st of June, 1792, that Porson resigned
his fellowship. Soon after, the professorship of Greek
became vacant by the resignation of Cooke, which had
been expected to take place some years before ; and
Postlethwaite, as if to make some atonement for his
previous conduct, wrote to Porson, even before the
vacancy occurred*, to inform him that it was likely to
happen, and observing that he would doubtless offer
himself a candidate for the office. Porson, supposing
that subscription to the Thirty-nine Articles would be
required for the tenure of the professorship, as for that
of the fellowship, replied to Postlethwaite, on the 6th
of October, 1792, in the following manner :

"SIR,—When I first received the favour of your letter, I
must own that I felt rather vexation and chagrin than hope
and satisfaction. I had looked upon myself so completely in
the light of an outcast from Alma Mater, that I had made up
my mind to have no further connection with the place. The
prospect you held out to me gave me more uneasiness than

* Parr's Works, vol. i. p. 385.

pleasure.   When I was younger than I now am, and my disposition more sanguine than it is at present, I was in daily
·expectation of Mr. Cooke's resignation, and I flattered myself
with the hope of succeeding to the honour he was going to
quit.   As hope and ambition are great castle-builders, I had
laid a scheme, partly, as I was willing to think, for the joint
credit, partly for the mutual advantage, of myself and the
University.   I had projected a plan of reading lectures, and
I persuaded myself that I should easily obtain a grace per-
mitting me to exact a certain sum from every person who
attended.   But seven years' waiting will tire out the most
patient temper; and all my ambition of this sort was long
ago laid asleep.   The sudden news of the vacant professorship
put me in mind of poor Jacob, who, having served seven
years in hopes of being rewarded with Rachel, awoke, and
behold it was Leah.

   " Such, Sir, I confess, were the first ideas that took possession of my mind.   But after a little reflection, I resolved to
refer a matter of this importance to my friends.   This circumstance has caused the delay, for which I ought before
now to have apologised.   My friends unanimously exhorted
me to embrace the good fortune which they conceived to
be within my grasp.   Their advice, therefore, joined to the
expectation I had entertained of doing some small good by
my exertions in the employment, together with the pardonable vanity which the honour annexed to the office inspired,
determined me; and I was on the point of troubling you, Sir,
and the other electors, with notice of my intentions to profess
myself a candidate, when an objection, which had escaped
me in the hurry of my thoughts, now occurred to my recollection.

   "The same reason which hindered me from keeping my
fellowship by the method you obligingly pointed out to me,
would, I am greatly afraid, prevent me from being Greek
Professor.   Whatever concern this may give me for myself,
it gives me none for the public.   I trust there are at least
twenty or thirty in the University equally able and willing
to undertake the office; possessed, many, of talents superior

to mine, and all of a more complying conscience. This I
speak upon the supposition that the next Greek professor
will be compelled to read lectures; but if the place remains·
a sinecure, the number of qualified persons will be greatly
increased. And though it were even granted that my industry and attention might possibly produce some benefit to
the interests of learning and the credit of the University, that
trifling gain would be as much exceeded by keeping the professorship a sinecure, and bestowing it on a sound believer,
as temporal considerations are outweighed by spiritual.
Having only a strong persuasion, not an absolute certainty,
that such a subscription is required of the professor elect, if
I am mistaken I hereby offer myself as a candidate; but if
I am right in my opinion, I shall beg of you to order my
name to be erased from the boards, and I shall esteem it a
favour conferred on, Sir,

" Your obliged humble servant,

" R. Porson.

"Essex Court, Temple, 6th October, 1792."

Postlethwaite immediately replied that no subscription
would be required.   " Dr. P.," writes Cleaver Banks to
Parr, " has acquainted Porson that his suspicions were
unfounded, and that the day appointed for his examination is Tuesday, *if any one will have the courage to
attempt it*, to use the doctor's words. The offer looks
very much like an atonement for past injuries, and I
am afraid the doctor would have us constrain it into a
compensation." Porson, when his scruples were proved
groundless, offered himself a candidate, and Cleaver
Banks accompanied him on the occasion to Cambridge.
He was elected on the 1st of November, 1792, by the
unanimous votes of the seven electors.

From every candidate for the Greek Professorship
is required a *prælectio*, or lecture, on some subject of

Greek literature, to be read publicly in the schools.
Porson took for the subject of his the character of
Euripides, which he sketched with admirable discernment, giving at the same time a full and clear view of
the comparative merits of the other two great tragic poets
of Greece. This lecture is printed in his " Adversaria,"
filling thirty large octavo pages, and containing many
quotations ; yet the composition of it occupied him only
two days.* When a friend expressed his surprise that
he could have produced it in so short a time, he replied
that the subject of it had long employed his thoughts.†
It is hoped that no apology is necessary for offering the
reader a specimen of it in English.

"Before the time when Euripides arrived at manhood,
Æschylus had elevated tragedy from the meanness of the
cart of Thespis, and had equipped her with her mask and
robe of dignity ; and Sophocles, having received her in this
condition from the hand of Æschylus, had embellished and
adorned her with such additional decoration, that no room
seemed left for any succeeding poet to obtain further honour
from the stage. Euripides, having imbibed, from his tenderest
years, the precepts of philosophy, was unwilling to waste
eloquence on the pursuit of public honours, and yet, being
warned by the fate of his master, Anaxagoras, was afraid to
apply his philosophy to eradicate from the public mind the
superstitions too deeply implanted in it.   That he might
not, however, pass his life in inglorious obscurity, and that
he might devote his powers of language and thought, as far
as circumstances would permit, to the advantage of his
fellow-creatures, he applied himself to the composition of
tragedies ; a pursuit which he cultivated with such diligence
and success as to dispute the preeminence in it, in the judgment of many, even with Sophocles himself. Trusting, there-

---

* Præf. in Advers. p. xii.   † Museum Criticum, vol. i. p. 119.

fore, to the protection of the theatre, and guarded and defended as it were by its shield, he instilled correctly into the minds of his countrymen that which it was not safe for him to express undisguisedly. The false notions of mankind in regard to religion, which had been consecrated by the profound veneration of ages, which had been established by length of time, and which he clearly perceived that his countrymen would have thought it infidelity to assail, he proceeded to weaken and undermine by means of characters which he brought upon the stage. Nor did he show greater indulgence to other prejudices with which he saw most of mankind overclouded, and under the influence of which they were driven

> ‘ Errare, atque viam palantes quærere vitæ,’
> ‘ To stray, and, wandering, seek the path of life.’

Hence, though he was by no means without reputation and honour among his countrymen, yet he received, during the whole of his life, no extraordinary favour from the multitude. Euripides, indeed, like many other great men, had to mourn over fame inadequate to his merits; for of seventy or more plays which he produced, fifteen only were awarded the prize. But the more unjustly his excellences, when his plays were offered for representation, were undervalued by the people, the more sincerely was he honoured by those who were better able to judge, and to whom poetry and philosophy were objects of esteem and delight. One of these, himself equivalent to a host, was Socrates, who, being some years younger than Euripides, looked up to him as a master, and, disregarding for the most part the plays of other dramatic poets, was a constant and attentive spectator of those of Euripides.

" By the unanimous consent of posterity, however, the name of Euripides deserves to be enrolled among those of the very greatest tragic poets; and even if we admit that he was inferior to Æschylus and Sophocles, we must allow that it was no small glory to have stood against rivals of such dignity and power.

" For my own part, if I may speak freely what I think, I consider that those who set Æschylus above Sophocles and Euripides are in error ; an error which, if it deserve pardon, must yet require correction.   Their mistake is certainly excusable, as it proceeds from a superabundance of regard, and honourable esteem, for the father of tragedy. All the dramas of Æschylus are distinguished by a grandiloquent, but rude, majesty ; and every one of them, if we contemplate it from beginning to end, falls in some degree short, we shall find, of the highest excellence. But such is the nature of the human mind, that, with a pardonable partiality, it exalts the merits of those who have originated any noble invention to an undue height, while their faults are either overlooked, or excused, or justified. We forgive them much for the sake of their excellences, but their greatest excellence generally is that they light the way for others to illustrate and improve what they have invented. Æschylus, if for nothing else, would be worthy of immortality for this, that he excited Sophocles and Euripides to produce the most faultless examples of tragic poetry ; for they, without his guidance, would never have been the great scenic poets that they were. In making comparisons of this kind we must always bear in mind which author was first in order of time. Æschylus may have been the greater poet ; but Sophocles and Euripides produced better plays. It is glory enough for Æschylus to be called the father and king of tragedy ; glory of which he himself was so far from being vain that, with admirable modesty, he wished nothing more to be engraved on his tomb than that he was present and bore himself bravely at the battle of Marathon.

*   *   *   *   *

" But if we would compare Sophocles and Euripides one with the other, we must proceed with greater caution, and shall find it more difficult to make an exact distinction between them ; for each is remarkable for his own peculiar excellences.   If Euripides has faults from which Sophocles is free, he makes amends for them by eminent good qualities. Sophocles offers no scene, and introduces no person, that does. not contribute to the progress of his drama ; his chorus chants nothing between the acts that does not, conformably with the precept of Horace, promote the plot, and suit with the subject; and his heroes are either exhibited for our imitation, as lovers of piety and justice, or subjected to punishment before our eyes as characters of an opposite kind. But we must admit that Euripides is frequently regardless of such proprieties; he attaches to the arguments of his plays episodes that have scarcely the slightest connexion with them; he frequently assigns to his chorus strains that are quite foreign to the purpose; he puts into the mouths of his characters many impious and immoral sentiments; and he cuts off a great part of the pleasure, which the spectator or reader would otherwise enjoy from his stories, by narrating in the introduction what is to occur in the sequel, so that hope and fear, if not entirely excluded, are in a great degree weakened. Yet of these faults there are some that easily admit of excuse. That he foretels the events which are to happen in the course of the play, is to be imputed to his desire of perspicuity; nor is it improbable that other tragic poets of that age, for the want of a proper introduction to their plays, were sometimes imperfectly understood by the audience, and that Euripides, through fear of this inconvenience, erred on the other side, and became too studious of clearness; for that he adopted this practice, not without thought, but with deliberation, not by chance, but with design, is evident from the fact that he brought on the stage no play without such an introduction; and though he was satirised for this practice by the comic poets, he was so obstinately attached to it that it was impossible to make him relinquish it.

*   *   *   *   *

"But there are other merits besides perspicuity, in which Euripides may justly be thought to have the superiority over Sophocles. His language pleases us by its natural simplicity and plainness; though I cannot deny that, from his constant preference of common words, he sometimes descends too much towards the humble and ordinary style. Sophocles, on the contrary, while he is anxious to avoid vulgar phraseology, and plebeian modes of expression, is somewhat too prone to indulge in forced metaphors, harsh inversions of language, and other faults of that nature, which render his verses, at times, too obscure to be pleasing. When we read Euripides we are delighted, and our thoughts and feelings are free from restraint; when we peruse Sophocles we seem to engage in severe literary study. The choruses too of Sophocles, though much easier to be understood than those of Æschylus, are by no means free from obscurity. . . . But the practice of Euripides, in using fewer tumid expressions and sesquipedalian words than Sophocles, may, I think, be readily excused, or rather defended; for by this means assuredly he approaches nearer to the truth of nature, and the usage of real life. If we could imagine a style formed of the excellences of both these poets; a style which should retain nothing of the prosaic phraseology of Euripides, and nothing of the stiffness of Sophocles, we should have perhaps such a style as would approach the perfection of tragic language. Meanwhile I admit that I receive greater pleasure from the natural grace and unaffected simplicity of Euripides than from the studied dignity and artificial accuracy of Sophocles. Sophocles, perhaps, has written better tragedies, but Euripides more pleasing poems. We approve Sophocles more than Euripides, but love Euripides more than Sophocles. Sophocles we praise, but Euripides we read."

In the conclusion of this passage Porson seems to have had in his mind the admirable judgment of Johnson on Dryden and Pitt as translators of Virgil.

"If the two versions are compared, perhaps the result would be that Dryden leads the reader forward by his general vigour and sprightliness, and Pitt often stops him to contemplate the excellence of a single couplet; that Dryden's faults are forgotten in the hurry of delight, and that Pitt's beauties are neglected in the languor of a cold and listless perusal; that Pitt pleases the critics, and Dryden the people; that Pitt is quoted, and Dryden read."*

* Life of Pitt.

The manuscript of this lecture, written in Porson's own neat hand, the only copy that he ever wrote, is now in the library of Trinity College.

For some time previous to his election to the professorship, his health had not been good. " Porson," writes Burney to Parr in December, " is in much better health than he has been for several months. His fancy, memory, taste, and philological powers are in as high vigour as ever ; though in a conversation lately, on the subject of the Greek Professorship, he complained of the difficulty of recalling the mind to a pursuit from which it has been torn ; and how hard a task it was, when a man's spirit had once been broken, to renovate it."* This statement seems to show that Beloe's assertion of Porson's despondency on the loss of his fellowship is nearer to the truth than Kidd's affirmation of his equanimity.

Parr, in his reply to Burney, says, " Why does Porson talk about resuming studies which, in fact, have never been interrupted ? and what is there in his professorship to call into action a sixth part of what he has read, or a third part of what he remembers ? If the Duke of Brunswick, at the head of his Huns and Vandals, were to burn every book of every library in Cambridge, Porson, being, as Longinus was said to be, a living library, would make the University hear without books more than they are likely to read with books. Again, injured as he has been, and persecuted, he ought not to let his spirits sink. His very enemies have never dared to quit their ranks as his admirers, and his friends

* Parr's Works, vol. vii. p. 413.

deserve to be weighed rather than to be numbered. Come, come, he will now have the εὔροια of life, and to this stoical abundance of the τὰ ἔξω let him add the Epicurean εὐθυμία, and then he will have no reason to complain of the τὰ ἔσω. Tell me, not in little broken sentences, but in detail, all the news about the professorship. The Cantab ὁ δεῖνα preferred his relation to Porson, and perhaps he might not wish Porson to interfere in college affairs as a fellow ; but when these two points [the annuity and the professorship] are secured, he will find himself no longer disposed to do evil, or prevented from doing good. Undoubtedly he [ὁ δεῖνα, Postlethwaite] is a man of sense, and, as times go, of virtue ; and though I never can approve, nor suffer others to extenuate, his conduct, I hope to retain some esteem for the man himself."*

"The distinction of this appointment was grateful to Porson," says his biographer in the Gentleman's Magazine. "The salary is but 40l. a year. It was his wish, however, to have made it an active and efficient office ; and it was his determination to give an annual course of lectures in the college, if rooms had been assigned him for the purpose. These lectures, as he designed, and had in truth made preparations for them, would have been invaluable ; for he would have found occasion to elucidate the languages in general, and to have displayed their relations, their differences, their near and remote connexions, their changes, their structure, their principles of etymology, and their causes of corruption. If any one man was qualified for this

* Parr's Works, vol. vii. p. 414.

gigantic task, it was Mr. Professor Porson; but his
wishes were counteracted." How many languages the
writer thinks that Porson would have thus illustrated, in
" this gigantic task," I know not; but he seems to have
thought him much nearer to omniscience in language
than he really was. Porson could have told much about
etymology, but his encomiast appears to have fancied
that he could have told everything.

That he intended to give lectures when he entered
on the professorship, he assured Mr. Maltby, who afterwards asked him why he had not given them. Porson
replied, "Because I have thought better on it; whatever originality my lectures might have had, people
would have cried out, *We knew all this before.*" This
was probably only a jocular reason; among the real
causes want of rooms might have had some influence,
and Porson's own indolence, and reluctance to begin,
had probably more. Lectures would doubtless have
greatly increased the income of his professorship, but
would have infinitely increased its labour.

It is no great honour to so wealthy a country as this,
that it should provide for the Greek professor of one
of its greatest universities, a man whom it necessarily
acknowledges among the most eminent of its scholars,
no larger an annual income than 40*l.* At that sum
the salary still stands; but there has recently been
attached to the office a canonry at Ely of 600*l.* a year,
from a desire, apparently, that the professor should
not again be a layman.

CHAP. IX.

NOTHING more appeared from Porson's pen till July
1793, when he published in the " Monthly Review " a
notice of Dr. Edwards's edition of the Treatise on Education attributed to Plutarch; a work which Muretus
suspected, and which Wyttenbach pronounced, to be
spurious. Dr. Edwards, however, without noticing these
adverse opinions, published it as the genuine production
of Plutarch.

The notes to this edition were partly in English and
partly in Latin. On this mixture of languages Porson
says, " This is a practice which we shall never fail to
reprehend. When an editor produces any observations
which merit the notice of the learned (and every editor
ought to believe at least as much), let him converse in
the common language of the learned; but when an
author writes on a subject of learning chiefly for the
benefit of his countrymen, let him compose wholly in
his mother tongue. Perhaps Dr. Edwards was induced
to write his notes in this piebald and patchwork man-

I

ner by the example of his father's Theocritus; but it is a fault that we neither can nor will excuse in any of the family. *Fallit te incautum pietas tua.*"

He accuses Dr. Edwards of being somewhat too timid in admitting into the text certain readings which he acknowledges would be improvements; and adds the following remarks, well worthy of transcription, on the duty of an editor.

"It may naturally be asked, Who shall decide which reading is indubitably certain? This decision must be in a great measure left to the discretion of the editor. 'What! are we to give to every man, who sets up for a critic, an unlimited right of correcting ancient books at his pleasure?' Not at his pleasure, but in conformity to certain laws well known and established by the general consent of the learned. He may transgress or misapply these laws, but without disowning their authority. No critic in his senses ever yet declared his resolution to put into the text what he at the time thought a wrong reading; and if a man, after perusing the works of his author perhaps ten times as often as the generality of readers, after diligently comparing manuscripts and editions, after examining what others have written relative to him professedly or incidentally, after a constant perusal of other authors with a special view to the elucidation of his own;— if, after all this, he must not be trusted with a discretionary power over the text, he never could be qualified to be an editor at all. Whatever editor (one, we mean, who aspires to that title) republishes a book from an old edition, when the text might be improved from subsequent discoveries, while he hopes to show his modesty and religion, only exposes his indolence, his ignorance, or his superstition. Dr. Edwards, after having, in his note on p. 3, approved an emendation by Casaubon, ὑπειπόντες for ἐπειπόντες, rejects it in his Addenda with this grave remark: 'I grow daily more and more sensible of the great caution which is requisite in adopting emendations.' This emendation has at least the warrant of a manuscript. Now, if ἐπειπόντες had been the common reading, which makes very good sense, and a manuscript gave ὑπειπόντες,· the same remark, inverted, would be equally just. The truth is, sometimes two readings have such equal claims, that it is very difficult to give a decisive preference to either. In this case, what blame can an editor deservedly incur, who inserts one in the text, if he faithfully informs us of the other?"

This review presents us with one of Porson's admirable emendations. Not far from the beginning of the treatise, the author, speaking of parents committing their boys to incompetent teachers, says, as the text stands in Dr. Edwards's edition, Ἐνίοτε γὰρ εἰδότες, αἰσθομένοις μᾶλλον αὐτοῖς τοῦτο λεγόντων, τὴν ἐνίων τῶν παιδευτῶν ἀπειρίαν ἅμα καὶ μοθχηρίαν, ὅμως τούτοις ἐπιτρέπουσι τοὺς παῖδας. For αἰσθομένοις some manuscripts have αἰσθομένων, of which Dr. Edwards, in his note on the passage, expresses approbation, and "which," says Porson, "he might more pardonably have admitted into the text than have left nonsense in its place. One manuscript," he continues, "gives αἰσθόμενοι ἄλλων, whence Brunck reads, with the slight addition of a letter, εἰδότες ἢ αἰσθόμενοι ἄλλων:—this, however, has not the good luck to please Dr. Edwards: *Friget Brunckii emendatio.* In spite of this censure, we must own that we think the correction true, as far as it goes, but perhaps it conveys not the whole truth. The right reading seems to be Ἐνίοτε γὰρ εἰδότες αὐτοί, ἢ αἰσθόμενοι ἄλλων τοῦτο λεγόντων." Some praise is due to Brunck, who saw part of what was required, but Porson has the merit of having seen the whole.

In the same year came forth a London edition of

Heyne's Virgil in four volumes octavo, published by Messrs. Payne and Co., for which Porson, it appears, had undertaken to correct the press.   This duty had at first been assumed, as Kidd tells us [*], by "a very learned and perspicacious scholar," but, after the third or fourth sheet of the index, with which the printers began, was finished, " the office devolved " upon Porson.   In regard to this work he has been accused of great negligence; the author of the " Short Account of Porson " says that Steevens detected four hundred and eighty errors in it; Gilbert Wakefield told Fox [†] that the same critic had discovered nine hundred ; and Steevens himself, if Kidd is not mistaken, was heard to say in an auction-room that he " had reckoned up six hundred errors, more or less."   One of the errors was *gravibus* for *gruibus*. All these faults were said to have arisen from Porson's per- functory discharge of his duty.   But the truth seems to be that Porson, whether from disgust at the drudgery, or from thinking he might trust the ordinary reader for the press, suffered the correction of the sheets to go altogether out of his hands.   According to a writer in the "Museum Criticum," [‡] the blame, on Porson's decla- ration, lay wholly with the booksellers, who, after they had obtained permission to use his name, paid, he said, no attention to his corrections.

It was while these rumours of Porson's carelessness were afloat, that Parr threw out the following remarks in his " Answer to Combe's Statement."   " Mr. Porson, the republisher of Heyne's Virgil, is a giant in literature,

* Tracts, p. lxv.   † Corresp. with Fox, p. 66.
‡ Vol. i. p. 395.

a prodigy in intellect, a critic whose mighty achievements leave imitation panting at a distance behind them,
and whose stupendous powers strike down all the
restless and aspiring suggestions of rivalry into silent
admiration and passive awe.   He that excels in great
things, so as not to be himself excelled, shall readily
have pardon from me, if he errs in little matters better
adapted to little minds.   But I should expect to see
the indignant shades of Bentley, Hemsterhuis, and
Valckenaer rise from their grave, and rescue their
illustrious successor from the grasp of his persecutors,
if any attempt were made to immolate him on the
altars of dulness and avarice for his sins of omission, or
his sins of commission, as a corrector of the press.
Enough, and more than enough, have I heard of his
little oversights, in the hum of those busy inspectors
who peep and pry after one class of defects only, in the
prattle of finical collectors, and the cavils of unlearned
and half-learned gossips.   But I know that spots of this
kind are lost in the splendour of this great man's
excellences.   I know that his character towers far
above the reach of such puny objectors.   I think that
his claims to public veneration are too vast to be
measured by their short and crooked rules, too massy
to be lifted by their feeble efforts, and even too sacred
to be touched by their unhallowed hands." *

The conclusion of this passage is stupendously
grandiose, but there were doubtless a large number
of literary pretenders, at that time as there are at all
times, who well deserved censure or ridicule for their

* Parr's Works, vol. iii. p. 518.

attention to one class of errors only, and who might justly be noted as finical and half-learned gossips. All such small-minded critics are ready in every age to assail, with their puny remarks, the fame of any great man, as the Lilliputians shot their tiny arrows at the huge body of Gulliver. Porson had perhaps been negligent, but he was not to be sunk into nothingness because he had not corrected the press with the diligence of a Cruden. If we may believe Beloe, indeed, the mistakes are chiefly confined to the notes, as those in the text do not exceed twenty in all the four volumes.*

A brief notice was prefixed, headed "Corrector Lectori," in which Porson stated that he had undertaken, not the duty of editing the work, but merely that of correcting the press ; that he had added nothing of his own, except a few conjectures of the learned with which Heyne seemed not to have met ; that though he had been anxious that the edition should be as free from errors as possible, he feared that more would be found than his readers or himself would approve ; and that a short preface had been received from Heyne, which the printers had carefully laid by, intending to prefix it to the work when completed, but which, when they sought for it, they were nowhere able to find.

In January and April 1794, Porson published in the "Monthly Review" a critique on Payne Knight's "Analytical Essay on the Greek Alphabet." Knight's book contains much that is fanciful in regard to the gradual formation of the Greek alphabet, and especially with regard to the digamma, of which he allowed himself a

---

* Sexagenarian, vol. i. p. 222.

more liberal use than any preceding critic had ventured to make. He also proposes a system of metrical quantity, founded chiefly on the practice of Homer, whose works, he says, " are composed of materials so pure and simple, and executed with such precision and regularity, that we can still trace the minutest touches of the master's hand, and ascertain, with almost mathematical certainty, the principles upon which he wrought." On this passage Porson very justly observes that " Homer's poetry, however exalted and embellished by learning and genius, must partake of that rudeness and simplicity which are always incident to the infancy of language and of society ;" and intimates that " the champions for Homer, who attribute to him all possible perfection, who find in him not only all other arts and sciences, but also a philosophical grammar, and a philosophical system of metre," attribute to him much more than they can substantiate, except to their own imaginations. The character of the book Porson sums up as follows :—" The author is a man of reading, learning, and inquiry. His taste and knowledge seem to predominate rather in the antiquarian's province, as it is generally called ; but, when he traces the history of language and the etymology of words, he gives too much scope to conjecture and imagination. In the execution of his plan he unnecessarily contracts his foundation by building only on the groundwork of Homer ; and, while he denies that particular changes of sounds and words can take place except in one certain prescribed mode, he allows too little to the changes, caprices, conveniences, &c., which produce the fluctuations. We have, however, perused his essay generally with entertainment, sometimes with instruc-

tion. and approbation ; and Mr. Knight may deserve, at
least, this praise, that the errors in his research are
sometimes more to the purpose than the successful
inquiries of others."

The book contains a remark on the faculties and attainments requisite for verbal criticism, which Porson
was very glad to quote, as a support to his own pursuits, at the head of his article :

" I cannot but think that the judgment of the public, upon
the respective merits of the different classes of critics, is peculiarly partial and unjust.

" Those among them who assume the office of pointing out
the beauties, and detecting the faults, of literary composition,
are placed with the orator and the historian in the highest
ranks ; while those who undertake the more laborious task
of washing away the rust and canker of time, and bringing
back those forms and colours which are the subject of criticism to their original purity and brightness, are degraded,
with the index-maker and antiquary, among the pioneers of
literature, whose business it is to clear the way for those who
are capable of more splendid and honourable enterprises.

" But, nevertheless, if we examine the effects produced by
these two classes of critics, we shall find that the first have
been of no use whatever, and that the last have rendered the
most important services to mankind. All persons of taste
and understanding know, from their own feelings, when to
approve and disapprove, and therefore stand in no need of
instruction from the critic ; and as for those who are destitute
of such faculties, they can never be taught to use them ; for
no one can be taught to exert faculties which he does not
possess. Every dunce may indeed be taught to repeat the
jargon of criticism, which of all jargons is the worst, as it joins
the tedious formality of methodical reasoning to the trite
frivolity of common-place observation. But, whatever may
be the taste and discernment of a reader, or the genius and
ability of a writer, neither the one nor the other can appear

while the text remains deformed by the corruptions of blun-
dering transcribers, and obscured by the glosses of ignorant
grammarians. It is then that the aid of the verbal critic is
required; and though his minute labour, in dissecting syllables, and analysing letters, may appear contemptible in its
operation, it will be found important in its effect."

The usefulness of verbal criticism, judiciously applied,
will not be questioned; but that elegant criticism,
which dwells on the beauties and defects of composition, and compares the merits of different authors, works,
and passages, is utterly useless, will not so readily be
admitted. The criticisms of Addison, Johnson, or Warton, which instruct or please us, cannot be regarded as
utterly valueless productions. Nor is verbal criticism
to be set above all other criticism simply because of its
usefulness; for the performances of mankind do not
rise in estimation merely in proportion to their utility;
else the labours of the agriculturist would exalt him
high above all other human agents.

CHAP. X.

PORSON'S INTENTIONS REGARDING ÆSCHYLUS. — PROJECTED EDITION BY
THE LONDON PUBLISHERS. — AN EDITION OF ÆSCHYLUS SURREPTI-
TIOUSLY PRINTED AT GLASGOW FROM PORSON'S CORRECTIONS. —
PORSON'S SAGACITY AND CAUTION EXHIBITED IN THE EMENDATIONS.

SOME time before this period, Porson had projected an
edition of Æschylus, to contain the fragments, and to
be accompanied with the scholia and notes*; and, says
the " Short Account of Porson," " he sent his Æschylus
to be printed at Glasgow in octavo." What he sent
was a copy of Pauw's Æschylus†, in which, according
to Dr. Young‡, he had made more than two hundred corrections. The text of the seven plays thus
corrected was printed by Foulis at Glasgow, as early as
1794, in two volumes octavo, for the London booksellers, who expected, apparently on Porson's promise,
that he would add notes and the fragments, but, having
waited for these accompaniments more than ten years,
they at last allowed the volumes, at the instance of
Porson's friends, to go forth in 1806 without them.
This text, says Kidd §, was *the substratum of Porson's
projected edition ;* " it was given to the world with his
knowledge, and, after unceasing importunity, with a
sort of half-faced consent." After it was published, he

* Monthly Review, Feb. 1796.
† Museum Criticum, vol. i. p. 110.
‡ Encyclop. Brit., art. " Porson."   § Tracts, p. lxix.

frequently and earnestly, according to the same authority, conversed about his intended preface to it; he had arranged the materials in his mind, and Kidd heard him twice detail the substance of them; and when he was entreated to prepare them for publication, he would promise to try, but added that he hated and abhorred composition.

In the mean time, with the date 1795, there had come forth a folio edition, presenting nearly the same text, at Glasgow, from the same printers, said to have been surreptitiously printed from the corrections for the other edition. According to a note on the Pursuits of Literature *, its origin was as follows: " Mr. Porson, the Greek Professor at Cambridge, lent his manuscript corrections and conjectures on the text of Æschylus to a friend in Scotland ; for he once had an intention of publishing that tragedian. His corrected text fell into the hands of the Scotch printer Foulis, and, without the Professor's leave or even knowledge, he published a magnificent edition of Æschylus from it without notes." Dibdin says that it was printed with the same types as the famous Glasgow Homer, and that there were only fifty-two copies struck off in all, and only eleven on the largest paper. He speaks with rapture of a large-paper copy, illustrated with Flaxman's designs, which he saw in the library at Althorp.

The account of the affair given by Hellenophilus, supposed to be Dr. Maltby, in Aikin's Athenæum, is that Porson concluded a treaty with Messrs. Elmsley and Payne, in consequence of which a new, but most improved edition, was to be printed at Glasgow. After

* Part II. p. 42.

the proofs of the first five or six plays had been regularly sent to the Professor, they suddenly stopped, and
some time after it was discovered that the Scotch printer
had used the paper for the folio edition.   Nor was it
known for a considerable time that the smaller edition
was in existence, till at length the English booksellers
discovered the fraud."   " A method was pursued by
Porson in this edition," observes the writer, " which we
earnestly recommend to the imitation of every critic.
Where the text appeared faulty, and no emendation
offered itself with sufficient authority to warrant its admission into the text, he marked the suspected place
with an obelus.   Of passages thus pointed out, both as
a warning to inexperienced readers, and a guide to
future critics, there are about one hundred and fifty ;
so that, unfortunate as this edition has been, the text is
still improved in a greater number of instances than
those in which it continues to be defective.   And in
regard to the remaining corruptions, we have little
doubt but Mr. Porson's acuteness would have pointed
out a probable remedy in most of the cases, had the
work gone on to its end, without the occurrence of that
calamitous fraud, which cannot be too much reprobated
or deplored."

" Porson," says a writer in the " Museum Criticum,"*
" never openly acknowledged this edition, but there
were too many marks of the master's hand for it to be
mistaken.   It is not to be supposed however that the
text of this edition is that which the Professor would
have given to the public, had he openly undertaken to
edit Æschylus."

* Vol. i. p. 111.

CHAP. XI.

PORSON had for some time been intimate with Perry, the
well-known editor of the "Morning Chronicle." In
November 1795, he married Mrs. Lunan, Perry's sister.
She survived the marriage about a year and a half,
dying of a decline in April 1797.*

Of the way in which the marriage came about, the
only account that we have is given in the "Personal
Memoirs" of Pryse Lockhart Gordon†, a Scotch soldier
of fortune, whose brother George, a mercantile agent,
was very intimate with Perry, who was also a Scotchman. It had been expected at one time, that Porson
would marry Dr. Raine's sister, but the doctor having
shown himself unfavourable to the match, it had not
afterwards been thought, by any of Porson's friends,
that he was at all likely to marry, for he appeared to
be a confirmed convivial bachelor.

But one night, while he was smoking his pipe with

* Sexagenarian, vol. i. p. 207.   † Vol. i. p. 280, seqq.

George Gordon at the Cider Cellar, he suddenly said, " Friend George, do you not think the widow Lunan an agreeable sort of personage as times go ? " Gordon said something in the affirmative. " In that case," continued Porson, " you must meet me to-morrow morning at St. Martin's-in-the-Fields at eight o'clock ;" and, without saying more, paid his reckoning and retired.

George Gordon was somewhat astonished, but, knowing that Porson was likely to mean what he said, determined to comply with the invitation, and repaired to the church at the hour specified, where he found Porson with Mrs. Lunan and a female friend, and the parson waiting to begin the ceremony. When service was ended, the parties separated, the bride and her friend retiring by one door, and Porson and George Gordon by another.

Pryse Gordon is however mistaken about the church at which the marriage took place, for the register of St. Martin's-in-the-Fields has been searched in vain for a record of it.

Gordon, on inquiry, found that it was some time since Porson had proposed, but that Mrs. Lunan, as he wished the ceremony to be performed without her brother's knowledge, had been unwilling to listen, and that it was only on finding that she must either yield to Porson's obstinacy on the point, or reject him altogether, that she was induced to give her consent. Gordon urged him to declare his marriage to Perry, but he declined, and they parted.

He was determined, however, that Perry should not be kept in ignorance of the affair, especially as he himself had taken part in it, and was preparing to go

to the " Morning Chronicle" Office to give intimation
of what had happened, when Porson returned, and said,
" Friend George, I shall for once take advice, which,
as you know, I seldom do, and hold out the olive-
branch, provided you will accompany me to the Court
of Lancaster; for you are a good peace-maker."   Lancaster Court, in the Strand, was Perry's place of residence, and hence Porson often called him " My Lord of
Lancaster."   Gordon agreed, and, as they found Perry at
home, Porson made him such a speech as inclined him,
though he was somewhat hurt at the secresy, to reconcilia-
tion, when a dinner was provided, as Pryse Gordon states,
and an apartment selected for the newly-married couple.

How long the Professor sat after the dinner, we are
not told; but, if Beloe may be believed, he soon sought
other company.   " What shall we call it," says he*,
" waywardness, inconsiderateness, or ungraciousness?
but it is a well-known fact that he spent the day " [it
could only have been the evening of the day] " of his
marriage with a very learned friend, now a judge,
without either communicating the circumstance of his
change of condition, or attempting to stir till the hour
prescribed by the family obliged him to depart."

On leaving this friend's house, he adjourned, as a
surgeon named Moore, an acquaintance of Barker's,
asserted, to the Cider Cellar, where he stayed till eight
the next morning.†

If this be true, it is perhaps greater neglect than was
ever before shown to a wife on the day of her marriage.

---

* Sexagenarian, vol. i. p. 229.
† Barker's Lit. Anecdotes, vol. i. p. 24.

Budæus, it is true, was said to have studied on his wedding-day as on other days ; Stothard went from the church to his easel ; and John Kemble, after performing at the theatre, required to be reminded to fetch his wife home.   But there are few instances, we believe, of the bridegroom having deliberately absented himself from the bride through the marriage night, for the mere sake of indulgence with his boon companions.

"One forenoon," says Maltby*, "I met Porson in Covent Garden, dressed in a pea-green coat.   He had been married that morning, as I afterwards learned from Raine, for he himself said nothing about it.   He was carrying a copy of *Le Moyen de Parvenir*, which he had just purchased off a stall ; and, holding it up, he called out jokingly, 'These are the sort of books to buy.' "

Mrs. Porson's first husband, a Scotchman, was a bookbinder, who had lived in Shire Lane, and with whom Perry had for some time been a lodger† ; but, proving a worthless fellow, she had been divorced from him by the Scotch law, and he was still alive, and had married again, when Porson took her.   She had had two or more children by Lunan, whom her brother had taken under his charge and sent to school.   At the time that Porson became acquainted with her, she was living with Perry as his housekeeper.   "She was amiable and good-tempered," says Colonel Gordon, "and the Professor treated her with all the kindness of which he was capable."

By the testimony of Kidd†, the death of Porson's

* Rogers's Table-Talk, "Porsoniana," p. 305.
† John Taylor's "Records of My Life," vol. i. p. 241.
‡ Tracts, p. xv.

wife was an event deeply to be regretted, since, during the short period of his marriage, " he evidently became more attentive to times and seasons, and might have been won by domestic comforts from the habit of tippling, which was doubtless as much a disease as the gout, and must have tended to impair a constitution naturally vigorous."

That he was not, with all his eccentricities, an ill husband, may be inferred from the fact that Perry, his brother-in-law, continued to be his firm friend, and to pay him the greatest attention, to the end of his life. Perry indeed is said to have had greater influence with him than any other person ; for he would listen to remonstrances from Perry which he would not have endured from any one else ; and he was sometimes induced, by Perry's intervention, to accept favours or attentions which the independence of his spirit would otherwise have spurned.

From the time of his wife's death, according to the memoir in the " Gentleman's Magazine," his asthma, with which he had been afflicted ever since he had the imposthume on his lungs, in the early part of his life, greatly increased, so as to prevent him from close or long-continued application to any kind of study. This malady, the writer suggests, may possibly have been aggravated by his sedentary habits.

While he was on a visit to Perry at Merton, a fire broke out in the house, which destroyed a performance on which he had bestowed the labour of at least ten months. He had borrowed the manuscript of the Greek Lexicon compiled by Photius, the patriarch of Constantinople, from the library of Trinity College, Cambridge, engaging to make a complete copy of it. This manuscript is known as the *Codex Galeanus*, from having been presented to Trinity College by the learned Gale, and, from its evident antiquity, may reasonably be supposed to be a transcript extremely valuable. Porson carried it with him wherever he went. On the morning of the day on which the fire occurred, he set out from Merton on a ride to London, taking with him the manuscript, but leaving the transcript, which he had just finished, behind him. As he was on the road, he felt, he thought, some apprehensions of approaching evil, and stopped three or four times on the way, deliberating whether he should return for his books and papers. Once he actually turned back his horse's head; but at last, trusting that his fears were idle, he resolved on continuing his journey. The following night, during his absence, the fire broke out, and the copy was destroyed. Dr. Raine was the first to inform him of his loss; and Porson, on hearing the news, inquired if any lives had been lost. Dr. Raine replied in the negative. "Then," rejoined Porson, "I will tell you what I have lost; twenty years of my life;" repeating, at the same time, the stanza of Gray,

> " To each his sufferings; all are men,
>   Condemn'd alike to groan,
>   The tender for another's pain,
>   The unfeeling for his own." *

How he meant these lines to be applied, we are left to conjecture. Among the effects destroyed at the same time were a copy of Kuster's Aristophanes, the margins

* Kidd, Tracts, p. xxxix.

of which were filled with notes and emendations, the letter of Ruhnken to which we have previously alluded, and many other literary treasures.

With the resolution of Bishop Cooper, who, when his wife, in a fit of rage, set fire to the manuscript of his Thesaurus on which he had spent eight years' labour, sat calmly down to write it over again, Porson devoted himself to make a second transcript of Photius equally accurate with the first. How long he took to his task is not related. The manuscript, a handsome quarto volume, he deposited in the library of his College. It was not printed till 1822, fourteen years after his death, when it came forth in quarto and octavo. Meanwhile, in 1808, an edition had been published, perhaps chiefly with a desire to anticipate Porson, by Hermann, but from very incorrect copies, and consequently with numerous blunders, and with a kind of sneer in the preface at those who would prefer to see it printed from the "Codex Galeanus." The edition has been reviewed, with no injustice perhaps to Hermann, but with some rather flippant censures on Photius himself, in the "Edinburgh Review,"* in an article attributed to the late Bishop Blomfield.

Porson's personal appearance, at the time of his marriage, was, when he was well dressed, very commanding. "His very look," says Mr. John Symmons, "impressed me with the idea of his being an extraordinary man; what is called, I believe, by artists, in the *Hercules*, 'the repose of strength,' appeared in his whole figure and face."† "His head," says Pryse

---

Gordon*, "was remarkably fine ; an expansive forehead, over which was smoothly combed (when in
dress) his shining brown hair. His nose was Roman,
with a keen and penetrating eye, shaded with long
lashes. His mouth was full of expression ; and altogether his countenance indicated deep thought. His
stature was nearly six feet." Mr. Maltby, who became
acquainted with him when he was under thirty, spoke
of him as having been then a handsome man.† His
ordinary dress, especially when alone, and engaged in
study, was careless and slovenly, but, on important
occasions, when he put on his blue coat, white waist-
coat, black satin breeches, silk stockings, and ruffled
shirt, "he looked," says Mr. Gordon, "quite the
gentleman."

This description of Porson is supported by the portraits of him that are to be seen at Cambridge ; one by
Kirkby, a painter of some note in his day, in the dining-
room of the Master's lodge at Trinity College ; and
another by Hoppner in the public library ; of which
an engraving is prefixed to this work. The marble
bust of him, by Chantrey, in the chapel of Trinity
College, is thought not to do him justice ; a plaster
bust, which was made from a cast taken immediately
after his death, and of which an engraving by Fittler
is given in the *Adversaria*, is considered to be a much
better representation of him.

There was also a portrait of him at the Cider Cellars
in Maiden Lane ; but we believe it has been removed,
and we know neither its author nor its merits.

* Personal Memoirs, vol. i. p. 288.
† Barker's Lit. Anecd. vol. ii. pp. 24, 186.

CHAP. XII.

IN 1796 Porson published in the " Morning Chronicle"
a Greek version of the nursery song of "Three Children
sliding on the Ice," with a short addition.   It was prefaced by the following letter to the Editor.

" SIR,
    " As a learned friend of mine was rummaging an old
trunk the other day, he discovered a false bottom, which on
examination proved to be full of old parchments.   But what
was his joy and surprise when he discovered that the contents
were neither more nor less than some of the lost tragedies of
Sophocles !   As the writing is difficult, and the traces of the
letters somewhat faded, he proceeds slowly in the task of
deciphering.   When he has finished, the entire tragedies will
be given to the public.   In the mean time I send you the
following fragment, which my friend communicated to me,
and which all critics will concur with me, I doubt not, in

determining to be the genuine production of that ancient dramatist. His characteristics are simplicity and sententiousness. For instance, what can be more simple and sententious than the opening of the ' Trachiniæ' ? ' It is an old saying that has appeared among mankind, that you cannot be certain of the life of mortals, before one dies, whether it be good or evil.' These qualities, too, are conspicuous in the following iambics, which contain a seasonable caution to parents against rashly trusting children out of their sight. Though your paper is chiefly occupied in plain English, you sometimes gratify your learned readers with a little Greek; you may therefore give them this, if you think that it will gratify them. For the benefit of those whose Greek is rather rusty with disuse, I have added a Latin version, which, I hope, is as pure and perspicuous as Latin versions of Greek tragedies commonly are.

"I am, Sir, &c.,

"S. ENGLAND."

ΚΡΥΣΤΑΛΛΟΠΗΚΤΟΥΣ τρίπτυχοι κόροι ῥοὰς
Ὥρᾳ θέρους ψαίροντες εὐτάρσοις ποσί,
Δίναις ἔπιπτον, οἷα δὴ πίπτειν φιλεῖ,
Ἅπαντες· εἶτ' ἔφευγον οἱ λελειμμένοι.
Ἀλλ' εἴπερ ἦσαν ἐγκεκλεισμένοι μοχλοῖς,
Ἢ ποσὶν ὀλισθάνοντες ἐν ξηρῷ πέδῳ,
Χρυσῶν ἂν ἠθέλησα περιδόσθαι σταθμῶν,
Εἰ μὴ μέρος τι τῶν νέων ἐσώζετο.
Ἀλλ', ὦ τοκεῖς, ὅσοις μὲν ὄντα τυγχάνει,
Ὅσοις δὲ μὴ, βλαστήματ' εὐτέκνου σπορᾶς,
Ἢν εὐτυχεῖς εὔχησθε τὰς θυράζ' ὁδοὺς
Τοῖς παισίν, εὖ σφᾶς ἐν δόμοις φυλάσσετε.

Glacie-durata triplices pueri fluenta
Tempestate æstatis radentes pulchras-plantas-habentibus pedibus,
In vortices ceciderunt, ut sanè accidere solet,
Omnes : deinde effugerunt reliqui.
Sin autem inclusi essent vectibus,
Aut pedibus labantes in arido campo,
Auri ponderis sponsione libenter contenderem
Partem aliquam juvenum servari potuisse.

I saw the Master of Emanuel this morning. I told him the needful. He said he should be in town to-morrow, and should see the curator, Mr. Smithies, but probably not Mr. Nicholls. Perhaps you could find out Mr. Smithies, and have some discourse with him. If not, you must manage with Mr. Nicholls, I suppose, as well as you can. For the Version, I mean the paper in which a letter appeared to the Editor of the M. C. containing Greek verses, Κρυσταλοπηκτοις τριπτυχοι κορος ρόας &c. with a Latin version. The letter is signed Iam. England; the time just after Ireland's humbug was exploded. I am, with remembrances to all friends,

Yours sincerely,

R. Porson.

2 June 1801
Trin. Coll.

From the original in the possession of the Rev. H. R. Luard, Trin. Coll. Cambridge.

At, O parentes, tum vos, quibus esse contigit,
Tum vos, quibus non contigit, germina pulchros-filios-procreantis
 segetis,
Si felices optatis extra-domos itiones
Pueris vestris, bene eos intra domos servate.

> Three children sliding on the ice
> All on a summer's day,
> It so fell out they all fell in :
> The rest they ran away.
> But had they stay'd within the house,
> Or play'd on solid ground,
> I'd wager seas and hills of gold,
> They had not then been drown'd.
> So, parents, that no children have,
> And eke ye that have some,
> If you would know they're safe abroad,
> Keep them lock'd up at home.

The signature "S. England" was used in sarcastic allusion to Samuel Ireland, who was then publishing the forged papers attributed to Shakspeare, which his son, William Henry Ireland, pretended to have discovered in a chest at the house of a gentleman in the country.

When these papers were exposed to the view of the public, Porson, among others, went to look at them. Being asked by Ireland, the father, to set his name to a declaration of his belief in their genuineness, he replied that he would rather be excused, as he was *slow to subscribe to articles of faith.* His caution, in this affair, stands in such felicitous contrast to the precipitancy of many of his contemporaries, that we cannot but feel inclined to fix our attention for a while on the subject.

Though there are many detached notices, and a fragmentary confession of the younger Ireland, concerning this imposture, a remarkable event in literary history, there has been hitherto, we believe, no clear and direct account of its origin and progress. Porson's judgment, as directed to the papers, is so admirably manifested, and so advantageously compared with that of Parr and others, that we are led to bestow our attention on the subject at such length as may seem to require some apology.

William Henry Ireland, the son of Samuel Ireland, an artist, having received a fair education, first at three schools in England, and afterwards, for three years, at the College of Eu in Normandy, had been articled, at the age of sixteen, to a solicitor in New Inn. From his father he derived a taste for old books, and paid more attention to booksellers' shops and stalls than to his legal studies; and as his father used to extol Shakspeare as a demigod, and frequently to express his wonder that no relic of his handwriting was to be found, except the signature to his will in the Commons, and his name attached to the mortgage-deed in the possession of Garrick, he was led to repeated perusals of Shakspeare's plays, and to conceive that if some apparently old writing could be produced as Shakspeare's, it might perhaps occasion some diversion by deceiving credulous searchers after the antique.

As his occupation often engaged him in the perusal of old deeds, he at length began to imagine the possibility of executing such a project. Securing some old paper, and getting from the journeyman of a bookbinder named Laurie a liquid to imitate faded ink, which was used in marbling the covers of books, and which, being held to the fire, became brown, he forged, as his first attempt, a letter of presentation to Queen Elizabeth, pretended to be written by the author of a thin pamphlet which he had picked up at a book-stall. This he showed to his father, who had no doubt of its genuineness.

Elated with his success in this attempt, he proceeded to the production of his Shakspeare papers. He invented a story, which he told his father and others, that he had formed an acquaintance with a gentleman in the country, who, learning his fondness for old writings, had invited him to his house, and offered him the liberty of turning over a chest-full of old deeds, which he had inherited from his father, an eminent lawyer; that he had been unwilling, for some time, to accept the invitation, lest the search should cause him only disappointment or ridicule; but that at length resolving to go, he was reproached for not coming sooner, and found a great quantity of papers tied up in bundles. Among these was the pretended lease of two houses from Shakspeare and Hemynge to Michael Fraser, which the gentleman gave him on condition that he should receive a copy of it, and promised him, at the same time, whatever else he should find worthy of notice.

Hearing it questioned whether Shakspeare had been a Catholic or a Protestant, he wrote a " Profession of Faith " for Shakspeare to prove him a Protestant; and then, to prove him, he says, a good-natured man, he wrote a letter for him, short but pleasant, to one Richard Cowley.

Other documents came forth in quick succession; a letter from Queen Elizabeth to Shakspeare; a note of hand and some theatrical receipts; a letter and some verses to Anne Hathaway; a letter to Lord Southampton and another from him; agreements with

John Lowine and Henry Condell; and, what was the most audacious of all the inventions, a deed of gift of certain plays in manuscript to one William Henry Ireland, for having saved Shakspeare's life when he was almost drowned through falling into the Thames. He was induced to forge this instrument by the remark that, if a descendant of Shakspeare should come forward, he might claim the papers, and said that the gentleman had observed that they formerly belonged to a Mr. Ireland, one of Ireland's own family, and were consequently Mr. Samuel Ireland's rightful property. For these writings he procured fly-leaves of old books, and other discoloured papers, from a bookseller named Verey in St. Martin's Lane. He used to lay before him, when writing, a deed of the time of James I., and cut off seals from old deeds to affix to his productions.

A young man of his acquaintance, named Montague Talbot, also articled to an attorney, suspected that all these documents were forgeries, and charged young Ireland with the execution of them. This charge he positively denied; but Montague, still retaining his suspicions, burst suddenly one day into Ireland's room, and surprised him in the act of forging. Ireland then entreated that he would not betray him, alleging his fear of his father's anger, when he should find that he had been deceived; and the two young fellows seem then to have acted in concert, the one continuing to forge writings, and the other furthering the deception among his friends and connexions.

Having heard some critics observe, that if a manuscript of one of Shakspeare's plays could be found, in his own handwriting, it would show whether he wrote all the mean language and ribaldry that had been attributed to him in print, he determined on transcribing the whole tragedy of " King Lear," substituting what he thought better language, in certain passages, for such as appeared low and poor.   Thus, for the couplet,

> " I have a journey shortly, Sir, to go;
> My master calls, and I must not say, No ! "

he gave Kent the words,

> " Thanks, Sir, but I go to that unknown land
> That chains each pilgrim fast within its soil,
> By living men most shunned, most dreaded ;
> Still my good master this same journey took ;
> He calls me ; I'm content, and straight obey.
> Then farewell, world ; the busy scene is done ;
> Kent liv'd most true ; Kent dies most like a man."

Such alterations led his father, and some others who inspected the manuscript, to suppose that Shakspeare's lines had been transformed, in many places, for the worse, by the players.

Growing still bolder, he conceived himself able to invent a whole play for Shakspeare, and, for the subject of it, fixed on the story of Vortigern and Rowena, which he found in a copy of Holinshed in his father's library. A part of this drama he at first produced in his own hand, and, being asked for the original, said that his friend in the country would not allow him to have it till he had made a transcript of the whole ; thus he gained time to write the entire play in an imitation of old hand.   At the time of its production, in 1796, he was nineteen years of age.

His friend Talbot, in the mean time, had deserted the law, gone off to Ireland, and turned actor ; and,

hearing of the noise that the fictitious documents were
making, wrote from Dublin to inquire particulars about
them.   Young Ireland replied, but not so as to satisfy
Talbot, who was displeased that so much had been
done without his knowledge ; and Ireland appears to
have afterwards acted wholly by himself.

The father now determined on publishing the papers,
that the world might not be deprived, as he said, of so
inestimable a treasure. The son told him that his friend
in the country would not sanction the publication,
and that he must therefore undertake it, if he undertook it at all, on his own risk ; a risk which the father
professed himself quite willing to incur.

But before printing the manuscripts, he resolved
on exhibiting them at his house to such as chose to
inspect them : and they were examined by a great
number both of the learned and the unlearned.   Sir
Frederick Eden was the first to pronounce the lease to
be a genuine lease, to Mr. Ireland's great joy, for if this
were genuine, why should the other papers be suspected ?   Among the earliest visitors was Mr. James
Boswell, who, when the papers were laid before him,
proceeded to peruse the fair copies made from the disguised handwriting, in order to judge of the style, and
then to consider the external appearance of the manuscripts, that he might form his opinion of their
antiquity.   As his examination was somewhat pro-
tracted, he became thirsty, and asked for a tumbler of
warm brandy and water.   Having nearly finished it, he
expressed himself, with great earnestness and fluency,
convinced, both by internal and external proofs, of the
genuineness of the manuscripts, which he could not but

regard with delight and reverence. Then, rising from his chair, he observed that he might well die contented, since he had lived to see that day ; and immediately afterwards, kneeling down before the papers, with his glass of brandy and water in his hand, and kissing the volume, he exclaimed, " I now kiss the invaluable relics of our bard, and thank God that I have lived to witness their discovery." Before he left the house, he gave Mr. Ireland a certificate expressing his belief in their authenticity.

Next day came Dr. Parr, who, after examining the papers, and being shown what Boswell had written the day before, remarked that it was too feebly expressed for the importance of the subject, and requested to be allowed to dictate the following form of certificate, to which he immediately subscribed his own name :

" We, whose names are hereunto subscribed, have, in the presence and by the favour of Mr. Ireland, inspected the Shakspeare papers, and are convinced of their authenticity."

Whether it was on this or on a previous occasion is not clear from young Ireland's confessions, but it would seem rather to have been some time before, that Dr. Parr came to see the papers in company with Dr. Joseph Warton, both of whom examined them, and put various questions both to the father and the son respecting the discovery of them, and the concealment of the gentleman's name in whose possession they had been found. The son having replied to their interrogatories, one of them, he says, he is not sure which, said, " Well, young man, the public will have just cause to admire you for the research you have made, which will

afford so much gratification to the literary world." The
" Profession of Faith " was then read aloud by the
father, both the doctors paying profound attention to
every syllable of it. When it was ended, Dr. Parr
exclaimed, addressing himself to the father, " Sir, we
have many fine passages in our Church-service, and our
Litany abounds with beauties ; but here, Sir, is a man
who has distanced us all ! " The son, on hearing
this extravagant encomium, could hardly refrain from
smiling, but felt his vanity, at the same time, wonderfully swollen.

It may be well to show, as a specimen of these productions, what sort of composition it was that called
forth so strong a eulogy from Dr. Parr. The spelling
is modernised.

"I, being now of sound mind, do hope that this my wish
will at my death be acceded to. As I now live in London,
and as my soul may perchance soon quit this poor body, it is
my desire that in such case I may be carried to my native place,
and that my body be there quietly interred with as little
pomp as can be ; and I do now, in these my serious moments,
make this my profession of faith, and which I do most
solemnly believe. I do first look to our loving and great
God, and to His glorious Son Jesus. I do also believe that
this my weak and frail body will return to dust, but for my
soul let God judge that as to Himself shall seem meet. O
omnipotent and great God, I am full of sin ; I do not think
myself worthy of Thy grace, and yet will I hope ; for even
the poor prisoner, when bound with galling irons, even he
will hope for pity, and when the tears of sweet repentance
bathe his wretched pillow, he then looks and hopes for pardon. Then rouse, my soul, and let hope, that sweet cherisher
of all, afford thee comfort also. O man, what art thou ?
Why considerest thou thyself thus greatly ? Where are thy

great, thy boasted attributes ?   Buried, lost for ever, in cold death.   O man, why attemptest thou to search the greatness of the Almighty ?   Thou dost but lose thy labour.   More thou attemptest, more art thou lost, till thy poor weak thoughts are elevated to the summit, and thence, as snow from the leafless tree, drop and distil themselves till they are no more. O God, man as I am, frail by nature, full of sin, yet, great God, receive me to Thy bosom, where all is sweet content and happiness; all is bliss ; where discontent is never heard, but where one bond of friendship unites all men.   Forgive, O Lord, all our sins, and with Thy great goodness take us all to Thy breast.   O cherish us like the sweet chicken that under the covert of her spreading wings receives her little brood, and, hovering o'er them, keeps them harmless and in safety.

" WM. SHAKSPEARE."

It was this weak whining rhapsody, declaring a belief that the body will return to dust, as if its fate had ever been doubtful ; expressing a trust that all may hope for forgiveness in another world because malefactors hope for forgiveness in this ; speaking of man's thoughts being *elevated to the summit*, and then *dropping and distilling till they are no more ;* and signifying that all men are united in one bond of friendship in a future state : it was such stuff as this that Parr pronounced, in the presence of Warton, to be superior to the finest passages of the Church-service !   Well might young Ireland, boy as he was, be scarcely able to restrain his laughter.   Well may we wonder that such trash could ever be believed to have proceeded from him who wrote the soliloquy of Hamlet.

The certificate which Parr wrote, afterwards appeared with the following names attached to it :

Samuel Parr.

John Tweddell.

Thomas Burgess.

John Byng.

James Brindley.

Herbert Croft.

Somerset.

Isaac Heard, Garter King at Arms.

F. Webb.

R. Valpy.

James Boswell.

Lauderdale.

Rev. J. Scott.

Kinnaird.

John Pinkerton.

Thomas Hunt.

Henry James Pye.

Rev. N. Thornbury.

John Hewlett, Translator of Old Records, Common Pleas Office, Temple.

Mat. Wyatt.

John Frank Newton.

It is observable that Dr. Warton's name does not appear in this list. Boswell, we may suppose, affixed his at a subsequent visit.

Parr, in his notice of the volume containing the forged papers in his "Bibliotheca Parriana," calls it "a great and impudent forgery," and says that he is " almost ashamed to insert this worthless and infamously trickish book " in his catalogue; adding, " Ireland told a lie when he imputed to me the words which Joseph Warton used the very morning I called on Ireland, and was inclined to admit the possibility of genuineness in his papers. In my subsequent conversation I told him my change of opinion. But I thought it not worth while to dispute in print with a detected impostor." To what words does Parr allude? If he means those about the research affording gratification to the literary world, Ireland says that he is uncertain by which of the two they were uttered; and they are, by whomsoever uttered, of little importance. But if he means those about the superiority of the " Profession of Faith " to the Litany, he surely would not have maintained that it was Warton who spurted forth that Johnsonian phraseology. If the

words were spoken at all, they must certainly have
been spoken by Parr. But even if Parr would have
affirmed that they were Warton's, he does not attempt
to deny that he himself proposed the form of certificate,
and set his hand to it.

Mr. E. H. Barker makes an effort to excuse Dr.
Parr's hasty decision by the following peculiar argumentation. "The question was one," he says, "on
which Porson was better qualified to give an opinion
than Parr, for he was more accustomed to examine
old manuscripts ; and, though Parr was a great admirer of Shakspeare, yet Porson was much better acquainted with his acknowledged works: now, *if Porson
entertained any opinion in favour of the genuineness and
authenticity of the papers*, Parr may be excused for
entertaining a stronger opinion in their favour." Yes,
Mr. Barker, *if Porson did entertain any opinion of their
genuineness*, a defender of Parr may build as much
reasoning upon that opinion of Porson's as he can ; but
it will be difficult to show that Porson ever even inclined to such opinion. What young Ireland says,
who was doubtless ready to swell the number of the
deceived as much as possible, is, that Porson, after inspecting the manuscripts, *appeared so perfectly well
satisfied respecting them*, that Mr. Ireland, his father,
"was emboldened to ask him whether he would be
unwilling to write his name among the list of believers
in their authenticity," when Porson very drily made the
reply that we have already mentioned. Young Ireland
does not say that Porson uttered a single word relating
to the papers, but merely that he *appeared satisfied
respecting them*, and the satisfaction which he felt was,

it seems, that they were spurious. Mr. Barker's reasoning would seem also to intimate that Porson inspected the papers before Parr, and that Parr, supposing Porson's opinion of them to be favourable, did not hesitate to express an opinion of them still more favourable; but that Porson's inspection of them preceded Parr's is nowhere told or intimated.

It was determined to bring "Vortigern and Rowena" on the stage. Sheridan, after much reluctance and hesitation, agreed that it should be acted at Drury Lane, and Kemble, who had never believed in the authenticity of the papers, consented to take the principal part. The terms were, that Sheridan should pay down 300l. for the manuscript, and that the profits of the performance for the first sixty nights should be equally divided between Mr. Samuel Ireland, as trustee for his son, and Sheridan. The transaction led to long conversations between Samuel Ireland and Sheridan, in which Ireland omitted no opportunity of extolling Shakspeare's transcendent genius; and Sheridan one day remarked that, however high Shakspeare might stand in general estimation, he had not, for his part, so lofty an opinion of him, though he allowed him "brilliancy of ideas and penetration of mind."

Shortly before the agreement was signed, Sheridan and Richardson went to Mr. Ireland's to inspect the fair copy of the play which had been made from the manuscript in the disguised hand. Sheridan, after perusing some portion, came to a line which, as young Ireland expresses it, "was not strictly poetic;" when, turning to Ireland the father, he exclaimed, "This is rather strange; for, though you are acquainted with my opinion as to Shakspeare, yet, be it as it may, he always wrote poetry." After reading a few pages further, he said, " There are certainly some bold ideas, but they are crude and undigested; one would be led to think that Shakspeare must have been very young when he wrote the play. As to doubting whether it be really his or not, who can possibly look at the papers, and not believe them ancient? " Another account says that Sheridan observed that Shakspeare must have been drunk when he wrote the play.

On the first night of the representation, Malone circulated a handbill, stating that he had never believed in the authenticity of the play, and that he was engaged in writing a work which would prove the whole of it a forgery. Samuel Ireland circulated another handbill, declaring that he knew what Malone was doing, and requesting every one to suspend his judgment till the play should be brought on the stage.

There was a vast conflux of persons to witness the exhibition. Sir James Bland Burgess wrote the prologue, in which he said,

> " The favour'd relics of your Shakspeare's hand
> Unrivall'd and inimitable stand."

And Mr. Merry had prepared an epilogue, which was to be spoken by Mrs. Jordan.

The piece proceeded, with some slight interruptions, until Kemble, in delivering a passage about death, came to the line,

> " And when this solemn mockery is o'er,"

which he delivered with more than necessary slowness,

and which seemed to be the signal for a general tumult of opposition among the unbelievers. Kemble waited till the noise had subsided, and then repeated the line in a similar manner, which was but a signal for a renewal of the tumult. Efforts were made to continue the representation, and the play was forced to its termination amid such storms of hisses and outcries as fairly overpowered all attempts at applause from the believers, Mrs. Jordan being hardly allowed to speak her epilogue. Kemble was thought, of course, to have desired the condemnation of the piece; and Sheridan expressed much dissatisfaction with Kemble's acting on the occasion, observing that, as a servant of the theatre, he ought to have done his best for its interests, whether he believed in the genuineness of the manuscripts or not.

After the night's performance was at an end, Sheridan and Samuel Ireland divided between them 206*l*., and the father handed to the son thirty pounds out of the half. The son had also sixty pounds out of the three hundred, clearing in all ninety pounds by his inventions. Whether the father put the rest in his pocket, or whether it went to pay expenses that had been incurred, nobody has related.

Barker, a bookseller of Russell Street, who afterwards published the play, said that if Ireland the father had brought him the manuscript ten days before the representation, he would have given him a thousand guineas for it; but, after the failure, it had very little sale; it appeared too late.

The volume in which Malone had threatened to prove the spuriousness of the papers made its appearance in

1796.   The first point which he attacked was the spelling.   There was, throughout all the performances, a
prodigious affectation of antiquated orthography, exhibiting clusters of consonants, and tails attached
to words, such as had never before met the public
eye.   " I have perused some thousand deeds and other
manuscripts," said Malone, " but never till now saw *and*
written with a final *e*, or *for* changed into *forre*, or *from*
into *fromme*, or *as* into *asse*, or *one* into *oune*, or *Master*
into *Masterre*.   I have seen," says he, " *Leicester* written
Leycestre, but never *Leycesterre*."   We find also *expenne-
ces, receyvedde, knottedde, thysse, nygheste, bllossoms,
bllooms;* and Shakspeare's mistress is called *Dearesste
Anna Hatherrewaye*.   But, in spelling, Ireland was not
consistent with himself; sometimes he forgets to write
forre in his peculiar way, and gives it in its present
form; the same is the case with *receyvedde*, and also
with *shyllynge;* and *this* is sometimes written, not *thysse*,
but *thys*.   As to the pretended handwriting of Queen
Elizabeth, it was totally different from her genuine
hand, with the exception of the signature, which was a
clumsy and imperfect imitation of it.   Arabic numerals
are used in specifying sums of money, whereas they
used to be noted thus :—xx^{li}. vs. viiid.   Shakspeare is
made to live at " the Blackfryers" before he had it.
Malone, in the course of his Shakspeare researches, had
disinterred, in the year 1790, the name of *William Ireland*, who probably gave designation to Ireland's Yard,
and young Ireland, seizing upon it, gave, as a contemporary name, *William Henry Ireland*, which is of itself,
as Malone observes, sufficient to make the " deede of
guyft " as he writes it, a *felo de se*, for second baptismal

names had not then come into use.   In this document, too, Shakspeare is made to say, "for the whyche service," [the preservation of his life when drowning,] "I doe herebye give hym as folowythe!!!," when no punctuation at all is employed in deeds, and the tripling of notes of admiration is an invention long subsequent to Shakspeare's time, first used perhaps by advertisers, and having in all probability never before had the honour of appearing in a legal instrument.

Let us extract, though we have perhaps already given enough, one more example of absurdity, with Malone's comment on it, as a specimen brick of his book.   The verses to Queen Elizabeth contain the following lines :

> " Queene of my thoughts by daye, my dreame by night,
>   My gracious mistress still is in my sight.
>   Her full perfections how shall I displaye ?
>   No words the bright idea can portraye.
>   *   *   *   *   *
>   So when some lowly swain essayes to prove
>   His humble duty and obsequious love,
>   The practised accents in his throat are lost,
>   And his best purpose by his virtue crost.
>   So, the dumb bard, the spangled courtier cries,
>   And, round me speechless, all St. James's flies ;
>   Each titled dame deserts her rolls and tea,
>   And all the Maids of Honour crye, Te ! He ! "

The reader will observe that the affectation of antiquated spelling is here almost wholly laid aside, though this may be attributed to the transcriber.   Malone comments thus :

"In the original there is a note, mentioning that this unfortunate miscarriage happened to our poet at a *breakfast* given by the queen to a select number of courtiers of both sexes. . . .   If the simile, ' So when a lowly swain,' should

be said to smell too strongly of one of our poet's plays, and
to be faulty in another respect, as being little more than
a comparison of a thing with itself, the answer, I suppose,
would be that Shakspeare, when he wrote these lines, had
probably recently composed his 'Midsummer Night's Dream;'
and as to the other point, that Addison's celebrated simile
of the angel was equally faulty; neither was the time of
Elizabeth an age of such nicety of criticism as the present.

"On my objecting to the word *idea* in the fourth line, my
friend," a gentleman who had procured a copy of these verses
for Malone from the unknown in the country, as they are
not among the printed specimens, and who expressed himself
quite convinced of their authenticity, " my friend told me he
had himself made the same objection to the gentleman who
had communicated these verses; on which he said he had
made a mistake, and that he had a *better copy* at home,
without that word; but as I would not venture to alter anything that even pretended to be the composition of our immortal bard, I have adhered to the first copy.   My friend
scrupled a little at the mention of *St. James's*, but there he
was certainly in an error; for Queen Elizabeth sometimes
resided at that palace.   The last line but two is more difficult to be got over; but those who may think those verses
genuine may *very consistently* maintain either that Shakspeare foresaw in this, as in many other instances that might
be produced from the 'Miscellaneous Papers,' what would be
written in the eighteenth century, or, which is full as probable, that the ingenious author of the 'Epistle to Sir William Chambers' had a peep some years ago at this curious
relique in the dark repository where it has been preserved,
and stole from it one of his best lines.

"Other objections were made by my friend to the omission
of the good chine and sirloin and manchet of Queen Elizabeth's days, and introducing our fragrant *Chinese beverage*,
with its proper accompaniment, in their room; and also to
the allusion to *balloons* and the *earthquake at Lisbon*, in a
subsequent part of these verses, which he had heard, though
he had not obtained a copy of them; but the *good believer* told

him that, a committee having been appointed to consider of these matters (consisting of Messrs. B. C. D. E. O. P. Q. and R.), these objections were overruled, and unanimously voted of no weight whatsoever." *

Some critics thought that the extraordinary deviations from probability in the papers tended to prove their genuineness, as a forger would have kept nearer to the appearance of truth.

Malone deserves great credit for his perspicacity and research in the exposure of the forgeries, but his attempts at wit and merriment, in his exultation over the vanquished, are often heavy and pointless.

But Malone was not to enjoy an unquestioned triumph. In the following year, 1797, George Chalmers, with the assistance of we know not whom, put forth his "Apology for the Believers in the Shakspeare Papers," a weighty octavo of more than six hundred pages, which is not so much a defence of those who had looked favourably on the papers, as an attack upon Malone for having spoken scornfully of them. If Tomline's Life of Pitt, as Macaulay declares, enjoys the reputation of being the worst biography in the English language, Chalmers's Apology may well be allowed the honour of being the dullest book of criticism in the English language. Chalmers shook one or two of Malone's absolute assertions, and dug up an exceptional *ande* and *forre*, but did the case of the believers, on the whole, very little good. Porson was fond of joking on those who, though forced to acknowledge that Shakspeare did not write the papers, yet wanted to prove that he might

---

* Malone's Inquiry, p. 100.

have written them.   Even Wakefield* launched a happy
couplet at Chalmers in his " Imitation of the First Satire
of Juvenal :"

> " See Chalmers urge with persevering page
>   To doubt and dulness a discerning age ; "

while the author of the " Pursuits of Literature "
applied to him Pope's lines,

> " So, forced from wind-guns, lead itself can fly,
>   And pond'rous slugs cut swiftly through the sky."

But the application is suitable only in part.   Chalmers's
pages were leaden enough, but no impulse gave them
a rapid flight.

An anonymous writer, about the same time, shot
forth this squib :

> " Chalmers, in every page thy readers trace
>   The heavy influence of thy leaden mace :
>   They all exclaim, when once thy book is read,
>   His ink is opium, and his pen is lead." †

Mason closed the controversy with the following
lines in the " Morning Herald :"

> " Four forgers, born in one prolific age,
>   Much critical acumen did engage ;
>   The first was soon by doughty Douglas scared,
>   Though Johnson would have screen'd him, had he dared ;
>   The next had all the cunning of a Scot ;
>   The third invention, genius, nay, what not ?
>   Fraud, now exhausted, only could dispense
>   To her fourth son their threefold impudence."

The first three were Lauder, Macpherson, and Chatterton.

---

* Memoirs, vol. ii. p. 425.
† Spirit of the Public Journals for 1800.

CHAP. XIII.

In 1797 came forth Porson's first edition of a Greek
play, the Hecuba of Euripides, in duodecimo, without
his name, though, to most of those who took interest in
classical publications, it was well known that it was his.
A short preface was prefixed, in which Porson observed
that nothing recondite, or of deep research, was to be
expected in the notes, as the edition was intended for the
use of *tiros;* that the text, if not everywhere correct,
was at least, he hoped, nearer to correctness than it had
previously been brought; that wherever the common
reading had been altered, the reason for the alteration
had been assigned ; and that no citation of the play by
any ancient author, presenting a variety of reading, had,
as far as the editor's memory served him, been omitted.
Some remarks on the iambic trimeter were added, in
which it was said that the tragic poets never admitted
an anapæst beyond the first place, or a dactyl beyond
the third, except in the case of a proper name.

The preface then concluded as follows :—

"The duty of explaining and illustrating I have forborne to take upon myself, partly lest what was intended to be but a pamphlet should swell into a volume. Imitations of Euripides by Latin writers I have, however, as they arose to my recollection, cited in the margin. The few passages where I have assumed the duty of the interpreter are such as allowed me to unite with it that of the critic. But if I shall be thought to have been, on any point, too sparing of annotation, I will endeavour, in the plays that are to follow, to avoid that fault; for the reader is to understand that the other plays of Euripides will soon be published in the usual order, if I shall find that the present specimen is not disapproved by the literary world; and, should I bring my work to a conclusion, I intend to add some remarks on the different metres of the tragic poets."

The preceding editors, Aldus, Barnes, King, Musgrave, and Beck, were duly consulted, and three new collations of manuscripts were given, two in the library of the Royal Society, and a third in the British Museum.

Among those who were not quite certain that the new edition was Porson's, was Gilbert Wakefield, with whom Porson maintained some intimacy, and who had previously published the five parts of his *Silva Critica*, and his *Tragœdiarum Delectus*, in both of which publications he had proposed some emendations of the Hecuba. Feeling persuaded however that Porson was the editor, and finding that he himself was not mentioned in the preface or annotations, he hastened, in great agitation, to the shop of Evans, the publisher, and asked him who the editor was. "Can you have any doubt?" replied Evans; "Mr. Porson, of course." "But," said Wakefield, "I want proof, positive proof." "Well, then," replied Evans, "I saw Mr. Porson present a large-paper copy to Mr. Cracherode, and heard him acknow-ledge himself the editor." Wakefield, having thus got sufficient evidence, went home and wrote *In Euripidis Hecubam Londini nuper publicatam Diatribe Extemporalis;* an effusion compounded of praise and censure, of complaint and apology.

"A few days before the appearance of this production," says Kidd, " Porson had met Wakefield at Payne's shop, from whence, conversing amicably on literary matters, they sauntered down to Egerton's, and afterwards parted in a friendly manner at Charing Cross. A few days afterwards, Porson left town for the country-house of a friend, where he was told that Wakefield was 'coming out with something against him.' He was surprised, but, on receiving a copy of the perform-ance, observed that it was as unskilful as it was rash, and that a column in a morning paper would be suffi-cient to show its want of solidity. 'But,' added he, 'if he goes on thus, he will tempt me to examine his *Silva Critica.* I hope we shall not meet ; for a violent quar-rel would be the consequence.'"*

On the eve of the publication of the *Diatribe*, Porson is said to have been at a club to which he belonged, consisting of seven members and a president; when, in the course of the evening, the president proposed that each of the members should toast a friend, accompany-ing his name with a suitable quotation from Shakspeare. When Porson's turn came, he said, "I'll give you my

* Rogers's Table Talk, "Porsoniana," p. 320. Kidd, Tracts, p. lxxi.

friend Gilbert Wakefield.   'What's Hecuba to him, or
he to Hecuba?'"

Wakefield's great reason for sending forth this pamphlet was, as he pretends, to remind the learned of that
kindness and courtesy which they ought to observe in
their conduct one towards another.

"The intercourse of scholars with scholars," he says, "in
which they have constant opportunities of praising, advising,
assisting, and recommending one another, conducting themselves, not as detractors from others' merits, but as sharers
and *competitors* in the same honourable labours, has always
appeared to me one of the most grateful consolations of the
unhappy lot of man. For my own part, whatever others
may think, if I should become insensible to the incitements
of honourable fame,

"' Quæ carmine gratior aurem
	Occupat humanam,'

I should consider that I lost by such privation one of the
noblest feelings of our common nature; nor would I object
to be pronounced by all upright and liberal-minded men, in
the words of Nestor,

'Αφρήτωρ, ἀθέμιστος, ἀνέστιος,

unfit to share the same social rites, the same laws, and the
same hearths with those around me. I would ask, therefore,
those whose minds are of the higher order, and who are actuated
by such kindly feelings as liberal studies ought to cherish,
to tell me candidly whether a man, who has always been
praised, honoured, and treated as a friend by me, is not altogether inexcusable, when, in writing on similar topics with
myself, and seeing a favourable opportunity for commending
me, he not only did not embrace it (for of that I should not
have complained), but let it pass with such utter disregard as
not obscurely to insinuate, but plainly to declare to all that
read his pages, that he thinks my services to Greek literature
utterly valueless, and considers me totally unworthy to have

my name enrolled among those of the learned. If I had left this insult, which, though silent, is more expressive than words, unresented, I might well be thought, through contemptible stolidity, ignorant of what is due to a high-minded man, and chargeable with the basest insensibility to ill treatment. But I am not deficient either in feeling or understanding ; and this edition of the Hecuba provokes me boldly to display the inscription on my standard, *Spectemur agendo,* which (having all my life laboured under many disadvantages, and not having enjoyed, what I should have considered the greatest happiness, an education at Eton,) I should before have been afraid to hold up to view."

The allusion to education at Eton was intended as something like a sneer at Porson.   Porson, in regard to his silence concerning Wakefield, told Burney that he had forborne to mention him from kindness, as he could have noticed him only with the severest censure.

Another reason which Wakefield gave for publishing the *Diatribe* was a desire that the relics of antiquity might be put in a more correct state, *aliquanto castigatiora,* into the hands of studious youth, for whom he sarcastically observes that Porson professed to write. He therefore proceeds to correct Porson's corrections, or to make remarks on passages which he thought that Porson should have altered. We shall produce a few of his animadversions ; the futility of many of them will be evident to those who know but little Greek ; and the mere English reader may wish to know something of the controversy.

His first assault is on Porson's patronage of the paragogic ν, inserted when the next word begins with a consonant. Thus he would read, at the end of an iambic verse,

$$\text{—— } εἴρηκε\ κακῶς, \text{ for } εἴρηκεν,$$

and, at the beginning,

Ζεὺς ὤλεσέ με, instead of ὤλεσεν,

asserting that it is manifest, both from manuscripts, and
from the earliest editors, that such a use of this letter
was unknown to the ancient Greeks, and had its origin
from modern transcribers. On this point he entered
also in his correspondence with Fox, and, as Fox desired full information concerning it, Wakefield enlarged
upon it in the following argumentation :

" It is not for us, at this time of day, to lay down the laws
of Greek composition and versification, but to inquire into
the actual practice of the ancients. Now it is most certain
that the old editions and old scholiasts so generally omit the
ν where modern editors interpolate the letter, as to induce a
most probable conviction that it was *universally* omitted by
the ancients; and the few present exceptions are the officious
insertions of transcribers and publishers, who would be ' wise
above what was written,' and modelled the manuscripts by
their own preconceptions of propriety. Whereas, from the
current persuasion among modern scholars of the necessity of
support to these short syllables by the application of consonants, it is perfectly inconceivable that they should have
left the syllables in question unsustained, had they found the
ν in their copies. Nay, it cannot be doubted but modern
editors, like Porson, would invariably supply the ν in all
those places where early editors were contented to omit it in
obedience to their authorities; and, if the early editions were
lost, all traces of the old practice, as it should seem to be,
would presently be obliterated beyond recovery." *

Again :

" It is universally allowed that the early editors adhered

* Wakefield's Correspondence with Fox, p. 98.

more closely to their manuscripts. In their editions the final ν is commonly omitted. In such works as scholia, of which few copies were circulated, that ν is *always* omitted. Good reasons may be assigned for the occasional insertion, but none possibly for the omission. Owners of manuscripts have perpetually corrected them, as we see at this day, according to their own fancy; and if Porson, for example, had them all, he would put in the ν throughout; and these manuscripts might go down as vouchers for the practice of antiquity. Very little learning would suffice to induce men to insert ν, from an appearance of vicious quantity; so that a very old manuscript now might abound in that insertion, though its prototype were without it; and so on. But the acknowledged omission in innumerable instances even now, and that obvious reason for its insertion in the rest, when no possible solution can be given for the regular omission, induce, to my apprehension, a probability of the highest kind, that the ancients never used it at all. More might be said, but this is the substance of the argument." *

Fox, who was not qualified by profundity of research to judge for himself on the matter, listened to Wakefield's representations, and believed that Porson, who adhered to his own practice, with regard to the ν, in the plays which he published subsequently, persisted in it only from obstinate opposition to Wakefield. Porson, in a note on the sixty-fourth verse of the Orestes,

Παρθένον, ἐμῇ τε μητρὶ παρέδωκεν τρέφειν,

disposed of the subject, and of Wakefield, but without naming him, thus :

" When a word ends in a short vowel, and the next word begins with two such consonants as would allow it to remain

* Wakefield's Correspondence with Fox, p. 114.

short, I scarcely think that any indisputable examples can be found of the final vowel being lengthened. Whoever should appeal to the authority of manuscripts in such cases would be extremely foolish, for the authority of manuscripts on the point is valueless; and I have only to entreat that nobody may abuse their testimony to overthrow my rule; for manuscripts neither agree with one another as to the practice, nor is the same manuscript always consistent with itself throughout."

In a note, too, on the Grenville Homer, for which he afterwards collated the Harleian manuscript of the Odyssey, he observes that "that manuscript observes no certain rule either as to adding or as to inserting the final ν. It often adds it at the end of a verse, when the next verse begins with a consonant; it often inserts it at a cæsura, when a liquid or two consonants follow; and it often omits it when the metre seems to demand its insertion.*

Wakefield then attacks Porson about the word ὀϊστός, which Porson made a dissyllable, but observed that it had always before been given as a trisyllable. This assertion, says Wakefield, is *in falsissimis habendum*, one of the greatest of falsehoods, for I myself edited it as a dissyllable in Herc. Fur. 194, so that I am almost tempted to address the present editor in the following words of Homer, nor should I, I think, incur the reader's censure by doing so:

> Ἀτρείδη, μὴ ψεύδε', ἐπιστάμενος σάφα εἰπεῖν.
> Atrides, lie not, when thou know'st the truth."

This savage language Porson noticed, when he edited the Medea, as follows, in his note on ver. 634. " Barnes

* Note on Odyss. i. 54.

observed, in his annotation on this verse, that ὀϊστὸς must be scanned as a dissyllable, and makes a similar remark on Androm. 1134; but in Herc. Fur. 196, having then grown bolder, he actually prints οἰστὸς instead of ὀϊστός. When, therefore, I said in the preface to the Hecuba that the word 'had always before been edited ὀϊστός,' *I made a mistake*, or, if you had rather, gentle reader, I TOLD A LIE, having been deceived by Musgrave's edition." Many young students, who knew nothing of Wakefield's "Diatribe," must have wondered why Porson thus expressed himself.

On verse 154, where Hecuba speaks of Polyxena being stained with a stream of blood ἐκ χρυσοφόρου δειρῆς, "from her gold-bearing neck," and where Porson observes, "it was customary among the ancients for virgins to wear a great deal of gold," Wakefield cries " *Nugæ!* how could Polyxena, a captive, have a great deal of gold?" and exults greatly in an emendation which he proposes, ἐκ χρυσοφόϐου δειρῆς, intending it to signify, " from her *golden-haired* neck." To this alteration Dr. Burney, in his critique on Wakefield and Porson in the " Monthly Review," justly made the following strong objections: 1. The compound χρυσοφόϐος is not found in what is left to us of the Greek language. 2. If it were found, it would signify *qui aurum timet*, as ὑδροφόϐος signifies *qui aquam timet*. 3. Or, if it had authority, and could signify *golden-haired*, it would not be applied to a mortal, for golden hair was attributed only to the deities, while the epithet ξανθὸς was applied to that of mortals. 4. But if it could justly be applied to a mortal, would Euripides have thought it a proper epithet for the *neck* of Polyxena? 5. That the captives had no valuable ornaments is refuted by a subsequent passage of the play, where Hecuba proposes to collect from the captives such valuables as they had concealed from their captors, to deck Polyxena's dead body. So numerous, in many cases, are the objections which he who would alter the text of an author has to anticipate.

We must notice another of Wakefield's flights.   On the passage,

$$\tau i \ \nu \acute{\epsilon} o \nu$$
$$\mathrm{K} \alpha \rho \acute{\nu} \xi \alpha \sigma' \ o \emph{\i} \kappa \omega \nu \ \mu', \ \emph{\"{\omega}} \sigma \tau' \ \emph{\"{o}} \rho \nu \iota \nu$$
$$\Theta \alpha \mu \beta \epsilon \emph{\i} \ \tau \tilde{\omega} \delta' \ \emph{\'{\epsilon}} \xi \acute{\epsilon} \pi \tau \alpha \xi \alpha \varsigma;$$

he offers these strictures :

"Awake, ye learned men, who have polished Euripides for us, and tell us, I pray, what sort of phrase is this, ἐκπτήσσειν οἴκων τινα; They are silent, having nothing to say. But perhaps, O most sagacious and accomplished editor, that friend of yours, who recently, with such deceit and want of firmness, attacked me from under cover in the review of the Glasgow ' Æschylus,'

Τυφλοῖς ὁρῶντας οὐτάσας τοξεύμασι,

(me, a humble individual, who have the greatest difficulty in these hard times, to scrape together a maintenance for myself and my family,) will vouchsafe us information on the subject, and throw light upon these and other astonishing matters ! Meanwhile I would say, and affirm with the utmost boldness, that this phrase is to be regarded as the merest and lowest barbarism, in support of which opinion the reader may consult my notes on Herc. Fur. 976, 987, and Ion. 1299. The word, indeed, must either be taken for ἐξέπτασας, from πτάω, πτῆμι, *volo*, or we must write, ἐξεπτόασας, from πτοιέω, *terreo*. Choose which you please."

On this passage Dr. Burney remarks:

" To whom Mr. Wakefield refers, and applies his quotation from the ' Hercules Furens,' it would be presumption in us to attempt to determine. *Let the gall'd jade wince; our withers are unwrung.* Mr. Wakefield cannot allude to the Monthly Reviewer's critique on the Glasgow ' Æschylus,' which should have been Mr. Porson's edition. Some critic has probably brought forward Schutz's remarks on Mr. Wakefield's Eumenides, and has been comparing the three editions and the Monthly Reviewer's strictures together. To some such animadversions this passage may perchance relate, though they have not reached us. . . . Our article, if we be not grossly misinformed, has been commended by liberal scholars, on account of the temperate observations which it contained. The person to whom Mr. Wakefield alludes may possibly reply; but, at all events, it is our duty to mention the passage and the note."

It is then observed that ἐξέπταξας, from ἐκπτήσσω, is sufficiently defended by Hom. Il. ξ. 40 :

$$\text{Ὁ δὲ ξύμβλητο γεραιὸς}$$
$$\text{Νέστωρ, πῆξε δὲ θυμὸν ἐνὶ στήθεσσιν Ἀχαιῶν,}$$

and by various other instances of neuter verbs used in an active signification.

In commenting on ver. 323,

$$\text{Τυμβὸν δὲ βουλοίμην ἄν ἀξιούμενον}$$
$$\text{Τὸν ἐμὸν ὁρᾶσθαι,}$$

he makes a curious blunder. He denies that ἀξιοῦσθαι can be used absolutely, or without its genitive case, and therefore proposes to read τιμῶν for τὸν ἐμόν: or, he adds, if γόνιμος might be used for γενναῖος, *noble*, we might read γόνιμον, which, as to its letters, has a greater resemblance to τὸν ἐμόν. He first says that ἀξιοῦσθαι ·cannot be used without its case, and then, by suggesting γόνιμον, proposes to use it without its case.

In ver. 490, Hecuba is represented as lying *with her back*, νῶτα, *on the ground*. Would she lie so indecently? says Wakefield. No: read χρῶτα, *with her body on the ground*. In ver. 500, she is represented as defiling her head, κάρα, with dust. Would she defile her head only? asks Wakefield. No: read χρόα, and make her defile her whole body. In ver. 164, the chorus is said to report πήματα, *woes*. No, says Wakefield, alter it to ῥήματα: people report *words*, not *woes*. In ver. 508, Porson, with other editors, leaves σε, *thee*, to be understood. Oh no! exclaims Wakefield, such negligence is highly criminal. Ought the lines of so correct a poet as Euripides to be put thus carelessly into the hands of studious youth? Attach the pronoun to the beginning of the verse:

Σ' Ἀγαμέμνονος πέμψαντος, ὦ γύναι, μέγα,

a position and elision of which the merest schoolboy can see the inelegance. In the first edition of the " Diatribe," indeed, the line was presented thus:

Ἀγαμέμνονος πέμψαντος σ᾽, ὦ γύναι, μέγα,

with a spondee in the fourth place; but afterwards a correction was made with a pen, and at last the page was cancelled, with some others*. One page was suppressed because *selexi* had been put for *selegi*; and another to alter *ad hoc scopulum* to *ad hunc scopulum*. In the earlier pages of the " Diatribe", on ver. 32, he

* Monthly Review, vol. xxviii. pp. 204, 442.

blunders, in his hurry, into writing τριταῖον ἡμέραν and τρίτον ἡμεράν.

We may now have done with this effusion of Wakefield's. About fifty alterations of the "Hecuba" are proposed in it, by not one of which would the text be improved. Wakefield said that his surprise at not being noticed by Porson in his Hecuba was the greater, as he had been noticed by him in the Appendix to *Toupii Emendationes in Suidam.* The notice was merely that Wakefield, in his *Silva Critica,* had hit upon a similar emendation of a word in Suidas with himself.* We have searched the *Silva Critica* for the readings which Wakefield had proposed before Porson published his Hecuba. They are five, and are, the reader may be assured, of the same character, trifling and venturesome, as those in the "Diatribe."

* Append. ad Toup. Emend. in Suid. tom. iv. p. 473.

CHAP. XIV.

BUT a more considerable antagonist than Wakefield was
rising against Porson on the other side of the Channel ;
a man, says Kidd, *neque meo judicio stultus et suo valde
sapiens.* Gottfried Hermann, then a very young member
of the University of Leipsic, had published, in 1789,
a treatise on the metres of the Greek and Latin poets,
and was preparing to put forth an edition of the "Nubes"
of Aristophanes, which appeared in 1799.   Meeting
with Porson's edition of the "Hecuba," he could not but
see that it had much merit, but observing that Porson,
in his preface, had proposed his *dicta* regarding the
metres without much proof, and seeing that many of
them were contrary to his own notions of what was
allowable, he resolved, in entire ignorance of Porson's
full strength, to publish a rival edition and preface, in
which he might pronounce his opinions, as a superior
on an inferior, regarding Porson's emendations and me-

trical tenets.   He accordingly mingled with his praise, in his prolegomena and annotations, an abundant quantity of censure.   It will be well to quote the commencement of his preface :

"Porson, although he warned his readers to expect from his edition nothing recondite, or of deep research, has yet done such service to Euripides as no one, who is not either unjust, or unskilled in Greek literature, will deny to be eminently worthy of a great critic.   But there is one point, and one only indeed, in which he has disappointed the expectation which rumour had excited regarding his publication.   He was said to have made many observations relating to the science of metres ; a subject which it was the more desirable to illustrate, as the text of Euripides, in this respect especially, is somewhat more difficult of emendation than that of the other tragic writers ; but though some remarks, indeed, on this department of classical learning, have been offered by Porson, yet he has chosen to state them arbitrarily and oracularly, rather than with the fulness of explanation which it is the duty of a critic to give.   The consequence of this method seems likely to be, that the greater number of those who read the 'Hecuba' of Porson, considering his character and authority as sufficient supports for his assertions, will be more ready, at least in this department of learning, to yield an implicit assent to his notions than to examine with care what he has somewhat too obscurely delivered. Whatever Porson, therefore, appears to me to have erred in asserting, I have taken upon myself to notice, not, however, for the purpose of censuring him, but for the benefit of those who take an interest in these studies.   Nothing absolutely perfect in any respect has ever been produced, we must remember, by any individual of the human race.   It is but right, therefore, that we should criticise the performances of others with freedom, nor should we, if we receive censure, be uneasy under it.   I do not plead my own cause, but that of literature and knowledge in general.

"I have thought proper, too, to take some notice of the

conjectures of Wakefield, whom Porson has .suddenly found, though not an equal, yet a determined, adversary; and who, as he exhibits not less rashness and presumption than ability, and not more exact knowledge of Greek than of Latin, is, though deserving of some consideration, yet quite unworthy to carry such authority as he has gained among my country-men, who are apt to be too favourable judges of foreigners."

After some remarks on Porson's spelling of certain words, and his adherence to Dawes's canon respecting the unlawfulness of omitting the augment in Attic Greek, a canon which Hermann labours to impugn as far as he is able, he proceeds to attack Porson's *dictum* regarding the inadmissibility of anapæsts into any place of a tragic senarius except the first, and of dactyls into any except the first and third, unless when proper names, which could not be subjected to this rule, were used. He fixes, first of all, on a passage of the preface which must be acknowledged to be indeed vulnerable. Porson says, "So far is it impossible, in my opinion, for an anapæst to constitute the second or fourth foot, that it cannot even constitute the third or the fifth. Whoever admits that this is true with regard to the third foot, will admit *à fortiori*, as logicians say, that it is true with regard to the fifth; for a dactyl, which is very often used in the third foot, is never seen in the fifth; and therefore the anapæst, if it is excluded from the third, will be excluded from the fifth." This reasoning is not sound, because there might not be the same objection to placing the long syllable of the ana-pæst before the final iambus as to placing the two short syllables of the dactyl before it. Porson, indeed, only showed that the anapæst was not used in the fifth foot,

(or in any foot but the first, except in the case of a
proper name,) not that it could not be used; and all
who have since written on the subject have shown no
more.   Hermann next, in the course of his dissertation,
proceeds to argue that an anapæst would be less toler-
able in the third place than in the fifth, but a schoolboy may see that what he advances for argument on
this point is mere fancy.

His conclusion is, that an anapæst may be admitted
indiscriminately into any place of a trimeter iambic;
nihil interesse quâ in sede trimetri anapœstus occurrat,
excepting of course the last; " and therefore," he adds,
" if all *senarii* that present an anapæst in the third place
are corrupt, it will not from thence be deducible that
all those require correction which present anapæsts in
other positions.   If indeed we resolve to eject the anapæst altogether, we must inquire whether it is to be
ejected for causes inherent in its own nature, or for
causes external to its nature.   As to its nature, it must
be allowed that though it is not altogether adapted to
the gravity of the tragic trimeter, yet that it is not
altogether at variance with it, since it is admitted with
such frequency in the case of proper names.   We must
suppose, accordingly, that it was not admitted except
under the strong obligation of necessity, as when the
poets were compelled to use words for which they could
not substitute others; of which kind of words there
might not only be proper names, but other words, that
could not conveniently be changed, and in the use of
such words who would be offended at the introduction
of an anapæst?"*   We need not follow Hermann's rea-

* Præf. in Hec. p. xlviii.

soning any further. If Porson did not prove that an anapæst could not be used in a tragic senarius elsewhere than in the first foot, he at least made all scholars believe that it was not elsewhere used. " Should any scholar of the nineteenth century," says Elmsley, " venture to maintain the admissibility of an anapæst, not included in a proper name, into any place of a Greek tragic senarius except the first foot, he would assuredly be ranked with those persons, if any such persons remain, who deny the motion of the earth, or the circulation of the blood. Before the appearance of the Preface to the ' Hecuba,' critics were divided into two sects upon this subject ; the more rigid of which excluded anapæsts from all the even places, whereas the other admitted them promiscuously into any place except the last. Mr. Porson, p. 6, with his usual strictness in attributing the merit of discoveries and improvements to the right owners, mentions an obscure hint of the true doctrine, which is contained in the preface to Morell's *Thesaurus Grœcœ Poëseos*." *　But that hint fell without effect on all Morell's successors until Porson.

In his note on ver. 343 Porson obscurely indicates his knowledge of that kind of cæsura of the fifth foot which he afterwards called the *pause*, to distinguish it, as he afterwards said, from the other cæsuras, because a verse which is without any of the other cæsuras is of necessity ill-modulated, but a verse may not strike the ear as ill-modulated which wants the pause. The verse is,

Κρύπτοντα χεῖρα, καὶ πρόσωπον ἔμπαλιν,

* Edinb. Rev. vol. xix. p. 65.

and the note,

> "Aldus reads τοὔμπαλιν, but several manuscripts, as well
> as Eustathius on Il. A. p. 129, 14 = 97, 31, have ἔμπαλιν,
> which makes indeed no difference as to the sense, but a very
> great difference as to the metre. What I mean will perhaps
> be better understood, if I assert that there occur in the Tragic
> poets very few verses resembling the first verse of the 'Ion,'
> Ἄτλας ὁ χαλκέοισι νώτοις οὐρανόν."

The rule regarding the pause he afterwards expressed
thus : *If a senarius end in a word which forms a cretic,
and a word of more than one syllable precede the cretic,
the fifth foot ought to be an iambus*, the variations and
exceptions, which we need not notice here, being subjoined. Porson discovered that the tragic poets observed this rule, but did not pretend to suggest any
reason for their observation of it. Hermann, in his
edition of the " Hecuba," said that the reason was as
follows :

> "The reason why such a position of the words, χαλκέοισι
> νώτοις οὐρανόν, must displease the ear, is this. Since at the end
> of a verse, when the lungs of an actor are almost exhausted,
> a gentler flow of pronunciation is required, all harsher sounds
> offend the ear, and offend it the more the greater the difficulty
> of uttering them, such a collocation of the words as disjoins
> the latter portion of the verse by too lengthened a sound
> from the former, and thus hinders and retards the easy flow
> of the numbers, is carefully avoided."

This solution of the difficulty receives great approbation from Elmsley. "It is by no means necessary,"
says he, " to have enacted the part of Mercury in the
'Ion' of Euripides, in order to be sensible of the relief
which is afforded to the 'exhausted lungs' of a corpu-

lent performer by that variation of the verse in question, Ἄτλας ὁ νώτοις χαλκέοισιν οὐρανόν. . . . Upon the whole it is not without reason that Mr. Hermann exults in the following terms over the inaptitude of his rival to investigate the causes of those facts which he himself had sufficient sagacity to discover. *Id sponte animadvertisset vir doctissimus, si non satis haberet observare, sed in caussas etiam earum rerum quas observaret inquirendum putârit.* This the learned critic would readily have discovered, if he had not been content merely to observe, but had thought proper to inquire into the causes of what he observed." *

But it will surely not appear to every one that this suggestion of Hermann's deserves all the commendation which Elmsley was so ready to bestow upon it. It supposes that an actor, when he began to pronounce a speech, took in just sufficient breath to carry him through the first verse; that when he reached the end of the verse his lungs were exhausted and emptied; that, consequently, he paused at the end of it, and inhaled another supply of breath to carry him through the second verse; and proceeded thus, pausing at the end of every verse for breath, through a whole speech, however long it might be. But doubtless pauses were made by actors, not at the end of every verse for breath, but in accordance with the requirements of the sense. The arrangement of the words in νώτοις οὐρανόν offended the ears of an audience because it violated a recognised principle of the iambic metre, not because the lungs of a corpulent performer would find a difficulty in pro-

* Edinb. Review, vol. xix. p. 82.

nouncing it; for performers in general are not corpulent, and we may consider that the lungs even of a
corpulent one would have been able to utter a verse
without beginning to feel exhaustion at the commencement of the fifth foot.   How did actors utter other
verses of which the fifth foot was a spondee?

Porson considered himself so disrespectfully treated
in Hermann's preface and notes to the " Hecuba," that
he chose to regard him, ever after, as a personal enemy.
He used to allude to Wakefield and Hermann together,
and appears to have been provoked at nothing, in the
whole course of his literary career, so much as at their
animadversions on his critical dogmata.   He would
speak of them as four-footed animals, and say that
whatever he wrote in future should be written in such
a manner that they should not reach it with their paws,
though they stood on their hind legs to get at it.*

Hermann's criticisms drew from Porson the Supplement to his Preface, in which he amply vindicated all
the metrical canons and opinions which he had before
delivered, and vindicated them at the expense of
Hermann, for though he is not named in the Supplement, yet almost every line of it, as Elmsley observes,
contains an allusion to some blunder committed by
Hermann either in his " Treatise on Metres," or in his
edition of the " Hecuba."   "Whoever wishes thoroughly
to understand," he adds, " the preface to Mr. Porson's
edition of the ' Hecuba,' ought ' to devote his days and
nights' to the study of Mr. Hermann's edition of the
same tragedy.   Those persons who possess both editions

---

* Short Account of Porson, p. 6.   •

will do well in binding them in one volume ; adding, if they think proper, the *Diatribe Extemporalis* of the vehement and injudicious Wakefield, and the excellent strictures on Mr. Porson's ' Hecuba' and Mr. Wakefield's ' Diatribe,' which appeared in the 'Monthly Review' for 1799, and which are well known to be written by a gentleman to whom Greek literature," Mr. Elmsley is pleased to say, " is more indebted than to any other living scholar." *

Hermann, on the publication of the Supplement, could not but feel convinced how imprudent and presumptuous he had been, and how much he had been mistaken in his estimate of the powers of him whose hostility he had provoked.   He became sensible of his errors, and repented them, and made his book on Greek and Latin metres a very different work from what it was at its first appearance.   Of the first edition Elmsley remarked that it was " a book of which too much ill cannot easily be said, and which contains a smaller quantity of useful and solid information, in proportion to its bulk, than any elementary treatise, on any subject, which we remember to have seen."   It was afterwards transformed into the Treatise so well known to scholars, which, though containing much that is visionary and fanciful, is yet admitted to be well worthy of perusal by all who are in pursuit of metrical knowledge.

  " The generous Hermann," according to Kidd †, " was wont to do justice " to the Supplement to the the Preface, for its exactness of research and clearness of induction, " in his lecture-room."   Yet he is said, on

---

* Edinb. Review, vol. xix. p. 65.
† Tracts, p. lxxiii.

the same authority, to have had in contemplation a
defence of the anapæst in the third place.   The truth
is, it would appear, that Hermann regarded Porson and
his work, throughout the rest of his life, with mingled
feelings of admiration and dislike.   He could not but
admit that Porson had immeasurably the advantage on
the point on which he had been excited to vindicate
himself, but he could but retain a sense of dissatisfaction at having been himself worsted in the encounter
which he had provoked.   Dr. Blomfield, in his strictures
on Valpy's reprint of Stephens's "Thesaurus" in the
" Quarterly Review," * took occasion to observe that
" Hermann and his school never miss an opportunity of
lavishing their censure on Porson, and on those English
scholars whom they facetiously enough term Porson's
disciples; while, on the other hand, it is a sufficient title
to their esteem to flatter the German critics at the
expense of the English."   Mr. Edmund Henry Barker,
who was one of the chief editors of the "Thesaurus," and
who had procured, it seems, a panegyrical epistle from
Hermann to prefix to it, resented Dr. Blomfield's censure
of that critic and his followers, in a pamphlet entitled
" Aristarchus Anti-Blomfieldianus," a pamphlet which
called forth, in the pages of the " Quarterly," another
article on the " Thesaurus " and on Hermann's " champion," written, not wholly, but probably in part, by
Dr. Blomfield himself, and containing the following
remarks, which it will not be unsuitable to our purpose to transcribe, that it may be seen what was the
opinion of the learned world, in regard to Hermann, at
the time when they were written :

* Vol. xxii. p. 340.

" Instead of defending Hermann," says the article, " Mr. Barker *justifies our assertion* by quoting at length several passages from his writings, in which he has spoken most slightingly and most unjustly of the scholars of this country, for the undisguised reason of their attachment to the name and the example of the late Professor Porson. As to the quarrel between Porson and Hermann (whom Mr. Barker styles ' these modern Goliahs'), it is perfectly well known to have originated in the attempt made by the latter to decry the edition of the Hecuba at the first publication ; an attempt which was as conspicuous for the bad feeling which dictated, as for the utter failure which attended it ; but which must always be regarded by scholars with some satisfaction, as being the means of calling forth from Porson that fund of accurate and clear observation which distinguishes the second edition of his Hecuba, and has given us more insight into the poetry of the scenic writers of Greece than all the volumes which ever preceded it.   Porson unquestionably resented what he considered a rude, presumptuous, and unprovoked attack from the German, whose errors and whose ignorance he exposes in the happiest and most complete manner, without condescending to name him ; but, in a note upon a verse of the Medea, he inflicts a severe chastisement by holding up to derision some of Hermann's blunders in caustic and taunting language ; which, however it might have been deserved, we think that he would have better consulted his own dignity by suppressing.   Hermann, who was then a young man, and had aspired to notice in a controversy with an adversary whose strength he had miscalculated, was deeply chagrined by his failure ; and, we are sorry to say, appears never to have been able to lay aside his feelings towards Porson, which had their origin twenty-five years ago.   Though he has subsequently profited as much, perhaps, as any one living, by the writings of Porson, though he has established a fame not only incomparably superior to that of which his early productions gave promise, but which is likely to be solid and durable, yet he cannot refrain from incessant attempts to pick faults in the criticisms of Porson, and from

almost indiscriminate censure of all who look up to him as
a guide. For this conduct he has neither provocation nor
excuse; all Mr. Barker's research in reviews and other
English publications has not succeeded in establishing the
least proof of ill-will towards Hermann. The nature, indeed,
of his philology, being too much founded on vague theory,
and his habit of dogmatising on the obscurest topics of
ancient metre, naturally occasion the frequent dissent of
other scholars, and, it may be added, lead to a perpetual fluc-
tuation in his own judgment; but, far from his being the
object of personal dislike or jealousy, we see him everywhere
noticed with the honour and deference due to an ingenious,
learned, and most industrious scholar, who has contributed
greatly to enlarge our knowledge of Greek literature.

"In almost all Professor Hermann's writings there are
proofs of a warm and irritable temper, and of a readiness to
take offence at the most trivial expressions; a foible which
is the more to be regretted, as he appears to be a man of an
honourable mind, and is certainly an object of great attachment, and even veneration, to the scholars who are his
intimates. The feelings entertained by Hermann towards
Porson are discovered from the writings of his pupils, particularly of Seidler and of Reisig, even more plainly than from
his own. That they study to flatter the prejudices of their
master by the condemnation of Porson, is too palpable in
everything which they have written. The professor himself
has lately made an ingenuous confession that he is disposed
to disapprove the criticisms of our countryman Mr. Elmsley,
(a gentleman who, by the by, is greatly his superior in every
line of scholarship,) because he finds them commended by
those who most respect the authority of Porson! This, we
think, is quite conclusive; and while we repeat our high
opinion of Professor Hermann's genius, learning, and industry, we must refuse the least credit to his judgment of
contemporary scholars." *

Parr was greatly offended at the disrespectful men-

---

* Quart. Rev. vol. xxiv. p. 392.

tion made of Heath in Hermann's notes on the Hecuba*,
and in his *Observationes Criticæ.*† " No man," said he,
" admires more sincerely than I do the genius and learning of Hermann. But I can never read without indignation the arrogant and contemptuous terms in which he
speaks of the late Mr. Heath, a man whose good sense,
good manners, and most meritorious labours ought to
have protected him from such indignities."‡ All English
scholars were moved with indignation or pity at the
foolish remark concerning Bentley on the 325th verse
of the Nubes : *Bentleius, summus alioqui criticus, sed
nullius auctoritatis in Aristophane, ad quem minimè
imbutus Attici sermonis cognitione accessit.* On the
whole it was considered that the castigations which
Hermann received from Porson, severe as they were,
were not at all heavier than his arrogance and audacity
had merited.

On the 28th of November in the preceding year,
1796, Hermann sent Porson a copy of his Treatise *De
Metris*, with a Latin letter, in which he praises Porson's
Æschylus, and says that he is contemplating an edition
of Plautus, and requests his good offices to procure him
access to the manuscripts of that author in the libraries
of Great Britain. He had ventured on this application,
he says, at the desire of Heyne, who had promised
to second it ; a promise which Heyne did not fail to
perform. The reader shall see both Hermann's letter
and Heyne's in such an English dress as I can give
them.

* Ver. 1002. † P. 59.
‡ Memoirs of Wakefield, vol. ii. p. 439.

" *To the much-celebrated* RICHARD PORSON,
    GODFREY HERMANN *wishes the greatest health.*

"My friend Heyne has given me an excellent proof of his
kindness in not only assuring me that you, a gentleman so
well known to fame, would not fail to regard me with favour,
but in not hesitating to induce you, by his own recommendation, to receive with indulgence the letter which I now
address to you. By this encouragement he has freed me
from great anxiety and apprehension; for though I had no
greater object of desire than that gentlemen of distinguished
merit in Great Britain should be willing to aid my literary
endeavours by their authority, yet I was extremely fearful,
either that I should find no means of access to them, or such
only as I should not be able to adopt without great presumption. Nor do I now, indeed, feel altogether free from
timidity on this account; though my fears have been much
allayed by the report of your kindness, which is said to be
extremely great; by the knowledge of your love of learning
and eminent literary merits, of which an illustrious specimen
has lately appeared in your edition of Æschylus; and by
your manifest zeal and readiness to serve all by whom learning is assiduously cultivated. I thought, too, that I might
more reasonably rest my hopes on your indulgence, if I should
submit to your exact and severe judgment some of the fruits
of my labours. I have therefore sent you a book which I
have written on the metres of the Greek and Latin poets;
though I am aware that, should it secure me any regard,
such regard must be attributable, not so much to what I
have done as to what I have endeavoured to do, and to the
good-will and consideration of the reader.

" If you, Sir, do not wholly disapprove of this work, your
sentence in its favour will be one of the greatest honours,
and your support of it one of the greatest pleasures, that can
happen to me in the whole course of my studies, especially
of those studies to which I have now devoted myself; for,
having felt, some years ago, from the example of Richard
Bentley, an extraordinary desire to edit Plautus, I was led,

some time afterwards, to contemplate that object the more eagerly, by observing that the method which that great man, formerly the ornament of his country, had adopted in editing Terence, had been abandoned by almost all other scholars. My desire, however, remained unaccomplished, as I gave precedence to Frederic Augustus Wolf, who entertained the same purpose, and than whom no more learned editor of Plautus could have been found. But when Wolf himself, after I had published my book on metres, gave up Plautus to me of his own accord, he inspired me with so much new ardour, while other learned friends also encouraged me, that there is no object which I would less willingly relinquish than that of giving a new edition of Plautus.

" Yet I have still one cause for great care and anxiety, since the manuscripts of Plautus, without which it is certain that no new light can be thrown on his text, are not only very few, but also, from the distance of the places in which they are kept, very difficult to be collated. But the excellence of the readings which Bentley has produced, on several occasions, from the manuscripts preserved throughout Great Britain, has fixed my hopes and expectations chiefly on them. If perchance Bentley, as he once thought of editing Plautus, made any collection of those readings, such a collection, both for its greater compendiousness, and because it is likely that the readings have been illustrated by the conjectures of their eminent possessor, would be not less acceptable to me than a collation of the manuscripts themselves. Should this request from me, therefore, or your regard for Heyne, have so much influence with you as to render you not unwilling to procure me, by your recommendation and authority, access to those manuscripts, there would certainly be no favour which I should account either a more fruitful cause for rejoicing, or a more worthy subject for gratitude.

" Leipsic, Nov. 28th, 1796."

Heyne's letter, in support of this request, was written on the 21st of the following December :

" *To the highly-famed* Mr. Porson,
      C. G. Heyne *wishes the greatest health.*

" As it is inconsistent alike with my disposition and practice to decline to do any service or kindness requested of me, especially when such request proceeds from a highly deserving person, you will, I hope, excuse me if I seem rather obtrusively to trespass on your occupation or your leisure. You have received from one of the most learned of my countrymen a book on the metres of the ancients, with a letter which he wrote to accompany it. That gentleman is deceived in supposing that I have so much influence with you as to prevail on you to grant to my entreaties what he so anxiously desires. He will more easily obtain his object by addressing himself to your kindness, provided there be but a possibility of accomplishing that which he has in view.

" You will see by the book that the learned writer has attached himself with great devotion to Plautus, and is eager to bring to effect what many, and especially the great Bentley, have conceived or attempted in regard to that author. As Bentley's papers are deposited somewhere with you, he is very anxious to be allowed the privilege of inspecting them. As to the attainment of his object, I know not whether you have any friendship or connexion with those gentlemen from whom permission for that purpose is to be obtained; but I am sure that you will not be wanting in inclination or zeal for the promotion of literature, and especially for the furtherance of a design to settle the text of Plautus, an author whose metres scarcely one mind in a century has sufficient learning, power, or will, to restore.

" So much for Hermann. For myself, be assured that I have availed myself, with so much the more eagerness, of this opportunity of addressing you by letter, as my sincere regard for you, and my high admiration of your recondite learning and exquisite judgment, are perpetually growing stronger; and to express these feelings to you, though but by a word or two, seemed to be to lighten myself of a great burden. Such indeed is human nature, that we delight to open our thoughts to any one to whom we are drawn by strong affection. It shall be my constant object to prove myself not unworthy of your kindness.

"Gottingen, Dec. 21st, 1796."

Whether Porson returned any answer to these letters is not known. It is not likely that he answered Hermann; but, with all his dislike to letter-writing, he may have favoured Heyne with a reply.

CHAP. XV.

PUBLICATION OF THE ORESTES.—ALLUSIONS TO WAKEFIELD IN THE NOTES;
TO INVERNIZIUS, AMMON, AND REISKE. — SOME REMARKS ON A PAS-
SAGE IN HOMER.

In the following year, 1798, appeared the Orestes.
Wakefield, at the end of his *Diatribe*, had recommended
Porson, if he continued to edit Euripides, not to make
his notes so dry and formal, but to render them more
entertaining by the interspersion of *amœnitates* and
lepores, and disquisitions on any matters that might
occur to him in the course of his reading ; to produce,
in fact, such annotations as Wakefield himself attached
to his Lucretius, where everything suitable or unsuitable
is seized upon for discussion, and the tail of a comment
has no more relation to the head of it than the tail of a
fish to the head of a woman. Porson gave a hint or
two, in his notes on the Orestes, that he remembered
this advice, but was little induced to follow it. Having
occasion, in his remarks on the fifth verse, to speak of
the discrepancies of the poets as to the punishment of
Tantalus, he concludes with saying, " I know not, gentle
reader, whether you have found your patience exhausted
in reading this note ; I have entirely exhausted mine
in writing it. But if you are not yet satisfied with
these *criticæ deliciæ*, these delicacies of criticism, read

what Guellius and Cerdanus have collected," &c.   In remarking, ver. 631, on σιγὴ λόγου κρείσσων, that one manuscript has κρείσσον, which perhaps some commentator, *paulo calidior*, may add to his store of such expressions, defending its elegance by the recondite *Dulce satis humor*, he makes an evident allusion to Wakefield, who was *calidus* enough, and who was fond of loading his pages with such illustrations.   And when he published the Medea, he observed that he " had intimated, in his note on the fifth verse of the Orestes, that he could have written long, nay very long, notes, having no connexion with his subjects ; but that he had hitherto so endeavoured to use his power as not to abuse it."

There are other allusions to Wakefield in the notes on the Orestes. Speaking of neuter verbs which assume an active signification, he mentions ἐκπτήσσειν and ῥεῖν, in Hec. 181, 532, as examples of this assumption, and says that it would be the act of a madman to disturb the reading in those passages ; but Wakefield had sought to disturb it in both passages. Another allusion to him is made, in reference to the same subject, on verse 1428, where it is said that περᾷ πόδα, in Hec. 53, is a much better reading than περᾷ ποδί, which Wakefield had wished to introduce. In ver. 435 of the Hecuba, Wakefield had taken under his patronage, in his *Diatribe*, a conjecture of Jacobs, ὄμμα for ὄνομα, on which Porson, at ver. 1081 of the Orestes, comments thus:

" As either of these two words is easily changed for the other by transcribers, it is sometimes difficult to determine, when manuscripts differ, which is the proper word; but, when manuscripts agree, I would make no alteration. I, therefore, in my note on Hec. 435, προσειπεῖν γὰρ σὸν ὄνομ' ἐξεστί μοι, omitted to notice the conjecture of Frederic Jacobs, ὄμμα for ὄνομα, as a useless alteration; but, as another opportunity of adverting to it now offers, I will give it a brief consideration. First, I would ask, what is wrong in the common reading? Is it wrong to say προσειπεῖν ὄνομα? If so, why? 'Because,' it may be answered, 'it occurs nowhere else.' Whether it occurs anywhere else or not, I do not know; but why do you not produce passages where your προσειπεῖν ὄμμα occurs? If you answer that this expression is nowhere to be found, I ask you again how it is reasonable to eject an expression of which there is one example in order to substitute another of which there is no example? However, to say the truth, προσαυδᾶν ὄμμα seems to present itself in Æschylus, Choeph. ver. 236; though there indeed Valckenaer reads ὄνομα: while concerning ὄμματος, in the 415th verse of the Phœnissæ, which is his own conjecture, he does not speak decidedly. To me it appears that in all these passages the received reading should be retained. Jacobs is a man not deficient either in ability or learning, but he often abuses both these qualifications to disturb sound readings. . . . Why, when the ignorance and audacity of transcribers have introduced so many solecisms and barbarisms, which nobody need hesitate to attack,

' Bella geri placuit nullos habitura triumphos?'

why should he engage in enterprises that can bring him no honour?"

Jacobs and Wakefield are not the only commentators that are attacked in the notes on the Orestes. Out of the various readings in verse 245, " may be constructed," says Porson, " this line:

Καὶ μὴ μόνον φρόνει, ἀλλὰ καὶ πρᾶσσε τάδε,

a most elegant line, which Le Clerc, Reiske, and Triller would adopt, I am sure, if they were alive; and which

I have no doubt will be adopted by Invernizius and
Ammonius, *Graiæ gentis decora*, those living ornaments
of Greek learning." Ammonius or Ammon had published
an edition of the Hecuba in 1789.   On ver. 1235, he
again takes occasion, in noticing a verse of Aristophanes,
to censure Invernizius, who, he says, has there introduced a bad reading from the excellent Ravenna manuscript, from which a man of but moderate sense and
learning could not have failed to extract the right reading. "For the information of tiros," he adds, "I will show
how the present corruption was caused. A transcriber,
after writing the line, found that he had accidentally
omitted two letters, which letters he put in the margin,
with a mark that they were to be inserted. A succeeding
transcriber, observing the letters and the mark, was
desirous to obey the admonition of his predecessor, but,
being made of the same clay as Invernizius, could not
see the right place for them, and put them in one which
they ought not to have occupied."   On ver. 273, he
makes another hit at Reiske, who, attempting to amend
the verse, (the end of which, by some failure in the
utterance of the actor, had been pronounced γαλῆν ὁρῶ
instead of γαλήν' ὁρῶ, *I see a weasel* instead of *I see a
calm*, and had consequently afforded a fertile subject
for jest to the comic writers,) observes that Euripides
might have escaped ridicule by writing ἐκ κυμάτων γὰρ
ὁρῶ γαλήνην αὖθις αὖ. "Yes," says Porson, alluding to
the words of Juvenal about Cicero, "he certainly might
have despised all the stings of Aristophanes, Sannyrio,
and Strattis, if he had constructed all his lines on such
a model."

Wakefield, on reviewing this play in the "British

Critic," * was at first completely deceived by Porson's irony, and took it for sober remark :

" 'Εκ κυμάτων γὰρ ὁρῶ γαλήνην αὖθις αὖ ·

Behold," says he, " in opposition to his own statutes, an anapæst, sanctioned by our metrical lawgiver, in the third foot :

> ' Quæ nemora, aut qui vos saltus habuere, puellæ
> Pierides,'

that ye should abandon the Professor to this dereliction of his own rules, and such failure of recollection? Besides, the inadvertency of the tragedian should be called, in strictness of speech, an ambiguity, and is denominated a solecism, we apprehend, with inaccuracy not pardonable in an instructor of such eminence." But after he had written this he began to feel misgivings that Porson might be playing the deceiver, and, to save himself from utter vilification, added, " After all, however, this may be no more than a piece of affected jocularity in the Professor to entrap the uninitiated in the mysteries of his witticisms."

On ver. 412 Porson remarks that Reiske, *quod cum risu mirere*, was the first that gave it metrical harmony ; an effect which the reader is to understand that Reiske produced by chance.

In his note on the ellipsis in the 664th verse, Ταύτης ἱκνοῦμαί σε, he turns aside to make a comment on the 283rd verse of the first book of the Iliad, λίσσομ' Ἀχιλῆϊ μεθέμεν χόλον: a comment which we will translate.

* Nov. 1800.

"Rollin* remarked (being perhaps instructed by Jean Boivin†) that λίσσομαι never governs a dative, and that consequently this passage of the Iliad ought to be rendered, *I entreat you to lay aside your anger towards Achilles.* Not that Rollin was the first to make this remark, for Henry Stephens had given nearly the true sense in his Thesaurus; but, when Rollin had made it, Bellenger started up to contradict it; and, in the supplement to the 'Essais de Critique de M. Vander Meulen' (the name under which Bellenger himself wrote), Amst. 1741, pp. 92—101, says that all interpreters had given the passage a different signification. He seems to have thought that if all interpreters go wrong, it is our business to perpetuate their errors, and transmit them to posterity! But he next accuses Rollin of plagiarism from Stephens. If he thought this accusation just, he ought at the same time to have acquitted Rollin of having introduced a new interpretation. But afterwards, in order to prove that λίσσομαι may govern a dative, he cites a verse from Phavorinus, where that verb is followed by a genitive, ἐπὶ or πρὸς being understood: λίσσομαι Ζηνὸς Ὀλυμπίου ἠδὲ Θέμιστος, a defective line of Homer, from which Bellenger argues thus: If λίσσομαι governs a genitive, with ἐπὶ or πρὸς understood, it may also govern a dative, since ἐπὶ or πρὸς governs also a dative. An egregious specimen of argumentation! And how astonishing that he should have adduced so lame a verse without remark; that one pretending to be a critic should not have remembered even the well-known words of Homer! In this note I acknowledge that I have deviated from my proper course; but I have done so for two reasons; the first is, because the true sense of this passage of Homer is not generally known, and a new one, but false, has recently been devised by certain Scotchmen; the second, that I might show, by a striking example, into what monstrous blunders learned men may fall, and what absurdities they may blurt forth, if they

---

* Manière d'Enseigner, tom. i. p. 191, éd. Amst. 1745.

† See Academiæ Inscriptionum Monument. tom. ii. p. 23; or Brunck ad Aristoph. Ran. 851.

once venture, under the influence of anger, hatred, envy, or any ill-feeling, to pass censure upon subjects which they cannot or will not understand."

The hint about writing under the influence of ill-feeling was probably directed as much against the living Wakefield as against the deceased Bellenger. Who the " certain Scotchmen " are, that had interpreted this passage of Homer falsely, we do not know ; for Dunbar, in his *Analecta Minora*, Professor Young, and Monboddo in his " Origin and Progress of Language,"* seem all to have understood it rightly.

For his note on 1121,

$$\text{"}Ωστ' ἐκδακρῦσαι γ' ἔνδοθεν κεχαρμένην,$$

" Κεχαρμένη Ald. κεχαρμένην plures MSS.   Utrumque probum,"

the German editors, Matthæi and Schæfer, have pronounced him guilty of a solecism, in sanctioning the nominative, in such a phrase, before the infinitive. " We will utter lamentations to Helen," says Pylades, in the preceding lines. " So that she may make a show of shedding tears," rejoins Orestes, " while she rejoices in her heart." Scholefield endeavours to defend Porson, by understanding καὶ αὐτὴ αἰσθήσεται, ὥστε αὐτὴ ἐκδακρῦσαι, " and she will see us lamenting, so that she may shed tears," &c. But this attempt at extrication, it is to be feared, will satisfy but few. How Porson himself would have vindicated the nominative must be left to conjecture.

* Vol. ii. p. 158.

CHAP. XVI.

PORSON'S CONTRIBUTIONS TO THE " MORNING CHRONICLE." — REMARKS
IN THE " PURSUITS OF LITERATURE." — HUMOROUS TRANSLATIONS OF
THREE ODES OF HORACE, IN REFERENCE TO THE POLITICS OF THE
DAY. — SOME ADDITIONAL OBSERVATIONS.

WE have noticed these two plays, the Hecuba and
Orestes, together ; but previously to the publication of
the Orestes, we must observe, there had appeared, in
the "Morning Chronicle," several squibs from Porson's
pen, the chief of which were burlesque "Imitations of
Horace," and some humorous papers on "The Orgies
of Bacchus." After his marriage he had become still
more intimate with Perry than he had previously been ;
Perry, valuing his intellectual powers, contributed in
various ways to his comfort ; and Porson, in requital,
furnished him with numerous paragraphs, chiefly of a
jocose and satirical kind, for his paper. Some have
considered that he gave up large portions of his time to
Perry, and that the columns of the "Morning Chronicle"
received numbers of contributions or corrections from
him ; but more has perhaps been supposed, in regard
to this point, than was really the case. The strongest
foundation for this supposition is found in the
"Pursuits of Literature,"* where Porson is charged

* Dialogue iv. p. 387.

with *giving up to Perry what he owed to the world*, and is exhorted to "write no more in Mr. Perry's little democratic closet fitted up for the wits at the 'Morning Chronicle' Office. It is beneath you," adds the author; "I speak seriously. I know your abilities. It may do well enough for Joseph Richardson, Esq., author of the comedy of *The Fugitive*, if a certain political dramatist's (Sheridan's) compotations will leave him any abilities at all, which I begin to doubt."

The "Imitations of Horace," consisting of whimsical translations of three entire odes, and some fragments, with remarks in prose, have been reprinted in the "Spirit of the Public Journals" for 1797, and in the fourth volume of the "Classical Journal." But they are so little known to the public in general, that we consider no apology necessary for introducing two of the odes, and some of the prose, here. They are excellent specimens of the dry sarcastic humour which Porson could so happily display. It is hardly necessary to observe that Pitt, the war with France, and the supposed danger of the country from the spread of French revolutionary principles, were the constant subjects of attack with Perry and his writers. We have altered two coarse expressions, in the passages italicised, a liberty for which we think that Porson would not have blamed us.

HORACE, *Carm.* lib. i. od. 14, translated.

The poet makes a voyage to Britain in pursuance of his promise, lib. iii. od. 4, ver. 33, *Visam Britannos hospitibus feros,* "I will visit the Britons inhospitable to strangers." The vessel in which he sailed was called the "Britannia,"

whether from the place of its destination, or from the circumstance of being built of British wood, I cannot determine;
but, I believe, for both reasons. After a tedious voyage, at
last he arrived safe at Portsmouth. The ship was grievously
shattered; but the captain determined to go out again immediately, before she was well refitted, and while the weather
was very unpromising. Several of the crew were heard to
mutter, in consequence of this proceeding; upon which the
captain, by advice of the pilot, put them in irons. But the
most curious incident was (if we may believe Quintilian) that
Horace was indicted for a libel, as if, under the allegory of
a ship, he had intended to paint the dangers and distresses
of the commonwealth. Whoever peruses my version will see
how groundless and absurd this accusation was. The reader
need only keep in mind that the poet, more safe at shore,
makes this pathetic address to the vessel in which his life
and fortunes were so lately risked.

To the good Ship Britannia.

Britannia, while fresh storms are brewing,
I wonder what the deuce you're doing!
Put back to harbour, might and main,
Nor venture out to sea again :
Your hull's toe tender long to last ;
You're fain to try a jury-mast ;
Your tackle's old, your timber's crazy,
The winds are high, the weather's hazy ;
Your anchor's lost ; you've sprung a leak ;
Hark, how the ropes and cordage creak !
A rag of canvas scarce remains ;
Your pilot idly beats his brains,
A cub that knows not stem from stern,
Too high t' obey, too proud to learn.
In vain you worry Heav'n with prayers ;
Think you that Heav'n one farthing cares
Whether a sailor prays or swears?
In vain you sport your threadbare joke,
And call yourself " Old Heart of Oak ; "
No seaman that can box his compass
Trusts to your daubs, or titles pompous.

O

Take heed lest Boreas play the mocker,
And cry, " This snug in Davy's locker."
Though while on board *so sick I fell*,
At shore, old girl, I wish you well.
Beware of shoals, of wind and weather,
And try to keep your planks together,
Or else the rav'nous sea will gorge,
And lodge you next the Royal George.

To this soon after succeeded the following :

Mr. Editor,

Understanding that my last translation of an " Ode of Horace " did not displease the best judges, I have taken the liberty to send you a second attempt, which I submit to your candour. It may seem matter of wonder to you, as it does to me, that neither Quintilian, nor Will Baxter, nor any other hunter of allegories, should find out the real drift of this Ode, which is so very easy to be discovered. The case, in short, is as follows : — Augustus, in the midst of peace and tranquillity, felt, or feigned, an alarm, on account of some books written by persons suspected of an attachment to the party of Cato and Brutus, and recommending republican principles. Now, Horace having been a colonel in Brutus's army, and being rather too free in expressing his religious sentiments, naturally passed for an atheist and a republican. Augustus published an edict to tell his subjects how happy they all were, in spite of the suggestions of malcontents ; commanding them to stick close to their old religions ; and threatening that whoever was not active in assisting the government should be treated as an enemy to church and state. Upon this occasion Horace read, or affected to read, for I will not take my oath to his sincerity, a recantation. In one part of the Ode he says, " Jupiter, who generally thunders and lightens in cloudy weather, now has driven his chariot through the serene air." This is so plain an emblem of Augustus fulminating his censures in a time of profound tranquillity, that it needs no further comment. Our author refers to this circumstance again, in the fifth Ode of the third Book, *Cœlo tonantem credidimus Jovem regnare.*

præsens divus habebitur Augustus: " We have believed that
Jupiter reigns thundering from heaven; Augustus shall be
esteemed a present god."   In another place he expressly
calls Augustus Jupiter, Epist. i. 19, 43: *Rides, ait, et Jovis
auribus ista servas:* " You joke," says he, " and reserve your
verses for the ear of Jove."   For all sovereigns, while they
are in power, are compared to the sovereign of the gods,
however weak, wicked, or worthless they may be:

> " Nihil est quod credere de se
> Non possit, cum laudatur Dîs æqua potestas."

I must not forget to add that this edict of the emperor was
followed by numerous addresses from large bodies of the men
who were once called Romans, allowing the reality of the
plots, lamenting the decay of piety, and promising to resist
all innovation, and to defend his sacred Cæsarean majesty
with their lives and fortunes.

Horace, book i. ode 34.

Till now I held free-thinking notions,
Gave little heed to my devotions,
Scarce went to church four times a year,
And then slept more than pray'd, I fear :
But now I'm quite an alter'd man ;
I quit the course I lately ran,
And, giving heterodoxy o'er,
Unlearn my irreligious lore.
Yet, lest you entertain a doubt,
I'll tell you how it came about.
Jove seldom lets his lightnings fly,
Except when clouds obscure the sky,
As well you know ; but, t'other morning,
He thunder'd without previous warning,
And flash'd in such a perfect calm,
It gave me a religious qualm.
Nor me alone ; the frightful sound
Reach'd to the country's utmost bound,
And every river in the nation
From concave shores made replication.*

---

* Shakspeare, *J. Cæs.* act i. sc. 1.

The brutish clods, in shape of cits,
Were almost frighten'd into fits.
Henceforth I bow to every altar,
And wish all infidels a halter.
I see what pow'r you gods can show,
Change low with high, and high with low;
Pull down the lofty from his place,
And in his stead exalt the base :
Thus Fortune's gifts some lose, some gain,
While mortals gaze and guess in vain.

The next specimen was offered as that of an intended translation of Horace, prefaced by some remarks.

Mr. Editor,

We have several translations of Horace; but none that I have seen appeared to do the author justice. There is in Horace a grace, a delicacy, a liveliness, a fulness of expression, and a harmony of versification, that at once captivate the ear and the heart. I need not explain to you how far short of these excellences our translators in general have fallen. Having myself studied this poet with uncommon attention, I have, with all my might, endeavoured to preserve these qualities in my version, of which I send you the enclosed Ode as a specimen. If you judge it to have less merit than the partial parent believes, you will still allow it, I hope, to soar above the common flights of modern poetry It is not heavy as lead, like Mr. ——; nor dull as ditchwater like Anna Matilda; nor mad as a March hare, like our present excellent laureate; nor stupid, — but I should never make an end if I went on with my comparisons. If this sample takes, I mean to publish a translation of the whole by subscription; it will be printed on wire-wove paper, and hot-pressed, not to exceed two volumes quarto. A great number of engravings will be added by the most eminent artists. The obscenities will be left out of the common copies, but printed separately for the use of the curious and critical readers. The passages that have an improper political tendency will be carefully omitted; such as,—

" Sed magis
Pugnas et exactos tyrannos
Densum humeris bibit aure vulgus."

" The clustering mob is more delighted to hear of battles and the expulsion of tyrants."

Or that address to Fortune:

" Purpurei metuunt tyranni,
Injurioso ne pede proruas
Stantem columnam ; neu populus frequens
Ad arma cessantes, ad arma,
Concitet, imperiumque frangat."

" Purple tyrants dread thee, O Fortune, lest thou shouldst kick down the standing pillar [of existing circumstances]; lest *the thronging populace should summon the loiterers to arms, to arms,* and demolish the empire."

But these passages, thank God, are very few, and shall be studiously suppressed. Luckily, Horace is full of loyal effusions, which I shall endeavour to render with spirit as well as fidelity. What, for instance, can be more applicable than the following passage to the present holy war?

" Diu
Latèque victrices catervæ,
Consiliis juvenis repressæ,
Sensere quid mens rite, quid indoles,
Nutrita faustis sub penetralibus,
Posset, quid Augusti *paternus*
In pueros *animus* Nerones."

" The armies, so long and so far victorious, were checked by the conduct of a young prince, and became sensible what could be done by a mind and a disposition duly nurtured under an auspicious roof; what could be achieved by the *paternal affection* of Augustus for the young Neros."

The specimen Ode, being of a somewhat gross character, we shall not republish.

CHAP. XVII.

OCCASION OF THE PUBLICATION OF THE " ORGIES OF BACCHUS." —
FREND'S PAMPHLET PUBLISHED AT CAMBRIDGE. — FREND ACCUSED OI
ATTACKING THE CHURCH. — IS TRIED IN THE VICE-CHANCELLOR'S
COURT, DR. KIPLING BEING PROSECUTOR. — FREND'S DISINGENUOUSNESS
— CHARACTER OF DR. KIPLING AS A SCHOLAR. — HIS PUBLICATION OI
THE " CODEX BEZÆ." — VERSES ON •HIS BAD LATIN. — EVENT OF
FREND'S TRIAL. — EXTRACTS FROM THE " ORGIES OF BACCHUS." —
OTHER CONTRIBUTIONS OF PORSON TO THE " MORNING CHRONICLE."—
" HYMN BY A NEW-MADE PEER."— " MISERIES OF KINGSHIP."— " ON
THE DUTIES OF GENTLEMEN-SOLDIERS." — A HUNDRED EPIGRAMS
WRITTEN BY PORSON IN ONE NIGHT.

THE circumstances that occasioned the publication of
the " Orgies of Bacchus " in the " Morning Chronicle "
deserve some notice.

In the year 1793, when the French Revolution was
spreading its influence, Mr. William Frend, a fellow
and tutor of Jesus College, Cambridge, published a
pamphlet entitled " Peace and Union recommended to
the Associated Bodies of Republicans and Anti-Re-
publicans." Shortly after its appearance, a deputation
of twenty-seven members of the University, afterwards
nicknamed "The Cube," two of whom were Dr. Kipling and Dr. Jowett, waited upon the Vice-Chancellor,
Isaac Milner, and represented that the pamphlet was
written to injure the Church, as it spoke disrespectfully
of ecclesiastical ranks and dignities, declared that the
Liturgy was far from purity, and pronounced the wor-

ship of the great body of the Christians to be idolatrous.   The Vice-Chancellor, after some deliberation,
consented .to proceed against Frend, and cited him
before his court, consisting of himself and ten assessors,
among whom were Farmer, the writer on Shakspeare,
and Postlethwaite, Porson's old enemy.   Kipling was
promoter or prosecutor, and Frend was accused under
the statute *De Concionibus,* made for the protection of
the established religion.   One of the strongest passages
of the pamphlet brought against him was a paragraph
in which he recommended the Dissenters to wait for a
change of religion for relief from persecution, adding,
" The most improbable tales were in early times invented of the Christians ; their meetings were burnt
down, and their persons were assaulted.   Is it to be
wondered at that the same practices should, by the
enlightened infidel, the interested churchman, and the
ignorant populace, be in our days both repeated and
applauded ?   The same passions will everywhere produce on certain minds the same effect ; and the priest,
in every age, whether he celebrates the orgies of Bacchus or solemnises the Eucharist, will, should either
his victims or his allowance fail, oppose in either case
every truth which threatens to undermine his altars or
weaken his sacerdotal authority."   Another was a passage in which he expressed objections to all ecclesiastical courts, dignities, and vestments, as contrary to the
spirit of Christianity, observing that the laity sat tamely,
"like brute beasts," under clerical usurpation ; that a
man could not pledge his faith to a woman without
the interference of the priest ; that his offspring must
be sprinkled by priestly hands ; and that he could not

be carried to his long home without " a spiritual incantation ;" practices which were highly advantageous to the clerical community, but of no benefit to the morals of the public.

The trial lasted eight days, much time being lost in proving the pamphlet to be Frend's ; a point which, as his name was in the title-page, it would have been but ingenuous in him to have admitted. But, observing that there was a volume of sermons in circulation which had Dr. White's name, of Oxford, on the title-page, but which were " in reality the production of a dissenting minister, and a member of Cambridge University," he threw on his adversaries the burden of proving the pamphlet to be his, and took advantage of the delay and discussion to annoy them, especially Kipling, with unpleasant remarks.

Kipling, unhappily for his peace, was extremely vulnerable. He had printed, some years before, a selection from Smith's Optics, with a preface, in which was this ridiculous passage : " The following treatise contains many inaccuracies, and even some errors, of which the editor was fully sensible before he sent it to the press, but was restrained from correcting them by the dread of reprehension." Surely he would not have been blamed for correcting errors, whether Smith's or his own, where accuracy was so necessary. He had also published, just before Frend's trial, a fac-simile of the Cambridge manuscript of the New Testament called Beza's, *Codex* (as he called it) *Theodori Bezæ Cantabrigiensis ;* an undertaking which Porson thought utterly useless, as the manuscript was in no respect valuable, and a chapter or two of it would have amply satisfied the curious as a specimen; and, while the work was in progress, he had made, in a letter to the " Gentleman's Magazine,"* the following uncomplimentary remarks on the editor : " I must own that if I could once perceive the use of such a work, I should readily grant that the University has pitched upon the fittest person in the world to be the editor.   Dr. Kipling (*quem honoris causâ nomino*) is, without any question, furnished with every accomplishment to get honour for the University, and money for himself. He has, from his earliest youth, applied himself diligently to all sorts of critical learning, but most diligently to sacred criticism, and, from a long acquaintance with manuscripts, aided by natural sagacity, has become such an adept in Greek palæography as few know, and few would believe.   It does not come within the plan of my present letter to say anything of his professorial and oratorical talents ; but I may venture to affirm without flattery (for I abhor it), that I never yet heard Dr. Kipling in the schools or the senate-house, that I had not the most lively remembrance of his principal, Dr. Watson."   Kipling had frequently acted as deputy of Dr. Watson when Regius Professor.

The ambiguity in the title of the Codex was a favourite object of attack with all who were adverse to Kipling; an ambiguity which did not escape Porson when he reviewed it in the " British Critic."   " I do not pretend," said Frend in his defence before the Vice-Chancellor, " to a deep knowledge of the Latin language, but I have been told by better critics than

* Oct. 1788, p. 876.

myself that it should be interpreted *The book of Theo
dore Beza, a Cambridge man;* but if any twenty-seven
members of the University should take a dislike to any
passage in the book, and cite Beza before the court as
a Cambridge man, the return would be 'non est in-
ventus.'" There was also in the preface some bad
Latinity, and Frend in consequence charged Kipling
with "inability to speak or write a single sentence of
pure Latin." One blunder was *paginibus*, on which
somebody, perhaps Porson, made this epigram, in the
style of the *Epistolæ obscurorum Virorum* :

> *Paginibus* nostris dicitis mihi menda quod insunt ;
>   At non in recto vos puto esse, viri.
> Nam, primum, jurat (cetera ut testimonia *omitto*)
>   Milnerus, quod sum doctus ego et sapiens.
> Classicus haud es, aiunt.   Quid si non sum ? in sacrosanctâ
>   Non *ullo* tergum verto theologiâ.

The last two words in italics exemplify some of the
Doctor's other inaccuracies. Kipling had " the paginibus sheet," as it was called, reprinted in the copies
that had not been issued, but in a large number the
blunder necessarily remained. The publication cost
the University nearly two thousand pounds, and Kipling is supposed to have cleared at least six hundred
guineas.

As to the observations regarding the clergy in Frend's
pamphlet, Frend sought to justify them by saying that
he designed them to bear chiefly, not on the Church of
England, but on the papists; and declared that all he
had said would have been thought innocent, but that
one of the twenty-seven, "a gentleman famous for his
eloquence," happened to light upon the words " Orgie

of Bacchus," when, like the man in Gil Blas, who was
written down a Jew on all kinds of frivolous pretences,
the author was marked as guilty of impiety.

The event of the trial was, that, as Frend refused to
admit that he had offended against the statute, and to
retract, he was sentenced to be expelled from the University.   He appealed ; and a court of five delegates,
of whom two were Dr. Barlow Seale and Dr. John Hey,
were appointed to reconsider the proceedings ; but the
result was that the Vice-Chancellor's sentence was confirmed.*

It was while the public press was making observations on these proceedings that Porson published his
" Orgies of Bacchus " in the " Morning Chronicle," in
three letters addressed to the editor, and signed " Mythologus."   The object of these jesting effusions is to
remark how many points of resemblance may be found,
if any one is disposed to find them, between the actions
of Bacchus, as related by poets and mythologists, and
those of the Messiah.   Porson draws a picture, and
leaves the reader to consider whether he has not seen
another picture containing objects similarly disposed ;
and the reader, struck with the comparison, will, according to his feeling or judgment, either tolerate or
condemn.   Mr. Maltby, whose opinion however we need
not adopt, pronounced that the letters could do nobody
any harm.   We shall offer a few specimens of them,
leaving those who wish to see the whole to consult
" The Spirit of the Public Journals " for 1797.

* Trial of Frend, by J. Beverley, Camb. 1793; Account of the
Proceedings against the Author of a Pamphlet, &c., Camb. 1793;
Sequel, Lond. 1795; Spirit of the Public Journals for 1797, p. 274.

The papers commence thus :

To the Editor of the " Morning Chronicle."

ORGIES OF BACCHUS.

Part I.

SIR,

  I learn from your paper that an expression in Mr. Frend's pamphlet, " The Orgies of Bacchus," has been much bandied about. As I apprehend that many of your readers may be in as great doubt as I was concerning these same Orgies of Bacchus, I have had recourse to my two excellent friends, the Rev. Thomas Kipling, would-be Professor of Divinity to his Majesty, and Thomas Taylor, self-created Polytheist of Great Britain.   These two amazing men, *quos longè sequor et vestigia semper adoro,* have kindly condescended to chalk out the plan of the following dissertation, and to furnish me with several valuable hints for its conduct.   Let me here indulge myself in giving a short character of these two worthies. The one, by the mere force of genius, without the slightest tincture of learning, has *sounded all the depths and shoals* of Christian theology ; the other, without staying even to learn the inflexions of Greek words, has plunged to the very bottom of pagan philosophy, *taught by the heavenly muse to venture down the dark descent, and up to reascend, though hard and rare.*   But to business.

A friend of ours has converted a portion of what follows into Latin.   We give a specimen of his translation :

Rumores hic illic sparsi sunt, Bacchum ab Ægypto oriundum fuisse ; quibus nihil auctoritatis tribuo.   Originem autem habuere ex eo quod Apollodorus narrat, Bacchum nempe in Ægypto aliquamdiù commoratum esse.   Vulgò creditur filius fuisse Jovis, deorum hominumque regis, et Semeles, mulieris Thebanæ.   Hoc, quanquam à discipulis ejus et comitibus affirmatum, negatum est à profanis aut derisum ; inter quos erant quidam ex ipsius cognatis, qui dictitabant Bacchum non magis à Jove genitum fuisse quàm semetipsos; Semelen autem, à mortali viro gravidam factam, Jovem infantis patrem dedecori suo prætexuisse. Hanc injuriam Bacchus ipse quàm gravissimè queritur, et minatur se in peccantes acerrimè vindicaturum; "cujus rei causâ," inquit, "mortalem speciem indutus sum, et formam propriam in hominis naturam mutavi," sive, ut aliàs loquitur, "Meipsum ex deo in formam verti humanam."

E numero illorum, qui hæc credere omnino nolebant, erant Alcathoë ejusque sorores, quæ Bacchum filium fuisse Jovis negabant, quasque minimè pudebat operari cùm sacerdos omnes festum celebrare jussisset. Ovidius, qui non ut historicus loquitur, sed in narrationibus poeticè luxuriatur, refert, more suo, ἀλληγορικῶς, has miseras sorores in vespertiliones mutatas esse; alii aiunt in noctuas et vespertiliones (vide Antonium Liberalem, fab. x.); sed utramlibet harum sententiarum accipiamus, res æquè manifesta est; hæ enim puellæ, quòd quæ sentiebant eloqui ausæ essent, ab ebriis comessatoribus, qui se Bacchantes vocabant, adeò crudeliter tractatæ sunt, ut ab ore hominum secedere, et in antris aliisque latebris lucem vitare, cogerentur.

Sed ne hæc quidem linguas scurrarum obstrinxerunt. Pentheus novum hunc deum, utpote falsum, ridebat; et consobrinum suum divinitus ortum esse negabat. Exitum hominis tam increduli facilè conjicias; secta enim Bacchantum, dum infirma erat, ab aliis vexata est; sed, cùm valuisset, alios vexabat; quod maximè secundum naturam est. Etenim Tiresias, augur iste, (qui, liceat obiter dicere, cæcus erat ut talpa,) hoc ipsum juveni prædixerat:

> Quem nisi templorum fueris dignatus honore,
> Mille lacer spargêre locis; et sanguine silvas
> Fœdabis, matremque tuam, matrisque sorores.

Cadmus etiam avus nepoti prudentissima consilia suaserat; sed ille, obstinato animo, deterrendus non erat. Argumenta autem senis sagacissimi, quibus homines religioni interdum morigerari jubebat, audire quàm maximè juvabit: " Si hic

non est deus, uti vobis non videtur esse, deus tamen à vobis
vocetur, et splendidè mendaces sitis; partim in Semeles
honorem, ut dicatur deum peperisse ; partim in nostrum, ut
ille decori omnibus sit nostratibus." Sed hæc omnia nihil
Pentheum movebant. Quandocunque ἐνθουσιασμὸς animum
humanum occupat, is omnem misericordiam, omnesque inter
cognatos caritates, exstinguit. Pentheus ergo membratim
dilaceratus est (uti Tiresias prædixerat, cujus verba forsan
eventûs causam dedêre) à turbâ mulierum Bacchantum ; et
mater Penthei ipsius, sororesque matris, dilacerationi adfu-
erunt.

The first letter concludes thus :

Here, Sir, I finish my scrap of mythology. In these
ticklish times, when to look or think awry is a most unpar-
donable crime, which can be expiated only by fine, banish-
ment, or durance, we are not yet, I trust, prohibited from
the discussion of philological questions. Talk of religion, it
is odds but you have infidel, blasphemer, atheist, or schis-
matic, thundered in your ears ; touch upon politics, you will
be in luck if you are only charged with a *tendency to treason.*
To wish that things may be better, is to assert, by *innuendo,*
that they are bad ; and whoever dares to disapprove of the
present war is *a deviser of sedition, and ought to have his
right hand struck off, pursuant to an Act of Parliament
made in the reign of Edward I., a statute not yet repealed.**
Nor is the innocence of your intention any safeguard. It is
not the publication that shows the character of the author,
but *the character of the author that shows the tendency of the
publication.* I have therefore endeavoured to steer clear of
all these rocks. I have sent you a simple recital of an
ancient fable, and, if it be received with approbation, shall
perhaps from time to time transmit similar communications.
If my paper is dull, it is at the same time perfectly harmless ;
if it is not recommended by the elegances of composition, it
is at least free from the contagion of pernicious opinions ; and

* An infamous paragraph to this purpose lately appeared in one
of the public papers.

though it may fail of conveying amusement or instruction, it cannot possibly give offence or scandal.

MYTHOLOGUS.

The second letter commences thus:

Part II.

SIR,

Perhaps you may remember, or perhaps you may have forgotten, that some time ago I sent you a short account of the *Orgies of Bacchus.* I chose this subject for two reasons; first, because it had of late been frequently mentioned; secondly, because I thought it totally unconnected with any public question, religious or political. But I begin now to perceive that I reckoned without my host. The principle *noscitur à socio* has been applied to my innocent lucubration with a vengeance. Though I knew that the "Morning Chronicle" was by many reputed a seditious jacobinical paper, I never dreamed that this character pervaded the whole of the work, but that it affected such parts only as might seem to animadvert on the supposed defects or abuses of the constitution; *supposed,* I repeat, for I believe that there are no *real* defects or abuses. I and Mr. Dymock defy to equal combat all malcontents who find flaws in the British Government and the British king's title. *Yet all this availeth me nothing, so long as* I have sent an article to that factious journal the "Morning Chronicle." *Who can touch pitch, and not be defiled?* Accordingly the defenders of liberty and property (of their own, I mean) took the alarm. Mr. Chairman Reeves found out that the dissertation aforesaid did, by dangerous insinuations, hint doubts concerning the Prince of Wales's hereditary right to the crown, and even glanced here and there at *Cæsar* himself. Is not this a brave fellow to see through a mill-stone? If these charges could be made good by evidence, I dare say this champion of the best possible system of government would shower down his tender mercies plentifully upon the offender's head. But my lord chief justice of Newfoundland's reasoning is so humorous and diverting, that I shall give you a taste of it for your entertainment. I had observed from the legend that "Bacchus was the son of Jupiter, king of gods and men." " Here," says this able expounder, " Jupiter plainly signifies his most gracious Majesty George the Third (whom God long preserve!); for mark the next words, 'king of gods and men.' Can any good subject doubt that by 'king of gods and men,' this rascal means *the supreme in church and state*, the legal title of the kings of England? But, as if this were not enough, the libeller proceeds, and adds 'by a mortal female.' Here he drops the mask, and discloses jacobinical sentiments in all their virulence. Here that horrid and diabolical position stares you full in the face, with all its native ugliness, *That a queen*, heaven bless us! *is no more than a woman, — a mortal female.* Here is no need of innuendos, implications, parallels, constructions, double meanings, &c., engines which we lawyers are sometimes obliged, in default of evidence, to employ for the public good. Here is treason in terms. Oho! Mr. Mythologus, you must not think of insulting with impunity whatever is great and venerable."

After some further remarks on Bacchus, he concludes as follows :

I have now, I trust, completely vindicated myself from the charge of disloyalty to the heir apparent ; and I beg leave to add a few words on the subject of innuendos. If we go on as we have begun, it will be impossible for a man to write or speak without incurring the danger of a prosecution either for a private or public libel. I was amusing myself lately with writing a set of fables, partly translated and partly original. While the rough copy of some of these fables lay on my table, who should come into my garret, before I had time to lock up my papers, but a member of the Crown and Anchor Association? You know the custom of that gang; they immediately lay hands on all the letters and papers they see, in order to get some information for the bloodhounds of the law. My friend, therefore, without ceremony, began reading, first to himself, and then aloud, " The dying lion then said, ' The insults of the noble beasts I could bear; but it embitters my last moments to think that I must patiently submit to be kicked by the heel of an ass.'"   " This is venomous enough," quoth my friend; " but it is no business of mine; let Dr. Kipling take it up if he pleases."   " Dr. Kipling!" hastily interrupted I.   " Ay, Dr. Kipling," answered he; " who can mistake it?   Mr. Frend, for he is plainly typified by the dying lion, would have been easy if any decent man had been his prosecutor; but he laments that he is expelled at the instance of such an animal as Dr. Kipling."

The third letter has this conclusion :   .

It is now time to take leave of Bacchus and his Orgies. However, by divine permission, and the aid of Tooke's Pantheon, I can send you, if you want them, some similar stories, full as authentic, and I hope as diverting, as the Arabian nights; at least they have one quality in common,—they are Oriental tales.   Whenever you can spare a column from religion, politics, the national debt, the king's bathing, and other matters in which the salvation of the public is concerned, I may perhaps trouble you with an explication of some other points of pagan theology, as they were (I will not say believed or understood, but) professed by the ancients.

MYTHOLOGUS.

No other papers of the kind were, however, made public.

Kidd says that Porson's mind, when he wrote these papers, must have been overclouded.   For this remark there is no foundation.   Porson's powers, when they were published, were in full vigour and energy; and they were written, or at least much of the portion of them relating to Bacchus, as early, according to Dr. Johnstone's testimony, as 1790.

The " Hymn to the Creator, by a new-made Peer," a contribution to the " Morning Chronicle " of the same

period, is supposed to be Porson's.   We give the first
six stanzas of it.

Hail, gracious Sire, to thee belong
My morning pray'r, my evening song;
   My heart and soul are thine:
Inspire me, while I chant thy praise
In zealous though in feeble lays,
   And show thy power divine.

Late, while I lay a senseless mass,
As. dull as peasant, ox, or ass,
   Unworthy note and name,
Methought thy fiat reached mine ear,
"Let Mr. Scrub become a peer,"
   And Scrub a peer became.

Of such a change in Nature's laws
What pow'r could be th' efficient cause,
   Inferior to a god?
All public virtue, private worth,
Conspicuous talents, splendid birth,
   Attend the sovereign's nod.

I'm now a member of that court
That settles, in the last resort,
   The business of the nation;
Where, since I'm kick'd upstairs by thee,
I'll clearly prove my pedigree
   As old as the creation.

But not omnipotence alone
Adorns the owner of a throne;
   His attributes pass counting;
Of justice, when he hangs poor knaves,
Of mercy, when rich rogues he saves,
   He's rightly called the fountain.

In part of payment for thy favours,
I'll tender thee my best endeavours,
   If haply thou shalt need 'em;

Nor shall I grudge thy shirt to air,
For all the bed-room lords declare
Thy service perfect freedom.*

We have also little doubt that the " Miseries of Kingship," a translation from Maphæus, which appeared in
the " Morning Chronicle " about the same time, was the
production of Porson. The words in italics are substi-
tutes for others of too little delicacy in the original.

MR. EDITOR,

Having lately seen an extract on the Miseries of Kingship, from Maphæus's additional canto to the Æneid, by one
of your contemporaries, who, I dare say, thought he had
found *a mare's nest* of recondite literature, I send you the
whole passage, with the translation, which, I hope you will
think with me, conveys the true spirit of the original.

Tunc sic illacrymans rex alto corde Latinus
Verba dabat: Quantos humana negotia motus,
Alternasque vices miscent! Quo turbine fertur
Vita hominum! O fragilis damnosa superbia sceptri!
O furor! O nimium dominandi innata cupido,
Mortalis quò cæca vehis? Quò, gloria, tantis
Inflatos transfers animos quæsita periclis?
Quot tecum insidias, quot mortes, quanta malorum
Magnorum tormenta geris! Quot tela, quot enses
Ante oculos (si cernis) habes! Heu dulce venenum,
Et mundi lethalis honos! Heu tristia regni
Munera, quæ haud parvo constent, et grandia rerum
Pondera, quæ nunquam placidam permittere pacem,
Nec requiem conferre queant! Heu sortis acerbæ
Et miseræ regale decus, magnoque timori
Suppositos regum casus, pacique negatos!

Latinus then, with leaking eyes,
Proceeded thus to sermonise:

---

* Spirit of the Public Journals for 1797, p. 250.

What clouds of ills, with whirlwinds surly,
Make human life a hurly-burly !
One while we're raised to highest pitch,
Now headlong thrown into a ditch !
Confound a sceptre !   He who takes it,
A million to a farthing breaks it.
Unhappy Love-rule, murd'rous hag,
Whither dost thou blind mortals drag ?
'Tis thou to battle eggest kings,
As well as louts to wrestling rings ;
What slaughters, blood, and wounds, and quarrels,
These heroes undertake for laurels !
Fantastic plant, that's chiefly found
To flourish in romantic ground ;
In short, this glory, that men greet,
Is but a vapour and a cheat.
Nor need folks envy us, God knows,
Our drums, and trumpets, and fine clothes ;
We've cause sufficient to abhor 'em,
We pay so cursed dearly for 'em :
Abroad we must not walk alone,
Or else we're pinn'd within the throne ;
While our state-nurses guard us there,
As children in the *baby's* chair,
And fill our heads with ghosts and sprites,
That will not let us sleep a-nights.
Such is our envied royal lot,
The blessed bargain kings have got.*

The style of a letter " On the Duties of Gentlemen-Soldiers," inserted in the same paper, manifestly indicates it to be Porson's.

   .   To all the British Dealers in Blood and Slaughter who are under the rank of Ensign.

[Dr. Gisborne having published a book intituled "The Duties of Gentlemen," this letter was to supply his omission of the duties of gentlemen-soldiers.]

* Spirit of the Public Journals for 1797, p. 403.

SOLDIERS, GENTLEMEN, HEROES,

For such you are, whatever was your former station or employment in life. He who was yesterday the ninth part of a man, by becoming a soldier to-day has multiplied his existence by at least three times three. Yet, hard fate! the integer of to-day is much more liable to be destroyed than the paltry fraction of yesterday. But what is that to your employers, you know? The more danger, the more honour; *needs must when the devil drives.* If you were till now the veriest wretches in nature; if you had been just excused from hanging, on condition you should enter into the army; if you had your choice from a justice of peace, whether you would be tried for felony or go for a soldier, and, in consequence of this obliging offer, freely chose to enlist; if your ankles were still galled with the irons of the prison; if, after a short confinement for perjury, you had gone into court again, in order to swear away an innocent man's life; in short, if you were the lowest, basest, most despicable of mankind, in your former occupation, you are now become, by a wonderful transformation, Gentlemen and Men of Honour.

But, that I may proceed with all possible method and clearness in my discourse, I shall first give you a definition of that most important and distinguished character, *a soldier.* A soldier, then, is a Yahoo, hired to kill in cold blood as many of his own species as he possibly can, who never did him any injury. From this definition necessarily flows a high sense of dignity. Your honour is your most precious possession, and of that it becomes you to be chary. You are the disposers of the world; the umpires of all differences; the defenders of the Defender of the Faith. But why do I say defenders of the Defender of the Faith? You are the defenders of the faith itself. It rests upon you to reinstate the empire of God, of religion, and of humanity, by means which God and Nature (and, I may add, the King of Corsica) have put into your hands. . . . If you will promote this godly work with all your might, though your sins were deeper than scarlet, yet shall they become whiter than snow; in short, you have nothing to do but to submit your lives to the disposal of the king and his officers, and your souls to your chaplain. After having made these trifling sacrifices, your way will be perfectly smooth and pleasant. If you survive, as you have a chance at least of one in twenty, you will come back laden with laurels to your native country, and there enjoy in full perfection all the blessings of civil government, which is the next best thing to military. If you die upon the spot, you fall a martyr to the glorious cause of God, of Christianity, of liberty, of property, of *subordinate order-liness*, and of *orderly subordination*. Nor need you be afraid of death, for I can assure you *in verbo sacerdotis*, i. e. on the word of a priest, that whoever dies in this contest shall instantly depart to Paradise, if ever thief from the gallows went thither. . . . .

And now for a few hints touching your general behaviour.

1. Be fluent in your oaths and curses upon all occasions. It will show a confidence in the goodness of your cause, and make people believe that you must be hand and glove with the person for whom you fight, when you use his name so familiarly, and appeal to him as an old acquaintance upon the most trivial occasions.

2. The Defenders of Religion must show that it never has any influence upon their practice. It is your duty, therefore, to be, what the canting methodistical people call, a profligate. What made the Christians victorious when they went to wrest the sepulchre of our Saviour from the idolatrous Turks, but a proper allowance of oaths and licentiousness? It is no sin in a holy warfare, or, if it were, it is the least of the seven deadly.

3. Keep up your spirits now and then with a cordial sup of liquor. You cannot imagine how this prescription will clear up your thoughts, and dissolve all scruples, if you ever had any, concerning the justice of the war. The liberal allowance which you receive, and the exactness with which it is paid, will amply furnish you with the means of procuring these cordials; and they will produce another good effect: they will recall your courage when it begins to ebb, and ooze, as it were, through the palms of your hands.

> For valour the stronger grows,
>   The stronger the liquor we're drinking;
> And how can we feel our woes,
>   When we've lost the power of thinking?

4. As you are men of nice honour, and it is a proverb that nothing is more delicate than a soldier's honour, I propose it as a case of conscience whether you should not tilt, as well as your officers, when an affront is offered you. For instance, if another soldier should call you a gaol-bird, and the truth of the fact be notorious, it appears to me that you ought to convince him of his mistake by running him through the body, or lodging a ball in his carcase. But perhaps your worthy superiors may deem this an infringement of their prerogatives. I speak therefore under correction.

5. Notwithstanding what I have said concerning the lawfulness, nay the duty, of drinking a drop of liquor now and then, I do not mean you should guzzle away all that large stock of money which is granted you by the bounty of the king and his Parliament. I would wish you to lay by a shilling or so of each day's pay; you who have wives and children, for the support of your wives and children; you who have poor relations, for the maintenance of your relations; and you who have neither, that, in your old age, if you should outlive the war, and return to your native country, you may purchase a snug annuity, and live in comfort upon the property you have acquired by valour.

I am, Soldiers, Gentlemen, and Heroes,

Your loving brother,

A JOHNIAN PRIEST.

It was in the " Morning Chronicle," too, that *the hundred and one epigrams* appeared, which Porson is said to have written in one night, about Pitt and Dundas going drunk to the House of Commons, on the evening when a message was to be delivered from his Majesty relative to war with France. The story is to be found in the effusion of frothy narrative called Warner's

" Literary Recollections,"* where it is said to have been
told by Perry to John Pearson, Esq., afterwards advo-
cate-general of Bengal. When the Minister and his friend
appeared before the House, Pitt tried to speak, but,
showing himself unable, was kindly pulled down into
his seat by those about him ; Dundas, who was equally
unfitted for eloquence, had sense enough left to sit
silent.   Perry witnessed the scene, and, on his return
from the House, gave a description of it to Porson, who,
being vastly amused, called for pen and ink, and,
musing over his pipe and tankard, produced the one
hundred and one pieces of verse before the day dawned.
There is, alas ! not one that can be called good among
them ; *sunt quædam mediocria, sunt mala plura.*   The
point of most of them lies in puns, and of course in bad
puns, for who could excogitate a hundred good puns,
supposing that there ever were such things, in one
night ?   The first epigram is,

> That *Ça Ira* in England will prevail,
>   All sober men deny with heart and hand ;
> To talk of *going's* sure a pretty tale,
>   When e'en our rulers can't so much as stand.

The following perhaps deserve preference over their
fellows :

> Your gentle brains with full libations drench ;
> You've *then* Pitt's title to the Treasury Bench.

> Your foe in war to overrate,
> A maxim is of ancient date :
> Then sure 'twas right, in time of trouble,
> That our good rulers should *see double.*

---

* Vol. ii. p. 6.

The mob are beasts, exclaims the *Knight of Daggers* :
What creature's he that's troubled with the *staggers* ?

When Billy found he scarce could stand,
" Help, help ! " he cried, and stretched his hand,
   To faithful Henry calling :
Quoth Hal, " My friend, I'm sorry for't ;
'Tis not my practice to support
   A minister that's falling."

" Who's up ? " inquired Burke of a friend at the door :
" Oh ! no one," says Paddy ; " though Pitt's *on the floor*."

CHAP. XVIII.

In 1799 came out the Phœnissæ. In the notes to this play Porson abstains from any allusions to Wakefield or Hermann, with the exception of one slight touch on Wakefield, and two animadversions on the lovers of anapæsts. The censure of Wakefield, whom he does not name, is given on ver. 1521, for having unadvisedly altered $\tau\acute{o}\nu\delta\epsilon$ $\lambda\acute{o}\gamma o\nu$ to $\tau o\acute{u}\sigma\delta\epsilon$ $\lambda\acute{o}\gamma o\upsilon\varsigma$, in the 548th verse of the Alcestis, on the faith of an unsound passage in Hesychius.

On ver. 1354, which, in Aldus's edition, commences with $\Sigma\tau\epsilon\acute{\iota}\chi o\nu\tau o\varsigma$, $\mathring{o}\varsigma$ $\mathring{\eta}\mu\acute{\iota}\nu$, but in all the manuscripts $\Sigma\tau\epsilon\acute{\iota}\chi o\nu\tau o\varsigma$ $\mathring{o}\varsigma$ $\pi\tilde{a}\nu$, he exclaims, " How savagely would the patrons of anapæsts have exulted over their enemies, if all the manuscripts had agreed with the edition of Aldus, or if the edition of Aldus had been the only surviving copy of the Phœnissæ!" On ver. 1371, which ends with $\tau\acute{e}\rho\mu o\nu$' $\mathrm{'I}o\varkappa\acute{a}\sigma\tau\eta$, $\beta\acute{\iota}o\upsilon$, but which Grotius had edited $\tau\acute{e}\rho\mu$' $\mathrm{'I}o\varkappa\acute{a}\sigma\tau\eta$, $\tau o\tilde{\upsilon}$ $\beta\acute{\iota}o\upsilon$, he observes, " If any one prefer Grotius's reading, I shall utter no heavier imprecation on him than that he may read in Orest. 590, $\mathrm{'E}\pi\epsilon\grave{\iota}$ $\gamma\grave{a}\rho$ $\grave{e}\xi\acute{e}\pi\nu\epsilon\upsilon\sigma$' $\mathrm{'A}\gamma a\mu\acute{e}\mu\nu\omega\nu$ $\tau\grave{o}\nu$ $\beta\acute{\iota}o\upsilon$."

In 1800 nothing is known, we believe, to have been
given to the public from the pen of Porson, except a
review of Pybus's "Sovereign," a poem addressed to
the Emperor of Russia. Mr. Kidd calls this "a truly
neat specimen of playful criticism," and says that when
Porson first opened the Laureate's splendid volume, he
exclaimed, in the hearing of several friends,

> I sing a song of sixpence,
>   A pocket-full of rye,
> Four-and-twenty blackbirds
>   Baked in a pie :
> When the pie was open'd
>   The birds began to sing :
> And was not this a dainty dish
>   To set before a king ?

The review is as follows. It appeared in the
" Monthly Review" for December 1800.

> *The Sovereign. Addressed to His Imperial Majesty*
> PAUL, *Emperor of all the Russias. By* CHARLES
> SMALL PYBUS, *M.P., one of the Lords Commis-*
> *sioners of the Treasury.* Folio, pp. 60. Price
> 1*l*. 1*s*., or, with a Portrait, 1*l*. 11*s*. 6*d*. White, 1800.

The inventive genius of modern times appears with peculiar
lustre in that new species of the *sublime*, of which the magnificent poem before us is an astonishing example. The
gigantic types, the folio wove paper, and the awe-inspiring
portrait, like the

Vultus instantis tyranni,

have superseded the old rules of Longinus, and have forced
admiration from the appalled beholder, even before he reads.
Mr. Pybus is certainly "as tall a poet of his hands" as any
wight that has issued from the press within our memory; and
he may vie for title-page, print, and margin, with the first of

our bards. When, however, we have bestowed this praise on his work, we have exhausted every source of panegyric; for his verses are formed only to be viewed, not to be perused; his poetry is so like a picture, according to the Horatian precept, that it will not bear the near approach of the eye.

The happy alliteration resulting from the title, *A Poem to Paul by the poet Pybus*, reminds us of the Latin work entitled *Pugna Porcorum, per Publium Porcium, Poetam.* Though this work is addressed to the Emperor Paul, it is, with inimitable dexterity, dedicated to our own king. This is a flight of courtly wit, which perhaps will never again be attempted; and the amazing resemblance which Mr. Pybus has asserted between the illustrious personages, to one of whom he *addresses* his *address* to the other, will be ranked by posterity among the most unexpected discoveries of the present age.

To compress the shining lines of Mr. Pybus into our narrow and unadorned pages, is, like translating Virgil, to lose all the beauty of the original. But we shall endeavour to gratify our friends in the country with a specimen of this state-performance, in the address to Peter I. and his ill-fated descendant:

> "Illustrious shade! Oh! could thy soul infuse
> Its faint resemblance in the anxious Muse,
> Then, in sublimer song, her voice should raise
> Strains less unequal to our hero's praise.
> But what at last avails the poet's fire?
> Vain are his honours, and his boasted lyre;
> Vain is the laurel that adorns his brow;
> Vain are his numbers; nor can all bestow,
> But from their deathless theme alone receive,
> The fame not e'en Mæonides could give.
> Since then establish'd glory thus defies
> The power of poesy that never dies,
> How much more vain are offerings alone,
> Composed of perishable brass and stone,
> Though quarries were consumed and millions spent,
> When the whole empire forms one monument.

" And thou, ill-fated prince, whom discord gave
An early victim to misfortune's grave,
Whate'er thy frailties were (and who has none ?),
Amply thy greater virtues shall atone,
Whose heralds on the wings of mercy cross'd
The trackless deserts of Siberian frost.
Thee coward cruelty in horrors dight,
And mean suspicion that avoids the light,
And persecution with tormenting flame,
Shall ever execrate, and hate thy name ;
While freedom's gratitude and pity's tear
Shall drop a tribute on thy mournful bier.
But Heaven will'd ! Nor let thy realms deplore
The mix'd event, that left one Peter more."

This *other Peter*, it seems, means the late empress; who, by a poetical licence, which can only be derived from royal authority, is here invested with the name of her husband. Perhaps Mr. Pybus had been thinking of a passage in Shakspeare :

" And if his name be *George*, I'll call him Peter."

In truth, the author seems liable to mistakes of this kind ; for we observe that some of his couplets terminate with words which have not even so much affinity with each other as that which subsisted between Peter and Catharine :

"Rhymes, like Scotch cousins, in such order placed,
The first scarce claims acquaintance with the last."

Considered in its political relations, Mr. Pybus's work is not less unfortunate than in its literary station. After the high and splendid hopes of curbing France, which are held out in the poem, comes a dolorous prose epilogue, to inform us that the glory of Europe is blasted, and that the Emperor has withdrawn his troops ! Subsequent occurrences have lamentably deepened the gloom of this disappointment ; and we sincerely condole with Mr. Pybus on the ungracious return which this northern Mecænas has made to the British treasury, both for *its solid pudding and its empty praise.*

A note adds, " The Imperial Balancer seems to have placed both [our pudding and our praise] in one scale, and to have counterpoised them with some other commodity, which has made our offerings kick the beam."

Porson used afterwards to repeat, very frequently, the following lines, which are universally supposed to have been his own composition :

> *Poetis nos lætamur tribus,*
> Pye, Petro Pindar, Parvo Pybus :
> *Si ulteriùs ire pergis,*
> *Adde his* Sir James Bland Burgess.

Which may be thus imitated :

> Three bards to praise them fain would bribe us,
> Pye, Peter Pindar, Charles Small Pybus :
> Three only ?   Lo, a fourth that urges
> His claim for praise, Sir James Bland Burgess.

The nursery lines, which Porson uttered when he opened Pybus's book, have been thus attempted in Greek, we know not by whom :

> Τετρώβολόν τι μέλπω,
> Κριθῶν τε πλήρη σάκκον,
> Καὶ κοττύλους δὶς δώδεκ'
> Ὀπτοὺς στέγει 'ν σιτευτῷ ·
> Στέγους δ' ἀναπτυχθέντος
> Ὄρνιθες ἐξεφώνευν,
> Ὅ δὴ δοκεῖ τι λαμπρὸν,
> Εἰ προσφέροιτ' ἄνακτι.*

In 1799 and 1800 Porson received from Gail, the French translator and editor of Xenophon, the two following letters, with presents of some of his works.

* Barker's Literary Anecdotes, vol. ii. p. 189.

" GAIL *to the illustrious* Mr. PORSON.

" SIR,

" M. Vellimenot the younger, a banker of Paris, ought, at his last trip to London, to have sent you, from me, my ' Treatise on Hunting, translated from the Greek of Xenophon.' In the apprehension that he may not have caused it to reach you safely, I address to you a second copy of it on vellum paper, accompanied with my ' Greek Roots ' and my 'Poetic Anthology.' Would you have the goodness, if I may venture to ask, to announce these three works, or to get them announced, in one of the most respectable of your journals ? May I request you especially, also, to cast your eye on two historical dissertations, which I think curious, and particularly on that relating to Hipparchus, Anacreon, &c. (p. 39 of my Anthology), the true sense of which the critics who have preceded me appear not to have caught ? I would also have you look at that on Epicharmus (p. 23 of the Anthology), and on my observations on M. Sturz's *Lexicon Xenophonteum* in the preface to the Anthology.

" I shall be flattered by having your opinion on these three articles; the rest would not recompense you for the trouble of perusal.

" Will you pardon me if I request you to read also my critical observations on Xenophon's object in his Symposium ?

" I send you a leaf of the *Décade Philosophique*, year x., third quarter, in which these observations have been inserted.

" I am working constantly at Xenophon. The six manuscripts of the *Hellenica* have occupied much time, and required incredible patience; but I have found valuable various readings, which have made me excellent amends. In another month I shall put forth a humble specimen of it, which will be inserted in my magazine by M. Millier.

" May my researches be thought useful ! May Mr. Porson say, when he reads them, that the author has not wholly wasted his time !

" GAIL, Professor of the Greek language
in the College of France.

" 15 Prair. an x. (1799)."

"GAIL *to the illustrious* Mr. PORSON.

"SIR,

"One of your countrymen, the amiable and learned Dr. Jones, is now at my house. He is willing to take charge of some works which I had last year the honour of sending you through the agency of Eisch the bookseller, but which probably never reached you.

"These books are, 1. My 'Greek Poetical Anthology.' The rest of the Greek course is not worth offering you. 2. My Theocritus in duodecimo; I do not offer you the fine edition in quarto, because I am not the proprietor of it. It has been printed at the expense of a banker of this country. 3. My Cynegetics. 4. A Letter to M. Schneider. 5. An extract from *La Décade Philosophique.*

"If I were not afraid, Sir, of trespassing on your time, I would ask you to favour me with your opinion, first, on the extract from *La Décade*, p. 281, which you will find in the parcel; an extract entitled 'Short Analysis of the Banquet of Xenophon;' secondly, on my dissertation relating to Anacreon, Hipparchus, &c., p. 39 of my 'Poetical Anthology;' thirdly, on my exposition regarding Epicharmus, p. 43 of the same work.

"This is a great deal to ask of you, Sir; it is perhaps to be extremely troublesome. But I presume upon your indulgence, and set a very high value on your opinion. In these two dissertations, I think a Socratic irony is apparent, and, if I am right, I have made an historical discovery. But I ought to distrust my own way of looking on these matters, as it differs from that of the greatest critics and historians both of our own and of other countries.

"To read and examine these three short pieces will not require more than an hour. I ask this of you, and entreat it as a favour. Do not reply till you have read them, and till you are able to send me your opinion.

"I beg the illustrious Mr. Porson to accept the tribute of my sincere and profound respect.

                    "GAIL, Professor of Greek Literature in
                          the College of France."

[No date.]

CHAP. XIX.

WHILE Porson was engaged about Euripides, the
splendid edition of Homer, known as the " Grenville
Homer," was being printed at the Clarendon Press, as
Kidd says, " for the three noble brothers ; " and those
who had the superintendence of it, being desirous that
there should be appended to it a collation of the
Harleian manuscript of the Odyssey (which had been
previously collated, but very negligently, by Thomas
Bentley), made application for that purpose to Porson,
who readily undertook the work, and devoted himself
to it with more than ordinary diligence.   He was then
living in Essex Court in the Temple, where he would,
on many occasions, shut himself up for two or three
days together ; but, while he was employed on the
Harleian manuscript, he was almost wholly inaccessible
even to his most intimate friends.   " One morning,"
says Mr. Maltby, " I went to call upon him there ; and,
having inquired at his barber's close by if Mr. Porson

was at home, was answered, 'Yes; but he has seen no
one for two days.' I, however, proceeded to his
chamber, and knocked at the door more than once. He
would not open it, and I came downstairs. As I was
re-crossing the court, Porson, who had perceived that I
was the visitor, opened the window, and stopped me."
His remuneration for the collation was fifty pounds, and
a large-paper copy. "I thought the payment too small,"
observes Maltby, "but Burney considered it as sufficient."* This collation has been reprinted in the
"Classical Journal." A few critical remarks are scattered through it. The passage regarding the final *v*
we have already extracted. He concludes, after making
some final corrections, with this paragraph :

"Thus I have at last, I hope, left no important error in
this collation; that there are no omissions, I will not assert.
If any one, however, shall take upon himself to supply my
deficiencies, and to correct, at the same time, such mistakes as
I have committed, let him be assured that he will do what is
acceptable to the republic of letters as well as to myself.
Whether he do it tenderly or harshly, will have no effect on
me, if he but do it accurately; but it may possibly have a
good effect on himself, if he be anxious to show that he undertook the task rather from a desire to be of service to letters
than to depress a rival."

The appearance of the Grenville Homer occasioned
Porson to receive the following application from Villoison :

"Sir,

"I beg you to have the goodness to excuse the forward-
ness of a foreigner who has not the happiness of being known
to you, but who has the highest admiration for your rare and

* Rogers's Table Talk, "Porsoniana," p. 311.

profound knowledge, your ἀγχίνοια and εὐστοχία, and who knows that you are the κριτικῆς κοίρανος τέχνης, and the most learned and most justly celebrated Hellenist of the country in which Greek learning is most cultivated.

"I have the honour, Sir, to be a member of your Royal Society of London, and of the Society of Antiquaries of the same city ; and I have been all my life employed on Homer, and have published the *Lexicon Homericum*, composed by Apollonius the Sophist, with my own Latin translation and notes. I have also put forth, at Venice, an edition of the Iliad, with the scholia, never before edited, of the most skilful grammarians of the Alexandrian school, and with the critical marks. Mons. Heyne, my learned friend, and *confrère* at the University of Gottingen, has done me the honour of acquainting me by letter that he has extracted a portion of these notes, as my friend Mr. Wolff had already done in his edition.

"On these grounds, Sir, I should very much wish to be able to obtain a copy of the beautiful edition of Homer which Lord Buckingham and Mr. Grenville are publishing at Cambridge, and which, if our journals may be trusted, is now to be distributed among amateurs.

"I have not the advantage of being known to Lord Buckingham or to Mr. Grenville. May I flatter myself that you, Sir, who certainly have the management of this valuable edition, would have the goodness to do a stranger so important a service as to mention him to these noble Mæcenases, and induce them to put me on the list of those for whom they intend copies of this excellent and superb edition ?

"For this kindness, Sir, I should feel so much the more under obligation to you, as it would be impossible for me to procure this book, even if it were obtainable in the way of trade ; for my fortune has been totally ruined by the Revolution, which has robbed me of a very considerable inheritance, and, what I regret much more, has left me no time to devote myself, as I should wish to do exclusively, to Greek literature, and to the composition of a work on ancient and modern Greece, the object of nine years' travels in Greece, Italy, and Germany, and of twenty years of research.

"I am waiting, Sir, with the greatest impatience, for the publication of your Æschylus and your Euripides, *Phidiaca opera*; and I request you, if you do me the honour to reply, and to mention me to my Lord Buckingham and Mr. Grenville, to have the goodness to write to me in Latin, French, or Italian, as I confess, to my shame, that I am unfortunate enough not to understand English.

"Forgive my indiscretion, or rather my temerity, and believe that I shall always think myself too happy in having embraced this opportunity of signifying to a learned critic of your distinguished merit the respect and admiration with which I have the honour to be,

                                  "Sir,
     "Your very humble and very obedient servant,
               "D'ANSSE DE VILLOISON,
          "of the Institute of France, of the Royal and
               Antiquarian Societies of London, &c. &c.

"Paris, Rue de Bièvre, No. 22,
     July 9, 1802."

Porson was successful in obtaining him a copy of the Homer, which he acknowledged as follows:

                         "Paris, Rue de Bièvre, No. 22,
                              Oct. 15, 1802.

"SIR,

     "I have received, with the most lively feelings of gratitude, the handsome present which you have made me of your noble and excellent edition of Homer. It is a masterpiece, Sir, of typography and accuracy; and your notes, abounding with proofs of sagacity, give it a value which nothing can equal. In your opinions, concisely expressed, but βεβρεγμένοις ἐν νῷ, on the various readings of your manuscript, we recognise, at every word, ἐξ ὄνυχος λέοντα. I am extremely flattered by owing this superb gift to the recommendation of a gentleman of your rare learning and merit, the worthy successor of Bentley and Toup, who have transmitted to you the sceptre of criticism.

"I delayed to send you my thanks, Sir, until I had studied your learned annotations, and until an opportunity occurred of sending, by a traveller who was to set out immediately, a letter which I have had some time written. But the traveller has put off his journey, and I cannot longer withhold from myself the pleasure of requesting you to present my tribute of respect and thankfulness to those generous noblemen who make so honourable a use of their wealth and knowledge, and of entreating you to believe that no one has the honour to be with more gratitude, attachment, and admiration,

"Sir,

"Your very humble and very obedient servant,

"D'Ansse de Villoison.

"À Monsieur Monsieur Porson,
   Professeur de Littérature Grecque
   dans l'Université de Cambridge."

Previously to the receipt of these letters had come forth the Medea, printed at the Cambridge University Press at the expense of the syndics. In the notes to this play, to which Porson set his name, he troubled his adversaries with a little more attention than he had paid them in the notes to the Orestes. In his comment on the first verse, after alluding to the mistakes often made by editors, and the old grammarians, in regard to accents, he proceeds to say, "Here is a rather long note, and on a subject, as some may think, of no great importance; and I might have diminished my labour, and perhaps consulted my quiet, by forbearing to offer these remarks, for I see that by some writers, very excellent men no doubt, but not over learned, and somewhat ill-tempered, the whole doctrine of accents is regarded as utterly valueless. But such persons are too old, I conceive, to be untaught anything wrong, or to learn anything right, by my instructions. It is to you YOUNG MEN, however, whom alone I consider under my charge, that I now address myself. I have occasionally touched on this subject before, as on the 632nd verse of the Orestes, and elsewhere, and shall touch on it again wherever it may be necessary. If any one of YOU, then, desires to gain an accurate knowledge of the Greek language, let him devote himself, without delay, to acquire a competent understanding of Greek accentuation, and persevere in the study, undeterred by the babble of railers and the laughter of fools; for *than foolish laughter nothing is more foolish*. One remark only, for the sake of admonition, I shall add at present. Whoever, without a knowledge of this subject, takes upon himself the office of collating manuscripts, will assuredly disappoint the literary world of much of that benefit which might justly be expected from his labours. Whoever is unacquainted with this science, is, while he ingenuously confesses his deficiency, blamable only for his ignorance; but he who, not content with merely avowing his want of knowledge, presumes to excuse it by affecting contempt for the study, is deserving of greater censure."

These observations, especially those relating to the " very excellent men, not over learned, and somewhat ill-tempered," *quidam viri, sed nec satis eruditi et paullo iracundiores*, are directed chiefly against Wakefield, who had published his Greek plays, and a small edition of Bion and Moschus, without accents, and had, in the preface to the latter work, offered, in his bold and wordy style, the following defence of his practice :

" If any one expresses surprise or indignation that I have discarded all the accents, grave, acute, and circumflex, as they are called, and thinks that he sees in them advantages which compensate for the trouble that they give the printer, I am not at all afraid to enter into a discussion with him on the subject. Let those who patronise accents, however, consider whether they are not catching at vain praise for possessing empty and useless knowledge, and giving importance to trifles that they may not be thought to have spent long study on trifles ; for, to borrow the words of a sensible rhetorician, it is not easy to alter notions which have been infused into us in boyhood (and especially those which flatter us with the appearance of learning), since every man had rather have learned formerly than learn now. From the defences of Foster and Primatt, ingenious and learned as they are, I collect nothing but that the controversy about accents is, if we look to solid utility, a mere question for grammarians, to whom, as they labour thus superfluously, we cannot give a better answer than the lines of Catullus :

> ' Turpe est difficiles habere nugas,
> Et stultus labor est ineptiarum.'

" How deeply must you be concerned, O ye learned professors, that the Latin tongue is destitute of these delights, which to you are sweeter than honey or the honeycomb ! "

It may be observed that Brunck had the same notion in regard to the uselessness of accents as Wakefield, for he would willingly, he said, discard them all, except such as denoted different significations of the same word.* Nor was Elmsley much more favourable to them, for he observed that to bestow extreme attention upon Greek accents is but lost labour, since they have no parentage but that of the Alexandrian grammarians, a set of men who were born to obscure the ancient Greek language rather than illustrate it.†

* Ad Eur. Bacch. 344.   † Ad Eur. Heracl. 403.

Porson's note on verses 139, 140, of the Medea, is one of the wonders of verbal criticism. He observes that the lines on which he is commenting are cited by the scholiast on Æschylus, but in such a way that they had previously escaped notice; and then proceeds to advert to various other quotations from poets which had experienced similar fortune, continuing latent in the text of authors or commentators, when editors ought to have detected them. " But," he remarks, "before I animadvert on the oversights of others, it will be well for me, perhaps, to correct my own errors, lest I be attacked with the old proverb, ' How is it, ill-conditioned man, that you look so keenly on other people's faults, and turn your glance away from your own ? '" He then observes that, in a note on the fourth verse of the Orestes, he had made a mistake, in saying that Bentley had commenced a verse with καὶ instead of ὡς : that he had arranged four verses of the same play in a wrong order; and that in one of them, the 676th, he had given παρὰ instead of πρὸς, not without judgment, as he thinks, but certainly without having given due notice of the change. " If a Le Clerc or a Pauw, however, had detected such an inadvertence, with what gentle words would he have addressed me ! But let those men, *et ceteræ ejusmodi quisquiliæ*, rest in peace. It is the reputation only

Præclarorum hominum ac primorum signiferumque

that I have determined to assail in this note." He then proceeds to point out various verses in Plutarch, Athenæus, Stobæus, and some of the scholiasts, which had been passed over unheeded by Bentley, Wyttenbach, and other eminent discerning spirits ; and concludes with saying that he might have produced more examples, but that what he has given may suffice for a specimen, and will at least, he hopes, not be displeasing to his readers ; " for," he continues, " though we very unwillingly allow our neighbour acuteness of judgment, or happiness of conception, yet I trust that credit for this labour, which depends only on industry and patience, or at best on a little tenacity of memory, will readily be granted me."

In alluding to the fourth verse of the Philoctetes, he would remark, he says, that the word Νεοπτόλεμε in it is to be taken as the first pæon, " if he thought any one of his pupils so dull and stupid as to be unable to see it for himself ; " a shaft which is supposed to be shot at Hermann.

Whether such a string of observations, which occupy, in the form of a note, the best part of eight pages, are properly appended to the lines of the Medea, may be questioned.   Doubtless some readers, who are not writers of notes, will think that a fitter place might have been found for them, and that a commentator should not be privileged to transfer whatever he pleases from his memory or his commonplace book to the margin of his author.   But if the criticism be misplaced, its sagacity is not the less worthy of admiration.

But Hermann was to receive a heavier castigation in a subsequent annotation.   Whatever remarks or allusions Porson had hitherto made in reference to him, he had not yet mentioned his name ; but now, in his note on ver. 675, after observing that the Attic writers, he thought, never allowed themselves to use γε after τοι, unless with a word between them, and noticing two exceptional passages requiring emendation, he says,

"These passages I would willingly submit to the correction of Godfrey Hermann, if I thought that he could as easily make corrupt places sound as he makes sound places corrupt. For who besides Hermann, in the fourth place of an iambic trimeter, ever — I will not say overlooked a dactyl (for of oversights we are all guilty), but — thrust in a dactyl by altering the text, as he has done in the 870th verse of the Nubes?   Who besides Hermann, for the excellent word χυτρεοῦν, ever substituted χυτροῦν, a word which is not Greek, which is supported by no authority, and which is ruinous to the metre?   But this Hermann has done in the 1476th verse of the Nubes; and his object, in doing so, was to throw obloquy on Dawes, *Cui si non aliqua nocuisset, mortuus esset.* These achievements, however, are nothing to his triumphant exploits with the innocent name of Hercules; for though, in his opinion, χυτροῦν is a proof of the lengthening of such syllables among the writers of comedy, nothing, he thinks, is more rare than the lengthening of such syllables among the writers of tragedy.   We may therefore imagine Hermann speaking thus with himself: 'We Germans, who understand the quantity of syllables much better than the English, will correct all the passages of Euripides in which Ἡρακλέης occurs with the second syllable long.'   Six passages accordingly, which were suffering from this disease, he proceeded to cure, if to cure is to assert disease where it is not, in order to show your own skill in manipulation.   These passages are in the Heraclidæ, the Ion, and the Hercules Furens; nor do I doubt that he would cure, with equal success, ten other passages, which I will cite that he may try his hand upon them."

Porson then enumerates ten places in which Ἡρακλέης occurs with the second syllable incontrovertibly long, but observes that Hermann will not be deterred by the fear of hiatus, or any other absurdity, from altering

them, since anything is to be endured rather than that
'Ηρακλέης should lengthen its second syllable. However justly Hermann deserved this exposure, it may be
thought that Porson would better have consulted his
own dignity by leaving him still unnamed.

In his note on ver. 750 he apologises for having
cited the 79th verse of the Hecuba as the 80th, and the
626th verse of the Orestes as the 633rd, and expresses
his surprise that the keen research of his critics had
allowed such mistakes to pass uncensured. " But," he
adds, " if any one shall hereafter animadvert on these
mistakes, and prepare to let loose the whole fierceness
of his anger upon them, let him, before he scorches me
with his fury, consult my *Addenda* and *Corrigenda.*"
And, on observing that the conjunction τε might be left
out of verse 750, he says, " Lest any one should charge
me, on this account, *with too great love of change, and
with altering good readings only for the sake of alteration,* know, excellent youths, that the conjunction is
not found in the edition of Lascaris." The words in
italics are a quotation from some criticism, but whose
we have not discovered.

In the 935th verse, the right reading, for the termination of the line, is ἐκτραφῶσι σῇ χερί, but Beck, following Aldus, had edited ἐκτραφῶσιν. Porson gives
this note: " Beck, who, with Aldus, reads ἐκτραφῶσιν,
gravely remarks, ' Brunck has ἐκτραφῶσι.' I therefore remark, with equal gravity, Lascaris has ἐκτραφῶσι."

Porson sent Villoison a copy of his Medea, for which
he thanked him in the same terms as for his other
present :

" Sir,

" I avail myself, with much eagerness, of an opportunity that occurs of repeating my obligations to you for your beautiful edition of Homer, and of thanking you for your excellent edition of the Medea of Euripides.   While you are at least equal to Bentley and Toup in profound knowledge of the Greek language, and in critical perspicacity, you are infinitely their superior in the knowledge of metre, without which it is impossible to touch a single Greek verse.   It is incumbent on you to handle this important subject thoroughly, and set forth the doctrine of metre, which is as yet a secret confined to you alone, in a separate methodical and didactic treatise, written in Latin, for the use of all Europe.   You would thus perform a signal service to Greek literature, a service which you only are able to perform.   I cannot too strongly request it of you for my own sake.

" I see by your Medea that you are going to give us a new edition of the Hecuba, which I do not yet possess, any more than your Orestes and your Phœnissæ.   I have the strongest desire to study these excellent works.

" I hope that you have received a letter which I had the honour to address to you some time ago at Cambridge, where I supposed that you were residing, to thank you for your Homer.   I beg you to believe that no one can have the honour to be with more grateful feelings,

" Sir,

" Your very humble and very obedient servant,

" D'Ansse de Villoison.

" Paris, Rue de Bièvre, No. 22,
     Oct. 24, 1802."

CHAP. XX.

In the early part of the year 1802, we find Porson addressing the following letter to his friend Dr. Davy,
enclosing proposals for a charitable subscription. For
whose benefit it was intended we do not know.

DEAR DOCTOR,

I cannot tell whether you are acquainted or not with
the object of the foregoing subscription. He was once of
Emmanuel, but choosing rather to trust his wits for a maintenance than the bounty of Holy Mother Church, you see
to what it has brought him. In the mean time, if you have
" a hand open as day for melting charity," you may contribute
what you see reasonable, and apply to any well-disposed
persons, that may fall in your way, for similar exertions of
benevolence. The amount of the subscription at present is,
I understand, between 400*l.* and 500*l.* ; so there will be something to purchase an annuity for the poor poet, after paying
his debts, and to give him food, which is necessary, in lieu of
fame, which is not necessary. God forbid it should ! How

many of us would then be in want of necessaries! We have been rather in expectation of you here in town this Christmas, but, I suppose, diseases, and consequently deaths, have been so rife, that you have had no leisure for jaunting or merry-making. I have got a copy of Coray's Hippocrates *de Aëribus, Aquis, et Locis,* which, if you come shortly to town, you may take with you; if not, I shall send it by Hole, when he passes this way in his return to Cambridge. I have been at death's door myself, but with a due neglect of the faculty, and plentiful use of my old remedy (powder of post), I am pretty well recovered, and am in any way but in medicine,

Dear Doctor,

Your humble servant to command,

R. PORSON.

Strand, No. 145 (Mr. Perry's),
  1st Feb. 1802.

Having recovered, as he says, he proceeded to publish a new edition of the Hecuba at Cambridge, in which the famous supplement to the preface made its first appearance. In his additions to the notes he twice bestows his attention on Wakefield. In the first passage, the 153rd verse, on which Wakefield, in making his foolish alteration of χρυσοφόρου into χρυσοφόβου, had cited a passage of Lycophronis, preserved in Athenæus, speaking rather against the alteration than for it, Porson very quietly quotes the passage, observing that he owes his knowledge of it to the fourteenth page of Gilbert Wakefield's *Diatribe Extemporalis in Hecubam;* a happy mode of showing how little he regarded Wakefield's attack, and how willing he was that all his readers should see what had been put forth against him. In the other passage, the 1164th verse, he treats the author of the *Diatribe* in a different way. Wakefield had sneered at Porson for calling the first syllable of ἀεὶ the

penultimate. "Whoever heard," says he, " of the penultimate of a dissyllable?" Porson remarks, "Pierson
on Mœris, p. 231, rightly states that *the penultima of
ἀεὶ is common;* and that no *scurra* or *sycophanta,* no
babbler or railer, may insult the shade of Pierson for
using the expression *penultimate of a dissyllable,* I will
here adduce two passages from two Latin grammarians."
He then transcribes passages from Valerius Probus and
Priscian, in which the word *penultima* is used in the
same way as Pierson had used it.

What Wakefield was, both as a man and a scholar,
has become tolerably apparent. In his boyhood he had
received a good education, both from his father, who
was a clergyman of some ability, and from Mr. Wooddeson, master, for nearly forty years, of the grammar-
school of Kingston-on-Thames, under whom Steevens,
Gibbon, Hayley, and Lovibond were educated. Of
Wooddeson's general tuition he spoke with approval,
but not of his instruction in writing Latin, which he did
not train his pupils to compose well, and which Wakefield, from the ill effects of early habit, says that he
never wrote without hesitation and difficulty. At about
seventeen he was sent, on a scholarship, to Jesus College,
Cambridge, where his father had been educated. The
mathematical and logical studies of the University he
did not like, but, though compelling himself to give
some attention to Euclid and algebra, devoted the chief
portion of his time to classical reading. In the third
year of his residence, he wrote for all Browne's three
medals, for the epigrams and the Greek and Latin ode,
but was in every case unsuccessful. His epigrams and
Greek ode he allows to have been justly rejected; but

accuses Dr. Cooke, who was then provost of King's, and whose judgment, as he had been head-master of Eton, was much regarded in such matters, of having set aside his Latin ode in favour of his own son's, which, he says, the friends of both parties afterwards acknowledged to be the inferior, and which he insinuates that the father had seen and corrected before it was sent in. Of the truth of this charge we cannot judge, unless we could bring both compositions to light; and both have probably long ago perished. Soon after, he commenced the study of Hebrew, reading it without points, of which he says that no words can sufficiently condemn the obstructions and inutility. When he took his degree, he had attained such proficiency in mathematics as to be second wrangler, and was consequently entitled to compete for the Chancellor's medals, of which he gained the second, Foster, afterwards master of Norwich school, being awarded the first. He was then elected to a fellowship, and in the same year published a small collection of Latin poems, partly original and partly translated. In the two following years he gained two prizes, offered to bachelors, for Latin prose, but stood on each occasion only second.

His fellowship, after holding it three years, he vacated by marriage; and, having been ordained, he devoted himself for some time to theological studies, but, conceiving a dislike for the forms of the Church of England, went over to the dissenters, and returned with great ardour to his classical pursuits, the results of which appeared in the five parts of his *Silva Critica*, which, *Vertumnis, quotquot sunt, natus iniquis*, he published when he was between thirty and forty. The

great characteristic of these miscellaneous criticisms is
an extravagant, and even insane, desire to make changes,
which their author calls emendations, in the texts of
writers.   The volumes never obtained much regard,
and have of late lain almost wholly unheeded ; nor
shall we disturb them to search for more examples of
the writer's pruriency for verbal alteration than those
which we have already extracted.   Sufficient instances
of it may be found elsewhere ; in his Virgil, his Horace
his Greek plays, and his Lucretius.   Whatever book h .
took up, indeed, he appears to have felt himself compelled to propose new readings for its pages.   Whatever
expression he saw susceptible of a plausible alteration,
he could not be content to leave unmolested.   He could
not allow what was good to be genuine or endura-
ble, if he himself could excogitate something that he
imagined better.   We have an excellent example of
this propensity in his letters to Fox.   He is reading
with one of his children the lines of Ovid's *Tristia*,

> Parve, nec invideo, sine me, liber, ibis in urbem;
>   Hei mihi ! quò domino non licet ire tuo.
> Vade, sed incultus, qualem decet exulis esse :
>   Infelix, habitum temporis hujus habe ;

and thinks that he perceives " something awkward and
obscure in the construction" of the third verse.   Surely,
he says, we ought to read *in cultu*.   Fox, in his reply,
says, " I showed your proposed alteration in the *Tristia*
to a very good judge, who approved of it very much. I
confess, myself, that I like the old reading best, and
think it more in Ovid's manner ; but this perhaps is
mere fancy."   The person to whom Fox showed the

R

alteration must have been one of Wakefield's own character; a man ready to pull to pieces, and to change
round for square or square for round; but Fox's good
sense inclined him to rest very well satisfied with what
had satisfied others.   Wakefield rejoins thus: " In reading the passage, I was struck with an instantaneous
repugnance of feeling to the connection of *qualem* with
the participle *incultus*; and I am very much inclined
to think (for confidence on these points, of all others, is
most inexcusable and absurd), that no similar instance
will easily be discovered." Strange delusion! Whoever
should seek for instances might find plenty of them;
and it is surprising that Wakefield should not have recollected the common passage,   .

> Facies non omnibus una,
> Nec diversa tamen, qualem decet esse sororum,

where the position of *diversa* with *qualem* is exactly the
same as that of *incultus* with *qualem*.

In editing Virgil he comes to

> Certent et cycnis ululæ; sit Tityrus Orpheus,

which is very good sense; and alters it to

> *Cantent* et cycnis ululæ,

which is mere absurdity.

In editing the Odes of Horace, he alters

> O beate Sexti

to

> O bea te, Sexti,

committing a false quantity that would disgrace a
schoolboy.

In the Epodes, he is caught by the difficulty in

> Fugit juventas; et verecundus color
> Reliquit ossa pelle amicta lurida,

but refuses to accept Bentley's conjecture of

> Reliquit ora,

and will have us read

> Fugit juventas; et verecundus color
> Reliquit; ossa pelle amicta lurida,

telling us that it is easy to understand *me* and *sunt*.
Most readers, we fear, will think it not at all easy, but
will be likely to consider the ellipsis very forced.

In the " Art of Poetry," the lines,

> Liber et ingenuus, præsertim census equestrem
> Summam nummorum, vitioque remotus ab omni,

had satisfied all critics till Wakefield fell upon them.
Even Bentley had left them undisturbed. But Gilbert
tells us that Horace must have written *vincloque* instead
of *vitioque*. We think that if Horace had written *vinclo*,
he would have used some other word than *remotus*
with it.

His Lucretius, which he published, to his credit, in
a handsome form, and, to his sorrow, with loss to his
purse, he disgraced, not only by this absurd rage for
conjecture, but by railing at Lambinus and others, far
better men than himself, as has been remarked in the
preface to the most recent English translation of that
author. But there was another point on which he exposed himself to censure; he made a great show of
having consulted manuscripts for various readings, but
did not always find in the manuscripts exactly what he

said that he found. This is shown in a review of the
edition in the " British Critic " for May 1801, of which
the chief part is understood to have been written by
Porson, and of which we must take due notice. It
commences thus :

" *Miror equidem doleoque, eò decidisse rem literariam, ut
à multis libri è chartis et typis magis quàm ex argumento
æstimentur.*

" ' We see with grief and astonishment the state of letters
so fallen, that, by multitudes, books are valued rather for the
type and paper than for the value of the contents.'

" It will readily be granted, by men of sense and judgment,
that an edition of a classical author is by no means to be
estimated from the beauty of the type, the fineness of the
paper, or the elegant proportions and arrangements of the
page. If these matters could afford foundation for a reasonable judgment, there could be no possible doubt about the
praises due to the present work. In its external form, the
book speaks abundantly for itself, nor can many editions of
the classics vie with it in that respect ; such only excepted
as exhibit merely a beautiful text, without any apparatus of
notes.

    *   *   *   *   *   *

" The notes of Mr. W. are indeed very numerous and
various ; philological, critical, illustrative, political ; such as
he always pours forth with a facility which judgment sometimes limps after in vain. A reader, however, must be more
than usually morose, who is not pleased with the strong and
lively relish which this annotator exhibits for the poetical
beauties of his author, and those of all the ancient classics ;
though, it is true, he sometimes rather overwhelms than
illustrates Lucretius by these incursions.

" But very distinct from the talent or feeling last mentioned is the power of reading with precision, and collating
with accuracy, a variety of ancient MSS. ; and on the degree
of success with which this difficult task has been performed,
must ultimately depend the characteristic value of the present

edition above others: the correction of the author's text, by these means, being particularly promised in the title-page and preface."

The reviewer then proceeds to remark that,

"with every allowance made for a labour in which the acutest eye will sometimes be deceived, and the most determined sagacity will sometimes remit its attention, Mr. Wakefield cannot receive the palm of a skilful or scrupulously accurate collator."

He observes that Mr. Wakefield had examined five manuscripts, one in the Public Library at Cambridge, one belonging to Edward Poore, Esq., and three Harleian manuscripts in the British Museum; that the first two of these were not within the reviewer's reach, but that he had examined the three Harleian manuscripts, taking the first two hundred and fifty lines of the first book, and a passage at hazard from the third book. After a few preliminary remarks on these collations, he says, on ver. 78,

"Mr. W. has published, 'Irritat animi virtutem, effringere ut arta;' and adds this note: 'Hanc constitutionem versûs, quam ex auctoritate librorum dederim, proprium acumen ingenii priùs expediverat. Verborum ordinem præbent G. B. L. M. Δ. Π. Σ.' (the three last being the Harleian MSS.). 'Solus Σ. conjecturam firmat, *effringere* scribens pro *confringere;* quam tamen necessariam reddidit codicum modo memoratorum ratio. In P. V. ed. (plurimis veteribus editionibus) Δ. Π. Σ. ordo est verborum *Irritât virtutem animi. Ω. irritant.*'

"The third sentence of this note forgets the second. If Δ. Π. Σ. and other MSS. give the order of words which Mr. W. has preferred, that is to say, *Irritât animi virtutem*, how can the same Δ. Π. Σ. give this other order, Irritât virtutem animi? Our collation furnishes the following account of the MSS., and we can fully assert its correctness, if the printer does but well and duly perform his part:

"Δ. Irritāt animi virtutē : effringere et arcta.

"Π. Irritat v̇ tutē āi cōfingere ut arcta.

"Σ. Irritat āi virtutē ëffrīge᾽ ut arcta.

The two points over the ë in *ëffringere* refer the reader to the margin, in which it is written *cöfrīgere.*

"In the sequel of the note, and in three sets of addenda, Mr. W. pours forth an army of examples to prove the frequent use of the word *effringere.* Nonius, in the word *cupiret,* x. 16., quotes the passage with *perfringere,* which, though much rarer than *effringere,* is good Latin. According therefore to the critical canon, which directs the more recondite reading to be preferred, *perfringere* would stand a good chance of success. But this canon has too often, and especially of late years, been pushed beyond all reason and modesty. 'Priscianus vulgatis consentit' (x. p. 879, 15), says Mr. W., but there Aldus gives *effringere.* Towards the end of the note Mr. W. says, 'Porro, pro *ut,* Δ. *et,* et in versu sequente *cuperet* G. B. L., *caperet* Π.'

"Here is an error, either of the editor or printer, for neither Π. nor any one of the Museum MSS. gives *caperet.* In Δ. it is plainly *cupiret;* in Π. and Σ. as plainly *aperiret.* It appears then that Mr. W., in his assertions concerning these three MSS., has been oftener in the wrong than in the right."

"V. 156. 'Versus 156, 157, 158 desunt in Π.,' says Mr. W. Verse 156 is not omitted in Π., but only 157, 158. The verses follow in this order : 154, 155, 159, 156, 160. In the 159th verse Mr. W. has noticed that Π. gives *divinum* for *divom;* but he should also have remarked that it gives *quocumque* for *quo quæque.*"

In regard to the collation of the passage in B. III. the reviewer says,

"V. 1006. Mr. W. conjectures Quem volucris, *lacerat.* This very reading, *totidem apicibus,* is in Π. This is therefore an error of omission.

"V. 1068. 'E : ita conjeceram legendum, et ita scribitur

in Vind. L. M. O. Ω. Cæteri libri, ut evulgari solet, habent *Et. Quoque noscere:* P. Π. *cognoscere,* ut *communes editi.'* All the three Harleian MSS. with one accord give *E;* two of them, Π. and Σ., *quoque noscere.* This therefore is an error of commission."

The conclusion of the article, whether wholly from Porson's hand or not, is as follows :

" In thus examining the present edition of Lucretius, we feel a strong confidence that we shall not be suspected of being actuated by any resentment against a person who must himself feel the chief evils of a restless, impatient, intolerant mind. We think it, indeed, most lamentable, that a man, whose proper occupations are study and polite literature, should be so little able to command himself, as to fall into extravagances of political conduct, injurious ultimately to himself and family. Too many instances of this spirit appear, completely out of their place, in this edition of Lucretius ; in the form of political verses, allusions to the glories of France, and aspirations after similar changes here, with prophetic intimations of their approach. In such a farrago, abuse of us and our work, as supporting all that Mr. W. wishes to see overthrown, is virtually the highest compliment; and though we owe no gratitude to the intentions of the author, we cannot but approve the tendency of his conduct towards us.

" We see, however, in his pages, not the slightest tincture of the character which he has, very early in his preface, bestowed upon himself, *si quis unquam, diffidens mei.* A most extravagant self-confidence, on the contrary, is everywhere conspicuous, except in a few of these prefatory flourishes ; and though his maturer judgment has enabled him to see in his own *Silva Critica,* 'plurima quæ sint juveniliter temeraria, ἀπροσδιόνυσα prorsus, et homine critico indigna,' yet the very same character, unimproved, will be found to prevail in his critical conjectures, scattered abundantly throughout the notes to this work, and readily accessible by means of his critical index. No author escapes his rage for correction ; and Horace and Virgil, in particular, would have as little know-

ledge of their own works, were they presented to them re-
formed *à la Wakefield,* as we should of the British constitution, were it given to his emendation. We can, however,
pity while we censure; and most sincerely wish that, with a
more temperate mind, even in literature, he would give himself exclusively, and without mixture, to those studies in
which, with all his failings, he has certainly made a proficiency not common among the scholars of this country."

By his political follies Wakefield brought on himself
a hard, but not unmerited, fate. He could see nothing
right in the administration of his country. He went
to the House of Commons to hear Mr. Pitt speak, and
thought him a monster, dire as any that had ever issued
from the Stygian flood, because he had not proved
himself the reformer that he had promised to be. He
adopted the vilest jacobinical notions, which he pro-
mulgated in English tracts, in his Latin prefaces and
notes to his editions of the classics, and in every other
method within his reach. His " Reply to the Bishop
of Llandaff's Address to the People of Great Britain"
contained such vehement abuse of the civil authorities,
and such treasonable expressions of hope that the
French would invade and conquer England, that the
ministry, who would have been weak to let it pass,
commenced a prosecution against the author, the termination of which was a sentence to two years' im-
prisonment in Dorchester gaol; a punishment which his
sedition fully deserved, though the gaoler seems to have
been permitted to treat him too tyrannically during
his confinement. Shortly after his release he died of a
fever, contracted by taking long walks, of which he had
been extremely fond before his incarceration, but for
which restraint and inaction had unfitted him. He is

to be pitied for his want of judgment and self-control, both as a scholar and a politician. Parr observed that he " united the simplicity of a child with the fortitude of a martyr ; " * that is, in plainer phrase, he combined great folly with great obstinacy.

In March 1801, Eichstädt despatched to Porson the first volume of his Diodorus Siculus, accompanied with the following highly complimentary letter. But, as the difficulty of transmission from the continent to England was at that time very great, the parcel was stopped at Hamburg. In May he sent it off again, attaching to his letter a postscript.

" *To the most celebrated* RICHARD PORSON,
     HENR. CAROLUS ABR. EICHSTÄDT, *Professor at*
     Jena, wishes health.

" Some time ago, when I was engaged in giving instruction at the University of Leipsic, I happened to form an intimate acquaintance with a very excellent man, Mr. Herbert Marsh, who, though he was distinguished by eminent merit of his own, both for talents and learning, seemed to me, nevertheless, to have still greater recommendation to notice from enjoying the friendship and regard of a gentleman so highly honoured as yourself. He spoke to me so frequently of your kindness, and in such handsome terms, that having long known and admired your extensive and exquisite learning, which is aided by eminent acuteness of judgment, I began, as I contemplated your excellent qualities of mind, even to conceive an affection for you. That feeling was strengthened by time, and, from your notes on Euripides, giving proofs alike of perspicacity and elegance, gradually assumed such force, that I often felt in my mind the most ardent desire to testify publicly my respect for you. Modesty caused long hesitation;

* Stephens's Memoirs of H orne Tooke, vol. i. p. 316.

but my good feeling towards you at length prevailed, and
gained such influence over me, that I resolved not only to
send you my Diodorus Siculus, which I have lately proceeded
to publish, but even to place it under your protection by a
public dedication. If you regard this determination of mine
as I should wish, I shall be extremely delighted, and, as I
have written with truth at the end of my preface to
Diodorus, shall consider it the commencement of a favourable
judgment from the world; or, if my hopes of praise be disappointed, you will nevertheless not wholly despise the affectionate expressions of a mind deeply devoted to you.

"But while I am speaking of my preface, let me say, most
excellent Porson, how much I should wish to ask another
favour of you, if I might do so without appearing presumptuous. There are illustrations, doubtless, either discoverable
in the libraries of your happy Britain, or the produce of your
own admirable genius, with which my edition of Diodorus
might be greatly improved. If your kindness would oblige
me with any portion of these, I should then, believe me, consider that I had done something useful in undertaking the
duty of an editor.

"This request, if I were not afraid of transgressing all
bounds of modesty, I would gladly extend to Lucretius, of
whom, at the will and pleasure of a bookseller, I have lately
commenced an edition, which is to be such as to present all
that is good in Wakefield's, with some additional annotations
of my own, if I can produce any. Wakefield's edition, indeed, has long been scarce among us, both because of Bentley's great name being connected with it, and because it is
sold at a price too heavy for German poverty. A man of
such knowledge as you, Sir, will easily be able to produce
abundance of matter to throw new light on Lucretius, and to
rectify the learning of your countryman, which has rather
been poured out rashly than drawn forth considerately. But
that my edition of that author should be graced with such
adornment, I venture rather to wish, than to hope or to request of you; for I know that Porsoniana cannot worthily be
attached to anything inferior to Toupiana. Farewell, illus-

trious Sir, and may you long enjoy with happiness the glory
which your merits have secured you.

"Jena, March 1, 1801."

" *To the honourable and most learned Professor of
the Greek Language,* Mr. RICHARD PORSON, *at Cambridge.*

" POSTSCRIPT.—It happens, with very unlucky omen, most
excellent Porson, that the letter which I sent you two months
ago, with a copy of Diodorus, has been sent back to me from
Hamburg; for some obstruction, I know not what, in the
public mode of conveyance, has prevented it from finding
its way into Great Britain. I have therefore sought for
another method of transmitting my communications to you,
and the opportunity of Leipsic fair has presented one. May
Apollo grant that the little offering which you should long
ago have received may not be returned to me a second time!
This delay, however, though for other reasons very disagreeable to me, is attended with this advantage, that, as the first
volume of my Lucretius has in the mean time issued from the
press, I have been enabled to add it, without hesitation, to
the Diodorus; for I hoped that if my plan of editing Lucretius should not be wholly disapproved by you, you would feel
more inclined to grant the favour which I asked of you somewhat too boldly in the preceding letter. Receive, therefore,
with favourable regard, that which I offer you with hopeful
anticipations, and bestow your good wishes on me and my
attempts.

"Jena, May 23, 1801.
    "Joined a Book signated M. R. P.,
                Cambridge.
Free.   Hamburg."

But Eichstädt had the same cause for complaint as
most of those who wrote letters to Porson. He waited
more than a year without receiving any notice that his
books had reached the end of their journey, and in

June 1802 addressed another letter to the silent Professor.

" *To the most learned and celebrated* Mr. RICHARD PORSON, HENR. CAROL. ABR. EICHSTÄDT, *Professor at Jena, wishes the greatest health.*

" It is almost a year, most excellent Porson, since I sent you a letter accompanied with the first volumes of Diodorus and Lucretius, which, through my efforts, such as they were, had made their way into the world.   To Diodorus I had prefixed your own honoured name, as a πρόσωπον τηλαυγές, that I might testify, at least by a respectful preface, that esteem for you which I had no other means of expressing. I prefixed the names also of Coray, Wolff, and Wyttenbach, who, with yourself, so eminently adorn and support the cause of learning, that no age, in my opinion, has ever seen a more illustrious quatuorvirate of critics.   Those three great men accepted my tribute of good-will in such a spirit as I desired, and viewed my work with such favour that they not only forgave the presumption of the dedicator, but contributed their efforts to illustrate the writer whom I had dedicated to them.   From you, most honoured Porson, I have received no answer, whether because my offerings are thought unworthy of your acceptance, or whether (as I would rather suppose) because my letter and books have not found their way into your hands; for the parcel of books, after having been detained a long time at Hamburg, was at length sent back to me with a note from the prefect of public transport at Hamburg, signifying that it could not be transmitted unless it bore the name of some Hamburg merchant, to whose charge it must be intrusted. I accordingly sent off the books a second time, addressed to Bohn, a Hamburg bookseller, by whom they were consigned to Geisweiler, a bookseller of London, who was then returning from Leipsic, and to whom they were intrusted on the express condition that they should be conveyed to you by his agency. I am therefore extremely desirous to know whether Geisweiler kept his promise, and took care that what was consigned to him, not without expense, was faithfully delivered.

" The second volume of my Diodorus has been recently published. I have a copy set apart for you, but keep it at home, through fear of trusting it to the hazards of travelling. I accordingly request you, most excellent Porson, unless my efforts find no favour with you, to let me know, as soon as possible, by what means this volume may be sent to London, and to whom it should be addressed. For, the more desirous I am to make my respect and esteem known to you, the more anxiously must I take care that my letters and books, the indications of my regard, may not fail of their purpose and object. Farewell, most worthy of men, and look on me with favour.

"Jena, June 1, 1802."

Whether Porson ever had the grace to acknowledge the receipt of the books, is unknown.

CHAP. XXI.

WITH the last edition of the Hecuba, the published labours of Porson on Euripides terminated. It has been stated in print that he left a transcript of the Hippolytus ready for the press, but, if he did so, it has never had the fortune to meet the eye of the public.

Maltby understood from Dr. Raine that such a transcript had been prepared, but it was not to be found among Porson's papers, he said, at his death. The doctor seems to have had a strong impression that it had been stolen, and to have intimated to Maltby whom he suspected; and Barker, from a conversation that he had with Maltby on the subject, concluded that either Upcott or Savage, the sub-librarian of the London Institution, was the object of Raine's suspicion.[*] Monk, when he published the play, had a portion of it,

* Barker's Lit. Anecdotes, vol. i. p. 63.

from ver. 176 to 266, corrected and written out in Porson's hand, and had heard Porson say that he felt no doubt of having restored that passage to the state in which it had come from Euripides himself.* No other portion is mentioned as having fallen into Monk's hands.

Some notes were also left by Porson on the two Iphigenias and the Supplices, but these had been made when he was very young, and required careful revision. Many of them are given in the Glasgow " Variorum " edition. Why he did not continue his attention to Euripides, and endeavour, as he expressed it, *to complete the web which he had begun to weave*, is a question that has often been asked. The true answer to it, we fear, is that he was fast falling, deeper and deeper, into habits which unfitted him for steady perseverance in any kind of mental labour, so that his days were either wasted in indolence, or employed only in desultory efforts that ended in little or nothing. A man who, in health that had long been far from good, spent his evenings, and perhaps his nights, in convivial indulgence, would be but ill fitted for toilsome research and calm disquisition. If he was naturally indolent, too, and averse to write, when he was in full vigour, and his head clear, how much more would this be the case when he was debilitated and overclouded!

About this period, or not long before, he was offered by the London booksellers 3000*l.* for an edition of Aristophanes, which, with his knowledge of that author, he might have completed, in Dr. Raine's opinion, in six months; but the money proved no inducement to him to commence it.

* Monk's Pref. to the Hippol.

During the six years, however, that elapsed between the appearance of the second edition of his Hecuba and his death, he was not wholly idle, but made exertions, from time to time, to do something. In October 1802, having observed that he had made a mistake in his note on the 782nd verse of the Hecuba by proposing to read, at the end of Androm. 1116, ἔτυχε δ' ὢν ἐν ἐμπύροις, without noticing that the commencement was εὔξαιτο Φοίβῳ, he wrote the following letter on the subject to the editor of the " Monthly Review ;" intending subsequently to translate it into Latin, and incorporate it in a body of *addenda* to the play, " which," in Mr. Kidd's phrase, " were appropriated to high matter seasoned with a little wholesome chastisement." This intention, however, he left wholly unexecuted.

" Sir,

" I agree with Mr. Cogan, that the passages of Euripides and Sophocles sufficiently defend one another, and prove, at least in poetry, the legitimate use of the verb τυγχάνειν, without the participle ὤν.

" My friend, Mr. C. Falconer, jun., pointed out to me another mistake in Mr. Porson's note, which Mr. Cogan has omitted to correct, either through forbearance or oversight. If in Euripides, Androm. 1116, we read [εὔξαιτο Φοίβῳ] ἔτυχε δ' ὢν ἐν ἐμπύροις, there will be an *hiatus valde deflendus*, which Mr. Porson will, I dare say, retract, when it is mentioned to him. I draw this conclusion from two of his own notes, one upon the 571st verse of the Hecuba, where he quotes with approbation my namesake's (Dawes, Misc. Crit. pp. 216, 217) censure of a similar mistake of King's ; the other on Orestes, v. 792, where Mr. Porson proposes a conjecture to remedy the same fault in a comic poet.

" While I am on this subject of the hiatus, it may not be improper to rescue another passage from the attacks of critics. Machon (Athenæus xiii. p. 580 D.) tells us that Gnathæna, seeing a young butcher, said to him, Μειράκιον ὁ καλός, φησί, πῶς ἵστης, φράσον; 'My pretty lad, tell me how you sell (your meat).' Your readers, Sir, who recollect Shallow's questions, 'How a good yoke of bullocks at Stamford fair?' 'How a score of ewes now?'[*] will readily agree that πῶς ἵστης is at least good English. But Lennep, in a note upon Phalaris, p. 95, 1, will not allow it to be good Greek; so corrects it to πόσου ἵστης, and falls into the error I have just exposed. Mr. Jacobs, in a note upon the Anthology, approves of Lennep's correction. Let us try to defend the vulgar reading by a quotation from Aristophanes, Eq. 478, Πῶς οὖν ὁ τυρὸς ἐν Βοιωτοῖς ὤνιος; but, see what a general prejudice has taken place in behalf of πόσου against poor πῶς! Gerard Horreus would read πόσου δ' ὁ τυρός. This conjecture Pierson (on Mœris, p. 424) refutes by producing Acharn. 768, Τί δ' ἄλλο, Μεγαροῖ πῶς ὁ σῖτος ὤνιος; to which when your readers have added a fragment of Strattis (apud Polluc. iv. 169), Τὰ δ' ἄλφιτ' ὑμῖν πῶς ἐπώλουν; τεττάρων Δραχμῶν μάλιστα τὸν κόφινον, they will consent to let Machon and Aristophanes enjoy their old reading.

"I am, Sir, &c.

"JOHN NIC. DAWES.[†]

"Oct. 1ĭ. 1802."

In July 1803, a fragment of a statue of Ceres, which had been brought from Eleusis, was to be placed in the vestibule of the Cambridge University Library, and Porson was requested to write the inscription for it:

SIMULACHRI . CERERIS . FRAGMENTUM
ELEUSINE . DEPORTATUM
POSUERUNT
EDVARDUS . DANIEL . CLARKE . ET
JOANNES . MARTEN . CRIPPS
JESU . COLLEGII . ALUMNI
A. D. M.DCCC.III.[‡]

---

[*] Shaksp. 2 Hen. IV. 3, 2.   [†] Kidd, Tracts, pp. 151—153.
[‡] Kidd, Tracts, p. lxxvii.

S

Some time previously, the famous Rosetta stone, a block of black marble, engraven with three inscriptions, in hieroglyphics, in the Coptic or native language of Egypt, and in Greek, all of the same import, setting forth the services which Ptolemy the Fifth had done to his country, and decreeing, in the name of the priests assembled at Memphis, various honours to be paid to him, had been brought to England, and deposited in the British Museum ; and Porson, fixing his attention on the Greek, the last twenty-six lines of which are considerably mutilated, restored it, in a great measure, by conjecture, and gave a translation of it. These results of his critical skill he presented, in January 1803, to the Antiquarian Society, who printed them, but not till several years after his death, in the sixteenth volume of their Transactions.* While he was exercising his sagacity on the stone, he visited the Museum so often, to read and consider it, that he got from the officials the name of "Judge Blackstone." †

In the "Monthly Review" for September 1801, James Tate, then a very young man, had made some remarks on Porson's Preface to the "Hecuba," and particularly on the subject of *the pause*. Having a great respect for Porson, he was pleased to find some of his observations supported in the Supplement to the Preface, which appeared in 1802 ; and Dalzel, to whom he was known, admitted a paper of his, on Greek metres, into the Preface to his "Analecta." Dalzel soon after wrote to Porson, and observed, in his letter, that he did not suppose Porson looked much into Reviews,

---

* Museum Criticum, vol. ii. pp. 159, 329.
† Short Account of Porson, p. 18.

or he would probably have taken some notice of Tate's paper.

These observations drew from Porson the following letter, which, passing into the hands of Tate, was by him sent to the "Museum Criticum."

R. PORSON *to* A. DALZEL.

"Essex Court, No. 5, Sep. 3, 1803.

"DEAR SIR,

"Our friend Mr. Laing being in town, and on the eve of his departure for the north, I could not find in my heart to take leave of him without troubling him to bear this trifling token of my esteem, public and private, for Mr. Dalzel.

"It is unpleasant enough at any rate to be engaged in controversy; unpleasant with an enemy; but still more unpleasant with a friend. A few minutes' conversation would generally decide a question better than volumes of dispute. I shall therefore be very concise, and only take the liberty of mentioning a very few points in which you seem to have either misconceived, or not fully conceived my meaning.

"You suppose me not to have seen (p. 164) the 'Monthly Review' for Sep. 1801. It is of no consequence whether I saw it or not. The Canon concerning the fifth foot of a Senarian was already published in the first edition of 'Hecuba.'

"A gentleman who sent me some anonymous remarks on the 'Hecuba' dated June 7th, 1798, has these words on v. 347. 'Nobody seemed to know the meaning of this note, till an imperfect account in the 'Monthly Review' (a short time since) appeared written, as it is said, by Dr Burney. It was mentioned to me three years ago by Dr. Goodall.' This last sentence is capable of two interpretations. 1. The editor of 'Hecuba' needed not to produce this observation as a discovery of his own, since it was already taught by an eminent scholar at our most famous school. 2. The editor of 'Hecuba' stole this observation from Dr. Goodall, and published it as his own.

"If our friends can indulge themselves in such candid in-

s 2

nuendoes, what are we to expect from our rivals and enemies? Godfrey Herman's note upon this passage is a model
of learning and liberality. He is exceedingly angry that I
made the remark at all. He is also very angry that I had
any remark to make upon iambic verses after his elaborate
treatise concerning metres. He is still more angry that I
wrapped up my Canon in studied obscurity. The fact, he
grants, is true; but, if I had given my mind to it, could I
not have discovered the reason of the fact? for if the editor
pretends that he passed by the reason, on account of its extreme easiness, Mr. Herman is resolved not to believe him.
'Now,' quoth he, 'what the editor reprehends in this verse,
if we retain τοὔμπαλιν, *cannot be any thing else* than the
spondee in the fifth place.' And then he goes on to say,
that a spondee in the fifth place has nothing in it reprehen-
sible.* I will consent to be called as ignorant of metre and
harmony as Leclerc, Reiske, and Herman, if I ever said or
thought any thing like the proposition that Mr. Herman has
fathered upon me. I must have been an accurate reader of
Euripides, to have disapproved of a Spondee in the fifth place
of a trimeter iambic, when, of the fifty-eight verses that
begin the 'Hecuba,' twenty-seven, at the lowest reckoning,
would oppose my Canon. To the candid observations of
Godfrey Herman, I shall only answer by a quotation from
Valckenaer's dissertation on the unpublished Scholia upon
Homer (post Ursini Virgilium cum Græcis collatum, Llo-
vardiæ, 1747, p. 147). 'Quum illud—monuerat *Canterus,*
biennio post, invidus sæpe virtutis alienæ obtrectator, *Henr.
Stephanus,* ita libello renovato præfatus est, ut cupidè velit
videri non ignoravisse quod Canterus detexerat.'

It may perhaps divert you to insert an epigram, made by
an Etonian, a friend of mine, upon the said Herman, in
imitation of Phocylides's saw†, (Strabo, X. p. 487, ed. Par.)

Νήϊδες ἐστὲ μέτρων, ὦ Τεύτονες·   οὐχ ὁ μὲν, ὃς δ' οὔ·
Πάντες, πλὴν "ΕΡΜΑΝΝΟΣ· ὁ δ' "ΕΡΜΑΝΝΟΣ σφόδρα Τεύτων.

---

* Vide Hecubam Hermanni, p. 108, quam totam perlegas velim.
† Καὶ τόδε Φωκυλίδεω.   Λέριοι κακοί· οὐχ ὁ μὲν, ὃς δ' οὔ·
     Πάντες, πλὴν Προκλέους· καὶ Προκλέης Λέριος.

Νή,δες ἐστὲ μέτρων, ὦ Τεύτονες, οὐχ ὁ μὲν, ὅσδου!
Πάντες, πλὴν Ἕρμαννος· ὁ δ' Ἕρμαννος σφόδρα Τεύτων.

The Germans in Greek
Are sadly to seek;
Not five in fivescore,
But ninety-five more:
ALL, save only Herman,
And *Herman's a German.

Καὶ τόδε Φωκυλίδεω· Λέριοι
κακοὶ, οὐχ ὁ μὲν, ὅσδ' οὐ·
Πάντες, πλὴν Προκλέους· καὶ
Προκλέης Λέριος.

* Or, "he is a."

ὁ μετρικός, ὁ σοφός, ἄτοπα γέγραφε περὶ μέτρων.
ὁ μετρικός ἄμετρος, ὁ σοφός ἄσοφος ἐγένετο.

From the original in the possession of the Rev. H. R. Luard, Trin. Coll. Cambridge.

which I thus endeavoured to do into English;

> ' The Germans in Greek
> Are sadly to seek ;
> Not five in five score,
> But ninety-five more :
> All ; save only HERMAN,
> And HERMAN's a German.'

"It is a known principle in iambic verse, that the iambic may be resolved into a tribrach, in any place but the last. As Mr. Herman has not given any striking instances of this resolution in his incomparable treatise, I shall try to supply the defect :

'Ο μετρικὸς, ὁ σοφὸς, ἄτοπα γέγραφε περὶ μέτρων.
'Ο μετρικὸς ἄμετρος, ὁ σοφὸς ἄσοφος ἐγένετο.

"But to return.   You say (p. 164) that I have not tried to correct the middle example,

"Ατλας ὁ χαλκέοισι νώτοις οὐρανόν.

What? I who had said in my preface, ed. 1, p. xv. "Tutissima proinde corrigendi ratio est, vocularum, si opus est, transpositio."—I could not change the situation of νώτοις and χαλκέοισι? Surely we wanted no Herman nor Tate to rise from the dead, and tell us this. I rank Herman among the dead, upon the strength of Aristophanes's authority :

Νυνὶ δὲ δημαγωγεῖ
'Εν τοῖς ἄνω νεκροῖσι·
Κἄστιν τὰ πρῶτα τῆς ἐκεῖ μοχθηρίας.   (Ran. 422.)

"But this fruitful article of transposition we will put off, if you, Sir, have no objection, to the postscript, and we will go on with the parœmiac anapæst. The anapæstic verses in which four short syllables meet are so few, that I thought it would be an impertinent digression to mention them; but I was partly induced to quote the Medea 1085, by having seen Mr. Tate's new-fangled Canon before its publication. At that time he seems not to have been aware of a prior exception in the same play, 114. But be that as it may, his emendations are both wrong, for this plain reason, that they utterly demolish the emphasis.   One of John Milton's answerers had reproached him with the heinous crime of being low of stature.   Milton in reply says, that to be sure he is not very tall, but he is nearer the middle size, than the small.   Where, however, adds he, would be the harm, if I were diminutive?   Which idea he expresses in these words, ' But what if I were little?'   Now it is impossible that Milton could arrange these words in this order.   He wrote, he could not help writing, ' But what, if little I were?'   On this head see more in the postscript.

" I could easily amend (that is to say, new write) all the parœmiacs that begin with a dactyl, because they are so very scarce; but let it be considered that the proportion of parœmiacs to other anapæsts is scarcely one in ten, and therefore, *a priori*, those which begin with a dactyl must be rare indeed. If we had only Sophocles's tragedies left us, I am doubtful whether we should have above one clear exception (Œd. C. 177),

$$\text{}^7\Omega\ \gamma\acute{\epsilon}\rho o\nu,\ \ddot{a}\kappa o\nu\tau\acute{a}\ \tau\iota\varsigma\ \ddot{a}\xi\epsilon\iota,$$

for the verse that follows a little after,

$$B\acute{\eta}\mu a\tau o\varsigma\ \ddot{\epsilon}\xi\omega\ \pi\acute{o}\delta a\ \kappa\lambda\acute{\iota}\nu\eta\varsigma,$$

may be easily eluded by aid of the Scholiast, $\kappa\iota\nu\acute{\eta}\sigma\eta\varsigma$.   But the whole quantity of anapæsts in Sophocles is so small, that it would be idle to frame a Canon upon such precarious foundations.   When I said that transposition was a very safe remedy, I did not mean that people might transpose as they liked.   Dawes lays down a rule, which, if he had been content with calling it general instead of universal, is perfectly right, that a syllable is long, in which the middle consonants β, γ, δ, and liquids, except ρ, meet.   But several passages, as well as the following, contradict this rule.   Œd. T. 717, $\pi a\iota\delta\grave{o}\varsigma\ \delta\grave{\epsilon}\ \beta\lambda a\sigma\tau\grave{a}\varsigma$ —   Elect. 440, $\pi a\sigma\hat{\omega}\nu\ \ddot{\epsilon}\beta\lambda a\sigma\tau\epsilon$.   These passages may be reduced to Dawes's Canon by transposition; but they will lose all their energy by the reduction.   See Brunck's note on Philoct. 222.

"V. 389. If I may believe Messrs. Dalzel and Tate, I have here forgotten my own rule, in not finding fault with σοφαί. — Certainly, if no stronger objections against Dawes's Canon can be produced, it will suffer no material hurt. In Soph. Electr. 399, Triclinius altered τιμωρούμενοι into the feminine. In Eurip. Hippol. 350, Brunck has rightly edited κεχρημένοι from his membranæ. πεφύκαμεν σοφαί is not ' I Medea am expert,' but, ' We women are expert.'—Euripides, the woman-hater, could not miss the opportunity of libelling the sex.   Ion. 629. ῞Οσας σφαγὰς δὴ, φαρμάκων τε θανασίμων Γυναῖκες εὖρον ἀνδράσιν διαφθοράς.   There is a stronger objection against Dawes's rule in Hippol. 1120, than can be brought, I believe, from any other quarter.

"But my friends have a very funny way of reasoning upon these subjects.   ' Mr. Porson says, that the Attic tragic poets seldom suffer such verses as, ῎Ατλας ὁ χαλκέοισι νώτοις οὐρανὸν—Ergo, he does not know of such verses as Ἀριόμαρδος Σάρδεσιν, μετώπων σωφρόνων, αἱματωποὺς ἐκβαλών, &c.' * ' Mr. Porson says that the tragic poets would not write such a verse as Ἀτὰρ τί ταῦτ' ὀδύρομαι τὰ δ' ἐν ποσὶν—Ergo, he did not remember, Εἰσῆλθε τοῖν τρισαθλίοιν ἔρις κακή. † ῾Η κάρτ' ἄρ' ἂν παρεσκόπεις χρησμῶν ἐμῶν, &c.'

"Another learned gentleman sends me some anonymous criticisms upon the 'Hecuba,' and on v. 639-640 says, 'Perhaps the learned Professor did not know that this passage is quoted by Eustathius (Il. Γ. p. 301, 16).'   Perhaps the learned Professor knew that not only that passage was quoted by Eustathius, but also another from the same play, 446, which has escaped the notice of the Monthly Reviewer, p. 332. This question may however be decided by any person, who will take the trouble of consulting the appendix to Toup, ed. Oxon. vol. IV. p. 504, compared with Brunck's Soph. Fragment. Helen.

" And now, Sir, I release you from a long and tedious letter. Notwithstanding the appearance of dissent my letter wears,

* British Critic, vol. x. Dec. 1797, p. 615.
† Ibid. p. 616.

be assured that there are very few men, for whom I entertain a greater respect and affection, than Mr. Dalzel; and I
trust he will believe me, when I affirm that I am his
obliged humble servant,

" R. Porson.

"P.S. Mr. Gilbert Wakefield, ὁ μακαρίτης, found a MS. in
the British Museum, containing an unedited hymn (as he
believed) of Proclus, which he therefore communicated with
the public in his Silva Critica, P. IV. p. 252, and printed
the four first verses thus:

Ὑμνος κοινος

Κλυτε, θεοι, ἱερης σοφιης οιηκας εχοντες·
Οἱ ψυχαις μεροπων αναγωγιον ἁψαμενοι φως,
Ἑλκτης αθανατων, σκοτιον κευθμωνα λιπουσαις,
Ὑμων αρρητῃσι καθηραμεναις τελετῃσι.

Annotatiunculæ quædam (a G. W. sc.):

vers. 2. ανθρωπων— MS. *Possis* ανδρων, *sed illud his Scripto-*
ribus usitatius.

vers. 3. ἑλκτης—*trahentibus*—*bibentibus*—*immortalia.* Ἐλκυτης
—ψυχας—λιπουσας—καθηραμενας. — MS.

"First and foremost, Mr. W. it seems, did not know that
this hymn was already extant in all the printed copies of
Proclus (vide Brunck. Analect. II. p. 443).

"Secondly, he might, even without the help of the editions,
have corrected the hiatus, by reading σοφίης ἱερῆς, if he had
an ear.

"Thirdly, he confesses to have made four conjectural emendations upon the third and fourth verses.

"Now, Sir, you may perhaps have some difficulty in believing that I have consulted this self-same individual MS., and

β   a

that in the first verse it is thus written, ἱερῆς σοφίης, by which
marks, very common in MSS., the scribe corrected his own
error.

"But if you believe this, I hardly expect you to believe that,
instead of ἑλκυτης, the MS. has ἕλκετ' ἐς ἀθανάτων as plain as

I have written it, and just as the printed books have it, except that they less elegantly give ἀθανάτους. Something too much of this.

"There is a passage of Sophocles three times quoted by Plutarch, and always in a different order, but so as in the three variations to remain a Senarian. Now the fragment consists of five words, and the sense is this: '(The physicians) wash away bitter bile with bitter drugs.' The five words, you know, will admit of one hundred and twenty permutations, and, what is extremely odd, these words will admit twenty transpositions, and still constitute a trimeter iambic.

"Now, as Sophocles certainly wrote these words in one order, and no more, the problem is, so to construct the verse as Sophocles wrote it. I shall first set down the words themselves in the English order, and then the different positions in which the words can be put, still retaining the iambic metre.

$$\begin{array}{ccccc} a & \beta & \gamma & \delta & \epsilon \end{array}$$

κλύζουσι πικρὰν χολὴν πικροῖς φαρμάκοις.

αβεγδ	βγαδε
αβεδγ	βγαεδ
αδεβγ	γβαδε
αδεγβ	δβαεγ Plut. 1.
αεβγδ	δγαβε
αεβδγ	δγαεβ
αεγβδ	γδαβε
αεγδβ	γδαεβ Plut. 2.
αεδβγ	
αεδγβ	

"The Scrap annexed you will understand, by comparing Euripides Iph. in Aul. Scen. 1, with Stobæus Serm. 103, in any edition but Grotius's.

"[The Scrap so annexed was a highly finished and exquisite copy of four different MSS. of Iph. Aul. vv. 29—33, illustrating what he calls the 'fruitful article of transposition,' and his own inimitable calligraphy, at one and the same time.—J. T.]"

In transmitting this letter to the "Muscum Criticum," Tate observed that his canon, as Porson called it, respecting the parœmiac anapæst, was so far from being "new-fangled," that it had been mentioned as well known by Bentley in his "Emendations on Menander,"* *anapæstos ubique terminari versu parœmiaco, qui posterius colon est hexametri.* "Verum Bernardus," he adds, "non vidit omnia." He admits, however, that the canon was "unquestionably wrong, unless he had been content with calling it general instead of universal."

Dalzel, in reply to Porson's epistle, which he calls γλυκύπικρος, wrote another of ten pages†, in which he addresses Porson with the greatest courtesy, saying that he had intended no innuendo against him, but had, on the contrary, spoken of him with the highest praise in the second edition of the "Analecta;" that, in noticing that he had not tried to correct the middle example, *secundum non moratur,* he meant only that he had left it as an easy matter for any ordinary scholar. He then tells a story of Reid, who, when a young man, travelling through Cambridge, sought an introduction to Bentley, who accosted him with "What, has my fame reached even your *ultima Thule?*" assuring Porson that not only had his fame reached Scotland, but that his name was had in honour by all who had any tincture of Greek literature. Of Wakefield he remarks that he "could never bring himself to think him a critic of any judgment," and that Porson has shown him to be altogether *sublestâ fide.* In regard to the passage of Sophocles, he very judiciously remarks, that to know the *proper collocation* of words in Greek and Latin is extremely difficult; that the order of the words in even the best modern writers of Latin, such as More, Erasmus, and Muretus, would not always have pleased an ancient ear; and that the words in the line of Sophocles could hardly be arranged in any order that would appear to be necessarily the order in which Sophocles put them.   He then concludes by lamenting that the public inclination is running so much towards chemistry, mineralogy, and such sciences, observing that there is some danger of our philosophers being reduced, when they meet with a piece of Greek, to say, like the monks of old, " Græcum est, non possum legere," but that he who, like Porson, is instrumental in preventing this kind of ignorance, is doing the greatest service to letters.

It was in 1803, also, that " Six More Letters to Granville Sharp, Esq., on his Remarks upon the Uses of the Article in the Greek Testament, by Gregory Blunt, Esq.," appeared; a pamphlet of about two hundred pages, which has been often said to have proceeded from the same hand that produced the Letters to Travis. The writer of the " Short Account of Porson " thought the style so like the Professor's that he felt " constrained to say either Blunt writes like Porson, or Porson like Blunt: Ἢ Λουθηρὸς Ἐρασμίζει, ἢ Ἔρασμος Λουθηρίζει :" either Luther Erasmizes or Erasmus Lutherizes.   Mr. Maltby had heard them asked for at a bookseller's shop as " Porson's Remarks on Sharp."   But the truth is, that he who seeks in these Letters for Porson's vigour, spirit, humour, and learning, as exhibited in the assault on Travis, will assuredly seek in vain; and he had little cause, as Mr. Kidd remarks, to thank such of his friends as paid him the compliment of pronouncing him the author. That he was not the author he assured Dr. Wordsworth, who mentions the fact in his preface to " Who wrote ΕΙΚΩΝ ΒΑΣΙΛΙΚΗ ?" But " he used to praise the work," according to Mr. Maltby, " and recommend it to his friends."

The chief design of these letters was to expose the fallacy of a proposition maintained by Granville Sharp, that " when, in Greek, the copulative καὶ connects two nouns of the same case, if the article is prefixed to the first of them, and is not repeated before the second, the second always relates to the same person that is expressed by the first." The writer who assumes the name of Blunt replies that, as the force and usage of the article in Greek are much the same as they are in modern languages, Mr. Sharp's rule might be tried in English as well as in Greek ; and that, unless mystery and obscurity had influenced his choice, he might have confined his examples within the pale of his own tongue, and thus have not only enabled every reader to judge of a question to which every person of common sense, though destitute of a knowledge of Greek, is competent, but might also, perhaps, have seen his own way more clearly before him. Thus he might have taken from St. Peter the phrase " the shepherd and bishop of your souls," and might have said that as the second noun has no article before it, it evidently refers to the same person as the first ; and might also have observed how different is the expression in Ezekiel, " the fatherless and the widow," where, as both nouns have articles, each denotes a different person. But some malicious questioner, adds Blunt, might ask Mr. Sharp whether he had no recollection of ever having seen such expressions as " the king and queen, the master and mistress, the son and daughter," and others of the same kind.   Or what would Mr. Sharp say, if one of those carnal spirits who are for "proving all things " should bring against him, from the book of Deuteronomy, the words " the judgment of the fatherless and widow? " His airy castle would be gone for ever, for one such puff would give it at once to the winds.

This will hardly serve for a confutation of Sharp's notions about the use of the article in Greek ; for the usage of the Greek article is less lax than that of the English.   Indeed the author of the Letters rather attempts to *play round the head* of the question than to *come to the heart* of it ; rather tries to amuse the reader by banter than to direct decisive attacks upon Sharp's position.   When Porson, however, was asked his opinion of Sharp's rule, he intimated distrust of it, and assigned such reasons for his distrust as appeared decisive to those that could judge of them.*

These Letters were called " Six More Letters to Granville Sharp," because "Six Letters " to him, in favour of his theory, had previously been published by Dr. Wordsworth.   Porson was perhaps the more ready to countenance the " Six More Letters " against the theory, as Bishop Burgess, whose scholarship he despised, had given it his support.

As to the authorship of these Letters, one of Dr. Disney's daughters has been heard to express her belief that they were written by an intimate friend of her father's, Mr. Thomas Pearne, Fellow and Tutor of St.

* Kidd, Tracts, p. 301.

Peter's College, Cambridge, a Unitarian, and good classical scholar. Dr. Disney himself knew who wrote them, but would not tell; but his daughter felt sure that she was right in her opinion as to the author.

In March 1804, Porson received a letter from Tittmann, Professor of Philosophy at Leipsic, and afterwards editor of Zonaras's Lexicon, stating that he designed to publish the Lexicon called Συναγώγη λεξέων χρησίμων, and soliciting Porson's assistance in finding a publisher, as well as any corrections or suggestions which he might be kind enough to supply, for the improvement of the work itself.* What was the result of the application we do not know. This is the last communication among Porson's papers from any Continental scholar.

* Porson's MSS. in the Library of Trin. Coll. Camb.

CHAP. XXII.

PORSON'S HABITS. — LORD BYRON'S ACCOUNT OF HIM AT COLLEGE. —
PORSON IN LONDON SOCIETY.—A LETTER OF HIS TO SURGEON JOY.—
HIS DRESS AND APPEARANCE. — VARIOUS ANECDOTES. — HIS VISIT TO
THE ASSEMBLY ROOMS AT BATH. — HIS FAVOURITE BEVERAGES. — HIS
CAPACITY FOR DRINKING AND SITTING UP AT NIGHT. — ENCOUNTER
WITH HORNE TOOKE.—ANECDOTE OF TOOKE AND BOSWELL.—PORSON'S
POTATION AT HOPPNER THE PAINTER'S. — HIS UNWILLINGNESS TO
RETIRE AT NIGHT FROM HIS FRIENDS' HOUSES. — FOND OF SMOKING.
—COULD OBSERVE ABSTINENCE.

OF Porson's habits at Cambridge something has been
seen in the earlier part of our biography. We are sorry
to find Lord Byron, at a later period, 1805, receiving
a still darker impression of them. It may be necessary
to make allowance, perhaps, for something of fastidiousness of taste in his lordship, but, with all reasonable
abatement, there must be some truth in what he tells
of the Professor. It is sad that such things should be
said, and sad that they cannot be fairly refuted. We
notice the passage with unwillingness, but we might be
accused of unjustifiable silence if we forbore to notice it.
It is to be found in a letter to Mr. Murray, written in
1818, after a perusal of the " Sexagenarian." *

His lordship says that he remembers to have seen
Porson at Cambridge, though not frequently ; that in
the hall, where he himself dined at the Vice-Master's
table, and Porson at the Dean's, he always appeared

* Moore's Byron, vol. iv. p. 94, ed. 1832.

sober in his demeanour, nor was he ever guilty, as far as
his lordship knew, of any excess or outrage in public ;
but that in an evening, with a party of undergraduates,
his behaviour would often be of a different character,
as he would, in fits of intoxication, get into violent
disputes with the young men, and revile them for not
knowing what he thought they might be expected to
know.   Lord Byron had seen him, he says, take up a
poker to one of them, using language corresponding in
violence to the action, and once saw him go away in
a rage because none of them knew the name of the
" Cobbler of Messina," insulting their ignorance with
the strongest terms of reprobation.   In this condition
his lordship used to see him, though but on a few
occasions, at William Bankes's (the Italian discoverer's)
rooms, where he would pour forth whole pages of
various languages, and distinguish himself especially by
copious floods of Greek.

Such is the description which Lord Byron gives of
Porson's evening displays. We have seen him brandishing the poker at an earlier period of his life ; but to the
character of the language used with the act there is no
testimony but his lordship's own opinion.   As the Professor, however, never injured any one with the poker,
we may suppose that the gesture and the words were
alike intended to be harmless.

Concerning the Professor's behaviour in London
society abundance of anecdotes are told.   To what we
have to say on this subject, the following letter, written
some time after 1804, and addressed to an eminent
surgeon, Mr. Joy, with whom Porson had long been
intimate, may serve as an appropriate introduction.

Dear Sir,

I should be very happy to obey your obliging summons;
I should equally approve of the commons, the company,
and the conversation; but, for some time past, my face, or
rather my nose, whether from good living or bad humours,
has been growing into a great resemblance of honest Bar-
dolph's, or, to keep still on the list of honest fellows, of honest
Richard Brinsley's. I have therefore put myself under a
regimen of abstinence till my poor nose recovers its *quondam*
colour and compass; after which I shall be happy to attend
your parties on the shortest notice. Thank you for returning
Mr. Ireland's, whom you justly call *an amiable youth*, and I
think you might have added *a modest*. Witness a publication of his that appeared in 1804, entitled *Rhapsodies, by
W. H. Ireland, author of the Shakspearian MSS., &c.*,
where he thus addresses his book:

> " As on thy title-page, poor little book,
> Full oft I cast a sad and pensive look,
>   I shake my head, and pity thee;
> For I, alas! no brazen front possess,
> Nor do I every potent art profess,
>   To send thee forth from censure free." *

Though I cannot help looking upon him as too modest in
the fourth verse; he certainly underrates the amount and
extent of his possessions. He is by no means *poor in his
own brass*. I was going to conclude with "And now to
dinner with what appetite you may," but first I bethought
me of a question: Do you see nothing extraordinary in this
note? nothing, perhaps you will say. Why then be amazed;
for it is written with a pen from the wing of an eagle. Ay,
and of an Irish eagle too, dear Joy. So no more at present,
but rests yours sincerely,

R. Porson.

In relation to his appearance, and especially that of
his nose, he would relate, with much good humour, the

---

* Barker's *Parriana*, vol. i. p. 418.

following anecdote. He went to call on one of the
judges with whom he was intimate, when a gentleman,
who did not know Porson, was waiting impatiently for
the barber. Porson, who was negligently dressed, and
had besides a patch of brown paper soaked in vinegar
on his inflamed nose, being shown into the room where
the gentleman was sitting, he started up suddenly, and
rushing towards Porson, exclaimed, "Are you the barber?" "No, sir," replied Porson, "but I am a cunning
shaver, very much at your service."

Mr. Maltby says, "He was generally ill-dressed and
dirty. But I never saw him such a figure as he was
one day at Leigh and Sotheby's auction-room; he evidently had been rolling in the kennel; and, on inquiry,
I found that he was just come from a party (at Robert
Heathcote's, I believe), with whom he had been sitting
up drinking for two nights."*

"Banks," says the same authority, "once invited
Porson (about a year before his death) to dine with
him at an hotel at the west end of London; but the
dinner passed away without the expected guest having
made his appearance. Afterwards, on Banks's asking
him why he had not kept his engagement, Porson replied (without entering into further particulars) that he
' had come;' and Banks could only conjecture that the
waiters, seeing Porson's shabby dress, and not knowing
who he was, had offered him some insult, which had
made him indignantly return home."†

He went one evening to a ball at the assembly-rooms
at Bath, escorted by Dr. Davis, a physician of the place,

* Rogers's Table-Talk, "Porsoniana," p. 305.
† Ibid. p. 321.

who introduced him to the Rev. Richard Warner.* When Porson separated from Warner, King, the master of the ceremonies, stepped forward and said, "Pray, Mr. Warner, who is that man you have been speaking to? I can't say I much like his appearance." "To own the truth," says Warner, "Porson, with lank un-combed locks, a loose neckcloth, and wrinkled stockings, exhibited a striking contrast to the gorgeous crowd around. I replied, however," he continues, "Who is that gentleman, Mr. King? The greatest man that has visited your rooms since their first erection. It is the celebrated Porson; the most profound scholar in Europe; who has more Greek under that mop of hair than can be found in all the heads in the room, ay, if we even include those of the orchestra." "Indeed," said the dancing-master, and went off to attend to his dancing, having no more conception of what is con-tained in the head of a scholar than the cat that looks at a king has of the value of the jewels in his crown.

Dr. Raine said that he had known him to be so very dirty at times that he has been refused admittance by servants at the houses of his friends.†

He was in this plight, on one occasion, in the "Morn-ing Chronicle" office, when a schoolmaster came to speak to Perry about some passage in a Greek author. When the schoolmaster had expressed his notions of it, Porson, who overheard it, said, "You are wrong, sir." The schoolmaster, being startled, and glancing at Por-son's mean appearance, asked Perry who he was. Perry told him, when, without venturing to defend his opi-

---

* Warner's Lit. Recollections, vol. ii. p. 6.
† Barker's Lit. Anecd. vol. ii. p. 14.

nion, he took his hat and walked off in reverential silence.*

He once walked out of town with Beloe to Highgate; and, as they were returning, they were overtaken by a violent shower of rain, and both drenched to the skin. As soon as they arrived at Beloe's residence, warm and dry clothes were prepared for them, but Porson obstinately refused to make any change in his dress. He drank three glasses of brandy, but sat in his wet garments the whole evening. "The exhalation, of course," says Beloe, "was not the most agreeable; but he did not apparently suffer any subsequent inconvenience." †

The redness of his nose, to which he alludes in the letter above, proceeded greatly from his indulgence in port, which he preferred to every other wine, as well at dinner as after it. ‡ Of liquors his favourite was brandy, the drink of heroes. Mrs. Parr said that more brandy was drunk during three weeks that Porson spent at Hatton than during all the time that she had kept house before.§

For tea and coffee he had no liking. At breakfast his favourite beverage was porter. One Sunday morning, when he was at Eton, he met Dr. Goodall, the provost, going to church, and asked him where Mrs. Goodall was? "At breakfast," replied the Doctor. "Very well, then," rejoined Porson, "I'll go and breakfast with her." He accordingly presented himself at Mrs. Goodall's table, and being asked what he chose to

* Barker's Lit. Anecd. vol. ii. p. 18.
† Sexagenarian, vol. i. p. 225.
‡ Rogers's Table Talk, " Porsoniana," p. 301.
§ Barker's Parriana, vol. i. p. 542.

take, answered " Porter." Porter was in consequence sent for, pot after pot, and the sixth pot was just being carried into the house, when Dr. Goodall returned from church.*

Mr. Upcott used to say that he was often to be seen at breakfast with a pot of porter and bread and cheese; and, in the latter part of his life, in the dirtiest attire, and with black patches on his nose.†

Of his capacities of drinking, and of sitting up at nights, extraordinary stories are told. He appears to have been, like Dr. Johnson, a bad sleeper, and to having been the readier, on that account, to consort with those who were willing to sit late. He had manifested his love of late hours even in his boyhood, at a visit to Mr. Norris, who, having invited him to spend an afternoon with him, expected him to take his leave in the evening, but finding him, after a hint or two as to the time, unwilling to move, was at last obliged to have him put to bed in the house. " In the former period of his early residence in the metropolis," says Beloe‡, " the absence of sleep hardly seemed to annoy him. The first evening which he spent with Horne Tooke, he never thought of retiring till the harbinger of day gave warning to depart. Horne Tooke, on another occasion, contrived to find out the opportunity of requesting his company when he knew that he had been sitting up the whole of the night before. This, however, made no difference; Porson sat up the second night also till the hour of sunrise."

* Rogers's Table Talk, " Porsoniana," p. 301.
† Barker's Lit. Anecd. vol. ii. p. 5.
‡ Sexagenarian, vol. i. p. 229.

His compotations with Horne Tooke, in the narrative of Mr. Maltby, assume a still more formidable aspect. " Horne Tooke told me," he states, " that he once asked Porson to dine with him in Richmond Buildings ; and, as he knew that Porson *had not been in bed for the three preceding nights*, he expected to get rid of him at an early hour. Porson, however, kept Tooke up the whole night ; and in the morning the latter, in perfect despair, said, 'Mr. Porson, I am engaged to meet a friend at breakfast at a coffee-house in Leicester Square.' 'Oh,' replied Porson, ' I will go with you ;' and he accordingly did so. Soon after they had reached the coffee-house, Tooke contrived to slip out, and, running home, ordered his servant not to let Mr. Porson in, even if he should attempt to batter down the door. 'A man,' observed Tooke, ' who could sit up four nights successively, could sit up forty.' "*

Porson called one day on Horne Tooke at Wimbledon, and accepted an invitation to stay to dine. Some dispute and ill-feeling arose between them at table, and Porson, after dinner, being called upon for a toast, said " I will give you the man who is just the reverse of John Horne Tooke." This provoked recrimination from Tooke, and Porson was at last so exasperated that he threatened to " kick and cuff" his host. Tooke, as Mr. Stephens† relates the affair, " after exhibiting his own brawny chest, sinewy arms, and muscular legs, to the best possible advantage, endeavoured to evince the prudence of deciding the question as to strength by recurring to a different species of combat. Accordingly,

* Rogers's Table Talk, " Porsoniana," p. 301.
† Memoirs of Horne Tooke, vol. ii. p. 315.

setting aside the port and sherry, then before them, he
ordered a couple of quarts of brandy ; and by the time
the second bottle was half-emptied, the Greek fell vanquished under the table.   On this, the victor at this
new species of Olympic game, taking hold of his antagonist's limbs in succession, exclaimed, ' This is the foot
that was to have kicked, and the hand that was to have
cuffed me ;' and then, drinking one glass more to the
speedy recovery of his prostrate adversary, ordered
' that great care should be taken of Mr. Professor Porson ;' after which he withdrew to the adjacent apartment, where tea and coffee had been prepared, with
the same seeming calmness as if nothing had occurred.
I should not have mentioned this scene," adds Stephens,
" but that it is well known to all Mr. Tooke's friends,
and almost to every one that ever visited Wimbledon."

How many times in his life Horne Tooke offered
such challenges, I cannot say; but he had previously
proposed one of the same kind to James Boswell, with
whom, on some occasion, he had had some serious
altercation.   Boswell, happening to meet him, not long
after, at a gentleman's house, expressed his willingness
to be reconciled to him, but only on condition that
between the toasts given after dinner they should each
drink a bottle of wine.   Horne Tooke refused to assent,
unless for wine should be substituted brandy.   Boswell
agreed, but, by the time he had swallowed a quart, fell
sprawling under the table.*

" I had once the pleasure of dining in company with
Porson," says one of Dr. Parr's old pupils, in a letter to
E. H. Barker, " in Benet-Combination, when I was a

---

* Stephens's Mem. of Horne Tooke, vol. ii. p. 439.

fellow. This most extraordinary man, who could in-struct and delight the most cultivated minds, could also make himself a very nuisance by certain degrading habits. After dinner he took a small book out of his pocket, containing some of his writing (in which he was exquisitely skilled), and it was handed round the table for us to look at. In the evening he entertained us with an account of some Greek manuscripts, till they got him down to the card-table, which soon almost neutralised this great man. Owing to his habits, it was almost as much desired to be rid of him at a seasonable hour, as to enjoy his earlier conversation. One of the company, now a bishop, undertook as a great favour to carry him off in good time ; without this precaution he would have stayed till the morning. As I had never been in his company before, I pleaded that he might be allowed to stay and *to drench himself with water, which he would do, when nothing else was before him.* I offered, for one, to sit up, not to talk with him, but to hear him talk, and was very sorry that I had none to second me." *

"When Porson dined with me," said Rogers, "I used to keep him within bounds ; but I frequently met him at various houses where he got completely drunk. He would not scruple to return to the dining-room after the company had left it, pour into a tumbler the drops remaining in the wine-glasses, and drink off the omnium gatherum." Maltby, who was present when Rogers said this, added that he had seen Porson do so.†

He would drink liquids of all kinds. " Horne Tooke

* Barker's Parriana, vol. i. p. 266.
† Rogers's Table Talk, p. 221.

used to say," as Mr. Maltby* tells us, "that 'Porson would drink ink rather than not drink at all.' Indeed," adds Mr. Maltby, "he would drink anything. He was sitting with a gentleman after dinner, in the chambers of a mutual friend, a Templar, who was then ill and confined to bed. A servant came into the room, sent thither by his master, for a bottle of embrocation which was on the chimney-piece. 'I drank it an hour ago,' said Porson."

"When Hoppner the painter was residing in a cottage a few miles from London, Porson, one afternoon, unexpectedly arrived there. Hoppner said that he could not offer him dinner, as Mrs. Hoppner had gone to town, and had carried with her the key of the closet which contained the wine. Porson, however, declared that he would be content with a mutton-chop, and beer from the next ale-house ; and accordingly stayed to dine. During the evening Porson said 'I am quite certain that Mrs. Hoppner keeps some nice bottle for her private drinking, in her own bed-room ; so, pray, try if you can lay your hands on it.' His host assured him that Mrs. Hoppner had no such secret stores ; but Porson insisting that a search should be made, a bottle was at last discovered in the lady's apartment, to the surprise of Hoppner, and the joy of Porson, who soon finished its contents, pronouncing it to be the best gin he had tasted for a long time. Next day Hoppner, somewhat out of temper, informed his wife that Porson had drunk every drop of her concealed dram. 'Drunk every drop of it!' cried she. 'My God, it was spirits of wine for the lamp!'"

* Rogers's Table Talk, "Porsoniana," p. 302.

Another of Maltby's anecdotes* respecting Porson's drinking, is this : " Gurney (the Baron) had chambers in Essex Court, Temple, under Porson's. One night, or rather morning, Gurney was awakened by a tremendous thump in the chambers above. Porson had just come home dead drunk, and had fallen on the floor. Having extinguished his candle in the fall, he presently staggered down stairs to relight it; and Gurney heard him keep dodging and poking with the candle at the staircase lamp for about five minutes, and all the while very lustily cursing the nature of things."

This story reminds us of Daniel Heinsius reeling home, and repeating, as he went up the stone staircase to his rooms,

" Sta pes, sta bone pes; sta pes, ne labere, mî pes;
    Sta pes, aut lapides hi mihi lectus erunt."

" Stand, stand, my trusty feet; firm be your tread;
    Stand firm, or else these stones must be my bed."

" Porson frequently spent his evenings," says Beloe†, with the present venerable Dean of Westminster, with Dr. Wingfield, with the late Bennet Langton, and with another friend in Westminster, with respect to whom the following line used to be facetiously applied from Homer :

" 'Ρίψε ποδὸς τεταγὼν ἀπὸ βήλου θεσπεσίοιο "—

meaning Beloe himself. " Yet he hardly ever failed passing some hours afterwards at the Cider Cellar in Maiden Lane.

" The above individuals being all of them very regu-

* Rogers's Table Talk, " Porsoniana," p. 304.
† Sexagenarian, vol. i. p. 228.

lar in their hours, used to give him to understand that
he was not to stay after eleven o'clock, with the exception of Bennet Langton, who suffered him to remain
till twelve, corrupted in this instance, perhaps, by Dr.
Johnson.   But so precise was Porson in this particular,
that although he never attempted to exceed the hour
limited, he would never stir before.   On one occasion,
when, from some incidental circumstance, the lady of
the house gave a gentle hint that she wished him to
retire a little earlier, he looked at the clock, and observed, with some quickness, that it wanted a quarter
of an hour of eleven."

"A brother of Bishop Maltby," relates Mr. Maltby,
"invited Porson and myself to spend the evening at his
house, and secretly requested me to take Porson away,
if possible, before the morning hours.   Accordingly at
twelve o'clock I held up my watch to Porson, saying,
'I think it is now full time for us to go home;' and
the host, of course, not pressing us to remain longer,
away we went.   When we got into the street, Porson's
indignation burst forth : 'I hate,' he said, 'to be turned
out of doors like a dog.'"*

He was greatly pleased with the encomium pronounced upon him by one of his companions at the
Cider Cellar : "Dick can beat us all; he can drink all
night, and spout all day."†

In 1798 Dr. Burney was meditating an edition of
Terentianus Maurus, and mentioned, in a letter to Parr,
his desire that Porson might consult some books for
him.   Parr replies, "The books may be consulted, and

* Rogers's Table Talk, "Porsoniana," p. 304.
† Short Account of Porson, p. 10.

Porson shall do it, and he will do it.   I know his price
when he bargains with me; two bottles instead of one,
six pipes instead of two, burgundy instead of claret,
liberty to sit till five in the morning instead of sneaking
into bed at one; these are his terms."*

"Porson," writes Maltby†, "was fond of smoking
and said that when smoking began to go out of fashion,
learning began to go out of fashion also." Had he lived
to the present day, he might have seen smoking revived
more than ever, but chiefly among those who have
little pretensions to learning.

Whatever was the extent of Porson's potations in
company, he was never accused of drinking to intem-
perance in solitude; and he could, when he thought
proper, observe total abstinence, for a considerable time,
from wine and spirituous liquors.

In his eating, as to the quality of his food, he was
easily satisfied.   He went once to the Bodleian to collate a manuscript, and, as the work would occupy him
several days, Routh, the President of Magdalen, who
was leaving home for the long vacation, said to him,
at his departure, "Make my house your home, Mr.
Porson, during my absence, for my servants will have
orders to be quite at your command, and to procure
you whatever you please."   When he returned, he
asked for the account of what the Professor had had
during his stay.   The servant brought the bill, and the
Doctor, glancing at it, observed a fowl entered in it
every day.   "What!" said he, "did you provide for
Mr. Porson no better than this, but oblige him to dine

* Parr's Works, vol. i. p. 730.
† Rogers's Table Talk, "Porsoniana," p. 305.

every day on fowl?" "No, sir," replied the servant,
" but we asked the gentleman the first day what he
would have for dinner, and, as he did not seem to know
very well what to order, we suggested a fowl.   When
we went to him about dinner any day afterwards, he
always said ' The same as yesterday,' and this was the
only answer we could get from him."

Dr. Raine used to say that he found Porson quite
manageable in his house ; and Dr. Maltby said the same
of him.*

In noticing these habits of Porson, we must remember that to drink to excess was one of the vices of the
day in which he lived; when a capacity for three
bottles was thought a necessary qualification for society ;
when noblemen and gentlemen fell senseless under the
dinner-table, and were carried to bed by their servants ;
and when Pitt and Dundas, on whom Porson made
his epigrams, rose reeling from a carouse to join the
Senate.   Yet, whatever allowances may be made on
account of the time, we must still admit that Porson's
drinking was enormous.   It should, however, be considered that he suffered from sleeplessness, which led
him frequently to protract his sittings ; and it may,
perhaps, be said that a craving for drink, which he
seems to have felt from an early period of life, was
with him a disease.

* Barker's Lit. Anecd. vol. ii. p. 13.

CHAP. XXIII.

PORSON'S WONDERFUL MEMORY. — ITS STORES ALWAYS READY FOR USE.
—DISPLAY OF IT AT A FRIEND'S HOUSE IN THE COUNTRY.—INSTANCE
OF IT GIVEN BY COXE. — HIS REPETITION OF POPE'S "ELOISA."—
WHETHER HE WAS THE AUTHOR OF "ELOISA IN DISHABILLE."—HIS
OWN REMARKS ON THE QUESTION. — "EPISTLE FROM QUEEN OBERCA
TO SIR JOSEPH BANKS."—PORSON ABLE TO REPEAT THE WHOLE OF
"RODERICK RANDOM."— HIS RECOLLECTION OF THE NAMES IN A
NOVEL.—OTHER PROOFS OF HIS MEMORY.— HIS VAUXHALL SONGS AT
AN EVENING PARTY.—WAS NOT VAIN OF HIS POWERS.—WISHED FOR
THE ART OF FORGETTING.

Of his memory, and its wonderful tenacity, innumerable
stories are told.   But what was most remarkable in regard to it, was, not so much its retentiveness, as its
power of producing at all times, and in all circumstances, the stores which it contained.   "Other scholars
may perhaps be quoted," says the author of the "Short
Account of Porson," "who have not fallen very short of
him in this particular," the ability to retain ; "scarce
any, however, can be found, who have possessed the
extraordinary talent of retaining everything they had
ever read, and carrying it about with them, and bringing it out, *à point nommé*, in all states and conditions,
whether sick or sorry, as Porson showed in numberless
instances that he could do, almost even to his latest
breath."   Whenever he fell into excess, he adds, "his
mind was less clouded, and his recollection more perfect,
than any other man's in the same circumstances."   *Quic-*

*quid legisset mente repositum servare, et in loco meditatè
et lucidè proferre, Porsoni fere proprium fuit.**

"Upon one occasion," says the "Short Account,"
"the Professor having spent an evening at a friend's
house, a little way out of town, where he arrived completely wet through, was brought the next morning to
visit his friend's neighbour, who had a learned library,
and a house full of books ; and, after apologising for
his dress and his shoes, which were not his own, but
supplied, with the rest of his clothes, by his companion,
and quoting Horace in two places for the awkwardness
or inconvenience of a shoe too tight or too loose, and
Theophrastus and Theocritus, he provoked one of the
company to observe, that the way to make the greatest
expedition was to run, as the French and Dutch and
Scotch women do, with their slippers in their hands,
when they are pressed for time ; and cited Æschylus,
where it is said, in the Prometheus, 'I hurried out of
the carriage without sandals.' Upon which the Professor started up upon his feet, and fired, as a strict
sportsman does, who hears a strange gun in the preserve
which he keeps for his own shooting. No sooner were
the three words pronounced, than he gave Stanley's
comment and parallel passages upon them ; for such
was the local mechanism of his memory, that, mention
a line in any classic, and he would not only tell which
side of the page it was on, but the previous and subsequent clause. But to proceed ; he quoted a similar
passage from Bion, which consisting of a broken line,
a whole verse, and a broken one, he made the most of
them, and thundered them out with a menacing gesture,

* Præf. in Adversaria.

and a strong emphasis on the last words 'without
sandals.' The person who had innocently begun this
capping match, and had never seen Porson before in a
room, was struck with the earnestness of his manner,
and apparent displeasure, and determined neither to
give up, nor sit still, but to follow the Professor, and do
as he did; he, therefore, too, stood on his legs, and
roared out, in the words of the next quotation in Stanley from Theocritus, 'Arise, nor stay to put your sandals
on your feet.' The Professor was startled at finding his
opponent on the same ground with himself, and so near
at his heels; but doubting if it were not by mere accident, he took the next passage from Horace that
followed in the commentator, to which he added the
remark of Stanley that concludes his note; namely, that
water-nymphs went unshod, for that reason Homer
gives Thetis the epithet of silver-footed. Here the Professor had as usual the last word, for he was in the
habit of seeing everybody and everything out."

When Coxe was at Cambridge, preparing his "Northern Travels" for the press, he formed an acquaintance
with Porson, who was then residing on his fellowship
at Trinity, and gives the following instance of his memory. "Taking tea one afternoon in his company at
Dockerell's coffee-house, I read a pamphlet written by
Ritson against Tom Warton. I was pleased with the
work, and after I had read it I gave it to Porson, who
began it, and I left him perusing it. On the ensuing
day he drank tea with me, with several other friends,
and the conversation happened to turn upon Ritson's
pamphlet. I alluded to one particular part about
Shakspeare which had greatly interested me, adding, to

those who had not read it, 'I wish I could convey to you a specific idea of the remainder.' Porson repeated a page and a half word for word. I expressed my surprise, and said, 'I suppose you studied the whole evening at the coffee-house, and got it by heart?' 'Not at all; I do assure you that I only read it once.' "*

He is said to have repeated at times, in company, the greater part of the " Rape of the Lock," with the various readings of the several editions, and a number of annotations, all delivered with such accuracy, that a person who heard it observed : " Had it been taken down as it came from his mouth, and printed, it would have formed the best edition of that poem ever published."†

Another poem of Pope's that he was fond of repeating was the " Eloisa ;" a repetition which Boaden once witnessed, and of which he gives the following account in his " Memoirs of Kemble."‡ " I was dining with him at the house of a mutual friend, when, over wine, a very dull man became outrageous in the praise of Pope's ' Eloisa to Abelard.' The Professor began upon the poem, and recited it, with some occasional accompaniments of imitations by two moderns, in Ovidian Latin ; and, as a perpetual or running commentary, he repeated the Macaronic version, called ' Eloisa in Dishabille,' which has stolen into print, and been attributed to Porson, as he assured me, erroneously. Our wise friend lost all patience at this outrage. ' He would not endure such a profanation of the work of an exalted genius. He would have satisfaction for the buffoon travesty of his favourite poem.' The man's head was

* Life and Posthumous Works of Archdeacon Coxe.
† Barker's Parriana, vol. i. p. 553.   ‡ Vol. ii. p. 337.

wrong; but, taking him aside, I did at last hit upon an argument that charmed away his anger. I asked him how he could think it possible for the Professor to undervalue the poem? and what proof he could give of his own veneration for it, equivalent to the committing it so accurately to memory, together with three rival versions of such different complexions? Goodman Dull then really laughed away his folly, and returned to table quite reconciled to his master."

We may here consider what has been said as to the authorship of the " Eloisa in Dishabille." It was generally thought to be Porson's own, from his frequent repetition of it, and from his silence as to any other parentage; but the writer of the " Short Account of Porson " was " inclined to think that the fondness of the Professor for the dirty brat was the fondness of adoption," and that it was really written by a Mr. Coffin of Exeter, a friend of Porson's. His grounds for this opinion the writer does not state, nor do we know where to find any particulars concerning Mr. Coffin, to indicate whether he were likely to be the author or not. On a fly-leaf of a copy of " My Pocket Book," a satire by Dubois on Sir John Carr's " Travels," which was published in 1807, and is now in the library of the London Institution, Porson has written some remarks as to the allegation that he was the author: " Such is the present eagerness of the public for anecdote, that, let an anonymous author tell the most scandalous and improbable falsehood of a known character, there will be no lack of readers to swallow it. In pages xii. and xiii. of the preface to this book the author charges the present Greek Professor of Cambridge with writing a parody on Pope's 'Eloisa.'　This statement is certainly false; for the parody in question was printed for Faulder in 1780, as appears from the 'Critical Review' for December 1780, and from the 'Monthly Review' for February 1781.　If therefore Mr. Porson wrote that parody, he must have written it when he was an undergraduate, many years before he became Greek Professor.　But if the author should say that he only meant that the person who wrote the parody is now the Greek Professor, I shall pass over the clumsiness of the expression, and only desire him to produce his proofs of the latter fact. This I know, that I have several times heard Mr. P. seriously disown all share whatever in the composition of that parody, and all knowledge of its author."　If Porson meant this as a denial that he was the author, a denial might have been made with less circumlocution. He made a denial of the authorship, however, to Boaden, and he made denials to others.　But Johnson said that if a man were asked whether he were the author of a book which he had written, but did not wish to acknowledge, he might justifiably assert that he was not the author; for if he made no reply to the question, it must be considered as an admission of the authorship.　In this persuasion Mathias denied the authorship of the " Pursuits of Literature," and Sir Walter Scott denied for a time the authorship of the " Waverley Novels."　Little more need be said upon the question. The production is no credit to its author.　No one can have much pleasure in seeing the delicate lines of Pope degraded into shamelessness.　The versification is smooth doggrel, and the few notes at the foot of the pages are trifling and nauseous.

If Porson denied that he knew who the author was, it is not probable that it was written by his friend Coffin, for such a denial would then have been a needless falsehood. But the denial of "all knowledge of the author" may have been made in some mystifying phrase, Coffin, or whoever wrote the thing, being perhaps already dead. John Taylor thought that "the warmth and frequency of Porson's obtrusive recitations evidently manifested parental dotage."* If Porson really wrote it, he must have written it when he was not more than twenty, and may have afterwards wished to be thought guiltless of its production. Moore, however, in his "Life of Byron," says that it was written by John Matthews, Esq., the father of Byron's friend, Charles Skinner Matthews; but that Porson "printed an edition" of it.

Another poem, of a somewhat similar character, "An Epistle from Oberea, Queen of Otaheite, to Joseph Banks, Esq., translated by T. Q. Z., Esq., professor of the Otaheite language in Dublin, and all languages of the undiscovered islands in the South-Sea," has been also confidently said to have been written by Porson. But Mr. Kidd declares that it has been improperly attributed to him; and, as the first edition of it appeared in 1774, when Porson was fourteen years of age, we may very well accept Mr. Kidd's declaration. The design of it was to ridicule certain highly descriptive passages in Hawkesworth's "Voyages," and it was written, if Mr. Kidd † be not mistaken, "by a late Member of Parliament well known in the walks of wit." This Member of Parliament, it appears‡, was Sir John

* Records of My Life, vol. i. p. 240.   † Tracts, p. lxiii.
‡ Barker's Lit. Anecd. vol. ii. p. 9.

Courtney ; and when Kidd remarked to Porson that Courtney was the author, Porson made no denial.   The versification is excellent, and, as Porson is said to have been extremely fond of repeating passages from it, the reader may not object to see a specimen of what he repeated.   It commences as follows.   " Opano," we should observe, was the form into which the Otaheitans metamorphosed Sir Joseph Banks's name.

> " Read, or oh ! say, does some more amorous fair
> Prevent *Opano*, and engage his care ?
> I, *Oberea*, from the Southern main,
> Of slighted vows, of injur'd faith, complain.
> Though now some European maid you woo,
> Of waist more taper, and of whiter hue,
> Yet oft with me you deign'd the night to pass
> Beneath yon bread-tree on the bending grass :
> Oft in the rocking boat we fondly lay,
> Nor fear'd the drizzly wind, or briny spray.
>   Who led thee through the wood's impervious shade,
> Pierc'd the thick covert, and explor'd the glade ;
> Taught thee each plant that sips the morning dew,
> And brought the latent minerals to thy view ?
> Still to those glades, those coverts, I repair,
> Trace every alley,— but thou art not there.
> Nor herb, nor salutary plant I find,
> To cool the burning fever of my mind.
> Ah ! I remember on the river's side,
> Whose babbling waters 'twixt the mountains glide,
> A bread-tree stands, on which, with sharpen'd stone
> To thy dear name I deign'd unite my own.
> Grow, bread-tree, grow, nor envious hand remove
> The sculptur'd symbols of my constant love."

" Whatsoever," says the " Short Account" of Porson*, " Whatsoever at any time pleased the Professor's fancy, he for the most part charged his memory with, and

---

* Page 22.

brought it out for the amusement of his company, whether in the shape of an Oration of Longolius on St. Louis, or Davis's Latin Hudibras, or the Pleader's Guide."

"Nothing," says the writer of the "Scraps from Porson's Rich Feast," "came amiss to his memory; he would set a child right in his twopenny fable-book, repeat the whole of the moral tale of the Dean of Badajos, or a page of Athenæus on cups, or Eustathius on Homer."

Dr. Dauney of Aberdeen told Mr. Maltby that, " during a visit to London, he *heard Porson declare* that he could repeat Smollett's ' Roderick Random ' from beginning to end :" and Mr. Richard Heber assured Maltby that " soon after the appearance of the ' Essay on Irish Bulls,' Porson used, when somewhat tipsy, to recite *whole pages of it verbatim* with great delight." * He said that he would undertake to learn by heart a copy of the " Morning Chronicle " in a week.†

Pryse Lockhart Gordon, in his " Personal Memoirs,"‡ says that Porson, having been invited to dine with him, and having come, by mistake, on Thursday instead of Friday, was kept to dinner on the Thursday, and, testifying no desire to go to bed when his host retired, was left with two bottles of wine before him, and an Italian novel, which he sat up all night reading, and of which, at a dinner party the following day, he gave a translation from memory, and though there were forty names mentioned in the story, he had forgotten only one of them. This slight failure in his recollection, however,

---

* Rogers's Table Talk, " Porsoniana," p. 310.
† Barker's Lit. Anecd. vol ii. p. 24.   ‡ Vol. i. p. 265.

annoyed him so much that he started up, and paced round the room for about ten minutes, when, stopping suddenly, he exclaimed : " Eureka ! The Count's name is Don Francesco Averrani." If this account is quite accurate, it shows that Porson was better acquainted with the Italian than was supposed by Mr. Maltby, who thought that he knew little or nothing of the language.*

On one occasion, when Porson, Reed, and some other of the literati, with John Kemble, were assembled at Dr. Burney's at Hammersmith, and were examining some old newspapers in which the execution of Charles I. was detailed, they observed some particulars stated in them which they doubted whether Hume or Rapin had mentioned. Reed, who, being versed in old literature, was consulted as the oracle on the point, could not recollect ; but Porson repeated a long passage from Rapin in which the circumstances were fully noticed. Archdeacon Burney, who favoured me with this anecdote, told me, at the same time, that he had often, when a boy, taken down Humphry Clinker, or Foote's plays, from his father's shelves, and heard Porson repeat whole pages of them walking about the room.

Basil Montague related that Porson, in his presence, and that of some other persons, read a page or two of a book, and then repeated what he had read from memory. " That is very well," said one of the company, " but could the Professor repeat it backwards ?" Porson immediately began to repeat it backwards, and failed only in two words.†

Priestley, the bookseller, used to relate that Porson

* Rogers's Table Talk, " Porsoniana," p. 329.
† Barker's Lit. Anecd. vol. ii. p. 18.

was once in his shop, when a gentleman came in, and asked for a particular edition of Demosthenes, of which Priestley was not in possession. The gentleman being somewhat disappointed, Porson, whose attention was directed towards him, asked him whether he wished to consult any passage in Demosthenes. The gentleman replied in the affirmative, and specified the passage. Porson then asked Priestley for a copy of the Aldine edition, and, having received it, and turned over a few leaves, put his finger on the passage, " showing," said Priestley, " not only his knowledge of the author, but his familiarity with the position of the passage in that particular edition." *

A similar anecdote used to be told by Mr. Cogan. One day Porson called on a friend who happened to be reading Thucydides, and who asked leave to consult him on the meaning of a word. Porson, on hearing the word, did not look at the book, but at once repeated the passage. His friend asked how he knew that it was that passage. " Because," replied Porson, " the word occurs only twice in Thucydides, once on the right hand page, in the edition which you are using, and once on the left. I observed on which side you looked, and accordingly knew to which passage you referred."†

" I once took him," relates Rogers, " to an evening party at William Spencer's, where he was introduced to several women of fashion, Lady Crewe, &c., who were very anxious to see the great Grecian. How do you suppose he entertained them? Chiefly by reciting an immense quantity of old forgotten Vauxhall songs.

* Barker's Lit. Anecd. vol. ii. p. 19. † Ibid. p. 23.

He was far from sober, and at last talked so oddly that
they all retired from him except Lady Crewe, who boldly
kept her ground.   I recollect her saying to him, " Mr.
Porson, that joke you have borrowed from 'Joe Miller,' "
and his rather angry reply, " Madam, it is not in ' Joe
Miller ; ' you will not find it either in the preface or in
the body of the work, no, nor in the index."   I brought
him home as far as Piccadilly, where, I am sorry to say,
I left him sick in the middle of the street." *

A writer in the " Public Ledger " said that he had
often seen him standing at night, in the midst of a
number of people, pouring forth, with dignified deport-
ment, and sonorous utterance, a number of lines of
Homer, apparently for no other purpose than to
excite the wonder of his audience at what few or none
of them could understand.†

Yet, like many other great men, who have excelled
in some particular faculty of the mind, he was far from
being vain of his peculiar excellence.   Sir Isaac Newton
claimed no other merit from his vast calculations than
that of persevering labour, and of keeping his subject
constantly before him till it was worked out; and
Porson would say that his memory was no better than
other men might make theirs.   He would sometimes
argue that all men are born with abilities nearly equal.
" Any one," he would say, " might become quite as
good a critic as I am, if he would only take the trouble
to make himself so.   I have made myself what I am
by intense labour ; sometimes, in order to impress a

---

* Rogers's Table Talk, p. 222.

† Public Ledger, Sept. 29, 1808.   Barker's Lit. Anecd. vol. ii.
p. 24.

thing upon my memory, I have read it a dozen times, and transcribed it six." *

A remark which he made to Mrs. Edwards, however, a friend of Dr. Parr's, intimates that he was quite conscious of the natural goodness of his memory.   He told her that "his memory was a source of misery to him, as he could never forget anything, even what he wished not to remember." †   Themistocles is not the only one that has longed for the art of forgetting.

* Rogers's Table Talk, " Porsoniana," p. 310.   Barker's Lit. Anecd. vol. ii. p. 25.   Hellenophilus (Bp. Maltby) in Aikin's Athenæum, Nov. 1808.

† Field's Memoirs of Parr, vol. i. p. 456.

CHAP. XXIV.

"IF," says the "Short Account of Porson," "a man
declared himself to be, or insinuated that he was, or
thought that he ought to be considered as, a hidalgo
in literature, *sese aliquem credens*, he was sure to be
attended to by the Professor in his own way; and if he
quoted the text of Homer, the Professor would give
him the scholiast on that text. Græculus, who had been
very free in his publications with professors in general,
once observed to Mr. Porson, rather too familiarly, in
regard to a vulgar saying, 'It is all the same in Greek,
Mr. Professor.' The Professor replied, gravely, "*You*
can't tell that, Sir.' At another time the same person
insisted upon it, that the Greek was an easy language.
The Professor said, ' Not to *you*, Sir.' "

This dislike of assumption may account perhaps, in
some degree, for Porson's want of cordiality for Parr.
He would observe to his intimate friends that he had

no very high opinion of Parr's intellectual powers; but he might have continued, we may suppose, on fair terms with him, as he continued with others of far less ability, had he not been alienated, apparently, by Parr's overbearingness in conversation, pretension to supremacy in literature, and overwhelming torrents of verbosity. As early as the time when Porson looked to the sheets of Heyne's Virgil, and when Parr, in his "Remarks on Combe's Statement," called him "a giant in literature," Porson drew back, in stately attitude, and said: "How should he be able to take measure of a giant?" Or, according to other accounts: "A man must be a giant himself to tell whether another is a giant." *

Let us contemplate, for a moment, Parr's literary character. He certainly was a man of learning and talent, but was as far from being a man of genius as any man of learning and talent ever was. He has not left on paper a single thought that can be called original. He has produced abundance of declamation, but declamation composed of material from other writers. An author he can scarcely be called. If we compare a page of Addison, or Locke, or Bacon, with a page of Parr, we see the difference between the productions of a writer who thinks for himself, and those of a writer who draws his supplies from the fountains of others. No man can say that he has gathered nutriment for his mind, or added to his intellectual stores, from the writings of Parr. Nor was his language more original than his matter; if he praised Burke, or abused Pitt, he delivered his praises or abuse in the

* Rogers's Table Talk, "Porsoniana," p. 318.

phrase of Cicero or Johnson.   His Preface to Bellendenus is but a cento, and his English efforts are of a
similar nature.   His sentences are full of sound, and
sometimes of fury, but the effect is altogether dispro-
portionate to the rage and noise.

It has been regretted that he gave up his time to
sermons and pamphlets, instead of devoting it to larger
works.   But if he had taken longer performances in
hand, it appears far from certain that he would have
carried any one of them to a successful conclusion.   His
ardour was excited only by fits, sufficing for the composition of a pamphlet, and for additions and improvements to it, but not burning long enough for the production of a work of magnitude.   He wanted the power
of what Garrick called concoction.   He collected a shelf
full of books for a life of Johnson, but either never
commenced it or commenced it to no purpose.

Even in classical reading, to which he was devoted
apparently more than to anything else, he has gained
himself no permanent reputation.   Of all the books
through which he roamed, he fixed on no one to edit,
nor is an original illustration of a single passage attached
to the name of Parr.

Let it be carefully remembered, however, that, when
we speak in depreciation of Parr, we refer only to his
literary character.   As a man, considered apart from
his writings and his talk, he was noble-minded and
generous, and always ready, with perhaps some few
whimsical exceptions, to do a service to any of his
fellow-creatures to the utmost of his power.   He gave
his contribution to the fund for Porson's annuity at a
time of his life when he could very ill afford it. Porson

himself remarked to Kidd that Parr was an excellent-hearted creature.

For Parr's literary character, then, it cannot be surprising that Porson, who could see very acutely into mankind, should feel no very great reverence, but should regard him very much as sounding brass.   One thing in Parr's conversation which particularly offended Porson was his proneness to disquisition and declamation on the origin of evil.   Once, in a large company, Parr said to Porson: " Pray what do you think, Mr. Porson, about the introduction of moral and physical evil into the world ?"   Porson, after a moment's pause, answered, with great dryness and solemnity of manner: " Why, Doctor, I think we should have done very well without them." *

This reminds us of Dr. Johnson's retort to Boswell, " What have you to do with liberty and necessity ? Or what more than to hold your tongue about them ?"

On another occasion, Parr said to Porson: " Mr. Porson, with all your learning, I do not think that you know much of metaphysics. " Not of your metaphysics, Doctor," was the reply.   Mr. Maltby, who knew Parr, as well as Porson, intimately, says that Parr was evidently afraid of Porson's intellectual powers.†

When Parr was uttering his effusions against the Rev. Charles Curtis and others, and the public prints were filled with paragraphs about them, Porson wrote the following lines, in allusion to the preface to Bellendenus :

---

* Barker's Parriana, vol. i. p. 543. Warner's Literary Recollections, vol. ii. p. 6.

† Rogers's Table Talk, " Porsoniana," p. 318.

> " Perturbed spirits, spare your ink,
>> And beat your stupid brains no longer,
> Then to oblivion soon will sink
>> Your persecuted preface-monger."

Which somebody has thus turned into Latin :

> " Turbata corda, jam papyro parcite,
> Nigroque latici; ne cerebrum tundite :
> Præfationis scriptor iste sic statim
> Oblivionis in nigros cadet sinus."

The reader who objects to *corda tundentia cerebrum* may also object to " spirits beating their brains."

Nothwithstanding the efforts which Parr made to secure Porson's pension, says Johnstone, " Porson privately sneered and jeered, and once lampooned him under the name of Dr. Bellenden."

Dr. Parr was not the only scholar of that day on whom Porson looked with aversion, or something like contempt. One whom he particularly disliked was Jacob Bryant. In the earlier part of his life, when he was meditating an edition of Æschylus, he had been introduced to Bryant by Coxe, and Bryant had exerted himself to procure subscriptions for the work. His efforts, however, were but little seconded by Porson, who was not much disposed to solicit assistance of any kind from any man. In this respect, as well as in some others, it was truly said of him by his fellow-collegian Walter Whiter, that " he would never do the thing that he was wanted to do." " I have tried a great deal to serve him," wrote Bryant to a friend, in a fit of vexation, " on account of his uncommon learning, but cannot obtain the least encouragement. He cannot carry on the scheme he has formed without assiduity and solicitation, and a proper respect to those from whom there is any expectation. But he visits nobody, and omits every necessary regard. A handsome gratuity from me shall certainly be ready when demanded, but I find a total disinclination in others." *

Bryant afterwards " used to abuse Porson," says Mr. Maltby†, " behind his back," as " they thought very differently, not only on the subject of Troy, but on most other subjects. One day, when he was violently attacking his character, the Bishop of Salisbury, Dr. Douglas, said to him : ' Mr. Bryant, you are speaking of a great man ; and you should remember, Sir, that even the greatest men are not without their failings.' Cleaver Banks, who was present on that occasion, remarked to me : ' I shall always think well of the Bishop for his generous defence of our friend.' "

Cleaver Banks tells the story himself, in a letter to Parr, thus : " I was exceedingly pleased with an instance of candour and liberality, which, as times go, are articles of rare occurrence in Bishops. Jacob Bryant takes every opportunity of showing his resentment against Porson, and was one day proceeding in his usual invectives, when the present Bishop of Salisbury checked him with a severe rebuke for his want of charity. Such things are not to be expected from Bishops now-a-days." ‡

The scholarship of Bishop Burgess he regarded with much contempt, which he took little care to conceal. During a visit to Oxford he gave strong offence to a

* Life and Posth. Works of Coxe ; Quart. Rev. vol. l. p. 110.
† Rogers's Table Talk, " Porsoniana," p. 309.
‡ Parr's Works, vol. i. p. 381.

party, with whom he was at supper, by speaking of Burgess with great disrespect. Holmes, the professor of poetry, was one of the number, and as he happened somehow to excite Porson's displeasure, Porson took up an oyster, which was gaping, and said *Quid dignum tanto feret hic* professor *hiatu ?* *

Paley he disliked, not perhaps for his want of classical scholarship, of which he might be said, however, to be almost destitute, but for his political opinions. It was once arranged by Maltby that he should meet Paley at a dinner which took place at the house of Dr. Davy, at Cambridge. Paley arrived first, and when Porson, who had never before seen him, came in, he seated himself in an arm-chair, and, looking very hard at Paley, said, "I am entitled to this chair, as being president of a society for the discovery of truth, of which I happen at present to be the only member."†

For Mackintosh also he had no liking. They differed in politics, and on other subjects their reading had but little in common. ‡

Tomline, the Bishop of Lincoln, he regarded with thorough detestation. "Meeting me," says Maltby, "one day at a book sale, Porson said, 'That ——, the Bishop of Lincoln, has just passed me in the street, and he shrunk from my eye like a wild animal. What do you think he has had the impudence to assert? Not long ago, he came to me, and, after informing me that Lord Elgin was appointed ambassador to the Porte, he asked me if I knew any one who was competent to

---

* Rogers's Table Talk, " Porsoniana," p. 324.
† Ibid. p. 308.   ‡ Ibid. p. 322.

examine the Greek manuscripts at Constantinople. I replied, that I did not; and he now tells everybody that I refused the proposal of government *that I should go out to examine those manuscripts.*' I do not believe," adds Maltby, " that Porson would have gone to Constantinople, if he had had the offer. He hated moving, and would not even accompany me to Paris. When I was going thither, he charged me with a message to Villoison." *

Tomline's name was originally Pretyman, and he changed it in consequence of having been left a considerable estate by a gentleman named Tomline, to whom he was in no way related, on condition that he should take the name of the testator. It was said that Tomline had seen him only once. When this was mentioned to Porson, he observed that " there would have been no such legacy if Tomline had seen him twice." †

Of Southey's epics, with their boasted freedom from " lion, tiger, bear, and boar similes," and with the absence indeed of almost all that renders true poetry what it is, Porson at once saw the value. " Mr. Southey," said he, " is indeed a wonderful writer ; his works will be read when Homer and Virgil are forgotten." To this remark Lord Byron is accused of having added " but not till then," and thus to have spoiled it. Mr. Kidd gives a specimen of similar apparent eulogy on Cumberland's tragedy of the " Carmelite ;" " the beauties of which," said some critic, " will be admired and felt when those of Shakspeare, Dryden, Otway,

* Rogers's Table Talk, " Porsoniana," p. 323.   † Ibid.

Southerne, and Rowe, shall be no longer held in estimation." *

Of a volume of poems not remarkable for originality
or elegance, he observed that they had in them much
of Horace and much of Virgil, but nothing Horatian
and nothing Virgilian.

The extravagant phrases in which Hayley and Miss
Seward complimented each other, frequently called
forth satirical remarks from Porson.   One day he
wrote for them the following dialogue :

Miss SEWARD *loquitur.*

Tuneful poet, Britain's glory,
Mr. Hayley, that is you.

HAYLEY *respondet.*

Ma'am, you carry all before you,
Trust me, Lichfield Swan, you do.

Miss SEWARD.

Ode, didactic, epic, sonnet,
Mr. Hayley, you're divine.

HAYLEY.

Ma'am, I'll take my oath upon it,
You yourself are all the Nine.†

It should be recorded that he had no liking for Wilkes.
Being present at a book sale, when Wilkes's " Characters
of Theophrastus " was put up, he observed that Wilkes,
a sponsor for "Characters," had no character himself.‡
But to such English scholars, or men of letters, as he

---

* Kidd, Tracts, p. lv.   † Sexagenarian, vol. ii. p. 314.
‡ Barker's Lit. Anecd. vol. ii. p. 11.

really esteemed, he was by no means a niggard of praise. One of those whom he most delighted to honour was Dr. Martin Davy, the Master of Gonville and Caius College, Cambridge, whom, in presenting to him a corrected fragment of a comic writer cited in the LXIVth Oration of Dion Chrysostom, he calls *acerrimum Græcarum literarum cultorem, patronum, vindicem, Cantabrigiæ nostræ decus et delicias*, adding τὰ ἱερὰ ἔοντα πρήγματα ἱεροῖσιν ἀνθρώποισι δείκνυται.

When Davy was elected Master of his College, Porson wrote him the following letter of congratulation :

DEAR DOCTOR,

I heartily congratulate you, and your friends, and the College, and the University, on your well-deserved promotion. Ζηλῶ τε σοῦ μὲν Ἑλλάδ᾽, Ἑλλάδος δέ σε. I shall not trespass upon your time with a long letter, occupied as I take it for granted you must be with the circumstances attendant on your elevation, and with the swarms of addresses that invade you from all quarters. Neither shall I amuse myself with foretelling the future glories of your reign. I never but once ventured on a similar prediction, and then my success was such as completely discouraged me from setting up for a prophet again. But a passage from Cicero had long been rusting in my mind, which passage I had almost despaired of introducing, when lo ! the occasion which the gods durst hardly have promised to my wishes, revolving time threw in my way. *Est tibi gravis adversaria constituta et parata, incredibilis quædam expectatio : quam tu unâ re facillimè vinces, si hoc statueris, Quarum laudum gloriam adamâris, quibus artibus eæ laudes comparantur, in iis esse laborandum.*

*   *   *   *   *

I have been lately studying anatomy. The last subject I cut up was human nature; and I discovered that all the wars, and murders, and bloodshed, and quarrels, and cruelties, that are incident to sickly mortals, *mortalibus œgris*, arise from their follies, and vices, and crimes; and if the doctors would undertake to purge and correct the humours which feed those follies, pamper those vices, and engender those crimes, the fee must be large indeed that I should grudge them:

Εἰ δ' 'Ασκληπιάδαις τοῦτό γ' ἔδωκε θεὸς,
'Ιᾶσθαι κακότητα καὶ ἀτηρὰς φρένας ἀνδρῶν,
Πολλοὺς ἂν μισθοὺς καὶ μεγάλους ἔφερον.

But I am committing the very fault I promised to avoid. I wish you long life and health to wear your new dignity to the mutual satisfaction of yourself and the public; and I remain,

Dear Doctor,
Your faithful friend and humble Servant,
R. Porson.*

Essex Court, No. 5, June 3, 1803.

Horne Tooke was another for whose mental powers and acquirements he had a high esteem. He used to observe that he had learned many valuable things from Tooke, but that he would not always take his assertions on trust. Horne Tooke, on the other hand, had a great opinion, and perhaps some dread, of Porson's intellectual force; for when disputes rose high between them over their cups, Porson would sometimes insult Tooke with the utmost violence and rudeness.† Tooke is reported to have said that he feared Porson in conversation, because he would often remain silent for a time, and then pounce upon him with his terrible memory.

Tyrwhitt he thought an admirable critic; and for

---

* Kidd, Tracts, p. 330. Parr's Works, vol. i. p. 544.
† See above, p. 278.

Markland he had such respect that he went to see the house near Dorking where he spent the latter years of his life.*

Of Bishop Pearson he said that "he would have been a first rate critic in Greek, equal even to Bentley, if he had not muddled his brains with divinity." †

Coray's scholarship he used to extol, and especially commended his edition of Hippocrates's "Treatise on Airs, Waters, and Places," in Greek and French. He also liked Larcher's Translation of Herodotus, as well as Larcher's other productions.‡

Elmsley he appears to have esteemed, until he found him too ready to make use of other men's emendations of authors without acknowledgment. In a critique on Schweighæuser's Athenæus, in the "Edinburgh Review," Elmsley inserted, as original, some restorations of passages that had defied the sagacity of that editor as well as his predecessors. When Porson saw the corrections, he at once recognised them as his own, but was unable to guess how the reviewer, whoever he was, had got hold of them, till he was reminded that he had some time before met Elmsley at a dinner party, where he had poured forth his emendations of Athenæus with great liberality.§ Another story says that he met Elmsley by chance in an umbrella shop, and, falling into conversation with him about Athenæus, told him of some emendations of which Elmsley took advantage.

---

* Rogers's Table Talk, "Porsoniana," p. 325.

† Ibid. p. 326.   Barker's Lit. Anecd. vol. ii. p. 24.

‡ Rogers's Table Talk, "Porsoniana," p. 326.

§ Quart. Rev. vol. v. p. 207.   Church of England Quart. Rev. vol. v. p. 413.

Both accounts may be true. But after the appearance of that review Porson would never open his mouth about Greek to Elmsley.

Dobree used to call Elmsley ἀρχικλεπτίστατος, *the most thievish of thieves;* and a story is told in the " Church of England Quarterly Review,"* which, if true, amply justifies the application of the epithet. When the authorities of Trinity College, Cambridge, after Porson's death, had selected that portion of his books which they were desirous to purchase, they were placed under the care of Mackinlay the bookseller, with strict injunctions· that nobody should have access to them. But Elmsley's uncle had been Mackinlay's partner, and Elmsley, being consequently well known to the servants, found entrance, by their means, to the literary treasures, and employed part of a Saturday, and the whole of a Sunday, during Mackinlay's absence, in transcribing what was likely to be useful to him as the editor of Aristophanes. Unhappily for the success of his schemes, however, many of the emendations, which he passed off as his own in his edition of the " Acharnenses," had been communicated by Porson to some of his friends ; and such wonderful coincidences led to a questioning of Mackinlay, who, on examining his cook, found that she had admitted Elmsley on the Saturday, and prepared his meals for him on the Sunday. Elmsley, in dread of exposure, attempted to suppress his "Acharnenses ;" but found, to his dismay, that it had been reprinted at Leipsic. Such is the tale told by the reviewer ; *ceterum fides ejus rei penes auctores erit.* Elmsley was a sound Greek scholar, but may have been too fond of purloining.

* Vol. v. p. 413.

Kidd he called " a very pretty scholar ;" and Kidd worshipped him as a deity. " It was amusing," says Mr. Maltby, " to see Kidd in Porson's company ; he bowed down before Porson with the veneration due to some being of a superior nature, and seemed absolutely to swallow every word that dropped from his mouth."[*]

One letter from Kidd to Porson, preserved among Porson's papers, at Cambridge, will show in what style Kidd used to write to him. It accompanied a list of some of Bentley's emendations of Aristophanes, compared with those of Porson's on the same passages. It is in a clear neat hand, an accomplishment in which he seems to have been desirous to imitate his master.

"Dear Sir,

" Vouchsafe to accept a transcript of certain emendations from the pen of Bentley, which furnish additional evidence in favour of those restorations with which every scholar is acquainted. The inclosed collation of a MS. of three tragedies of Æschylus was found in a copy of Aristophanes, ed. 1. Bas. which belonged formerly to Matth. Raper ; it is not of much value, but it may lead to inquiry about the MS.

" On Thursday next at about eleven o'clock permit me to submit to you materials for an edition of Dawes's *Miscellanea Critica*. Mr. Heber's copy of Dawes's proposals for publishing a Greek translation of the first book of Milton's Paradise Lost with a specimen is mislaid ; to wait for it any longer would not, I fear, be prudent ; I cannot, however, but regret the absence of that paper, since appearing with the M. C., it would evince the rapid progress as well as real candour of Dawes's mind. The remarks upon Askew's projected edition of Æschylus, which were inserted in a weekly

* Rogers's Table Talk, " Porsoniana," p. 325.

paper published at Newcastle-upon-Tyne, are irretrievably
lost; the copies of those fragments, which the late Mr. Brand
had preserved, did not turn up at the sale of his library;
they were announced at the end of a pamphlet entitled
'Tittle-tattle-Mongers,' printed at Newcastle, 1747. 'Speedily will be published: *Philonoi Antipolypragmonis epi-*
stola ad juvenem ἀλαζονοχαυνοφλύαρον *Antonium Askew,*
M.B., Coll. Emman. apud Cantabrigienses non ita pridem
Pseudo-Socio-Commensalem, Æschyli editionis promisso-
rem. In quo ὁ δεῖνα *obiter, festivum caput, ex suis virtu-*
tibus ornatur.'

> "I am, dear Sir,
> Your very obliged
> and most obedient humble Servant,
> Tho. Kidd.

"3 Hoxton Square, 11th June 1808."

Malone's diligence and accuracy as a critic Porson
greatly admired, and said that he thought the Essay on
the Three Parts of Henry VI., the object of which was
to prove that those plays were not original compositions
of Shakspeare, but had merely received an infusion of
his spirit after they were written, was "one of the most
convincing pieces of criticism that he ever read." *

For Dr. Raine, master of the Charter House School,
who had been his fellow collegian, he had always a
high esteem ; and with him, Dr. Davy, Cleaver Banks,
and William Maltby, he seems to have held closer intercourse than with any other persons.

To such intimate friends he sometimes expressed his
regret that he had not, instead of devoting himself to
learning, gone out to the wilds of America, and settled

---

* Nichols's Illustr. of Lit. History, vol. v. p. 455.   Prior's Life
of Malone, p. 131.

there.   At other times he would wish that he had been brought up as a farmer, or to some kind of business. As he was once speaking thus, Maltby said to him, "What would you then have done without books?" He replied, "I should have done without them." *

* Rogers's Table Talk, "Porsoniana," p. 309.

CHAP. XXV.

IN 1806 was established, by a Company of Shareholders, the London Institution, in the Old Jewry; and Porson was thought the most eligible man to be its Principal Librarian. He was accordingly appointed to that office by a unanimous resolution of the Governors, and the announcement of his election was made to him by "Conversation Sharp," one of their number. Professor Young of Glasgow, writing to Burney about that time, says, "Of Devil Dick you will say nothing. I see by the newspapers they have given him a post; a handsome salary, I hope; a suite of chambers, coal and candle, &c. Porter and cider, I trust, are among the *et cæteras.*" His emoluments were 200*l.* a year and a suite of rooms.

The Library of the Institution is large and valuable, and Porson's handwriting is to be seen in a few of the books.   We have already mentioned what he has written in " My Pocket Book ;" some critical remarks written in Anderson's " British Poets " will be found below ; and there were some notes in a copy of Simplicius's " Commentary on Epictetus." All these are printed by Kidd in his " Tracts and Criticisms." A remark on a fly-leaf of Walter Moyle's Works, regarding a printer's blunder, *Proandcopius Agathias,* for *Procopius and Agathias,* has not escaped Mr. Barker.   There is also a copy of the Aldine Herodotus, in which Porson has marked the chapters in the margin in Arabic numerals, with such nicety and regularity that the eye of the reader, unless upon the closest examination, takes them for print.   For most courteous assistance in inspecting these volumes I am much indebted to Mr. Thomson, the present excellent librarian of the Institution.

But the Porson of that day was no longer the Porson of the time when he edited the Hecuba and the Orestes. His asthma had increased ; the paroxysms of it, as early as 1804, had grown so violent that his friends were often afraid he would expire in their presence *; his habits had originated other diseases ; and he was in a condition rather to rest than to act.   He used " to attend in his place," however, according to Dr. Thomas Young, " when the reading-room was open, and to communicate very readily all the literary information that was required by those who consulted him respect-

* Sexagenarian, vol. i. p. 220.

ing the object of their researches." Many resorted to
his rooms to confer with him on matters of literature,
both ancient and modern, and whatever he knew he was
ready, when he was in sufficient health, and his faculties
were unclouded, to tell. But of his general mode of
discharging the duties of his office, Mr. Maltby, who
had ample means of knowing, gives a very unfavourable
account. His attendance was irregular ; he made no
efforts, such as had been expected from him, to purchase
books to augment the library ; and he was often
brought home, in a state of helpless insensibility, long
after midnight. Had his life been prolonged, it is
hardly to be supposed that he would have been suffered
to continue in his office. " I once read a letter," says
Mr. Maltby, " which he received from the Directors of
the Institution, and which contained, among other severe
things, this cutting remark, 'We only know you are our
librarian by seeing your name attached to the receipts
for your salary.' His intimate friend Dr. Raine was one
of those who signed that letter; and Raine, speaking of it
to me, said, 'Porson well deserved it.'"* He became dis-
satisfied with the Directors, and used to call them "mercantile and mean beyond merchandise and meanness."

During the two years that he held this appointment,
he made occasional visits to Cambridge and Eton, but
seems to have applied himself to no regular study or
occupation. His last visit to Norfolk was made in
1806, when he is said to have carried with him for
perusal a manuscript of some portion of Plato, which
he had borrowed from Dr. E. D. Clarke.

* Rogers's Table Talk, " Porsoniana," p. 337.

In the early part of 1808 his memory had begun to fail; and later in the year symptoms of intermittent fever appeared. In September he complained of being quite out of order, and feeling as if he had the ague.

On the morning of Monday the 19th of that month, he left the Institution to call on his brother-in-law, Mr. Perry, in the Strand, and reached his house about half past one, but, not finding him at home, proceeded along the Strand towards Charing Cross, and at the corner of Northumberland Street was seized with an apoplectic fit, which deprived him of speech and of the power of motion.

For our knowledge of what befel him on that occasion, we are indebted chiefly to Mr. Savage, the Under Librarian of the London Institution, who was then editing a periodical publication called " The Librarian," in which he inserted an account of the commencement of Porson's illness. The work reached only two volumes, and is now scarce.

As none of those who gathered round Porson, when he fell senseless, knew who he was, and as nothing was found upon him to indicate his residence, he was conveyed to the workhouse in Castle Street, St. Martin's Lane, where medical assistance was immediately given, and he was partially restored to consciousness. But as he was still unable to speak, and was unknown there also, it was thought proper to insert an advertisement, describing his person, in the public papers, that his friends might be apprised of his condition. On the following morning, accordingly, a notice appeared in the " British Press," in which he was described as " a tall man, apparently about forty-five years of age, dressed in a blue coat and black breeches, and having in his pocket a gold watch, a trifling quantity of silver, and a memorandum-book, the leaves of which were filled chiefly with Greek lines written in pencil, and partly effaced ; two or three lines of Latin, and an algebraical calculation ; the Greek extracts being principally from ancient medical works."

This account was seen by Mr. Savage, who, knowing that Porson had not slept at home the preceding night, had no doubt that he was the person described in the advertisement. He therefore hastened to the workhouse in Castle Street, where he found Porson, still extremely feeble, but sufficiently recovered to be able to walk. After asking a few questions, Mr. Savage proposed to call a coach, but Porson would not allow Mr. Savage to leave him for a moment, saying that he would rather walk and take one in the street. They therefore proceeded through the King's Mews to Charing Cross, and, getting into a vehicle, drove from thence towards the Old Jewry.

On the way, he spoke of his sudden attack in the street, and congratulated himself on having fallen into the hands of honest people, who had left him his gold watch, and everything else about him, in safety. He also adverted to the fire that had destroyed Covent Garden Theatre a few hours before, of which he had heard from those about him in the morning, and seemed much concerned at the account that Mr. Savage gave him of the loss of lives and property with which the catastrophe had been attended. He conversed, indeed, during the whole of the journey, in his usual pleasant and instructive manner, giving no indication that his mental faculties had suffered any serious injury from his apoplectic seizure. On coming in sight of St. Paul's, he began to speak of Sir Christopher Wren, lamenting the treatment that he had received in the latter part of his life, and observing that " even in our days we were too apt to neglect modest unassuming merit."

About a quarter past nine they reached the house of the Institution, when, on getting out of the coach, his bodily debility was very observable, but he was able to walk, with some effort, to his room, where he took a slight breakfast, consisting of two cups of green tea, which he always preferred, and two small slices of toast. Soon afterwards he went down into the Library, and happened to be met by Dr. Adam Clarke, who published an account of the meeting, as well as of Porson's "last illness and death," and from whose narration it will be proper to give some considerable extracts.

"That his prodigious memory had failed a little for some months before," he observes, "I had myself noticed, and spoken of it with regret to some of my friends; but neither then, nor at the time of which I am now writing, could any other symptom of mental decay be discovered. What follows will probably appear a sufficient proof that he was not only in possession of his ordinary faculties, but that his critical powers were vigorous, and capable of embracing and discerning the nicest distinctions.

" Having that morning occasion to call at the Institution, to consult an edition of a work to which the course of my reading had obliged me to refer, on returning from one of the inner rooms, I found, that, since my entrance, Mr. Porson had walked into that room through which I had just before passed. I went up to him, shook hands, and, seeing him look extremely ill, and not knowing what had happened, I expressed both my surprise and regret. He then drew near to the window, and began in a low, tremulous, interrupted voice, to account for his present appearance; but his speech was so much affected, that I found it difficult to understand what he said.   He proceeded however to give me, as well as he could, an account of his late seizure, and two or three times, with particular emphasis, said, 'I have just escaped death.'

"When he had finished his account of the fit into which he had lately fallen, and on which he seemed unwilling to dwell, except merely to satisfy my inquiries, he suddenly turned the conversation by saying, 'Dr. Clarke, you once promised, but probably you have forgotten, to let me see the stone with the Greek inscription, which was brought from Eleusis.' I replied, 'I have not, Sir, forgotten my promise, but I am now getting a *fac simile* of the stone and inscription engraved, and hope soon to have the pleasure of presenting you with an accurate copy.'   To which he answered, 'I thank you, but I should rather see the stone itself.' I said, 'Then, Sir, you shall see it.   When will you be most at leisure, and I shall wait upon you at the Institution, and bring the stone with me?   Will to-morrow do?' After considering a little, he said, 'On Thursday morning, about eleven o'clock, for at that time of the day I am generally in the library in my official capacity.' This time was accordingly fixed, though from his present appearance I had small hopes of being gratified with that luminous criticism with which, I well knew, he could illustrate and dignify even this small relic of Grecian antiquity.

"It may be necessary here to state that, *about twelve months ago,* when this stone came into my possession, I took a copy one morning of the inscription to the Institution to show it to the Professor. He was not up, but one of the sub-librarians carried it up to his room.   Having examined it, he expressed himself much pleased with it, observing that it afforded a very fair specimen of the Greek character after the time that Greece fell under the power of the Romans; 'for it was evident,' he said, 'that the inscription was not prior to that period.'   Some days afterwards, I met him in

Y

the library of the Institution, and he surprised me by saying, 'I can show you a printed copy of the inscription on your stone.' He then led me up stairs to his study, and, taking down Meursius's *Theseus*, showed me in the tract *de Pagis Atticis*, at the end, the very inscription, which had been taken down from the stone, then at Eleusis, by Dr. Spon, in 1676. From this time he wished particularly to see it, as by it the existence of the village *Besa*, and the proper method of writing it with a single *s*, to distinguish it from a village called Bissa, in Locris, was confirmed; and he considered the character to be curious."

The stone exhibited the inscription ΤΙΒΕΡΙΟΣ ΚΛΑΥΔΙΟΣ ΘΕΟΦΙΛΟΣ ΤΙΒΕΡΙΟΥ ΚΛΑΔΙΟΥ ΘΕΜΙΣΤΟΚΛΕΟΣ ΒΗΣΑΙΕΩΣ. It was found in the kitchen of an old house in North Green, Worship Street, by a young man surveying the premises, who, noticing the letters on it, procured it from the tenant, and presented it to Dr. Clarke. The Doctor supposes that it was brought from Eleusis by Sir George Wheeler, who accompanied Spon in his travels through Greece, and that it passed from him to John Kemp, a great antiquary, at whose death it was sold, among other curiosities, by auction.

"After having fixed Thursday morning," proceeds Dr. Clarke, "to wait on him with the stone, I approached the table, and took up the quarto edition of Dr. Shaw's Travels, and, unfolding the plate containing the *Lithostroton Palæstrinum*, (a copy of a mosaic pavement, found at Palæstrini, now Preneste, in Italy,) said, 'I wish just to look at the title of this plate, as I have got a copy of it, collated with that in Montfaucon, engraved for a work which I am just now about to publish.' Whether this part of Dr. Shaw's work had ever attracted his notice before, I cannot tell; but seeing several words in the uncial Greek character interspersed through the plate, he appeared particularly struck with an animal of the *lutra* species, there denominated ΕΝΗΤΔΡΙΣ, where the η evidently serves as an aspirate to the υ, and immediately observed, 'If this be authentic, here is an additional proof that the η was anciently used and pronounced as we do our aspirated H.' I replied, it certainly was; and as to the authenticity of the *Prenestine Pavement*, I believed it could not reasonably be called in question.

"He seemed to wish to converse further on the subject, though his speech was greatly affected, so that he was a long time before he could complete a sentence, not only because of the paralytic affection of all the organs of speech, but also through extreme debility, and the dryness of the tongue and fauces, his lips being parched so as almost to resemble a cinder. Though I wished to hear his remarks, yet feeling a desire to save him from the great pain he appeared to have in speaking, I would have withdrawn, but felt reluctant on account of his appearing pleased with my visit. I endeavoured therefore to change the conversation, in order to divert him as much as possible from feeling the necessity of any mental exertion; and, taking occasion from the remark he had made on the power of the η in the ΕΝΗΤΔΡΙΣ, I observed that I had noticed a very curious peculiarity in the formation of an *omega* on my Eleusinian stone; it resembles, said I, a kappa lying on its left perpendicular limb, with a semicircle drawn between the two arms on the left, thus, Ⴗ, making the form with my pen on a piece of paper. I then asked him if he had ever noticed this form of the omega in any ancient inscription. He said, 'No, but it may serve to form a system from;' and then began to relate with considerable pleasantry the story of the critic, who, having found some peculiarity in writing one of the tenses of the verb γράφω, made an entire *new person* of it. I said I wish the system-makers, especially in literature, would have done, as they are continually perplexing and retarding science, and embarrassing one another. To this he answered, 'Your wish is the wish of all, and yet each in his turn will produce his system; but you recollect those lines in the Greek Anthology,

Οὐκ ἔστι γήμας ὅστις οὐ χειμάζεται,
Λέγουσι πάντες, καὶ γαμοῦσιν εἰδότες.

As soon as he had repeated these lines, which he did, considering his circumstances, with a readiness that surprised me, he proceeded, as was his general custom, when he quoted any author in the learned languages, to give a translation of what he had quoted. This was a peculiar delicacy in his character. He could not bear to see a man confounded, unless he knew him to be a pedant; and therefore, though he might presume that the person to whom he spoke understood the language, yet, because it might possibly be otherwise, and the man feel embarrassed on the occasion, he always paid him the compliment of being acquainted with the subject, and saved him, if ignorant, from confusion, by translating it. This however, in the above case, cost him extreme pain, as he was *some minutes* in expressing its meaning, which astonished me the more, because, notwithstanding his debility, and the paralysis under which the organs of speech laboured, he had so shortly before quoted the original in *a few seconds*, and with comparatively little hesitation. The truth is, so imbued was his mind with Grecian literature, that he *thought*, as well as *spoke*, in that language, and found it much more easy at this time, from the power of habit and association, to pronounce Greek than to pronounce his mother-tongue.

"Seeing him so very ill and weak, I thought it best to withdraw, and, having shook hands with him, (which, alas! was the last time that I was to have that satisfaction,) and, with a pained heart, earnestly wished him a speedy restoration to health, I walked out of the room, promising to visit him, if possible, on Thursday morning, with the Greek inscription. He accompanied me to the head of the great staircase, making some remarks on his indisposition, which I did not distinctly hear; and then, leaning over the balustrade, he continued speaking to me till I was more than halfway down stairs. When nearly at the bottom, I looked np, and saw him still leaning over the balustrade; I stopped a moment, as if to take a last view of a man to whose erudition and astonishing critical acumen my mind had ever bowed down with becoming reverence, and then said, ' Sir, I am truly sorry to see you so low.' To which he answered, ' I have had a narrow escape from death.' And then leaving the stair-head, he returned towards the library. This was the *last conversation* he was ever capable of holding on any subject. On matters of *religion*, except in a *critical* way, he was, I believe, never forward to converse. I should have been glad to have known his views at this solemn time; but as there were some gentlemen present when we met in the library, the place and time were improper."

What occurred at the Institution, after Dr. Clarke's departure, must be sought in the narrative of Mr. Savage. " On Dr. Clarke taking leave of him, the Professor soon afterwards went up stairs into his own room, and, stopping a short time, came down again, apparently going out; when Mrs. Savage observed to him that she thought from his indisposition he would consult his own ease and quiet by remaining at home, and that she could provide him for dinner anything that he should prefer; with this he seemingly acquiesced; but, as I was led to believe, the Professor fancied himself to be under some restraint, and, to convince himself of the contrary, walked out, and soon after went into the African, or Cole's Coffee-house, in St. Michael's Alley, Cornhill."

On entering this house, he was so greatly exhausted, as we find on recurring to Dr. Clarke's narrative, that he must have fallen, had he not caught hold of the

brass rod of one of the boxes, when he was noticed by
a gentleman, Mr. J. P. Leigh, with whom he had frequently dined at the same place, and who communicated
to Dr. Clarke what happened on the occasion.

" A chair being given him, he sat down and stared around
with a vacant and ghastly countenance; Mr. Leigh, addressing him, asked how he was, but he did not recollect him,
and gave no answer.   He then invited him to have dinner,
but this he refused.   He asked him to have a glass of wine;
this he also declined; but on Mr. Leigh's assuring him that
it would serve to revive him, he smiled, and said, ' Do you
think it will? " and then drank about one half of it, giving
back the glass to Mr. Leigh again, which he appeared scarcely
able to hold.   Previously to this, from his coming into the
Coffee-house, his head lay down on his breast, and he was
continually muttering something, but in so low and indistinct
a tone as not to be audible; but after taking the wine he
seemed a little revived, and was able to hold his head more
erect.   Mr. Leigh then pressed him much to have some
dinner, but he declined it, shaking his head.   As he appeared
to be much exhausted, and very cold, Mr. Leigh ordered a
jelly to be put in a wine-glass of warm water, with a very
little brandy in it, and begged him to drink it; he refused
at first, but on Mr. Leigh's entreaties, and assuring him it
would do him much good, he took the tumbler, drank about
two spoonfuls of it, and returned the glass.   He seemed now
considerably roused, but would make no answer to several
questions addressed to him by Mr. Leigh, except these words,
which he repeated probably twenty times: ' The gentleman
said it was a ludicrous piece of business, and *I* think so too.'
These words he uttered in so low a tone, that Mr. Leigh was
obliged to put his ear nearly to his mouth in order to hear
them.   ' Not thinking,' says Mr. Leigh, ' that a Coffee-house
was a proper place to witness the wreck of so great a mind,
I ordered a coach to be brought to take him to the Institution.   He refused for some time to go into the coach, but

at last was helped in by the landlord, and the waiter accompanied him home. When they came to the Old Jewry, the waiter asked him where they should stop. He then put his head out of the window, and waved with his hand when they came opposite to the door of the Institution. The waiter says that, previous to this, he appeared quite senseless all the way, and did not utter a word. How quick the transition from the highest degrees of intellect to the lowest apprehensions of sense ! On what a precarious tenure does frail humanity hold even its choicest and most necessary gifts !"

Another account, in the "Gentleman's Magazine," states that on his return to the London Institution on the morning of the Tuesday, he entered, after taking his slight breakfast, into conversation with some gentlemen there, and remarked that "the keeper of the workhouse was a wag, and had endeavoured to pose him with his wit." "They observed," continues the statement, "much incoherence, both in his manner and matter, and, fearing that he was labouring under some fatal disorder, they thought it right to recommend him to prepare his will. He at first seemed reluctant, but afterwards assented to the propriety of it, and entered into general conversation on the moral obligation of disposing of our property after death ; adding that the subject had often been treated in a legal way, but scarcely ever in the manner he wished, except in a work entitled 'Symbolæography ;' and he afterwards left the room and brought one of his Catalogues, in which that book was described. He remained in conversation in this way during five hours, sometimes in the full exercise of his powers, at others wild and wandering."

'Symbolæography' is a work published by William West, a lawyer, in 1590, containing forms of all kinds of legal instruments. It passed through fifteen editions, according to Watt's "Bibliotheca Britannica," but is now little valued.

This conversation about the book might have taken place on some previous morning, but could not have occurred on the morning of the Tuesday after he came from the workhouse, for it is evident from the narratives of Mr. Savage and Dr. Clarke that he was at that time far too weak to hold such discourse.

The account proceeds to say that after taking leave of the gentlemen, with whom he had been discoursing on wills, he went to Cole's Coffee-house, and, having talked some time to a friend there, suddenly left the place, and took his way to Cornhill, " where, looking up at the vane and clock of the Exchange, which had been under repair, a number of persons assembled round him, surprised at his fixed attention, the motive of which he did not explain. The porter of the London Institution, happening to observe him in this situation, conducted him back to Cole's, where, on taking two glasses of wine, the paroxysm and insensibility returned; and he was carried home in a coach to the Old Jewry."

When he was brought into the Institution, Mr. Savage went immediately for Mr. Norris, a surgeon, who lived near, and was one of Porson's intimate friends. Mr. Norris afterwards wrote an account of his attendance on Porson, in which he states that he had seen him on the preceding Friday, when " his countenance was pale, his skin hot, his pulse quick and

feeble, and his tongue white," and he complained of
having been ill for some time of *ague and fever*, but
thought himself then growing better. "I told him,"
says Mr. Norris, "that I supposed his reason for using
the term ague was his having had cold fits succeeded
by heat (to which he assented); that these symptoms
were common to almost all fevers, however excited;
that he was at that moment very seriously ill from a
cause entirely different from what he imagined; and I
concluded by begging him to send for my friend Mr.
Upton, who was just at hand, or for some physician of
his own acquaintance. To this however he would not
consent, as he said he was now better, but I so far
prevailed as to obtain his promise to do what I desired
the next morning, if he should not continue to improve.
To a message which I sent the next day, he returned
for an answer that he was better."

When Mr. Norris saw him on the Tuesday, in compliance with Mr. Savage's summons, he found him
"sitting up, and staring about him, as if surprised.
The only answer I could obtain," he says, "to any
question, was, 'Well! How! What!' and he appeared
to be utterly incapable of reasoning, or of comprehend-
ing what was said to him.

"In this state he was put to bed, and I sent immediate notice of his situation to his brother-in-law Mr.
Perry, who soon arrived, and who continued to the last
to pay him the kindest attention, with the most affectionate solicitude."

After specifying the medicines given, which afforded
relief for a time, Mr. Norris proceeds to say that "Dr.
Babington and Mr. Upton now saw him, when stupor

had again returned, accompanied by general debility. Blisters and sinapisms were applied, which procured transient relief, and it was endeavoured to support his strength by wine and cordial medicines, of which, however, very little was swallowed. He continued, with a few slight and short appearances of amendment, to grow weaker until Sunday night, when he died; having gradually lost the power of speech and sight, so that some time before his death his eyes were perfectly insensible to the light of a candle.

Dr. Clarke saw him once during his illness, on Friday the 23rd, when he appeared more collected in mind than he had been since the Tuesday evening. "I went into his room," says he, "and drawing close to his bedside, asked him how he did. He fixed his eyes on me at first with a wild and vacant stare, and seemed to labour to recollect me. At last he recognised me, but was too much exhausted to speak, though he appeared comparatively sensible."

He expired on the night of the 25th of September 1808, exactly as the clock struck twelve, with a deep groan, but without any struggle, in the forty-ninth year of his age.

His friends thought it proper that the body should be opened; an operation which was accordingly performed on the following Tuesday, in the presence of Dr. Babington, Sir William Blizard, Mr. Thomas Blizard, Mr. Upton, and Mr. Norris. Their report was as follows:

" The body was emaciated.
" The dura mater did not exhibit any unusual appearance.

" Under the tunica arachnoides a clear fluid was seen to be generally diffused over the surface of the brain; and upon separating the pia mater, lymph, to the quantity of about an ounce, issued from between the convolutions of the brain.

" The brain was of an unusually firm texture; its cortical part was of a lighter colour, and its medullary part less white, than is common.

" The ventricles did not seem to contain more than one ounce of lymph; but upon removing the whole of the brain, at least an ounce and a half more lymph remained at the basis of the skull.

" The abdominal viscera did not present anything particularly worthy of notice. The substance of the intestines, indeed, was unusually thick, as was that of the bladder; there was an adhesion of the omentum to the liver, and several more-between it and the diaphragm; and on its peritoneal covering there was a small ossification. The pylorus was very narrow, but without disease. To none of these circumstances do we attach any consequence, as they do not appear to have had any share in producing death.

" The heart was sound, and the pericardium contained the usual quantity of lymph.

" The left lung had many adhesions to the pleura, and bore visible marks of former inflammation. The right lung was in a perfectly sound state.

" From a due consideration of these circumstances, and of the symptoms observed during the short period of his confinement, as well as what we know of his sedentary mode of living, we are of opinion that *the effused lymph in and upon the brain,* which we believe to have been the effect of recent inflammation, *was the immediate cause of his death.* It may also be observed that his health had been in a declining state during some months, so as to have been visible to his friends.

" It is very clear that during the indisposition which he called ague and fever, a slow inflammatory action was going on within the head, the result of which was the effusion above noticed. The first effect of compression from this cause that was noticed was on Monday the 19th of September, on which day he walked from the Old Jewry to the west end of the town, when he fell in the street."

The adhesions of the left lung to the pleura, says Dr. Clarke, are supposed to have been the effect of the illness which he had when a boy at Eton. " The healthy state of the viscera," observes the Doctor, " may be attributed to his general abstinence from ardent spirits, which, I am assured by one of his intimate friends, he very rarely drank, and scarcely ever to excess." For this notion it is to be feared that there was too little ground ; though he may have been more abstinent from spirituous liquors during the later part of his life than he had been for some time previous. As to the skull, which some reports stated to be uncommonly thick and others uncommonly thin, it was, in reality, much like those of other men.

The " algebraical calculation" found in his memorandum-book, is supposed to have been the following equation, which he had presented, but a short time before, to Mr. Charles Butler, having copied it from a memorandum-book which he carried about him, at Mr. Butler's request :

$$xy + zu = 444$$
$$xz + yu = 180$$
$$xu + yz = 156$$
$$xyzu = 5184$$

In the conversation which he held with Mr. Butler on that occasion, he intimated that he meditated a new edition of the *Arithmetica* of Diophantus, as well as some addition to the Letters on 1 John v. 7, as some thought that the argument for the authenticity of the text, drawn from the Confession of Faith presented by the African clergy to Hunneric King of the Ostrogoths, had not been satisfactorily answered. The solution to the equation is $u = 36$, $x = 3$, $y = 4$, $z = 12$.

On the Monday after his death, October 3, his remains were removed from the London Institution, to be deposited in the chapel of Trinity College, Cambridge. The hearse was followed, as it left London, by four mourning coaches and six private carriages, in which were many of Porson's relatives and intimate friends, and was received at the gate of Trinity College, in due form, at half past two, on Tuesday afternoon. From hence the coffin was removed to the hall, where, according to the ancient usage, when distinguished respect is paid to a deceased member of the College, the body lay in state till five o'clock. At that hour Dr. Mansel, the Master of the College, who was then Bishop of Bristol, the Vice-Master, the senior and junior fellows, and many others desirous to show honour to the dead, advanced into the hall, and walked in procession round the coffin, the pall being borne by the eight senior fellows, among whom were two of his own standing, Hailstone and Raine, and his old examiner Lambert, and having attached to it several copies of verses in Greek and English, celebrating, as was then common in the universities at the funerals of eminent men, the abilities and merits of the deceased. The service at the grave was read by the Bishop of Bristol. His remains repose at the foot of the statue of Newton, in the same chapel with those of Bentley. *His epitaph* there *is his name alone*, inscribed on a plain slab.

On a brass plate on the coffin were engraved the following words :

RICARDUS . PORSON

APUD . CANTABRIGIENSES

LINGUÆ . GRÆCÆ . PROFESSOR

ET

COLL. TRIN. S.S. ET . IND. OLIM . SOCIUS

APUD . LONDINENSES

INSTITUTIONIS . LITTERARIÆ

BIBLIOTHECARIUS . PRINCEPS

NATUS . VIII. CAL. JAN. MDCCLIX.

OBIIT . VII. CAL. OCT. MDCCCVIII.*

Of the Greek verses affixed to the pall, one copy, written by Mr. George Burges, has been preserved in the " Classical Journal."†

Εἰ μὲν τὰ θνητῶν πράγμαθ', ὅστις εὖ ποίῃ,
Δύναμιν ἔχοι τιν' ὥστε σωθῆναι θανεῖν,
Πόρσων ἂν ἔζη δὴ πολὺν βίου χρόνον ·
Νῦν δ', εἰ καλῶς τις εἴτε μὴ καλῶς πονεῖ,
Οὐδέν τι μᾶλλόν ἐστιν ἀποφυγὴ μόρου ·
Οὐκοῦν ἐγείρων θρῆνον οἴκτρον ἐπὶ τάφῳ
Τοιοῦδε φῶτος οὐκ ἐπαιδεσθήσομαι·
"Αλλοι γὰρ ὥσπερ δένδρ' ἀχρεῖ', ὅδε δ' ἔπεσεν
Ὑπερτενὴς ὡς δρῦς, ἀγάλμαθ' Ἑλλάδος.
'Αλλ' ἡδόνη τις ἐστὶ τοῖσδε γ' ἐν κακοῖς·
Τὰ τοῦδε γὰρ πάντ' ἀνδρὸς οὐ τεθνήξεται·
"Εχει μὲν Ἄδης σῶμα, περιμένει δ' ἔτι
Ψυχή τις οὖσ' ἄφθαρτος ἐν τοῖς γράμμασιν.

Another copy of Greek verses on Porson, which, as Dr. Young has observed, declines Πόρσων with a long o, and Νεύτων with a short, is preserved in the same journal, but whether it is a relic of the offerings at the

---

* Kidd, Tracts, p. xxiv.   † Vol. i. p. 81.

funeral, or was composed since, or who was the author of it, I know not.

A. Τίς ποτ' ἀνὴρ περίσημος, ὃν ἐνθάδε τύμβος ἐέργει,
   Ἦ παρὰ Βεντλείῳ Νεύτονος εἰσὶ ταφαί;
B. Ὦ ξεῖν', αἰδεσθεὶς ὄνομα κλυτὸν ἀνδρὸς ἄκουσον,
   Ἀτθίσιν ὃς Μούσαις λαμπρὸν ἔτειλε φάος.
   Τῷ δὲ θεαὶ κατέδειξαν, ἀμειβόμεναι χάριν ἀνδρὸς,
   Οἵ ἐν Ἀθηναίοις θεῖον ἄγοντο χορόν.
   Ἐκ τῶνδ' οὖν μελέων τε θέσιν θεσμόν τε κοθόρνου
   Εὑρὼν ὀψιγόνοις γνωστὸν ἔθηκεν ἰδεῖν.
   Πόρσωνος δ' ὄνομ' ἐστί· τρίτος δ' ἐπὶ τοῖσιν ἀπελθὼν
   Οὓς εἶπας δόξης ἴσον ἀνεῖλε μέρος.

The last of the Cantabrigian heroes whose funerals were honoured with verses is said to have been the Professor of Mineralogy, Dr. E. D. Clarke, who was buried at Jesus College in 1821.

Beloe and Pryse Gordon have related that Porson, to the surprise of his friends, left at his death nearly 2000*l.* of his own property in the funds, to which his relatives became heirs; and Gordon blames him for having left no tokens of his good-will to his wife's orphans, or to Perry, who had cherished him like a brother for twenty years. But both these writers, though they may be thought to have had ample means of informing themselves, were yet mistaken, for though Porson did surprise his friends by leaving money in the funds, the sum was only 888*l.* 17*s.* 7*d.* The 2000*l.* which led Gordon and Beloe into error, was the money, amounting to nearly that sum, which had been subscribed for his annuity, and which, as the contributors, or their heirs, declined to receive any of it back, was ultimately devoted to founding the *Porson Prize* and the *Porson Scholarship.*

But out of this fund, first of all, certain expenses
were to be paid ; the expenses of Porson's funeral ; of
a bust by Chantrey, which is now in the library of
Trinity College, Cambridge; and of engraving the
portrait by Hoppner, an impression of which, executed
by Sharpe, was sent to each of the subscribers to the
fund, or their executors. After this deduction, enough
was left to purchase Bank annuities to a considerable
amount.

In 1816 it was proposed to the University of Cambridge, by the Rev. Dr. Burney and the Rev. J. Cleaver
Banks, who, at the time of Porson's death, were the only
surviving trustees of the fund, that, as the contributors
had left to the trustees to apply the fund to whatever purposes they should think fit, so much of it should be trans-
ferred into the names of the Vice-chancellor, Masters,
and Scholars of the University, as would produce the
yearly sum of twenty pounds, for the foundation of an
annual prize, to be called the Porson University Prize,
consisting of a Greek book or books, to be given for the
translation of a passage from Shakspeare, Ben Jonson,
Massinger, or Beaumont and Fletcher, into Greek
iambics. This proposal the authorities readily accepted, and the Vice-chancellor, the Greek Professor,
and the Public Orator, with four Heads of colleges,
were appointed examiners for the prize.

After this endowment was made, it was thought
proper that the rest of the fund should be left to
accumulate at compound interest, being invested in the
names of the Chancellor, Masters, and Scholars of the
University, until it should reach such a sum as would
be sufficient to found a handsome scholarship; and

accordingly, in 1848, an agreement was made, between the executors of Dr. Burney and Cleaver Banks, and the authorities of the University, that as soon as the annual interest of the money invested should amount to 65*l.* such scholarship, to be called the Porson University Scholarship, should be founded, the examiners for it being the same as for the Porson University Prize. In 1854 the sum amounted to 2250*l.* 3 per cent consols; and on March 24th, 1855, Mr. Herbert Snow, of St. John's College, was elected the first Porson scholar.

Of Porson's library, between two and three hundred of the most valuable volumes, and those most enriched with notes, with the whole of his papers, were purchased, at the suggestion of Dr. Raine, by Trinity College, Cambridge, for a thousand guineas.* The rest were sold by auction, but none fetched very large prices, except the Grenville Homer, which brought eighty-three guineas.† The produce of the whole was however 1032*l.* 17*s.* 3*d.* The value of all that he left was,

	£	s.	d.
Library sold to Cambridge - - - -	1050	0	0
——— sold in London - - - -	1032	17	3
Copyright of plays to Wilkie and Robinson - -	200	0	0
888*l.* 17*s.* 7*d.* in 5 per cents, at 97 - -	862	3	7
Furniture and effects, after deducting all expenses -	211	14	10
	£3356	15	8

This sum, as he died intestate, was equally divided between his sister, Mrs. Hawes, and the three children of his brother Henry, Julius, Frederick, and a daughter.

* Museum Criticum, vol. i. p. 116.
† Classical Journal, vol. i. p. 385.

All these have since died, the last in 1814, so that the name is extinct. Mr. Siday Hawes, Porson's brother-in-law, administered to the estate, and hence was erroneously reported to have inherited the property.

How Porson, with his habits and means, could have observed sufficient economy to save so much, is wonderful. He bought many books; his annual income from his fellowship during the ten years that he held it was not more than 100*l.*, and he had certainly saved nothing when he resigned it; his annuity from the subscription was of about the same amount; the value of his professorship was only 40*l.* a year; and though his salary at the London Institution was 200*l.* a year, he held the appointment there not more than two years. His friends might therefore well be astonished at finding that he had the greater part of nine hundred pounds in the funds at his death.

As to Perry's conduct towards Porson, Porson's surviving connexions do not represent it to have been quite so disinterested as it has generally been considered. He contrived to get into his hands 600*l.* of Porson's money, which he declined, with mean excuses, to restore to Porson's relatives, till a threat of legal proceedings alarmed him.

From the papers, and the margins of the books, were collected by Monk and Blomfield those annotations on the tragic and other poets which were published in 1812, under the title of *Porson's Adversaria;* and, as the notes on Aristophanes were extremely numerous, a separate collection was made of them by Dobree, entitled *Aristophanica.* The difficulty of arranging these observations was very great, for none of the manuscripts were left in a state for publication ; some of the remarks were written in copy-books, in so small a hand that one page would contain forty or fifty complete notes ; some were on detached scraps of paper ; and all had been noted down at different periods of his life, on the suggestion of the moment, and left to be put in order when time should serve.* How well the editors performed their task the public has long known.

The notes on Pausanias were printed at the end of Gaisford's *Lectiones Platonicæ* in 1820 ; the Photius was published by Dobree in 1822; and the emendations of Suidas were appended to Gaisford's edition of that lexicographer in 1834. Some annotations on the Greek historians, the lexicographers, particularly Hesychius, and on some of the Latin authors, still remain unpublished.

* Mus. Crit. vol. i. p. 116.   Month. Rev. Dec. 1817, p. 421.

CHAP. XXVI.

PORSON'S reading extended to all kinds of books in
Greek, Latin, French, and English, beyond which
tongues he seems to have attempted few or no linguistic
conquests. These are the four languages which he
intimates that he can speak in the macaronic doggrel entitled *Oracula Echûs de Bello et Statu Nationis*, printed
in Beloe's "Sexagenarian."* His favourite authors
in Greek were the tragic poets and Aristophanes, and
perhaps, next to these, Athenæus. He was fond of
reading the Greek physicians, one of whose folios,
especially Galen's, he sometimes put under his pillow
at night; not, as he used to observe, because he expected medicinal virtue from it, but because his asthma
required that his head should be kept high.† Of
Thucydides he confessed, according to Mr. Maltby, that
he knew comparatively little, and that, when he read
him, he was obliged to mark with a pencil, in almost

* Vol i. p. 249.   † Short Account of Porson, p. 11.

every page, passages which he did not understand. Being once asked whether he had read all Plutarch, he replied, " He is too much for me." To Plato he seems to have given great attention, and sent Thomas Taylor, when he was employed about his translation, several corrections of the Greek text, which Taylor, from his superficial acquaintance with the Greek language, either undervalued, or knew not how to use.* As to Aristophanes, Dr. Burney said that no man had ever understood him so well at thirty years of age as Porson.† Lucian, though his matter might have been thought attractive to Porson, he appears to have read but little, disliking his Greek as not being of the golden age.

On Athenæus he bestowed such critical care that the editors of his *Adversaria* affirm that more errors were removed from the text by the single hand of Porson than by the whole series of critics that preceded him.‡ " Every scholar knows," says the reviewer of his *Adversaria* in the " Monthly Review,"§ " the miserably corrupt state in which so many valuable fragments of the Greek dramatic writers have been preserved to us in the text of Athenæus ; and we also know how greatly the learning and industry of Casaubon have contributed to illustrate the meaning of the author and improve the text, though still leaving innumerable passages in utter obscurity, and frequently confounding the verses of the poets with the prose text in which they are quoted. Infinite as are the merits of Casaubon in illustrating things, it must be acknowledged that, in

* Rogers's Table Talk, " Porsoniana," p. 327.
† Barker's Literary Anecdotes, vol. ii. p. 188.
‡ Præf. in Adversar. p. xiii.   § Dec. 1817, p. 426.

the less highly valuable, but not unimportant department of arranging words and syllables, he was not,
and, from the state of Greek literature in the age in
which he lived, he *could not*, be always equally successful; nor has the late German editor (Schweighæuser)
succeeded much better in the task.   It was reserved
for the accurate and accomplished scholar, whose lucu-
brations are now before us, to pour a flood of light on
the almost impenetrable obscurities of a text so often
corrupt in itself, and sometimes still more vitiated by
the attempts of preceding commentators to improve it.
By the peculiar penetration of his mind, the accuracy
of his ear, and the felicity of his conjectures, we find
verse detected in its latent prosaic garb, and prose
degraded from its poetic stilts ; order rising from confusion; and metre and harmony resulting from intricate
and apparently hopeless corruption."   Porson had
meditated an entire edition of Athenæus *, but the
project, like many of his other designs, was doomed
not to be accomplished.

Of the Latin authors, it is not apparent in which he
delighted most, unless it were Cicero, whose Tusculan
Disputations he sometimes quoted, especially the senti-
ment of Epicharmus from the first book,

> " Emori nolo, sed me esse mortuum nihil æstimo."
> Ἀπό μου θανεῖν ἤ, θνήσκειν δ' οὔ μοι διαφέρει.

Nor did he forget to couple with it Juvenal's lines,

> " Esse aliquos manes, et subterranea regna,
> Et contum, et Stygio ranas in gurgite nigras,

---

* Adversaria, pp. 83—87.

Atque unâ transire vadum tot millia cymbâ,
Nec pueri credunt, nisi qui nondum ære lavantur."

Of all the Latin dictionaries, extant in his time, he gave the preference to Gesner's *Thesaurus*. As to Greek Lexicons, he set a high value on that of Scapula, which he recommended a gentleman, who wished to commence Greek at the age of forty, and asked him what books he should use, to read through from the first page to the last.* He valued the Geneva edition most, and said that there were words in it not to be found in Stephens's *Thesaurus*.†

For all modern Latin and Greek poetry he expressed supreme contempt, and said of the *Musæ Etonenses*, when the publication came out, that it was "all trash, fit only to be put behind the fire." This judgment he passed as a utilitarian, considering that it added nothing to the stock of human knowledge, presenting only well-known thoughts in a garb emulating that of antiquity.

In French he read a great number of books, and said that if he had a son, he would "endeavour to make him familiar with French and English authors rather than with the classics, as Greek and Latin are only luxuries."‡

Many English authors he had read with very great attention. Swift was a great favourite with him. He could repeat large quantities of Swift's verses, and pointed out a remarkable correspondence of a passage in the "Tale of a Tub," which he was very fond of

* Rogers's Table Talk, "Porsoniana," p. 329.
† Kidd, Tracts, p. 403.
‡ Rogers's Table Talk, "Porsoniana," p. 329.

reading, with another in "Gulliver's Travels;" a correspondence which none of Swift's critics had noticed.
In the Introduction to the "Tale of a Tub," it is said,
"Fourscore and eleven pamphlets have I writ under three
reigns, and for the service of six and thirty factions."
In "Gulliver's Travels," not far from the beginning, it is
said, "On each side of the gate was a small window
not above six inches from the ground ; into that on the
left side the king's smiths conveyed fourscore and
eleven chains, like those that hang to a lady's watch
in Europe, and almost as large, which were locked to
my left leg with six and thirty padlocks."   "From the
curious coincidence of the numbers in these two
passages," says Dobree, "Professor Porson inferred that
both were written by the same person, that is, that
Swift was the author of the 'Tale of a Tub.' " *

He was very fond of repeating a defence of a passage
of Boyle against Bentley, which Bentley had charged
with a ludicrous mistake, when it contained none :

"To show Stobæus's approbation of Phalaris's Epistles,"
says Bentley †, "I had observed that he quoted three of
them, under the title of Phalaris.   The gentleman adds
one more ; and I should thank him for his liberality, had
not any one of those three I mentioned been sufficient for
my purpose ; but where he says, 'It is Tit. 218, and again
in the collection of Antonius and Maximus, and that I overlooked it,' for that I must beg his pardon ; for I could
hardly overlook the 218th title of Stobæus, when there are
but 121 in all.   It is not *title* 218th but *page* 218th ; and
not of Stobæus, but of Antonius that is printed at the end
of him ; but the *title* of Stobæus, that the Examiner would
cite, is 84.   How far 'the assistant that consulted books

* Kidd, Tracts, p. 316.   † Dissert. on Phalaris, p. 15.

for the Examiner may be chargeable with this mistake, or how far it goes towards a discovery that Mr. B. himself never looked into Stobæus, I leave for others to determine."

On this charge Porson used frequently to observe :

"Mr. Boyle and his assistants are so often in the wrong, that it is barely doing justice to defend them when they are in the right.   Boyle used the Frankfort edition of Stobæus, folio, 1581, in which the collections of *Stobæus, Antonius,* and *Maximus* are blended together, so that the title of Stobæus, where the quotation from Phalaris occurs, is in other editions the 84th, but in the Frankfort the 218th. The singular coincidence of the number 218 led Bentley into this mistake." *

Junius was an author that he often read, and of whose letters he carried many portions in his memory. On one passage he proposed an excellent emendation.   " Your zeal in the cause of an unfortunate prince was expressed with sincerity of wine, and some of the solemnities of religion."   Before " the sincerity " Porson supposed that the word *all* had dropped out, being necessary to complete the antithesis to " *some* of the solemnities." †

Respecting Dryden, as given in Anderson's edition of the British Poets, he had written, on a blank leaf of a volume of that publication, now in the Library of the London Institution, the following remarks. " The editor has with singular good faith suppressed above seven hundred of Dryden's verses, to wit, the twenty-seventh idyllium of Theocritus, with the translations from the third and fourth books of Lucretius.   If the indecency of some passages was the cause of their suppression,

* Kidd, Tracts, p. 314.   † Ibid. p. 208.

why were not the verses against the love of life, and
the fear of death, retained ?   Dr. Anderson has also
omitted near two octavo pages of preface ; but, to be
consistent, he should have cancelled the paragraph in
which mention is made of that part of the third book.
However, to make Dryden some amends for depriving
him of his own, he has given him two poems that are
not his : *Tarquin and Tullia*, and *Suum Cuique*. *Suum
Cuique* was written by some staunch Jacobite, but I
know not whom ; 'Tarquin and Tullia' was written by
Arthur Mainwaring, who afterwards turned Whig, and
expiated his youthful heresy in 'The Medley.'—See
Malone's ' Life of Dryden,' p. 546.

" The accuracy of the editor is equal to his good
faith.   P. 679, *Horace* de Arte Amandi, for *Ovid*."*

He liked Milton.   In the passage of the second book
of " Paradise Lost " describing the opening of the
infernal gates he has restored to Milton an expression
which had unjustly been taken from him.   The phrase
on their hinges grate harsh thunder was generally supposed, on the authority of Johnson in his "Miscellaneous
Observations on Macbeth," to have been copied from
the " Romance of Don Bellianis," where the gates of a
castle are mentioned as " grating harsh thunder on their
brazen hinges ;" but Porson discovered that there were
two editions of " Don Bellianis," one published before
the " Paradise Lost," and the other after it ; that the
second contained that phrase, but not the first; and that
consequently Milton did not borrow from the author of
the romance, but the author of the romance from
Milton.

* Kidd, Tracts, p. 326.

He said that if he lived, he would write an essay to show the world how unjustly Milton had been treated by Johnson.*

This referred to Lauder's charge of plagiarism against Milton, to which Johnson is generally thought to have listened with too great willingness, and in which Porson thought that he could prove him guilty of criminal participation. He told Holt White that he intended to publish something on the subject, and that he was only waiting to procure a pamphlet bearing on the controversy. Two of the arguments which he meant to use Holt White thought decisive of the question. First, That, as Johnson was always eager for inquiry on every subject connected with literature, and always ready to find cause for depreciating Milton, it is strange that he should not have desired the satisfaction of seeing with his own eyes the passages which Lauder declared Milton to have copied. Secondly, That Johnson has preserved, throughout his biography of Milton, a deep silence on the story of Lauder and his falsified quotations.†

Numberless portions of Shakspeare's language he had always ready for application, as may be seen in his "Letters on Hawkins's Johnson," and his "Letters to Travis." He did not class himself, doubtless, with those who worship Shakspeare as a god, but he must have been greatly fascinated with much of his phraseology. He was fond of asserting, however, that the fine passage in the "Tempest" about *the cloud-capp'd towers, the*

---

* Rogers's Table Talk, " Porsoniana," p. 329.

† Holt White's Review of Johnson's Criticism on Milton's Prose, p. 30.

gorgeous palaces, &c., is excelled by some lines in Sir Alexander (afterwards Lord) Sterling's tragedy of "Darius," of which he called Shakspeare's verses an imitation :

> " Let greatness of her glassy sceptres vaunt,
>   Not sceptres, no, but reeds, soon bruised, soon broken ;
> And let this worldly pomp our wits enchant ;—
>   All fades, and scarcely leaves behind a token.
>
> These golden palaces, these gorgeous halls,
>   With furniture superficiously fair ;
> Those stately courts, those sky-encount'ring walls,
>   Vanish, all ; like vapour in the air." *

" Darius " was first published in 1603 ; the " Tempest " in 1623 ; and it would appear, from the resemblance in the thought, and in some of the words, that Shakspeare must have seen Lord Sterling's verses.   But if Porson thought that Shakspeare falls below Sterling in power and grandeur, few will be found to concur in his notion.

He added one note to the mass of published comment on Shakspeare.†   In most copies of " Othello "‡ we read,

> " Be not you known of 't ——."

But the oldest reading is,

> " Be not *acknown* of 't,"

that is, *Be not acknowledged of it, do not appear informed or aware of it;* a reading which is confirmed,

---

* Moore's Diary, vol. ii.
† Malone's Supplement to Shakspeare, vol. i. p. 867.
‡ Act iii. sc. 3.

as Malone observed, by a passage in " Cornelia," a
Tragedy by Thomas Kyd, 1594 :

> " Our friends' misfortunes doth increase our own,
>   But ours of others will not be *acknown*."

That is, *acknowledged*, *felt*. Porson added another
instance, still more apt, from the " Life of Ariosto " subjoined to Sir John Harrington's translation of "Orlando,"
p. 418, edit. 1607 : " Some say he was married to her
privilie, but durst not be *acknowne* of it."   Malone's
book was printed in 1780, when Porson was but twenty-
one years of age.

From a few unpublished notes of his on the same
author, preserved in the library of his college, a friend
has selected for us the following as worthy of being
made known.

On the words " To fall and blast her pride," " King
Lear," act ii. sc. 4, he observes that the whole passage
should be read thus :

> " You nimble lightnings, dart your blinding flames
>   Into her scornful eyes; infect her beauty !
>   You fen-suck'd fogs, drawn by the powerful sun,
>   To-fall and blast her pride ! "

To-fall being taken as one word ; as in the " Merry
Wives of Windsor," act iv. sc. 4 :

> " Then let them all encircle him about,
>   And, fairy-like, *to-pinch* the unclean knight."

And in " 2 Henry VI.," act v. sc. 2 :

> " Now let the general trumpet blow his blast,—
>   Particularities and petty sounds
>   *To-cease*."

And in " Hamlet," act i. sc. 4 :

> " That you, at such times seeing me never shall
> .   .   .   .   .   *to-note*
> That you know aught of me."

In " Macbeth," act i. sc. 3,

> " If you can look into the seeds of time,
>   And say which grain will grow, and which will not,"
>   .

he reads *rot* instead of *not*.

In " Love's Labour's Lost," act iii. *sub fin.*, instead of

> " A whitely wanton with a velvet brow,"

> " A *whiteless* wanton."

With the line in " A Midsummer Night's Dream,"
act i. sc. 1,
> " To you your father should be as a god,"

he compares

> Νόμιζε σαυτῷ τοὺς γονεῖς εἶναι θεούς.
>   Auctor apud Grot. in Excerptis, p. 929.

On " King Lear," act iv. sc. 4,

> " I pray you, father, being weak, seem so,"

he cites from Euripides, Troad. ver. 729,

> Μηδὲ σθένοντα μηδὲν ἰσχύειν δόκει.

But of all English authors he seems to have had the
greatest liking for Pope. He admired, with all the
world, Pope's vigour of thought and accuracy and
beauty of language. Mr. Maltby has seen the tears

roll down his cheeks while he was repeating Pope's "Epistle to the Earl of Oxford," prefixed to Parnell's Poems.   Walking with Maltby and Rogers over Pope's Villa at Twickenham, he exclaimed, "Oh, how I should like to pass the remainder of my days in a house which was the abode of a man so deservedly celebrated!"*

Foote's plays he liked, and would recite whole scenes from the "Mayor of Garrat."   Moore's "Fables for the Female Sex" was also a favourite book with him. Smollett's "Roderick Random" he could repeat, as we have seen, from beginning to end.

He was fond of reciting, it has been often said†, the following passage from Middleton's "Free Inquiry."

"I persuade myself that the life and faculties of man, at the best but short and limited, cannot be employed more rationally or laudably than in the search of knowledge; and especially of that sort which relates to our duty, and conduces to our happiness.   In these inquiries, therefore, whenever I perceive any glimmering of truth before me, I readily pursue and endeavour to trace it to its source, without any reserve or caution of pushing the discovery too far, or opening too great a glare of it to the public.   I look upon the discovery of anything which is true as a valuable acquisition to society; which cannot possibly hurt or obstruct the good effect of any other truth whatsoever; for they all partake of one common essence, and necessarily coincide with each other; and like the drops of rain, which fall separately into the river, mix themselves at once with the stream, and strengthen the general current."

The subjoined passage from Lewis's "Historical

* Rogers's Table Talk, "Porsoniana," p. 313.
† Memoirs of Holcroft, vol. ii. p. 240.

Essay on the Consecration of Churches,"* he had honoured with several references :

" He alone, who is the only and best Son of the best and greatest Father, in compliance with His Father's love to mankind, most willingly clothed Himself with our nature, who were buried in corruption, and like a careful physician, (who for the health's sake of his patients looks into the wounds, lightly stroketh the sores, and from other many calamities attracteth grievances upon Himself,) He Himself hath saved us."

The references indicating that the words in the parenthesis owe their origin to Hippocrates, and that they are cited by Plutarch, by Lucian, by Eusebius, by Gregory Nazianzen, by Tzetzes in his Chiliads, and by Simplicius on Epictetus.†

An extract, given below, from Barrow's " Second Sermon on Evil Speaking," containing remarks on *facetiousness*, from which Sheridan is said to have taken hints for Puff's descant on puffing in " The Critic," Porson had copied into a blank book, as Mr. Boaden tells us‡, with one line at the top of each page, intending to exemplify and illustrate every one of its positions from ancient and modern literature :

" It is indeed a thing so versatile and multiform, that it seemeth no less hard to settle a clear and certain notion thereof, than to make a portrait of Proteus, or to define the figure of the fleeting air. Sometimes it lieth in pat allusion to a known story, or in seasonable application of a trivial saying, or in forging an apposite tale; sometimes it playeth in words and phrases, taking advantage from the

* P. 41.   † Kidd, Tracts, p. 317.
‡ Memoirs of Kemble, vol. i. p. 67.

ambiguity of their sense, or the affinity of their sound;
sometimes it is wrapped in a dress of humorous expression;
sometimes it lurketh under an odd similitude; sometimes it
is lodged in a sly question, in a smart answer, in a quirkish
reason, in a shrewd imitation, in cunningly diverting or
cleverly retorting an objection; sometimes it is couched in
a bold scheme of speech, in a tart irony, in a lusty hyper-
bole, in a startling metaphor, in a plausible reconciling of
contradictions, or in acuté nonsense; sometimes a scenical
representation of persons or things, a counterfeit speech, a
mimical look or gesture passeth for it; sometimes an affected simplicity, sometimes a presumptuous bluntness gives
it being; often it consisteth in one knows not what, and
springeth up one can hardly tell how. Its ways are unac-
countable and inexplicable, being answerable to the numberless rovings of fancy and windings of language. It raiseth
admiration as signifying a nimble sagacity of apprehension,
a special felicity of invention, a vivacity of spirit, and reach
of wit more than vulgar: it procureth delight by gratifying
curiosity with its rareness, or semblance of difficulty; by
directing the mind from its road of serious thoughts; by
instilling gaiety and airiness of spirit; by provoking to such
dispositions of spirit, in the way of emulation or complai-
sance; and by seasoning matters, otherwise distasteful or
insipid, with an unusual and thence grateful fancy."

How copiously Porson could have illustrated each of
these phrases, is easily imagined.

Two of the books which he was fond of carrying
about him were "The Pillars of Priestcraft and Ortho-
doxy Shaken," and "A Cordial for Low Spirits," collections of Humorous Political Tracts written wholly or
chiefly by Thomas Gordon, the translator of Tacitus,
and professedly edited by Richard Barrow, Esq. As
these effusions seem to have had some influence in the
formation of that sarcastic style which Porson adopted in

his " Letters to Travis," and his papers in the " Morning
Chronicle," we shall give a few extracts as specimens of
their quality.   One of the pamphlets is called " An
Apology for the Danger of the Church, proving that
the Church is, and ought to be, always in Danger, and
that it would be dangerous for her to be out of Danger."
Specifying who are friends of the Church, the writer
says,

" The Lord Syntax is past forty, and has all the rules of
grammar by heart, but, notwithstanding this great accomplishment, the caul is not yet taken off his face, and he is
still a minor.   But, being a babe in common sense, he is
consequently a resolute high churchman.

" Lord Gemini does likewise demand honourable mention
on this occasion.   Nature was very negligent when she
made this great man, for he is *an unfinished piece of brown
earth*, and his mind, if he has one, tallies exactly with his
outside.   He cannot shut his mouth, nor hold his tongue.
However, half made as he is, he is full of bright zeal; and
when he is in the house, he seems to mean several speeches
for the church, but no mortal is so well bred as to hear him :
and yet his mouth, as I said, being always ready open, he
proceeds eternally.

" I confess that Earl Talman, though he is a churchman,
wants two essential qualifications for that character.   He
has sense, and he is never drunk.   But, quoth Cato, who
had not a due respect for priesthood and tyranny, *Solus
Cæsar ad evertendam rempublicam sobrius accessit.*   To be
just to Earl Talman, I grant he was twice a whig upon
valuable considerations, and once out of a pique.   But at
present he is a great churchman, because he has not a *proper*
reason to be otherwise."

*   *   *   *   *

" A traitorous enemy to the church hath been the weather.
. . .   There has not been a blast of wind, or a shower of
rain these five years, but what has been drawn, head over

heels, into the party and interest of the church.   It thundered
for the church, and snowed for the church, and froze for the
church. And yet the whigs, who have got all the money in the
nation, have so brib'd the elements, that they have quite forsook
the Catholic cause.   We had last summer very hot weather,
which, in the opinion of all the orthodox, boded nothing
less to the nation than a general famine and pestilence, for
the martyrdom of the blessed martyr, and the keeping out
of the pretender.   But these pestilential friends of the
church, though earnestly wished for, and positively foretold,
have not done the church the least service, by laying waste
their native country. How often was the king's army to
have been frozen up in Scotland, during the late rebellion !
And most of the parsons in the kingdom had pawned their
word and faith upon it. But, in the issue, neither the frost
nor the snow help'd the church and the pretender.

" In last autumn, word was brought to the parson of a
certain parish, that such a boy was just then killed with
thunder and lightning. ' Is he ? ' says the parson. ' It is
what I always foretold, that that boy would come to a dismal
end, for he went constantly to a fanatical conventicle, and
neither I nor his schoolmaster could dissuade him from it.'
' Ay, but Sir,' replied the messenger, who brought the
Doctor these glad tidings, ' Gaffer Pitchfork is murdered
too with thick same toady clap of thunder, and you do know,
Sir, he was a main man for the church, and fought bravely for
putting up the May-pole.' At this the Doctor scratched his
head, and said, ' It is appointed unto all men once to die.' "

CHAP. XXVII.

THE great feature in Porson's character was honesty ;
honesty in all his doings, as a critic and as a man.   He
was once, however it happened, arrested for debt, but
took extreme care never to incur that disaster a second
time.[*]

As a critic, he used to say, " whatever you quote or
collate, do it fairly and accurately, whether it be Joe
Miller, or Tom Thumb, or The Three Children Sliding
on the Ice ; "[†] and his practice was in conformity with
his precept. As a man, he appears to have wronged no
one in any way, at any time of his life.   He was " true
and just in all his dealings," if we except, perhaps, too
little attention to his duties at the London Institution,

---

[*] Barker's Lit. Anecdotes, vol. ii. p. 25.
[†] Short Account of Porson, p. 11.

though, in making this exception, we must consider the
state of his health when he was appointed; and he
injured none by unmerited censure, but was as free as
even Turner the painter himself from seeking to raise
his own reputation by depreciating that of others.   He
blamed no efforts in literature, but such as it would
have been folly to praise; and would probably have
said nothing against Hermann or Wakefield, had not
their presumption prompted them to aggression on
him.

" He is not only a matchless scholar," said Parr *, who
thought more highly of Porson than Porson thought of
him, " but an honest, a very honest man."   " I think
him," he observes, in another place, " a sincere and
well-principled man ; with all his oddities, and all his
fastidiousness, he is quite exempt from base and ran-
corous malignity; he shows, without concern, what
may be the weaker parts of his character to vulgar
minds; and he leaves men of wisdom and genius to
discover, and to feel, and to admire, the brighter
qualities of his head and his heart." †.   " There is one
quality of the mind," says Bishop Turton, " in which it
may be confidently affirmed that Mr. Porson had no
superior; I mean, the most pure and inflexible love of
truth.   Under the influence of this principle, he was
cautious, and patient, and persevering in his researches;
and scrupulously accurate in stating facts as he found
them.   All who were intimate with him bear witness
to this noble part of his character; and his works
confirm the testimony of his friends."‡

* Works, vol. vii. p. 403.   † Ibid. p. 407.
‡ Vindication of Porson's Lit. Character, p. 348.

Kindliness of feeling he has been less readily allowed, his head being considered to have predominated over his heart. Pryse Gordon even says that he had no heart. The following elaborate character of him, by Wakefield *, though doubtless darkened by prejudice, has been thought, by a writer in the "Quarterly Review," to contain in it a large portion of truth:

"I have been furnished with many opportunities of observing Porson, by a near inspection. He has been at my house several times, and once for an entire summer's day. Our intercourse would have been frequent, but for three reasons: 1. His extreme irregularity, and inattention to times and seasons, which did not at all comport with the methodical arrangement of my time and family. 2. His gross addiction to that lowest and least excusable of all sensualities, immoderate drinking. And, 3. The uninteresting insipidity of his society; as it is impossible to engage his mind on any topic of mutual inquiry, to procure his opinion on any author or any passage of an author, or to elicit any conversation of any kind to compensate for the time and attendance of his company. And as for Homer, Virgil, and Horace, I never could hear of the least critical effort on them in his life. He is, in general, devoid of all human affections; but such as are of a misanthropic quality; nor do I think that any man exists for whom his propensities rise to the lowest pitch of affection and esteem. He much resembles Proteus in Lycophron:

$$\tilde{\omega} \; \gamma \acute{\epsilon} \lambda \omega \varsigma \; \dot{\alpha} \pi \acute{\epsilon} \chi \theta \epsilon \tau \alpha \iota,$$
Καὶ δάκρυ·

though, I believe, he has satirical verses in his treasury for Dr. Bellenden, as he calls him (Parr), and all his most intimate associates. But in his knowledge of the Greek tragedies, and Aristophanes; in his judgment of manuscripts and

* Correspondence with Fox, p. 99.

all that relates to the metrical properties of dramatic and lyric versification, with whatever is connected with this species of reading, none of his contemporaries must pretend to equal him.   His grammatical knowledge also, and his acquaintance with the ancient Lexicographers and Etymologists, is most accurate and profound; and his intimacy with Shakspeare, Ben Jonson, and other dramatic writers, is probably unequalled.   He is, in short, a most extraordinary person in every view, but unamiable; and has been debarred of a comprehensive intercourse with Greek and Roman authors by his excesses, which have made those acquirements impossible to him, from the want of that time which must necessarily be expended in laborious reading, and for which no genius can be made a substitute.   No man has ever paid a more voluntary and respectful homage to his talents, at all times, both publicly and privately, in writings and conversation, than myself; and I will be content to forfeit the esteem and affection of all mankind, whenever the least particle of envy and malignity is found to mingle itself with my opinions.   My first reverence is to virtue; my second only, to talents and erudition; where both unite, that man is estimable indeed to me, and shall receive the full tribute of honour and affection."

The charge of being " misanthropic, and devoid of all human affections," is ridiculed by Beloe, as utterly groundless, being refuted by abundance of passages in Porson's life. · A man could not be inhuman or unfeeling, he observes, who was so fond of society, and who was so often drawn by his love of company into excesses.   By his friend George Dyer, the writer of the notice of him in the " Public Characters," it is said that " to the credit of his heart, he can discuss a subject that respects the interests of the poor, and the cause of benevolence, as readily as he can a question relative to the harmony of language, the authority of manuscripts, and the niceties of Greek criticism." By Mr. Kidd he is said to have " possessed a heart filled with sensibility," and to have been in company the gentlest being that he ever met. But a writer in the " Monthly Review *, who had often been in company with Porson, remarks, that, though he could be mild and civil, he could also be otherwise; that, if he was the gentlest being that Kidd ever met, a sad inference must be drawn as to the rest of Kidd's society; and that Kidd himself may be congratulated on having always escaped the Professor's grasp, which may be supposed less " gentle " than that of *the Russian bear or Hyrcan tiger*. As to his kindness, the same writer says that, " as far as we know and have heard, he said and did no more kind things than men less gifted than he was with the power and opportunity of doing them." All these opinions have doubtless something of truth and justice in them; Porson varied, like other men, at different times, and with different people; he could be kind and open; he could be reserved and severe. " He felt towards others," said Dr. Maltby, " more benevolence than he expressed."

That his society was insipid, or that it was impossible "to engage his mind on any topic of mutual inquiry," or to elicit his opinion on a passage of an author, can be understood only of his behaviour in company with Wakefield. He did not care to communicate his opinions to Wakefield, lest Wakefield should turn them to his own purposes, or misrepresent what he could not understand. That he was ready to afford his aid to those who consulted him in literary difficulties, we

* Jan. 1818.

have already seen instances. "His mode of communication, liberal in the extreme," says the writer of the "Short Account of Porson,"* was truly amiable, as he told you all you wanted to know in a plain and direct manner, without any attempt to display his own superiority, but merely to inform you. Whereas great. scholars are sometimes apt to be brilliant themselves, and leave you unenlightened."

That his reading was not so comprehensive as it might have been with other habits, and that he effected so much less for classical literature than he might have effected, must always be a subject of regret to scholars. "Were we to estimate what he might have done," says the writer of the "Short Account," "had he taken all his advantages, in twenty years, allowing his powers to have been perfected at the age of thirty-one, of which we have abundant proof, our loss is incalculable, since I am convinced that he could have gone through all the plays of Euripides, published his Aristophanes, Athenæus, and Photius, and elucidated his Æschylus, in the time; and all without any violent exertions on his part, since, like Menander, though he had not written a line, he had it all in his head." When we contemplate how much such men as Heyne and Ernesti achieved, we cannot but lament that Porson, with superior powers, accomplished so much less.

One mode in which he wasted much time, was in the practice of mere penmanship. He excelled, as all men know, in writing with neatness and beauty. He wrote notes on the margins of books with such studied accuracy that they rivalled print. He used to say that

* Page 10.

Dr. Young had the advantage in "command of hand," but that he preferred the shape of his own letters to that of Dr. Young's.* "His rage for calligraphy was such," says Mr. Maltby, "that he once offered to letter the backs of some of Mr. Richard Heber's vellum-bound classics. "No," said Heber, "I won't let you do that; but I shall be most thankful if you will write into an Athenæus some of those excellent emendations which I have heard from you in conversation."† Porson having consented, Heber sent him an interleaved copy of Casaubon's edition, which had belonged to Brunck, and in which Porson inserted the notes that were afterwards published in his *Adversaria*. The Athenæus is now in the library of the Rev. Alexander Dyce.

Wakefield's charge of want of feeling in Porson, has been thought to be somewhat substantiated by his conduct towards his relatives. When he went from Eton to Cambridge, he suffered a long time to elapse before he resumed any intercourse with his family. Having a great dislike to writing letters, he maintained little correspondence with them ; and his silence gave them great offence. He was generous to the utmost of his means to the orphan children of his brother Henry; but his presents were accompanied with no epistles ; not only his own relations, but their neighbours in that part of Norfolk, censured him for this apparent insensibility. Yet of his father, if he paid him no open attention, he always thought with due respect. When he married, he was anxious that his father should approve

---

* Encycl. Britann. art. "Porson."

† Barker's Lit. Anecd. vol. ii. p. 56. Rogers's Table Talk, "Porsoniana, p. 311.

of the match.   When his father was ill, and his sister, whom he had not seen for twenty-two years, wrote to inform him that the old man was in danger, Porson immediately set off into Norfolk, and resided with his sister for seven weeks, till their father recovered.   Two years afterwards, when he was seized with his last illness, Porson, on receiving notice of it, went down and stayed with him till he died.*

When he was in Norfolk with his sister, he went regularly to church, except when the violence of his asthma prevented him.   During his first visit, he accompanied Mr. Hawes, his brother-in-law, to the church of Horstead ; when they found that preparations were made for administering the Sacrament.   As they were leaving the church after the sermon, Porson stopped suddenly, and asked Mr. Hawes if he thought that there would be any impropriety in his receiving the Sacrament.   Mr. Hawes replying in the negative, they turned back, and partook of the Communion together.†

This is mentioned by Beloe as an example of his readiness to accommodate himself to the ways and habits of the people with whom he happened to be associated.   We consider that it was so ; and his abstemiousness during his residence with his sister, is to be regarded as another instance of the same disposition.   While he lived in her house, he abstained wholly from spirits, and never drank more than two glasses of wine after dinner.   He conversed without restraint with the family, and accompanied them in their walks.

But the truth is, that, when a man of reading and

* Sexagenarian, vol. i. p. 214.   † Ibid. p. 220.

thought, sprung from a humble family, is once detached from it, and transplanted into a more cultivated and intellectual society, he can in general feel but little inclination to return to it, except for very short periods, and at long intervals. He finds himself in his proper place in his new condition, and cannot, without uneasiness, be long kept away from it. Besides, whatever honour or regard he obtains elsewhere, he will find little, though he may be a nine days' object of remark, in his own country. His visits will be like that of Lady Staunton to the wife of Butler, of which both were glad to see the termination. His daily studies, too, demand his daily attention, for no man can pursue literature with success, unless he give his mind and his time constantly to it. Pope said that he who would cultivate poetry, must leave father and mother, and cleave to it as his own flesh; and the same may be said of any other intellectual pursuit.

Porson's dislike to writing, not only epistolary, but of all kinds, has been previously noticed. His slowness in writing was proportioned to his aversion to it. He never attained anything like ease in composition, but, to whatever subject he applied his thoughts, always felt embarrassment in expressing himself. "Upon one occasion," says Beloe, "he undertook to write a dozen lines on a subject which he had much turned in his mind, and with which he was exceedingly familiar. But the number of erasures and interlineations was so great as to render it hardly legible; yet, when completed, it was, and is, a memorial of his sagacity, acuteness, and erudition." *

* Sexagenarian, vol. i. p. 218.

These remarks refer, we believe, to the following expression of opinion on the causes which apparently brought on the premature death of Raphael. Mr. Duppa, wishing to insert this opinion, in a Latin dress, in his Life of Michael Angelo, requested Porson to translate it for him; a request with which Porson readily complied, on condition that he should be allowed to correct the press, as he " cared not to be answerable for any nonsense but his own."*

De Obitu Raphaelis.

Cùm minùs robustâ valetudine uteretur Raphael, effusiùs quàm vires suæ ferebant, veneri operam dedisse videtur, unde calorem et debilitatem consequi nihil mirum.   Medici (pluralem enim Vasari numerum adhibet, alii unum modò memorant) existimationi suæ et quæstui fortasse metuentes, si tanto viro mortem accelerâsse crederentur, hanc excusationem prætexebant, se a Raphaële, quâ erat verecundiâ, veram febris causam celatos esse, caloremque ex aliâ et ordinariâ causâ ortum putantes, sanguinem misisse, et ἐξ ἀφαιρέσεως curâsse, aliter facturos, si sibi rem candidè, ut erat, narrâsset.   Quicquid est hujus, ex ambiguo sermonis usu gravis error prognatus est et vulgares libros pervagatus, Raphaëlem scilicet non, quod verum esse jam vidimus, ex nimiâ veneris indulgentiâ, sed ex turpis morbi contagione mortem obiisse.

Nor did he speak, in general, with greater facility than he wrote.   " His elocution," says the same authority, was " perplexed and embarrassed, except where he was exceedingly intimate ; " though " whatever he said was manifestly founded on judgment, sense, and knowledge."

Of that intellectual fermentation and excitement,

* Kidd, Tracts, p. 327.

which are perpetually engendering thoughts in the mind, and urging them forth into utterance, he felt but little.   Nature has not given all things to all men. The greatest commanders in the domain of thought have made but moderate excursions into the regions of language; and he who had extended his knowledge over forty languages is said, perhaps with truth, to have produced nothing like an original thought in any one of them.

> " Where beams of warm imagination play,
>   The memory's soft traces melt away ; "

and when the memory keeps the mind full of extraneous matter, the imagination has no room to disport, and produce its creations.   What Porson wrote with the greatest facility, was the ludicrous.   Walpole said of Gray, that he wrote nothing with ease but pieces of humour; and the same may apparently be said of Porson.

But his want of imagination only qualified him the better, perhaps, for those occupations to which he devoted himself.   His thoughts being enticed but little into the regions of fancy, were the more easily fixed on the subject which he had before him.   He was at liberty to give his attention undisturbed to the author whom he was perusing; to weigh his sense, and consider the soundness or corruption of his language. His memory could bring its stores to work in tranquillity, and his judgment apply its sagacity without interruption.   Of such calm exercise of his faculties, we see the fruits in his emendations.   No one, since men began to distinguish wrong from right, and sense from nonsense, in written pages, has brought to the critical art greater power of discernment, or a happier facility in substituting soundness for corruption. His corrections are of that character which insures the reader's instant acquiescence. He was slow to alter, but, when he made an alteration, made it with unquestionable success.

"The justness of a happy restoration," said Johnson, in reference to attempted emendations of Shakspeare, "strikes at once." This is the case with Porson's restitutions in the Greek writers; we feel that the text has received either that which the author wrote, or something with which the author might very well have been satisfied.

One of the most felicitous corrections that criticism has ever produced, is that of Bentley on the Scholiast of Homer, by the addition of half a letter. On Odyss. xi. 546, there occurs in the Scholia this passage :— Αἰχμαλώτους τῶν Τρώων ἀγαγὼν ἐρώτησεν ἀπὸ ὁποτέρου τῶν Τρώων μᾶλλον ἐλυπήθησαν· εἰπόντων δὲ 'Οδυσσέα, κ.τ.λ. "Agamemnon, to ascertain whether Ajax or Ulysses had the better title to the armour of Achilles, brought forward the Trojan captives, and asked them from which *of the Trojans* they had suffered the greater harm; and, as they replied "Ulysses," he gave the armour to him." The words τῶν Τρώων, Barnes could think of no better way of correcting than by turning them into αὐτῶν οἱ Τρῶες: at which Bentley sneered, and by altering T into H, making it ὁποτέρου τῶν 'Ηρώων, "from which of the two heroes," restored soundness to the passage at once.

Porson produced one admirable emendation without

the change of any part of a letter. In the 218th verse of the Eumenides of Æschylus, finding, in Aldus's edition, the words, Ὄρχους τι —, he altered them to Ὄρχου 'στι, making the passage stand thus :

Εὐνὴ γὰρ ἀνδρὶ καὶ γυναικὶ μορσίμη
Ὄρκου 'στι μείζων τῇ δίκῃ φρουρουμένη,

a reading which editors have joyfully adopted. By the alteration only of one letter, he has in several instances produced the happiest effects. *Vide quid faciat unius litterulæ mutatio*, he exclaims, on altering σθένειν into στένειν, in the 293rd verse of the Medea. Another happy effect, produced by the addition of a single letter, is exhibited in the 1393rd verse of the same play, μένε καὶ γήρασκ' for μένε καὶ γῆρας, a correction by which the sense and the metre are aided at the same time. In the Republic of Plato*, he finds πάσας δὲ διεξόδους διεξελθὼν ἀποστραφῆναι λογιζόμενος, which had satisfied all preceding critics, but which he, with a change of one letter in the last word, improves into λυγιζόμενος, making the passage to signify " pursuing every means of evasion by writhing himself in all directions." In the Philoctetes of Sophocles, he lights on καὶ σοῦ δ' ἔγωγε θαυμάσας ἔχω τάδε, and observing that it is adverse to a rule which he has discovered for himself (that when the speaker suddenly turns his discourse from one person to another, as is the case here, he expresses the name or other noun first, the pronoun next, and the particle next), he transforms it into παῖ, σοῦ δ' ἔγωγε, κ.τ.λ.

Another happy emendation or two may properly

* Book ii. c. 14.

be noticed. In the Hercules Furens, verse 310, he finds

Ὅ χρὴ γὰρ οὐδεὶς μὴ θεῶν θήσει ποτέ.

"This," he says, "nobody, I suppose, understands," and metamorphoses it, by a very slight change, into excellent sense,

Ὅ χρὴ γὰρ οὐδεὶς μὴ χρεὼν θήσει ποτέ.*

In Hesychius he meets with the mass of corruption, Πολυβοτραφεῖ. τῷ ἀναθρέψαντι Πόλυβον νάματι, and, with the aid of a suggestion from a manuscript, Πο-λυβοονάμα, gives it the sensible form of Πολύβῳ τροφεῖ. τῷ ἀναθρέψαντι, Πολύβῳ ὄνομα.†

A scholion on a verse of the Phœnissæ,

πολλοῖς δ' ἐπῆει δάκρυα τῆς τύχης ὅση,

which is now thought spurious, but which the scholiast had not rejected, he finds standing thus : λείπει γὰρ τὸ ἕνεκεν τῆς τύχης ἡ δίκη ἦν, and corrects it to λείπει γὰρ τὸ ἕνεκεν. ἕνεκεν τῆς τύχης, ἡλίκη ἦν.‡

On a line of Statius,

—— " Matremque recens circumvolat umbra,"

the scholiast has "Et hoc poeticè, ut Euripides, Syrseen opersu." This no man had attempted to correct or explain. Porson finds no difficulty ; he remembers that it is a reference to Phœniss. 668, [*ποτωμένην*] *ψυχὴν ὑπὲρ σοῦ.*

A longer specimen of the acuteness of his criticism

---

* Ad Phœniss. ver. 5.   † Ib. ver. 45.   ‡ Ib. ver. 1386.

may be seen in Kidd's Tracts; an admirable recon-
struction of a passage of Dion Chrysostom's LXIVth
Oration, where the words of a comic poet are mixed
with prose. It is an effort of excogitation, superior,
indeed, but of a similar character, to those displayed
in the note on the 139th verse of the Medea.

In one alteration only is he found to have erred. In
the 937th verse of the Medea he found Οὐκ οἶδ᾽ ἂν εἰ
πείσαιμι, and, thinking the position of the ἂν offensive,
ejected it, and wrote οὐκ οἶδ ἄρ᾽ εἰ πείσαιμι. But Elmsley
has justified the common reading by two exactly
similar passages, one in Euripides himself, and another
in Plato, and has well observed that in such phrases
the optative could not be used without ἄν.*

In the 1095th verse of the Hecuba,

εἰ δὲ μὴ Φρυγῶν
Πύργους πεσόντας ᾖσμεν Ἑλλήνων δορί,
Φόβον παρέσχεν οὐ μέσως ὅδε κτύπος,

he very properly introduced ἄν, reading παρέσχ᾽ ἄν,
with Heath, Brunck, Markland, and three manuscripts.
Hermann, merely for the purpose, apparently, of
differing from Porson, omitted the ἄν, asserting that it
was unnecessary; but who would now support this
assertion?

Nor has Porson given, like many other critics, other
men's emendations as his own. Only in one instance
has he thus transgressed, having been detected by Mr.
Burges in appropriating, unconsciously, a conjecture of
Markland's.

Nor should the style of his notes be left without its

---

* Eurip. Med. 937.   Museum Criticum, vol. ii. p. 31.

commendation. It is clear, plain, and unaffected; and is free, as has been well observed, from those trite phrases and expressions of which the constant recurrence offends and wearies the reader in the majority of Latin annotations. He drew from his own mind, and expressed himself in his own way.

The faults that have been found with his style are, that it wants ease; that it is too dry and stiff to be pleasing; and that the thoughts seem to have been conceived in English, and translated, not always without difficulty, into Latin. A critic, who carefully noted the minutiæ of Porson's phraseology, adduced from the *Prælectio in Euripidem* the expressions *studio perspicuitatis*, "the study of perspicuity," *gradus probabilitatis*, "the degree of probability," *calumnias professi inimici*, "the calumnies of a professed enemy," *in historiæ circumstantiis*, "in the circumstances of history," as examples of such English Latinity; expressions which, though they may be justified by the authority of Cicero or Quintilian, partake so much of the idiom of English as to give a modern air to that which ought to exhibit the obvious guise of antiquity. These blemishes, however, as he observes, are merely *nævi in corpore egregio*, and are to be noticed only lest they should give authority to a mode of writing which ought to be avoided.*

The emendations of Bentley, notwithstanding the master stroke which has just been cited, do not in general make the same impression on the reader with those of Porson. Porson appears to alter the text because alteration was evidently necessary; Bentley, because he

* Monthly Review, Dec. 1817, p. 423.

himself thought that it was necessary. Porson, as a corrector, offers *good wine that needs no bush;* Bentley is a host that must often use argument to recommend his fare. As Porson's touches remind us of Johnson's remark about a just restoration, Bentley's recal his saying about doubtful alterations, for we cannot help "suspecting that the reading is right which requires many words to prove it wrong, and that the emendation is wrong, which cannot without so much labour appear to be right." Thus in one of his earliest emendations of Horace, *strictis* for *sectis,* in *virginum strictis in juvenes unguibus acrium,* we can hardly, though the alteration is good, forbear from fancying, as we read his note in its justification, that he upholds it rather to show his own ingenuity than with a conviction that it was necessary to the text of his author; and our minds can scarcely be cleared from a doubt that *sectis* may be the right reading. This is still more forcibly the case, when we contemplate one of his more venturous emendations, such as

Ut silvis folia privos mutantur in annos,

instead of

Ut silvæ foliis pronos mutantur in annos,

for though we can scarcely feel satisfied with *foliis mutantur,* yet we are impressed with the persuasion, when we see Bentley's vindication of the changes which he has made, that he had the ostentation of his own acuteness in view, more than the sincere infusion of soundness into Horace's line. Such a notion never takes possession of us as we contemplate Porson's corrections; we feel that what he has done proceeded from an honest desire to serve his author ; that no sophistry is needed to advocate his treatment of the text. We are often pleased with Bentley's notes on his corrections, but are always pleased with Porson's corrections for themselves.

Bentley was often presumptuous and rash ; Porson was to all critics an example of caution. *Priusquam incipias consulto opus*, and *nihil contemnendum est neque in bello, neque in re criticâ*, were his maxims. Before he operated on a passage himself, he took care to ascertain what others had done. He consulted not only commentaries, but translations, and, according to Mr. Maltby, " never wrote a note on any passage of an ancient author without carefully looking how it had been rendered by the different translators."*

He was not insensible to the honours of authorship, but never felt in himself the ability to attain them. Once, when he was asked why he had produced so little original matter, he answered, " I doubt if I could produce any original work that would command the attention of posterity. I can be known only by my notes; and I am quite satisfied if, three hundred years hence, it shall be said that one Porson lived towards the close of the eighteenth century, who did a good deal for the text of Euripides." †

Bentley had much the same feeling with regard to original composition. He had no hope of attaining permanent reputation by it, and said that he thought it safer for him to try for distinction by getting on the shoulders of the ancients.

* Rogers's Table Talk, " Porsoniana," p. 326.   † Ibid. p. 334.

But while we allow Porson greater nicety and happiness of correction, we must, on deliberation, concede to Bentley the larger range of reading and of thought. Porson was one, in Parr's phrase, " to whom the hat of Bentley would have vailed ; " but Bentley would have felt called to do him homage only for his sagacity in emendation, and perhaps for somewhat greater nicety of ear in respect to Greek metre. Bentley could collect his materials in equal profusion with Porson, and could animate them with something more of spirit.

As to the works of each, it is idle to make a comparison between them. Bentley, we must acknowledge, wrote more than Porson, and had written more, even at the age at which Porson died. But Bentley's manner of life was different from Porson's ; Bentley lived in such a way as to secure and cherish health and strength, mental and bodily ; Porson indulged in such lax habits as render it wonderful how any vigorous tone of mind could be so long maintained throughout them. What more he might have done, had his practice been different, it is superfluous to inquire ; we see what he has done, and allow it its excellence ; we see that Bentley's mind produced a larger offspring, and must admit that its aggregate value must be greater, though no equal quantity of it be comparable to the quantity that has proceeded from Porson.

Some who compare Porson with the continental scholars, such as Wyttenbach, Heyne, or Valckenaer, who have edited large and numerous volumes, are apt to consider that he must be far inferior to them, because he has published less. But the merit of a critic, like that of a painter, is to be judged, not from the number, but the excellence of his productions. *Ponderanda, non numeranda.* A limner may cover many thousand feet of canvas, and a commentator many thousand pages of paper, without proving their superiority over those of far less extensive performance. If we examine what these voluminous annotators have written, we shall find that a large portion of it is illustration; Heyne, for instance, in his Apollodorus, is not content with affixing critical notes to the text, but adds a whole volume of expository observations, three or four times the bulk of Apollodorus's own matter. From this department of the critic Porson generally held aloof; not because he could not have engaged in it with success, for how ably he could have fulfilled its duties he has shown on several occasions, but because, from dislike of labour, he was little inclined to do that which inferior minds, devoted to patient research, could do with ease. A German is far more willing *to write about it and about it* than an Englishman; a German is profuse of words, of which an Englishman is sparing. In comparing the merit of commentaries we must ascertain where most proofs of sagacity appear.

Had he lived somewhat later, when comparative philology had begun to be more studied, he might have engaged in that branch of research, and, if he had devoted himself heartily to it, would doubtless have pursued it with great success.

As far as his labour, however, extended, he is to be praised for bestowing it on that which he knew that he could do well. *Quam quisque nôrit artem, in hac se exerceat.* It has been said that he might probably have obtained greater honour, and done more good,

by directing his talents and industry to law or to
statesmanship; but whether he would have attained
great success in such pursuits with his habits of life,
must be considered as extremely doubtful. If he
cannot be ranked among the greatest benefactors of
mankind, he must certainly be allowed to have done
much good to his country by the promotion of its
learning, and especially of that species of it called
classical learning. That the advancement and maintenance of this kind of knowledge is a benefit to
society, will be admitted by all who can judge how
much advantage the man who possesses some acquaintance, however little, with Latin and Greek, has
over the man who is destitute of it. So many words
in our own language are derived from the languages of
antiquity, that he who is utterly ignorant of those
tongues cannot be said to understand his own. Nor
are classical studies to be stigmatised as the mere
study of words, to the disregard of things; for if words
are the signs of things, no one can think of words without being led at the same time to think of things. We
therefore do wisely in maintaining and encouraging
the study of the classics, as much as is practicable,
throughout the nation, believing that it is the best
possible basis for a sound and liberal education. We
are somewhat too negligent, perhaps, as to the nature
of some portions of the books that we put into the
hands of boys; we think too little of Quintilian's
Horatium in quibusdam nolim interpretari; we might
certainly be more careful to expurgate, and thus give
less ground of objection to such critics as the Abbé
Gaume. Perhaps, also, we give rather too much

attention to Greek plays, to the scanning of choruses, and the fabrication of Greek iambics, when the perusal of parts of Aristotle and Plato might be attended with more benefit to the mind of youth. But verse and prose composition, in both languages, and especially in Latin, ought to be diligently cultivated, as leading to a better understanding of the languages themselves, and to a nice discrimination of the sense of words in general.

CHAP. XXVIII.

A NATURAL concomitant of Porson's honesty was a sturdy independence of spirit. He yielded submission to no man. He would accept no favours but such as friend might reasonably receive from friend; and, as he was unwilling to bestow praise, except such as merit demanded, he was reluctant to receive praise to which he did not conceive himself fully entitled.

" Of every thing mean, base, insolent, treacherous, or selfish, whether practised towards others or towards himself," says Dr. Maltby, " he had a quick discernment, and a most rooted abhorrence ; and the terms of bitter contempt, or of severe indignation, in which he expressed himself upon such occasions, may have given rise to opinions concerning the real bent of his feelings, which those, who had frequent opportunities of observing him, can safely pronounce to be unfounded." * " Never did he swerve," adds the same authority, " from his undeviating attachment to truth, nor ever was he known to betray a secret."

* Hellenophilus, Aikin's Athenæum, Nov. 1808.

A man of such high spirit had, as might be expected, a great dislike to being invited by his acquaintance merely for show.   He was once dining with Mackintosh, who expressed a wish that he should accompany him on the following day to a dinner at Holland House, to meet Fox.   Porson made some reply that sounded like consent, and Mackintosh, meeting Mr. Maltby the next morning, told him that Porson was going to Lord Holland's.   Maltby coming in contact with Porson shortly after, observed to him, " I hear that you are to dine at Holland House to-day." " Who told you so?" " Mackintosh." " But I certainly shall not go," rejoined Porson ; " they invite me merely out of curiosity, and, after they have satisfied it, would like to kick me down stairs." " But," said Maltby, " Fox is coming expressly from St. Ann's Hill to be introduced to you." The attraction, however, was ineffective ; Porson persisted in staying away ; and Lord Holland told Rogers, many years afterwards, that Fox had been greatly disappointed at not meeting Porson on that occasion.*

It was this kind of feeling that prompted his extraordinary reception of two visitors at Cambridge.   Two gentlemen called upon him one day at his rooms, and said that they had come to see him.   Porson made no reply, but rang his bell and ordered a pair of candles. When they were brought, he said, " Now then, gentlemen, you will be able to see me better."   It has been stated in a recent version of this anecdote †, that one

* Rogers's Table Talk, " Porsoniana," p. 322.   Barker's Lit. Anecd. vol. ii. p. 13.

† Notes and Queries, Feb. 11, 1860.

of these visitors was Mr. Summers, his old school-master; but this is utterly improbable, for Porson always spoke of Mr. Summers with regard, as he appears, indeed, to have spoken of all from whom he had received any real kindness. Mr. Summers used to say, that Porson " had been too hardly censured by the world; that his nature was not unkind; " but that " he was too often accosted from motives of curiosity, which could not escape his penetration; and at times, perhaps, when his mind was alienated from the common forms of life," as was frequently the case, " by some deep subject" that occupied his thoughts.*

Another story is, that two farmers from East Ruston, passing through Cambridge, called at his rooms, and, when he came in, told him that they did not like to leave the town " without seeing Mr. Porson." " Well, now then, gentlemen," rejoined Porson, " you have seen me; I wish you good morning; " and walked off.

A man of such a temper was not likely to be very tolerant of admonition. We have seen how much he had been befriended by Sir George Baker; Sir George's house was always open to him, and his assistance and encouragement always ready to promote any design that he might take in hand. All this kind-ness and attention Porson fully acknowledged; yet, after visiting him regularly for some years, he suddenly ceased to visit him at all. For this withdrawal Sir George expressed himself quite unable to account; there had been no quarrel, and Porson had given him no cause to speak of him otherwise than with kind-

---

* Letter of Rev. W. Gunn to Dawson Turner, Barker's Parriana, vol. ii. p. 736.

ness.   But it is supposed by Mr. Maltby that some words of remonstrance, which fell from Sir George respecting Porson's irregularities, were the cause of his change of conduct.

Such absolute independence was not unfrequently attended with waywardness and caprice. He would show likings and dislikings without much apparent reason. He was kind to children, says Beloe, but would be at no pains to conceal his partiality, if he felt any, where there were several in one family. " In one, which he often visited, there was a little girl of whom he was exceedingly fond ; he often brought her trifling presents, wrote in her books, and distinguished her on every occasion, but she had a brother, to whom, for no assignable reason, he never spoke, nor would in any respect notice." *

The little girl, going one day into the kitchen to deliver a message to a servant, took Porson by the hand, and led him in with her. A young woman, whose name was Susan, and who was much regarded by the family, was ironing linen. The child asked Porson to make some verses upon her ; and, on his return to the sitting-room, he said,

> When lovely Susan irons smocks,
>   No damsel e'er looked neater,
> Her eyes are brighter than her box,
>   And burn me like a heater.†

When contradicted in argument, he was, if the " Sexagenarian " may be credited, not easily provoked to asperity of language. " By precept," said Bishop

---

* Sexagenarian, vol. i. p. 217.   † Ibid. vol. ii. p. 313.

Maltby, " as well as by example, he discountenanced all violent emotions of the mind, and particularly anger." *
But Beloe mentions one occasion in which he was moved, and, as it appeared, with justice, to express himself with great exasperation. " A person of some literary pretensions, but who either did not know Porson's value, or neglected to show the estimate of it which it merited, at a dinner-party, harassed, teazed, and tormented him, till at length he could endure it no longer, and, rising from his chair, exclaimed with vehemence, ' It is not in the power of thought to conceive, or words to express, the contempt I have for you, Mr. *   *   *.' "

This scene is represented, in a key to the " Sexagenarian," published in " Notes and Queries,"† to have occurred at the house of Mr. Hill in Henrietta Street, Covent Garden, in the presence of Mr. Morris, Mr. Kemble, Mr. Dubois, Mr. Fillingham, and Mr. Perry; and the offender is said to have been Mr. Isaac Disraeli, who, in return for Porson's expressions of severity, retorted on the Professor in an ill-natured note in his novel called " Flim-Flams."   Barker, in his Literary Anecdotes ‡, gives a somewhat different account, saying that Disraeli, on some occasion when Porson had fallen intoxicated under the table, had started up and made a sarcastic speech over him ; and that Porson, hearing of this insult, took an opportunity of retorting upon Disraeli, and concluded an address to him with the same words that Beloe has given.   That Mr. Disraeli

---

* Aikin's Athenæum, vol. iv. Oct. 1808.
† April 21, 1860.   ‡ Vol. ii. p. 14.

was the author of the novel of " Flim-Flams," published
anonymously in three volumes by Murray, in 1805, a
production filled with pointless attempts at satirical
description and dialogue, and abortive efforts at wit,
and written altogether in a style and manner utterly at
variance with Disraeli's acknowledged works, it seems
extremely difficult to believe ; but he is universally said
to have been concerned in its composition.   The attack
on Porson, however, is made, not in a note, but in the
text, where the Professor, Dr. Parr, Mr. Godwin, and
Mr. Malthus, under the names of Pours-on, Græculus,
Caconous, and Toomany, are represented as meeting,
with some other public characters, at a large dinner-
party, given by " My Uncle," who, by a remark about
a Greek word in Athenæus, sets the Doctor and the
Professor at strife, when, after much discussion and
quotation, the Professor is made to catch at the word
tatyras used by the Doctor, and, uttering " a shrill
whew ! " to say, " You dare not tell us that *tatyras* is
the true word for pheasant ; Ptolemy Euerge*tus* reads
tetarton, others *tatyron*."   " You lie, and you know you
lie," retorts the Doctor ; when the Professor empties
his wine-glass on the Doctor's wig, and the Doctor
hurls back his wig, saturated with wine, in the Professor's face.   The Professor then challenges the Doctor
to drink brandy with him *in a pair of shoes;* and the
Doctor retorts by offering to drink brandy with the
Professor *in a pair of boots;* a pair of new boots are
accordingly sent for, and the operation commences, the
Professor singing Greek epigrams, and the Doctor
spouting passages from Lysias ; but, amidst a great
hubbub with which the party closes, the two com-

batants are left sitting, each with his boot before him, and the match undecided.

From the universally received character of Isaac Disraeli, he would seem as little likely to have given the offence as to have written the novel. " The philosophic sweetness of his disposition," says his son, " the serenity of his lot, and the elevating nature of his pursuits, combined to enable him to pass through life without an evil act, almost without an evil thought." * The novel is the offspring of injudicious satire, ill-natured, but weak, and casting disgrace, not on those who are caricatured in its pages, but on him or them that gave it being.

I have been assured, on trustworthy authority, that what was done or said with reference to Porson, in his state of insensibility, was in reality harmless and trifling, but was reported to the Professor with great exaggeration; and I have been given to understand, on the same authority, that the passage of the novel, in which Porson is introduced, was probably written by Dubois.

For Fitzgerald, the " small beer poet," who had one evening *bawled his creaking couplets* at a dinner of the Literary Fund Society, Porson, who was present, showed his want of respect in a somewhat Johnsonian manner. A gentleman brought Fitzgerald up to Porson to introduce him. " Sir," said he, " I have the honour to present to you Mr. Fitzgerald." Porson was silent. " Sir," recommenced that gentleman, " I have the honour to present to you Mr. Fitzgerald, who

* Memoir prefixed to Routledge's edition of Disraeli's Works, 1860.

recited the verses you have just heard." Porson was silent. "Sir," persisted the gentleman, "I have the honour to present to you Mr. Fitzgerald, who himself composed the verses which you have just heard." "Sir," said Porson, very gently, "I am quite deaf." *

To a lady who annoyed him with impertinent questions at a dinner, asking him the Greek for a knife, a fork, and other matters, he made a more playful retort, replying to her last interrogatory, "To me, madam, it is *heautontimoroumenos*, to you *heauteentimoroumenee*."

To a gentleman, who, at the close of a fierce dispute with Porson, exclaimed, "My opinion of you is most contemptible, Sir;" he retorted, "I never knew an opinion of yours that was not contemptible."

The following letter † to Mr. Upcott, from the Rev. T. Smart Hughes, detailing an interview which he had had with Porson in 1807, shows exactly what Porson was in the latter part of his life. Mr. Hughes's tutor, who is mentioned in it, was the Rev. J. D. Hustler, a fellow of Trinity College. ‡

"My dear Sir,
        "I wish it was in my power to give you a more detailed account of my interview with your celebrated predecessor than my memory will now permit. It was the only one I ever had with him. It occurred when I was an undergraduate; and I unfortunately made no notes of it at the time, being then busily engaged in reading for my degree, which occupied almost all my thoughts. This interview

---

* Butler's Reminiscences, p. 169.
† Notes and Queries, 2nd S. vol. iii. p. 62.
‡ Rev. H. R. Luard, Cambridge Essays, 1857.

took place in the rooms of my private tutor, between whom
and Porson a great intimacy subsisted.

"After about an hour spent in various subjects of conversation, during which the Professor recited a great many
beautiful passages from [his] authors in Greek, Latin, French,
and English, my tutor, seeing the visitation that was evidently intended for him, feigned an excuse for going into
the town, and left Porson and myself together. I ought to
have observed that he had already produced one bottle of
sherry to moisten the Professor's throat, and that he left out
another, in case it should be required. Porson's spirits being
by this time elevated by the juice of the grape, and being
pleased with a well-timed compliment which I had the good
luck to address to him, he became very communicative;
said he was glad that we had met together; desired me
to take up my pen and paper, and directed me to write
down, from his dictation, many curious algebraical problems,
with their solutions; gave me several ingenious methods of
summing series; and ran through a great variety of the
properties of numbers.

"After almost an hour's occupation in this manner, he
said, 'Lay aside your pen, and listen to the history of a
man of letters, — how he became a sordid miser from a
thoughtless prodigal, a . . . from a . . ., and a
misanthrope from a morbid excess of sensibility.' (I forget
the intermediate step in the climax.) He then commenced
a narrative of his own life, from his entrance at Eton school,
through all the most remarkable periods, to the day of our
conversation. I was particularly amused with the account
of his school anecdotes, the tricks he used to play upon his
master and schoolfellows, and the little dramatic pieces
which he wrote for private representation. From these he
passed to his academical pursuits and studies, his election
to the Greek professorship, and his ejection from his fellowship through the influence of Dr. Postlethwaite, who, though
he had promised it to Porson, exerted it for a relation of his
own. 'I was then,' said the Professor, 'almost destitute in
the wide world, with less than 40l. a year for my support,

and without a profession, for I never could bring myself to subscribe Articles of Faith. I used often to lie awake through the whole night, and wish for a large pearl.'

"He then gave me a history of his life in London, when he took chambers in the Temple, and read at times immoderately hard. He very much interested me by a curious interview which he had with a girl of the town, who came into his chambers by mistake, and who showed so much cleverness and ability in a long conversation with him, that he declared she might with proper cultivation have become another Aspasia. He also recited to me, word for word, the speech with which he accosted Dr. Postlethwaite when he called at his chambers, and which he had long prepared against such an occurrence. At the end of this oration the Doctor said not a word, but burst into tears and left the room. Porson also burst into tears when he finished the recital of it to me.

"In this manner five hours passed away; at the end of which the Professor, who had finished the second bottle of my friend's sherry, began to clip the king's English, to cry like a child at the close of his periods, and in other respects to show marks of extreme debility. At length he rose from his chair, staggered to the door, and made his way down stairs without taking the slightest notice of his companion. I retired to my college; and next morning was informed by my friend that he had been out upon a search, the previous evening, for the Greek Professor, whom he discovered near the outskirts of the town, leaning upon the arm of a dirty bargeman, and amusing him by the most humorous and laughable anecdotes. I never even saw Porson after this day, but I shall never cease to regret that I did not commit his history to writing whilst it was fresh in my memory.

"I am, my dear Sir, with great regard,
"Yours sincerely,
"T. S. HUGHES.
"Cambridge, Oct. 1826."

Great as were Porson's deviations from the even tenour of sobriety, great as were his disagreements with the social habits of the generality of mankind, great also must have been his merit, which, with such aberrations and eccentricities, secured him, not only the praise, but the regard, of all men of learning and intellect that had intercourse with him. Whoever knew Richard Porson, felt that he knew a man of high and noble mind, who, with all his irregularities, and all his inclination to sarcasm and jest, had a sincere love of truth and honesty, and who, with an utter contempt for pretence and presumption, was ever ready to do justice to genuine worth.

His life is an example, and an admonition, how much a man may injure himself by indulgence in one unhappy propensity, and how much an elevated mind may suffer by long association with those of an inferior order. A Porson cannot day after day descend to the level of a Hewardine, without finding it difficult at length to recover his original position above it.

APPENDIX

APPENDIX.

Porson's Family.

THAT we might not interrupt the narrative of Porson's biography, we have said but little in it of his family, thinking it sufficient to add some notice of it here.

He had, as we have said, two brothers and a sister, the sister older, and the brothers younger, than himself. The second brother's name was Henry, who seems to have shown no inclination for literature, but being, in his boyhood, ready at accounts, was sent to Norwich to qualify himself for an exciseman, in which character he lived for about a year at Debenham in Suffolk, where he married the daughter of a farmer, and then took a farm for himself near Colchester. While he was here, the accounts of the corporation of Norwich were found to be in disorder, and Henry Porson, being known to some of the aldermen as a good arithmetician, was sent for to examine the books, and make a report upon them; an undertaking which he executed with great success. He died of consumption at the early age of thirty-three.

Thomas, the other brother, eleven years younger than Richard, was thought to have possessed great qualifications for becoming a scholar. He received the same educational advantages, under Mr. Summers and Mr. Hewitt, as Richard. He became assistant to the Rev. Mr. Hepworth, who had a school at Wymondham, in Norfolk, and was afterwards master of the grammar school at North Walsham. On parting from Mr. Hepworth, he set up a boarding-school for himself at Fakenham, also in Norfolk, where he married, and, being con-

sidered to possess extraordinary talent, was likely to succeed,
but died in his twenty-fourth year.   Dr. Davy, indeed, the
Master of Caius, who knew the brothers well, was of opinion
that Thomas was fully equal in ability to Richard.   If
Thomas, then, had lived to enlarge his reading like Richard,
what might not have been done for Greek literature by two
Porsons, especially if Thomas had been more inclined to
steady work than Richard ?

The sister was about four years older than Porson, and
married Mr. Siday Hawes, a brewer, at Coltishall, in Norfolk.
She had, says Beloe *, a strong personal resemblance to
Richard, particularly in the lower features of her face, her
tone of voice, and peculiarity of smile.   In an account of
Porson, which appeared in the " Morning Chronicle" the day
after his death, she was described as "amiable and accomplished."   When this eulogy was communicated to her, she
expressed herself to this effect: "I wish it had been suppressed.   The editor, I have no doubt, had the most obliging
intentions in the world, when he represented me as an amiable
and accomplished woman ; but I really have no taste for such
flattery.   He must have known, from my situation in early
life, that it was impossible I could possess any accomplish-
ments.   I wish not to be brought before the public ; my only
ambition is, at the close of life, to have deserved the character of having been a good wife to my husband, and a
good mother to my children."   These sentiments, as Beloe
observes, show that she had much congeniality of feeling
with her brother, than whom no man had more dislike,
during his whole life, to compliment and adulation.   She had
the wonderful Porson memory.   When she was married, the
clergyman, on concluding the ceremony, said to her, " Mrs.
Hawes, you have given away a great name to-day."

Her eldest son, Mr. Siday Hawes, was for some time a
member of Corpus Christi College, Cambridge, but being,
like his uncle, reluctant to subscribe to the Articles of the
Church of England, withdrew from collegiate life, and en-

---

* Sexagenarian, vol. i. p. 202.

gaged in more active occupation. After having resided in
South and North America, he now lives on his property as
an agriculturist, at Hayes, near Horsham, in Sussex.

Porson's mother died in 1783, and his father in 1806.

Oration on the Character of Charles II.

[A Latin oration on the character of Charles II. is given by
Beloe in his " Sexagenarian" as one of the earliest specimens
to be found of Porson's Latinity. It "was probably delivered," he says, "in the Chapel of Trinity College, at the
time when it is dated," namely, May 29, 1784, when Porson
was in his twenty-fourth year. We cannot learn, nor do we
suppose, that it was ever delivered; but it was perhaps written
by Porson, with a view to delivery on some occasion, for some
other person; and it contains so much strong satire and
invective, of that kind which Porson could so easily use, and
built on so large a foundation of truth, that we have thought
the reader would not be displeased to see an English version
of it.]

Though the opinions of private individuals respecting the
merits of Charles II. are, in the present day, many and
various, yet, if we look back to the testimony of the church,
and of the whole nation, in his own time, we shall esteem
this day not only as deserving *to be marked with white*, but
as worthy of being celebrated every year by a solemn thanks-
giving. And since no law or custom takes deeper root, or
continues longer in force, than that which protects itself
under the name of religion, it may be no unsuitable employment of the present occasion to examine and contemplate,
with some closeness of attention, Charles's character and
disposition, and to inquire, calmly and dispassionately, how
much he contributed to the good of his country; by what
virtues, public and private, he was distinguished; by what
services he promoted liberty and religion; and how meri-

toriously, in a word, he fulfilled the duties of a sovereign and of a man.

If there ever was a king that commenced his reign with the best and happiest possible omens, that king must assuredly have been Charles II.; so strong and so unanimous was the consent of the whole nation to exalt him to the throne of his ancestors. And as *the quarrels of lovers*, according to the proverb, *are the renewing of love*, the people, whatever offences they had committed against his father, or of whatever deficiencies in duty they had been guilty towards him, endeavoured to atone or compensate for all by the extraordinary affection which they displayed towards the son. They who had groaned, for so many years, under the rule of a cruel and suspicious tyrant, consoled themselves with the expectation of happier fortune when the rightful prince should be recalled from his exile; and thought it better, even if they were to experience the rule of a tyrant again, to submit to one to whom arbitrary power seemed in some degree to belong by the law of hereditary succession. As soon as Cromwell therefore was dead, all sects and factions prepared with the utmost eagerness to restore the king. They hoped, doubtless, that the new sovereign would bear in mind, with feelings of gratitude, how much he owed to the favour of his country, and would some day show, as well by actions as by words, his sensibility of the obligation; that, being admonished by the unhappy fortune and premature death of his father, he would, when he took the helm of government, avoid, by cautious and prudent steering, the rocks and shoals on which his parent had struck; that he would neither curtail the rights and liberties of the people, nor extend the limits of his own prerogative beyond the sanctions of divine and human law; and that, having long and bitterly contended with adversity, he would enjoy prosperity without vain or intemperate exultation.

It was in reliance on these expectations, apparently, that they pronounced his right to the throne established in perpetuity, and appropriated, for the supply of his regal expenses, such a portion of the revenue as would suffice, not merely for maintaining, but for exhibiting in full splendour, the pomp and dignity of a powerful prince. Nor did they fail to contribute largely from their own private resources, giving, by this means, the most noble proofs of strong affection for their sovereign, and not making the slightest mention of any conditions to be imposed on him. So eagerly did they hasten to show their zeal and obedience, that they forgot alike what they owed to the memory of their ancestors, to themselves, and to posterity; and that nothing might be wanting to testify their obedience and submission to the voice of their king, those who had the chief share in the glory of his restoration, took upon themselves, in the name of the whole nation, the guilt of the murder of the Blessed Martyr, as they called him, and besought the clemency of their sovereign to pardon the crime which they had committed. Yet the sovereign did not so far yield to clemency as to deem all deserving of forgiveness, but tempered his natural inclination to mercy by just severity, and sentenced such of his father's judges as had consented to his death from principle, and because they thought it for the good of the state, to suffer the severest punishment; while to those who had voted for his decapitation from the pressure of the time, and who, he thought, might afterwards prove subservient agents in his own schemes, he vouchsafed, by a prudent and generous sentence, a full and complete pardon. But for my own part, to say what I think freely and without disguise, it must be acknowledged, I consider, by those whose feelings do not mislead their judgment, that Charles offended alike against kingly dignity and sound policy, in not consigning all past transgressions to oblivion. Or even if the favourers of the Stuarts should deny this, they will surely not deny (for they neither can nor dare) that, of the punishments which the law inflicts upon rebels, the severer portion, as being of a nature at variance with the laws of humanity, ought to have been remitted.

Although the people, as we have already observed, had granted what was enough, and more than enough, for the expense of a properly conducted royal household; yet,

that they might give the richest proof of love for their
new king, they proceeded to vote extraordinary supplies, to
fill, not only his coffers, but those of his brother. Lest anything should be wanting, too, to indicate their feelings as
fond subjects, they abrogated, by a resolution not less ridiculous than foolish, whatever acts the Parliament of Cromwell had passed during the preceding twenty years. If the
historians of that period are to be trusted, however, these
extravagances may be in some degree excused, as having
been committed, for the most part, by men of easy principles
and morals, careless and half-intoxicated; though the laxity,
which admitted such characters into all but the highest
council of the nation, appears not altogether deserving of
praise.

There is also another matter, not indeed to be too much
regarded, and yet not wholly to be neglected; I mean a
certain thirst and eagerness for bloodshed, by which Charles
was strongly influenced through the whole course of his
reign; yet we can scarcely conceive it was from innate
cruelty, in a prince of such a character, that so many innocent men were put to death in violation of divine and human
laws, and in violation even at times of his own promises; it
seems more probable that such spectacles were to this king a
source of jest and amusement. Nor should I greatly wonder,
indeed, if Charles, who had often witnessed, when in France,
how easily the king of that country condemned his subjects
to death, exile, or confiscation of property, and whom the
people of England greeted with no less flattery than the
French paid to Louis, wished to exercise in this respect the
same arbitrary power as the King of France. Assuredly,
unless we allow some force to these palliations, we must
admit that there are scarce any acts related in all history,
concerning the worst and most odious of tyrants, which are
more opposed to humanity, or more at variance with all
lenity and prudence, to say nothing of regard for law, than
those proceedings of the reign of Charles. Among the noblemen brought to the bar in his days, the most eminent were
Vane, Russell, and Sidney, whose unjust and cruel deaths

will stamp eternal infamy on Charles's memory. If we look on acts of such atrocity with the indignation that they deserve, we shall imagine ourselves reading the crimes of another Tiberius or Nero.

But if we had no cause to complain of the administration of the government at home, the disgrace of the wars which Charles undertook, and the treaties which he concluded, is such as was scarcely incurred by King John when he begged the Pope to restore him his crown. By sending an army against the Dutch, from whom he had experienced the most noble hospitality, he met with the just punishment of avarice and ingratitude; for, as the Dutch proved victorious, Charles was forced to make peace on the most unfavourable terms. What induced him to engage in war was, if we speak the truth, the desire of gain, a desire which in the end was not ungratified; for though he got nothing from the States of Holland but ignominy, he had the art to convert to his own use the money which the liberality of his subjects had voted for the expenses of the war. Many of his faults, too, which, if committed by any other prince, would have been called crimes, are designated by a lighter name from being compared with his greater and more flagrant offences; among which the shameful resignation to the enemy of Dunkirk and Tangier, two of the greatest fortresses and defences of the empire, justly holds a prominent position. But all his basenesses are crowned by his compact with Louis, by which he submitted to become a pensioner of France.

It is well enough known in the present day that Charles had attached himself to the same religious faith as his brother James, the faith of Rome, which, when opportunity should serve, he had determined, with the aid of the King of France, to disseminate through Great Britain, substituting the doctrines of the Pope for those of the Reformers, and overthrowing at the same time the whole constitution, and establishing tyranny in the place of civil liberty. But he pursued that object so timidly and coldly, he concealed his intentions with such cunning (shall I say?) or malice, that many of the Catholics suffered the severest punishments under the sanction of a king who had embraced the same faith with themselves.

These examples of the public virtues of Charles we have selected from an infinite number. Let us see if his conduct as a man made amends for his deficiencies as a ruler. His father, whatever were the errors of his government, atoned for them in some degree by his private virtues. But in this respect he left a son sadly degenerate and dissimilar; a son who visited no country in Europe but to bring away from it new follies and new vices. His grandfather James used to be called by his flatterers a second Solomon. That which was wanting to complete the likeness to Solomon in the grandfather was supplied by the grandson, for no one that counts the number of Solomon's concubines and Charles's, will deny that Charles resembled Solomon in this particular. With women of loose character, and men equally depraved, he amused his leisure in every kind of luxury and licentiousness. What sort of man he really was, was shown, as some one has not unhappily remarked, by the words which he uttered at the point of death, when he spoke, not of his country, nor of any of his friends or relatives, but of a harlot.

But perhaps it will be said he devoted his resources to supply the wants of the followers and supporters of his father and himself, and seized with eagerness opportunities of testifying how grateful he felt towards all who had assisted him, whether in adversity or prosperity, with their money, swords, or publications. Nothing was ever further from his thoughts; the most faithful advocates of kingly power he either neglected, like Cowley and Butler, or drove, like Clarendon, from their country, exposed to all the perils and sufferings of exile.

Those who strain every nerve to free the memory of Charles in some degree, by fair means or by foul, from the infamy that hangs over it, enlarge on his affability and suavity of manner, and tell, with delight, how witty and full of humour he was at the festal board. Witty and full of humour doubtless he was, if we take scurrility and buffoonery for wit and humour; for those he had in the greatest abundance, since he made no attempt at wit but to offend modesty, and thought nothing a jest that was not directed against religion. Through the whole of this prince's reign, indeed, there was not the slightest regard paid to modesty, chastity, sincerity, temperance, or piety; nor was there any shorter or surer road to the favour of the king than by becoming notorious for buffoonery, irreligion, drunkenness, and prodigality. To embrace his history in a few words, he was, before he obtained the crown, a beggar; when he had obtained it, he was not a king; he had neither dignity, nor wisdom, nor courage; he had no sense either of friendship or of honour; he was neither affectionate to his brother, nor true to his wife; he lived an atheist, and died a papist. Such was Charles the Second.

> " Manibus date lilia plenis;
> Purpureos spargam flores, animamque tyranni
> His saltem accumulem donis."

Porson's Charades.

Porson had, as Beloe observes, " a great talent for splendid trifles." He exercised this talent, at times, in making charades to amuse ladies with whom he was intimate, and whom he wished to please, for he was not equally ready to please all. Some of these were written for Mrs. Gordon and Mrs. Perry, others for Miss Raine and Mrs. Goodall. One of the best, on the word *Cornix*, was composed for Mrs. Clarke, on a small piece of vellum shaped like a heart. It was first printed in the " Gentleman's Magazine," for Sept. 1808, sent by a correspondent who signs himself " W. P."

> Te Primum incauto nimiùm, propiùsque tuenti,
> Laura mihi furtim surripuisse queror.
> Nec tamen hoc furtum tibi condonare recusem,
> Si pretium tali solvere merce velis.

Sed quo plus candoris habent tibi colla SECUNDO,
   Hoc tibi plus PRIMUM frigoris intus habet.
Sæpe sinistra cavâ cantavit ab ilice TOTUM
   Omina, et audaces spes vetat esse ratas.

The correspondent adds this, his own, translation:

  " Whilst thoughtless, all too near, I gaz'd on thee,
     Laura, you stole my heart; for this I grieve;
  Yet to forgive 's not difficult in me,
     Would you an equal pledge but deign to leave.
  But as the snow thy whiter neck transcends,
  Thy heart, still colder, harbours no amends.
     These, a dissyllable in Latin, hold
  Many quite purpose-stay'd by left-hand croaks
  (Of raven, rook, and crow, the same is told,)
  Foreboding nought but harm from hollow blasted oaks."

The following are given in the "Sexagenarian," and in
Barker's "Literary Anecdotes."

  If Nature and Fortune had placed me with you
    On my first, we my second might hope to obtain;
  I might marry you, were I my third, it is true,
    But the marriage would only embitter my pain.
                    [Parson.]

    My first is the lot that is destin'd by fate,
    For my second to meet with in every state;
    My third is by many philosophers reckon'd
    To bring very often my first to my second.
                 [Woman.]

My first, though your house, nay your life, he defends,
  You ungratefully name like the wretch you despise;
My second, I speak it with grief, comprehends
  All the brave, and the good, and the learn'd, and the wise.
Of my third I have little or nothing to say
Except that it tolls the departure of day.
                 [Curfew.]

  The child of a peasant, Rose thought it no shame
    To toil at my first all the day;
  When her father grew rich, and a farmer became,
    My first to my second gave way.

Then she married a merchant, who brought her to town :
  To this eminent station preferr'd,
Of my first and my second unmindful she's grown,
  And gives all her time to my third.
                              [Spinnet.]

My first is the nymph I adore,
  The sum of her charms is my second,
    I was going to call it my third,
But I counted a million and more,
  Till I found they could never be reckon'd ;
    So I quickly rejected the word.
                              [Thousand.]

My first in ghosts, 'tis said, abounds,
And, wheresoe'er she walks her rounds,
My second never fails to go,
Yet oft attends her mortal foe.
If with my third you quench your thirst,
You sink for ever in my first.
                              [Nightshade.]

My first is expressive of no disrespect,
  Yet I never shall call you it while you are by ;
If my second you still are resolv'd to reject,
  As dead as my third I shall speedily lie.
                              [Herring.]

    My first of unity's a sign ;
      My second ere we knew to plant,
    We used upon my third to dine,
      " If all be true the poets chant."
                              [Acorn.]

Your cat does my first in your ear ;
O that I were admitted as near !
For my second I've held you, my fair,
So long that I almost despair.
But my prey if at last I o'ertake,
What a glorious third I shall make !
                              [Purchase.]

My first with more than quaker's pride,
  At your most solemn duty,
You keep, nor deign to lay aside,
  E'en though it veils your beauty :

D D

My second, on your cheek or lip,
  May kindle Cupid's fire,
While from your eye, or nose's tip,
  · It ne'er provokes desire.
But if my third you entertain
  For your unhappy poet,
In mercy, Chloe, spare his pain,
  Nor ever let him know it. ·

                    [Hatred.]

There are a few riddles, also, given as Porson's, by Beloe, in his "Sexagenarian;" but whether rightly attributed to him or not, it is not worth while to inquire. They are such as any one might make with a very little trouble.

Catechism for the use of the Swinish Multitude.

Of this composition some extracts are given by Beloe in the "Sexagenarian,"* and have been reprinted in the *Facetiæ Cantabrigienses.* Porson never denied that he was the author of it; he allowed Maltby to make a transcript from a copy in his own hand. It was printed with Porson's knowledge, and Carlile of Fleet Street republished it. The origin of it was the term "Swinish Multitude," applied by Burke to the common people, in his "Reflections on the French Revolution." The art with which Porson has introduced the common sayings about pigs is highly worthy of notice.

Q. What is your name?
A. Hog or *Swine.*
Q. Did God make you a *Hog?*
A. No. God made me man in his own image; the *Right Honourable* SUBLIME BEAUTIFUL made me a Swine.
Q. How did he make you a Swine?
A. By muttering obscure and uncouth spells. He is a dealer in the black art.

* Vol. ii. p. 322.

Q. Who feeds you?

A. Our drivers, the only real *men* in this COUNTRY.

Q. How many hogs are you in all?

A. Seven or eight millions.

Q. How many drivers?

A. Two or three hundred thousand.

Q. With what do they feed you?

A. Generally with husks, swill, draff, malt, grains, and now and then with a little barley-meal and a few potatoes; and, when they have too much buttermilk themselves, they give us some.

Q. What are your occupations?

A. To be yoked to the plough; to do all hard work; for which purpose we still, as you see, retain enough of our original form, speech, and reason to carry our drivers on our shoulders, or to draw them in carriages.

Q. Are your drivers independent of each other?

A. No; our immediate drivers are driven by a smaller number, and that number by a still smaller, and so on, till at last you come to the Chief Hog Driver.

Q. Has your Chief Driver any marks of his office?

A. A brass helmet on his head, and an iron poker in his hand.

Q. By what title does he wear his helmet?

A. In contempt of the choice of the hogs.

Q. Do the drivers wear badges of distinction?

A. Many; some have particular frocks and slops; others garter below the knee; some have a red rag across their jackets; and some carry sticks and poles.

Q. How do they look in their trappings?

A. *Like a sow on a side-saddle.*

Q. What is the use of that iron ring in your snout?

A. To hinder us from rooting in our drivers' gardens.

Q. What is the use of that wooden yoke on your neck?

A. To keep us from breaking through our drivers' fences; but both ring and yoke are principally intended to diminish our strength and spirits, and to prevent our resistance, if at any time we fancy we have too little victuals or too much whipping.

Q. What is the use of those whips and cudgels that some of your drivers bear ?

A. To beat us when we grunt too loud for the slumbers of the Upper Driver.

Q. Do your drivers ever meet to transact business ?

A. Yes; formerly their meetings continued only *three weeks*, but of late they have been prolonged to *seven*.

Q. What do they do at these meetings ?

A. They sell us.

Q. You seem to me too lean to be very profitable.

A. The greatest profit to our drivers lies in our work; besides, most of them agree, at the meeting, that *we enjoy an unexampled degree of fatness, plumpness, and sleekness;* and that methods should be taken rather to starve than to pamper us, lest we should grow fat and kick.

Q. Where do they meet ?

A. In a rotten house. The nominal president is the Chief Hog Driver, otherwise called Father of the Hogs; but the true president, otherwise the *Step-father* of the hogs, is the governor of the *sub-meeting*. Everything is done by the latter, and attributed to the former. The latter raises the price of pork at his pleasure.

Q. Truly the gentleman seems *to have brought his hogs to a fine market*. But you mentioned the sub-meeting ?

A. Yes; there is also an *upper-meeting*.

Q. Are the members of it skilful in pork ?

A. They are born (or created) skilful in all branches of *butchery*.

Q. Of whom consists the sub-meeting ?

A. Of middle drivers chosen by us, and sent on behalf of the poor herd of swine; to take care that they be not starved to death, but only kept as lean as possible; to see that no undue cruelty is used, but only that they be whipped within an inch of their lives.

Q. Do you choose and send agents that can make no better terms for you than these ?

A. We did not choose and send them.

Q. Why you said even now that they were chosen and sent by you.

A. They are chosen and not chosen.

Q. A paradox ! Try to explain.

A. You know that the country is parcelled out into farms, some overstocked with hogs, and some almost empty. Some of these hogs have a bit of potato ground allowed them by their drivers, and others have none. Now only the potato'd hogs are allowed to nominate an agent for the meeting. A few of the farms send each one or two agents, and consequently all the agents may be sent by a very few hogs.

Q. When the herd is small, the driver will make himself agent by threatening to starve you, or will otherwise win you to his purpose; but how do they manage you when you are numerous ?

A. They praise our beauty, good sense, good nature, gentleness, and great superiority to all other hogs; they kiss the old sows and the young pigs; they give us our belly-full of new beer, till we are *as drunk as David's sow*, and wallow in the mire. In this condition they make us choose them, while we really know nothing at all of the matter.

Q. Do they promise beforehand to take care of you?

A. Yes; and forget to perform it afterwards.

Q. But you choose another agent when one has betrayed you.

A. Very often we cannot. Nay, one of the drivers the other day told the hogs on his farm that he had bought them, and would sell them.

Q. What is the advantage of being an agent ?

A. Some court the office merely for the honour, but all the knowing ones are hired by the governors to say none of them are hired, and that they are all chosen by *the free sense of the swinish multitude.*

Q. How many are hired ?

A. A majority.

Q. How much is reckoned decent wages ?

A. Nothing under the price of several hundred hogs.

Q. Do they ever graciously condescend to inform you of their resolutions ?

A. They write copies of them and send them about.

Q. Gratis, of course ?

A. No; but they will let us have a copy for a few dozens of potatoes.

Q. The resolutions, however, are easy to read ?

A. Scarcely one of us in twenty can read at all, for we are told by our drivers that we ought to be ignorant.

Q. Are they sincere in this ?

A. Very sincere; for they are constantly rewarded in proportion to their own ignorance. But, alas ! if we could read, it would be nothing, for the resolutions are not written in English.

Q. No; they are written, I know, in *Hog Latin,* but that I took for granted you understand.

A. Shameful aspersion on the hogs ! The most inarticulate grunting of our tribe is sense and harmony compared to such jargon.

Q. Do not your drivers, then, appoint interpreters for you ?

A. Yes; that they would call in their own case *buying a pig in a poke.*

Q. What are the interpreters called ?

A. The BLACK LETTER SISTERHOOD.

Q. Why do you give the office to women ?

A. Because they have a fluent tongue and a knack of scolding.

Q. How are they dressed ?

A. In gowns and false hair.

Q. What are the principal orders ?

A. Three: *Writers, Talkers,* and *Hearers,* which last are also called *Deciders.*

Q. What is their general business ?

A. To discuss the mutual quarrels of the hogs, and to punish their affronts to any or all of the drivers.

Q. How can one hog affront all the drivers ?

A. By speaking the truth.

Q. What is the truth?

A. What is that to you?

Q. If two hogs quarrel, how do they apply to the sister-hood?

A. Each hog goes separately to a *Writer*.

Q. What does the *Writer?*

A. She goes to a *Talker*.

Q. What does the *Talker*.

A. She goes to a *Hearer* or *Decider*.

Q. What does the *Hearer* decide?

A. What she pleases.

Q. If a hog is decided to be in the *right*, what is the consequence?

A. He is *almost* ruined.

Q. If in the *wrong*, what?

A. He is quite ruined.

Q. What is the true reason of this practice?

A. The ease and interest of the sisterhood. If it were otherwise, they would have more work and less wages.

Q. What is the pretended reason?

A. That they are afraid we should never have done quarrelling, if they could easily settle our disputes.

Q. That is, they pull out your tusks that you may not bite each other. Is not this reason mockery as well as oppression?

A. No; they tell us that what has been done ought to be done again.

Q. Do none of the drivers take compassion on you, when they see you thus *grunt and sweat under a weary life?*

A. Several agents in the sub-meeting have proposed schemes for our relief, but have always been overpowered by a great majority.

Q. Could that majority give any reasons for their behaviour?

A. Nine.

Q. Name the first.

A. They said, for their parts, they were very well contented as they were.

Q. The second?

A. They believed the present system of hog driving would last out their time.

Q. The third?

A. The Chief Hog Driver had published an advertisement against giving the hogs any relief.

Q. The fourth?

A. The hogs were very desirous to have some relief.

Q. The fifth?

A. The hogs were in perfect tranquillity at present.

Q. The sixth?

A. The hogs were in a violent ferment at present.

Q. The seventh?

A. The hogs were too good to need relief.

Q. The eighth?

A. The hogs were too bad to deserve relief.

Q. The ninth?

A. If they gave us what was right, they could not help giving us what was wrong.

Q. How do you look when you hear such a mass of lies and nonsense?

A. We stare like stuck pigs.

Q. But you are vastly superior in numbers and strength; how are you kept quiet under such complicated injuries?

A. By force and by art.

Q. By what force?

A. By twenty thousand *hogs in armour.*

Q. By what art?

A. By sowing the seeds of discord among us.

Q. Whom do they employ to sow the seeds of discord?

A. The ministers of peace.

Q. How do these ministers execute their commission?

A. They tell the simpler hogs that their brethren mean to cut the throats of their drivers, and then to turn drivers themselves.

Q. How do these hogs treat the obnoxious swine?

A. They burn down their sties, and eat up their meal and potatoes.

Q. Have the *ministers of peace,* as you call them, any other employment?

A. Yes; they tell us from time to time that unless we believe all that they say, and do all that our drivers bid us, we shall infallibly go to the devil.

*   *   *   *   *

Q. How are these *peace-makers* rewarded?

A. With our potatoes.

Q. What with all?

A. Ten per cent. only.

Q. Then you have still ninety left in the hundred?

A. No; we have but forty left.

Q. What becomes of the odd fifty?

A. The drivers take them partly as a small recompence for their trouble in protecting us, and partly to make money of them, for the prosecution of lawsuits with the neighbouring farmers.

Q. Do they not reserve for their own use ten times as many as they want?

A. They eat till they are full, and pelt each other with the remainder.

Q. You talk very sensibly for a hog. Whence had you your information?

A. From a *learned pig.*

Q. Are there many learned pigs in the country?

A. Many, and the number daily increases.

Q. What say they of the treatment which you suffer?

A. That it is shameful and ought instantly to be redressed.

Q. What do the drivers say to these pigs?

A. That the devil is in them.

Q. It is a devil of their own conjuring: but what do the drivers do to these pigs?

A. They knock them down.

Q. Do all the learned pigs make the same complaint?

A. All; for the instant a pig defends the contrary opinion, he resumes his old form, and becomes *a real master and tormentor-general of innocent animals.*

Q. Are there any other methods of recovering the human shape ?

A. None, but a promise to treat the herd we have left with exemplary severity.

Q. Who disenchants you ?

A. The governor of the sub-meeting must always consent, but the ceremonies of transformation vary.

Q. Give me an instance of a ceremony.

A. The hog that is going to be disenchanted, grovels before the *Chief Driver*, who holds an iron skewer over him, and gives him a smart blow on the shoulder, to remind him at once of his former subjection and future submission. Immediately he starts up, like the devil from Ithuriel's spear, in his proper shape, and ever after goes about with a nickname. He then beats his hogs without mercy, and, when they implore his compassion, and beg him to recollect that he was once their *fellow-swine*, he denies that he ever was a hog.

Q. What are the rights of a hog ?

A. To be whipt and bled by men.

Q. What are the duties of a man ?

A. To whip and bleed hogs.

Q. Do they ever whip and bleed you to death ?

A. Not always; the common method is to bleed us by intervals.

Q. How many ounces do they take at a time ?

A. That depends upon the state of the patient. As soon as he faints, they bind up the wound; but they open his veins afresh when he has a little recovered his loss; hence comes the proverb *to bleed like a pig.*

Q. What is the liberty of a hog ?

A. To choose between half starving and whole starving.

Q. What is the property of a hog ?

A. A wooden trough; food and drink just enough to keep in life; and a truss of musty straw, on which ten or a dozen of us *pig together.*

Q. What dish is most delicious to a driver's palate ?

A. A hog's pudding.

Q. What music is sweetest to a driver's ear?

A. Our shrieks in bleeding.

Q. What is a driver's favourite diversion?

A. To set his dogs upon us.

Q. What is the general wish of the hogs at present?

A. To save their bacon.

Chorus of Hogs. Amen.

The Salt-Box,

A satire on the mode of examination at Oxford, has been commonly attributed to Porson, and is so much in his manner, that there can hardly be a doubt of its being his.

METAPHYSICS.

Professor.—What is a salt-box?

Student.—It is a box made to contain salt.

Professor.—How is it divided?

Student.—Into a salt-box and a box of salt.

Professor.—Very well; show the distinction.

Student.—A salt-box may be where there is no salt; but salt is absolutely necessary to the existence of a box of salt.

Professor.—Are not salt-boxes otherwise divided?

Student.—Yes, by a partition.

Professor.—What is the use of this division?

Student.—To separate the *coarse* from the *fine*.

Professor. How! Think a little.

Student.—To separate the *fine* from the *coarse*.

Professor.—To be sure: to separate the *fine* from the *coarse*. But are not salt-boxes otherwise distinguished?

Student.—Yes, into possible, probable, and positive.

Professor.—Define these several kinds of salt-boxes.

Student.—A possible salt-box is a salt-box yet unsold, in the joiner's hands.

Professor.—Why so ?

Student.—Because it hath not yet become a salt-box, having never had any salt in it, and it may probably be applied to some other use.

Professor.—Very true; for a salt-box which never had, hath not now, and perhaps may never have, any salt in it, can only be termed a possible salt-box. What is a probable salt-box?

Student.—It is a salt-box in the hands of one going to buy salt, and who has sixpence in his pocket to pay the shopkeeper; and a positive salt-box is one which hath actually and *bona fide* got salt in it.

Professor.—Very good ; and what other divisions of the salt-box do you recollect?

Student.—They are divided into *substantive* and *pendent.* A substantive salt-box is that which stands by itself on a table or dresser; and the pendent is that which hangs against the wall.

Professor.—What is the *idea* of a salt-box?

Student.—It is that image which the mind conceives of a salt-box, when no salt-box is present.

Professor.—What is the *abstract* idea of a salt-box?

Student.—It is the idea of a salt-box *abstracted* from the idea of a box, or of salt, or of a salt-box, or of a box of salt.

Professor.—Very right: by this you may acquire a proper knowledge of a salt-box: but tell me, is the idea of a salt-box a *salt idea*?

Student.—Not unless the idea hath the idea of salt contained in it.

Professor.—True: and therefore an *abstract* idea cannot be either *salt or fresh, round or square, long or short:* and this shows the difference of a salt idea, and an idea of salt. Is an aptitude to hold salt an *essential* or an *accidental* property of a salt-box?

Student.—It is essential: but if there should be a crack in the bottom of the box, the aptitude to spill salt would be termed an accidental property of that box.

Professor.—Very well, very well indeed. What is the salt called with respect to the box?

Student.—It is called its contents.

Professor.—Why so?

Student.—Because the cook is content, *quoad hoc*, to find plenty of salt in the box.

Professor.—You are very right. Now let us proceed to—

LOGIC.

Professor.—How many *modes* are there in a salt-box?

Student.—Three: bottom, top, and sides.

Professor.—How many modes are there in salt-boxes?

Student.—Four: the *formal*, the *substantive*, the *accidental*, and the *topsy-turvy*.

Professor.—Define these several modes.

Student.—The formal respects the figure or shape of the box, such as a *circle*, a *square*, an *oblong*, &c.; the substantive respects the work of the joiner; and the accidental respects the string by which the box is hung against the wall.

Professor.—Very well: what are the consequences of the accidental mode?

Student.—If the *string* should break, the box would fall, and the salt be spilt, the salt-box broken, and the cook in a passion; and this is the accidental mode and its consequences.

Professor.—How do you distinguish between the bottom and the top of a salt-box?

Student.—The top of a salt-box is that part which is uppermost, and the bottom is that which is the lowest in all positions.

Professor.—You should rather say the uppermost part is the top, and the lowest part the bottom. How is it, then, if the *bottom* should be *uppermost*?

Student.—The top would then be lowermost, so that the bottom would become the top, and the top the bottom; and this is called the *topsy-turvy* mode, and is nearly allied to the accidental, and frequently arises from it.

Professor.—Very good: but are not salt-boxes sometimes single, and sometimes double?

Student.—Yes.

Professor.—Well, then, mention the several combinations of salt-boxes, with respect to the having *salt or not.*

Second Professor.—Hold! hold! you are going too far.

Governors of the Institution.—We can't allow further time for logic; proceed, if you please, to—

NATURAL PHILOSOPHY.

Professor.—What is a salt-box?

Student.—It is a combination of matter, fitted, framed, and joined, by the hands of a workman, in the form of a box, and adapted for the purpose of receiving and containing salt.

Professor.—Very good. What are the *mechanical powers* engaged in the construction of a salt-box?

Student.—The *axe*, the *saw*, the *plane*, and the *hammer.*

Professor.—How are these powers applied to the purpose intended?

Student.—The *axe* to fell the trees, the *saw* to split the timber, the—

Professor.—Consider! It is the property of the mallet and wedge to split.

Student.—The *saw* to slit the timber, and the *plane* to smooth and thin the boards.

Professor.—How! Take time, take time.

Student.—To thin and smooth the boards.

Professor.—To be sure: the boards are first thinned and then smoothed. Go on.

Student.—The plane to thin and smooth, and the hammer to drive the nails.

Professor.—Or rather tacks. Have not some *philosophers* considered *glue* as one of the mechanical powers?

Student.—Yes; and it is still so considered: but it is called an inverse mechanical power; because, whereas it is the property of direct mechanical powers to generate motion, *glue*, on the contrary, prevents motion, by keeping the parts to which it is applied fixed to each other.

Professor.—Very true. What is the mechanical law of the *saw?*

Student.—The power is to resist as the number of *teeth* and *force* impressed, multiplied by the number of strokes in a given time.

Professor.—Is the *saw* only used in slitting timber into boards?

Student.—Yes; it is also used in cutting boards into lengths.

Professor.—Not lengths. A thing cannot be said to be cut into lengths.

Student.—Shortnesses.

Professor.—Very right. What are the mechanical laws of the *hammer?*

Governor.—We have just received intelligence that dinner is nearly ready; and as the medical class is yet to be examined, let the medical gentlemen come forward.

Porson has always had the credit of being the author of the following verses on Dr. Jowett, Fellow of St. John's, who, having a taste for horticulture, was permitted by the head of his College to turn a strip of vacant ground into a garden. Some jokes being passed on its diminutiveness, he turned it into a plot of gravel.

> A *little* garden *little* Jowett made,
> And fenced it with a *little* palisade;
> Because this garden made a *little* talk,
> He changed it to a *little* gravel walk :
> And now, if more you'd know of *little* Jowett,
> A *little* time, it will a *little* show it.

In "Blackwood's Magazine" the lines were given in a briefer form :

A *little* garden *little* Jowett made,
And fenced it with a *little* palisade ;
A *little* taste hath *little* Doctor Jowett ;
This *little* garden doth a *little* show it.

With this Latin version:

Exiguum hunc hortum fecit Jowettulus iste
Exiguus, vallo et muniit *exiguo :*
Exiguo hoc horto forsan Jowettulus iste
Exiguus mentem prodidit *exiguam.*

Many sayings have been attributed to Porson that are not his. We have seen the punning observation on Brutus killing Cæsar, *Nec bene fecit, nec male fecit, sed interfecit,* ascribed to him; when it is certainly not his. In Charles Phillips's " Recollections of Curran and his Contemporaries," it is attributed, with as little ground, we believe, to Curran. The application of Horace's *quos et aquæ subeunt et auræ* to a pair of breeches, was long circulated as his, when it was Glasse's. In Barker's " Literary Anecdotes," * it is said that Porson, hearing a child of Major Revell repeat Cowley's translation of an ode of Anacreon, took her on his knee, and repeated to her the ode in *Greek, German, French,* and *Italian.* Porson, it is well known, had no acquaintance with German, and, according to Mr. Maltby, very little with Italian.

The following story of Porson, which has been often printed, rests wholly upon the authority of the Rev. Charles Caleb Colton, who published it in his " Lacon." Whether what he tells really occurred, or whether it is wholly or partly invention, we do not know.

" Porson was once travelling in a stage-coach, when a young Oxonian, fresh from College, was amusing the ladies with a variety of talk, and, amongst other things, with a quotation, as he said, from Sophocles. A Greek quotation, and in a coach too, roused our slumbering Professor from a kind of dog-sleep in a snug corner of the vehicle. Shaking

* Vol. ii. p. 22.

his ears, and rubbing his eyes, ' I think, young gentleman,' said he, ' you favoured us just now with a quotation from Sophocles; I do not happen to recollect it there.' 'Oh, Sir,' replied our tiro, the quotation is word for word as I have repeated it, and in Sophocles too ; but I suspect, Sir, that it is some time since you were at college.' The Professor, applying his hand to his great-coat, and taking out a small pocket-edition of Sophocles, quietly asked him if he would be kind enough to show him the passage in question, in that little book. After rummaging the pages for some time, he replied, ' On second thoughts, I now recollect that the passage is in Euripides.' ' Then perhaps, Sir,' said the Professor, putting his hand into his pocket, and handing him a similar edition of Euripides, ' you will be so good as to find it for me in that little book.' The young Oxonian returned to his task, but with no better success. The tittering of the ladies informed him that he had got into a hobble. At last, ' Bless me, Sir,' said he, ' how dull I am ! I recollect now, yes, I perfectly remember that the passage is in Æschylus.' The inexorable Professor returned again to his inexhaustible pocket, and was in the act of handing him an Æschylus, when our astonished freshman vociferated: 'Stop the coach ! Holloah, coachman, let me out, I say, instantly, let me out ! There's a fellow here has got the whole Bodleian library in his pocket; let me out, I say, let me out; he must be Porson or the devil ! ' "

The play upon the Latin gerunds *di -do -dum,* one of the neatest plays on words that was ever made, has never been assigned to any one but Porson. It is said to have been produced in a company who were making puns or rhymes on words. Porson said that he would make, some say a rhyme, others a pun, on anything. Some one said that he had better try one on the Latin gerunds. He immediately replied,

E E

> When Dido found Æneas would not come,
> She mourn'd in silence, and was *Di -do -dum.**

The following playful epitaph has, we believe, never appeared in print:

> Here lies a Doctor of Divinity;
> He was a Fellow too of Trinity:
> He knew as much about Divinity,
> As other Fellows do of Trinity.

In illustration of Porson's mathematical qualifications, the following communication was made to the "Classical Journal."†

" It is well known that Porson's proficiency in Algebra was very considerable; and that the solving of such problems as are commonly heard of by the appellation of Diophantine, was to him a source of particular entertainment. It is even said that some of these were found upon his person at his death. His celebrated equation given in the former part of your journal, is in every one's hands. It has, however, been urged that his knowledge of geometry was only superficial. But this, it should seem, is little better than mere idle report; as is sufficiently evident from the nature of the annexed problem, composed by him, *en capricieux*, as a sort of challenge to the then fellows of Trinity College.

V. L.

" Cambridge, October, 1814.

" PROBLEM.—In Euclid, I. 47, the point in which the straight lines CF, BK, intersect, is in AL, the perpendicular drawn from the right angle to the base, BC.

R. P.

-----

* Barker's Lit. Anecd. vol. i. p. 90. Facetiæ Cantabrigienses, p. 95.
† Vol. x. p. 401.

" If not, let CF, BK, intersect in any point P, which is nôt in AL; that is, let the points *r*, *s*, not coincide. Produce BC

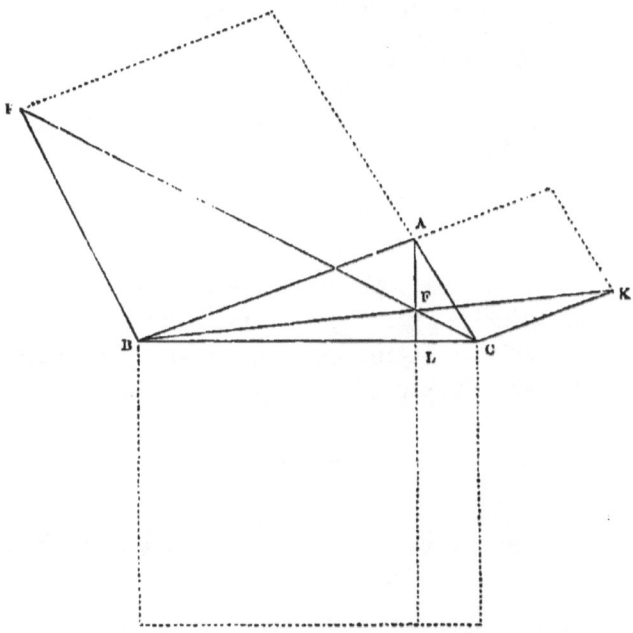

both ways, and from F and K let fall the perpendiculars FM, KN.

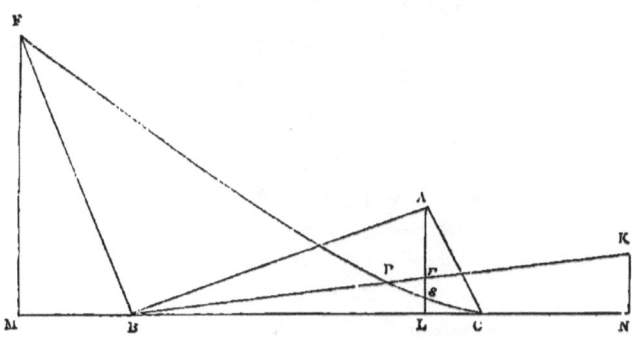

" Then because (Eucl. I. 29 and VI. 8, or I. 13 and 32) the triangle BFM is similar to the triangle ABL, and that BF is equal to AB, ∴ BM = AL. Similarly, CN = AL, ∴.

$BM = CN$, and therefore the whole $MC =$ the whole BN. Also $FM = BL$, and $KN = LC$.   Then

$$FM \; : \; MC \; :: \; sL \; : \; LC, \text{ and}$$
$$BN \; : \; NK \; :: \; BL \; : \; Lr$$
$$\therefore \; \overline{FM \; : \; NK} \; :: \; \overline{sL.BL} \; : \; LC.Lr$$
$$\therefore \; \frac{FM}{BL} \; : \; \frac{NK}{LC} \; :: \; sL \; : \; Lr, \text{ that is, (since}$$
$$FM = BL, \text{ and } NK = LC,)$$
$$1 \; : \; 1 \; :: \; sL \; : \; Lr,$$
$$\therefore \; sL = Lr,$$

the less $=$ the greater, which is absurd.   Therefore r and s cannot but coincide; that is, the lines must cut in AL.   And a similar proof may be applied, if the point of intersection be taken anywhere else out of the right line AL.   Q. E. D."

Beloe has preserved an equation composed by Porson in Greek.[*]

Τίς ὁ ἀριθμός, οὗ τενομένου εἰς δύο ἀνίσους μερίδας, ἡ τῆς μεί- ζονος μερίδος δύναμις μετὰ τῆς ἐλάττονος μεταλαμβανομένη ἴση ἔσεται τῇ τῆς ἐλάττονος δυνάμει μετὰ τῆς μείζονος μεταλαμβανομένῃ.

Required the number, which being divided into two un- equal parts, the square of the greater added to the less shall be equal to the square of the less added to the greater.   Let x be the number, and y one of the parts.   Then $x - y =$ the other part.

$$\therefore \; (x - y)^2 + y = y^2 + (x - y),$$
$$\text{Or, } x^2 - 2\,x\,y + y^2 = y^2 + x - y,$$
$$x^2 - 2\,x\,y = x - 2\,y,$$
$$x\,(x - 2y) = (x - 2y),$$
$$\therefore \; x = 1.$$

showing that practically there are no positive values of the two parts.

---

* Sexagenarian, vol. ii. p. 309.

Since the pages relating to Porson's early years were printed off, we have been favoured with the following anecdote by the Rev. John Gunn, of Irstead, near Norfolk.

During Porson's boyhood, a proposal was made at a vestry-meeting to take down the north side of East Ruston Church, and build the brick wall which is now standing on the north side of the nave. But before any resolution was passed, it was desirable to know how many bricks would be required for the purpose; and none of the parishioners present could make a calculation. At last one of them said, " Send for young Porson," who, when he was found, soon told them the requisite number.

Of his mode of examining, when he took part in the University examinations, we can give one anecdote. When Blomfield, afterwards Bishop of London, was candidate, with several others, for the Craven Scholarship, Porson desired them to be at his rooms by a certain hour in the forenoon. On assembling, they had to wait some time for the Professor, who was then greatly sunk in health, being within a year of his death, and found, though the morning was cold, no fire lighted; nor were any other preparations made for their reception. On Porson's appearance, however, the deficiencies were soon supplied, and he proceeded to dictate to them several corrupt verses, which they were to show their skill in correcting. Blomfield was able to correct six of the number, and was declared the successful candidate.

As an instance of his critical perspicacity, it may be mentioned that he was of opinion, as he often told Mr. Kidd, that the account of the woman taken in adultery, in the seventh and eighth chapters of St. John's Gospel, must be a pure interpolation; an opinion happily supported by the recently discovered *Codex Sinaiticus*, a manuscript which is considered to be as old as the fourth century, and in which that passage is not found. This manuscript, also, it may be added, wants the text of the Three Heavenly Witnesses, which Porson so triumphantly proved spurious.

In regard to his fondness for nice penmanship, it may be remarked, in addition to what has been already said, that he often wasted time, not only in writing with superfluous care, but in producing extremely small writing. Mr. Norgate, the publisher, brother-in-law to Mr. Siday Hawes, has a specimen of his minute writing, comprising, in a circle of an inch and a half in diameter, the Greek verses on music from the Medea of Euripides, with Johnson's translation of them for Burney's History of Music, in all more than 220 words, with a considerable space left blank in the centre. It is written on vellum, a portion of a leaf which fell from the Photius which he copied.

In p. 54, where Heyne's application to Cambridge for the loan of Bentley's manuscripts on Homer is mentioned, it might have been added that the request of Heyne was readily granted, and that the Gottingen professor, in his edition of Homer, acknowledged himself greatly indebted to Bentley's labours, of the merits of which he spoke in the highest terms.

INDEX.

E E 4

Budæus's Commentaries on the Greek Language, Porson inclined to publish, 37.

Burges, George, his Greek verses on Porson, 334.

Burgess, Bishop, attacked Porson after his death on the " Letters to Travis," 82. Answered by Bishop Turton, *ib.* His patronage of a notion of Granville Sharp's, 269. His classical scholarship despised by Porson, 304.

Burgess, Sir James Bland, writes a prologue to Ireland's " Vortigern," 147.

Burney, Dr. Charles, his review of Huntingford's " Monostrophica," 45. His opinion of the " Letters to Travis," 79. Promotes the subscription for Porson's annuity, 95, 98, 100. Trustee of the annuity fund, 336.

Butler, Charles, Porson's conversation with, 332.

Byron, Lord, his account of Porson's habits at Cambridge, 271, 272. His addition to a remark of Porson's about Southey, 306.

Carthew, Rev. T., requested to examine Porson, 11. His letter to Professor Lambert, *ib.*

Casaubon, merits of his Athenæus, 341.

" *Catechism for Swinish Multitude,*" 402.

Ceres, fragment of a statue of, Porson's inscription for, 257.

Chalmers, George, his dull " Apology for the Believers " in the Shakspeare papers, 152, 153.

Chantrey's bust of Porson, 336.

Charades, some of Porson's, 399.

Charles II., Porson's oration on, 393.

Cicero, Porson's liking for, 342.

Clarke, Dr. Adam, his opinion of the age of the Dublin MS. of the New Testament, 71. His account of Porson's last illness and death, 320, *seqq.* Exhibits a stone from Eleusis to Porson, 321, 322.

Clarke, Dr. E. D., honoured with verses at his funeral, 335.

Classical literature, advantages of an acquaintance with, 267, 376.

Codex Sinaiticus, 421.

Coray, Porson's respect for his scholarship, 310.

Coffin, Mr., said to be the author of " Eloisa in Dishabille," 290.

Coli æus's Greek Testament omitted 1 John v. 7, 59.

Collier, Rev. Mr., assists in examining

Porson as a boy at Cambridge, 14. Is one of his examiners for the Craven scholarship, 32.

Colton, Rev. C. C., his story of Porson, 416.

Complutensian edition of the Greek Testament, 59, 60.

Coxe, Archdeacon, gives an instance of Porson's memory, 288. Introduced Porson to Jacob Bryant, 303.

Cooke, Greek professor at Cambridge, 102. Had been head master at Eton, 240.

Courtney, Sir John, wrote the " Epistle of Oberea to Sir Joseph Banks," 292.

Criticism, elegant, 120, 121. Verbal, *ib.*

Cyprian, no authority in favour of 1 John v. 7, 65.

Dalzel, Andrew, Porson's letter to, 259 —265. Dalzel's reply, 266.

Davies, Dr., head master of Eton, presents Porson with Toup's Longinus, 28.

Davy, Dr. Martin, letter of Porson to him, 237. Another, 308. Porson's esteem for him, *ib.*

Dawes, author of the " Miscellanea Critica," Porson's esteem for, 28, 45. Disrespectfully mentioned by Huntingford, 45. Satirises Askew, 313.

Dawes, J. N., a letter of Porson's with that signature, 256, 257.

Disney, Colonel, intimate with Porson, 21.

Disraeli, Isaac, offends Porson, 382. Concerned in the novel of " Flim-Flams," 383. His character, 384.

Dobree, P. P., publishes Porson's " Aristophanica," and " Photius," 338, 339.

Don Bellianis, the romance of, 346.

Douglas, Bishop of Salisbury, defends Porson against Jacob Bryant, 304.

Dryden, Anderson's edition of, 346.

Dublin manuscript of the New Testament, 58.

Dubois concerned in the novel of " Flim-Flams," 384.

Dyer, George, wrote notice of Porson in the " Public Characters," 359.

Editor, duty of an, 114.

Edwards, Dr., his edition of Plutarch on Education reviewed, 113.

Egerton, the " black-letter bookseller," publishes Porson's " Letters to Travis," 58, 84.

letter to Porson on a contemplated edition of Plautus, 179—181. Attacked in the notes to the "Medea," 233—235. Porson's remarks on him, 260, 261. An alteration of his, 370.
Hermesianax, Weston's, Porson's review of, 44.
Hewitt, Rev. Chas., curate of Bacton and East Ruston, finds Porson's mother reading Congreve, 6. Takes Porson under his tuition, 9. His qualifications for an instructor, 10, 11. Speaks of Porson to Mr. Norris, 11. His letter to Professor Hewitt, 12.
Hey, Dr. John, a delegate to reconsider Frend's sentence, 203.
Heyne, Professor, requests the loan of Bentley's papers on Homer, 53, 422. His Virgil reprinted in London, 115. His letter to Porson on behalf of Hermann, 182.
Homer, absurd to attribute to him all perfections, 119. Grenville edition of, 161, 225.
Horace, Porson's burlesque "Imitations" of, 191--197.
Hoppner, his portrait of Porson, 132. Engraved by Sharpe, 336.
Hughes, Rev. T. S., letter from, concerning Porson, 385.
Huntingford's "Apology for his Monostrophics" severely criticised by Porson, 45—47.
Hutchinson's Xenophon, Porson's notes to, 49.
"Hymn by a new-made Peer," 209, 210.

Invernizius censured, 187.
Ireland, Samuel, exhibits his son's forged Shakspeare papers, 140.
Ireland, Wm. Henry, his Shakspeare forgeries, 135—153. His profits, 144.
"*Italic Version*" of the New Testament does not support 1 John, v. 7, 63, 64.

Jacobs, Frederic, 185, 186.
Jerome, St., his version of the New Testament, 66. Revision of it by Alcuin, 67. No support in it for 1 John, v. 7, 68. Nor in Jerome's "Prologue to the Canonical Epistles," 68—70. That "Prologue" probably not his, *ib.*
Johnson, Dr., his silence about Lauder in his Life of Milton, 347.
Johnstone, Dr., meets Porson at Hatton, 91, 92.

Jowett, Dr., joins in the prosecution of Frend, 198. His little garden, 415.
Joy, Surgeon, Porson's letter to, 273.
"*Junius,*" a favourite with Porson, 345. Emendation of a passage in, 345.

Kemble, John, acts in Ireland's "Vortigern," 147, 148.
Kidd, Rev. T., his remark about Porson at Eton, 19. An observation of his on the "Orgies of Bacchus," 209. Porson's esteem for his scholarship, 312. Letter from him to Porson, *ib.*
Kipling, Dr., prosecutes Frend, 198. His publication of Smith's "Optics" and Beza's Codex, 200. Porson's satirical notices of him, 201, 204, 209. His bad Latin, 202.
Kirkby, his portrait of Porson, 132.
Knight, Payne, character of his "Essay on the Greek Alphabet," 118—121.

Lambert, Rev. James, Professor of Greek at Cambridge, examines Porson, 14. His account of the examination, *ib.* His willingness to serve Porson, 15. Present at Porson's funeral, 333.
Langton, Bennet, tolerates Porson's late habits, 283.
Leigh, Mr. J., his attention to Porson in his illness, 326.
Lewis, "On the Consecration of Churches," passage from, illustrated by Porson, 352.
London Institution, its establishment, 315. Its Library, 316.
Luther's New Testament omitted 1 John v. 7, 59.

Mackintosh, Sir James, disliked by Porson, 305.
Malone, Edmund, not deceived by Ireland's forgeries, 147. His volume exposing them, 144—152. Commended by Porson, 313.
Maltby, Bishop, his praise of Porson's *obeli* in Æschylus, 124. His praise of Porson's honesty, 378.
Maltby, Mr. William, his anecdotes of Porson; one of them, at least, unfounded, 35. Porson's intimacy with, 313.
Mansel, Bishop, reads the service at Porson's funeral, 333.
Marsh, Bishop, intimate with Porson in his youth, 249.
Martin, a Frenchman, defends 1 John

THE END.

LONDON
PRINTED BY SPOTTISWOODE AND CO.
NEW-STREET SQUARE

LIST

OF

WORKS IN GENERAL LITERATURE

PUBLISHED BY

MESSRS. LONGMAN, GREEN, LONGMAN, AND ROBERTS

39 PATERNOSTER ROW, LONDON.

CLASSIFIED INDEX.

ALPHABETICAL CATALOGUE

of

NEW WORKS and NEW EDITIONS

PUBLISHED BY

MESSRS. LONGMAN, GREEN, LONGMAN, AND ROBERTS,

PATERNOSTER ROW, LONDON.

Miss Acton's Modern Cookery for Private Families, reduced to a System of Easy Practice in a Series of carefully-tested Receipts, in which the Principles of Baron Liebig and other eminent Writers have been as much as possible applied and explained. Newly-revised and enlarged Edition ; with 8 Plates, comprising 27 Figures, and 150 Woodcuts. Fcp. 8vo. 7s. 6d.

The Afternoon of Life. By the Author of *Morning Clouds.* Second and cheaper Edition, revised throughout. Fcp. 8vo. 5s.

Agassiz. — An Essay on Classification [The Mutual Relation of Organised Beings]. By LOUIS AGASSIZ. 8vo. 12s.

Aikin. — Select Works of the British Poets, from Ben Jonson to Beattie : With Biographical and Critical Prefaces by Dr. AIKIN. Including a Supplement of Selections from more recent Poets. 8vo. 18s.

Alexander.—Salmon-Fishing in Canada. By a RESIDENT. Edited by Colonel Sir JAMES EDWARD ALEXANDER, K.C.L.S., F.R.G.S. ; Author of "Travels in Africa, Persia, America," &c. With Map and 40 Woodcuts. Post 8vo. 10s. 6d.

Arago (F.)—Biographies of Distinguished Scientific Men. Translated by Admiral W. H. SMYTH, D.C.L., F.R.S., &c. ; the Rev. BADEN POWELL, M.A.; and ROBERT GRANT, M.A., F.R.A.S. 8vo. 18s.

Arago's Meteorological Essays. With an Introduction by Baron HUMBOLDT. Translated under the superintendence of Major-General E. SABINE, R.A., Treasurer and V.P.R.S. 8vo. 18s.

Arago's Popular Astronomy. Translated and edited by Admiral W. H. SMYTH, D.C.L., F.R.S.; and ROBERT GRANT, M.A., F.R.A.S.

Arnold.—Poems. By Matthew Arnold. FIRST SERIES, Third Edition. Fcp. 8vo. price 5s. 6d. SECOND SERIES, price 5s.

Arnold.— Merope, a Tragedy. By Matthew ARNOLD. With a Preface and an Historical Introduction. Fcp. 8vo. 5s.

Lord Bacon's Works. A New Edition, revised and elucidated; and enlarged by the addition of many pieces not printed before. Collected and edited by ROBERT LESLIE ELLIS, M.A.; JAMES SPEDDING, M.A.; and DOUGLAS DENON HEATH, Esq., Barrister-at-Law. VOLS. I. to V., comprising the Division of *Philosophical Works ;* with a copious INDEX. 5 vols. 8vo. price £4. 6s. VOLS. VI. and VII., comprising the Division of *Literary and Professional Works ;* with a full INDEX. 2 vols. 8vo. price £1. 16s.

Baker. — The Rifle and the Hound in Ceylon. By S. W. BAKER, Esq. New Edition, with 13 Illustrations engraved on Wood. Fcp. 8vo. 4s. 6d.

Baker. — Eight Years' Wanderings in Ceylon. By S. W. BAKER, Esq. With 6 coloured Plates. 8vo. price 15s.

Barth. — Travels and Discoveries in North and Central Africa : Being the Journal of an Expedition undertaken under the auspices of Her Britannic Majesty's Government in the Years 1849—1855. By HENRY BARTH, Ph.D., D.C.L., &c. With numerous Maps, Wood Engravings, and Illustrations in tinted Lithography. 5 vols. 8vo. price £5. 5s.

Bate.—Memoir of Capt. W. Thornton Bate, R.N. By the Rev. JOHN BAILLIE, Author of "Memoirs of Hewitson," "Memoir of Adelaide Newton," &c. *New*

Bayldon's Art of Valuing Rents and Tillages, and Claims of Tenants upon Quitting Farms, at both Michaelmas and Lady-Day ; as revised by Mr. DONALDSON. *Seventh Edition,* enlarged and adapted to the Present Time : With the Principles and Mode of Valuing Land and other Property for Parochial Assessment and Enfranchisement of Copyholds, under the recent Acts of Parliament. By ROBERT BAKER, Land-Agent and Valuer. 8vo. 10s. 6d.

Black's Practical Treatise on Brewing, based on Chemical and Economical Principles : With Formulæ for Public Brewers, and Instructions for Private Families. New Edition, with Additions. 8vo. 10s. 6d.

Blaine's Encyclopædia of Rural Sports ; or, a complete Account, Historical, Practical, and Descriptive, of Hunting, Shooting, Fishing, Racing, &c. *New Edition,* revised and corrected ; with above 600 Woodcut Illustrations, including 20 from Designs by JOHN LEECH. 8vo. price 42s. half-bound.

Bloomfield. — The Greek Testament, with copious English Notes, Critical, Philological, and Explanatory. Especially adapted to the use of Theological Students and Ministers. By the Rev. S. T. BLOOM-FIELD, D.D., F.S.A. Ninth Edition, revised. 2 vols. 8vo. with Map, price £2. 8s.

Dr. Bloomfield's Critical Annotations on the New Testament, being a Supplemental Volume to the Ninth Edition. 8vo. 14s.

Dr. Bloomfield's College and School Edition of the *Greek Testament :* With brief English Notes, chiefly Philological and Explanatory. Seventh Edition. Fcp. 8vo. 7s. 6d.

Dr. Bloomfield's College and School Lexicon to the Greek Testament. Third Edition, carefully revised. Fcp. 8vo. 7s. 6d.

Boase.—The Philosophy of Nature : a Systematic Treatise on the Causes and Laws of Natural Phenomena. By HENRY S. BOASE, M.D., F.R.S., and G.S. 8vo. 12s.

Bourne.—A Treatise on the Steam-Engine, in its Application to Mines, Mills, Steam-Navigation, and Railways. By the Artisan Club. Edited by JOHN BOURNE, C.E. New and greatly improved Edition ; with numerous Steel Plates and Wood Engravings. 4to. [*Nearly ready.*]

Boyd. — A Manual for Naval Cadets. Published with the sanction and approval of the Lords Commissioners of the Admiralty. By JOHN M°NEILL BOYD, Captain R.N. Second Edition ; with 253 Illustrations (13 coloured). Fcp. 8vo. 12s. 6d.

Brande.—A Dictionary of Science, Literature, and Art : Comprising the History, Description, and Scientific Principles of every Branch of Human Knowledge ; with the Derivation and Definition of all the Terms in general use. Edited by W. T. BRANDE, F.R.S.L. and E. ; assisted by DR. J. CAUVIN. Third Edition, revised and corrected ; with numerous Woodcuts. 8vo. 60s.

Professor Brande's Lectures on Organic Chemistry, as applied to Manufactures ; including Dyeing, Bleaching, Calico-Printing, Sugar-Manufacture, the Preservation of Wood, Tanning, &c. ; delivered before the Members of the Royal Institution. Edited by J. SCOFFERN, M.B. Fcp. 8vo. with Woodcuts, price 7s. 6d.

Bray.—The Education of the Feelings or Affections. By CHARLES BRAY. Third Edition, revised and enlarged. 8vo. 5s.

Brewer. — An Atlas of History and Geography, from the Commencement of the Christian Era to the Present Time : Comprising a Series of Sixteen coloured Maps, arranged in Chronological Order, with Illustrative Memoirs. By the Rev. J. S. BREWER, M.A., Professor of English History and Literature in King's College, London. Royal 8vo. 12s. 6d. half-bound.

Brialmont and Gleig's Life of Wellington. History of the Life of Arthur Duke of Wellington : the Military Memoirs from the French of Captain BRIALMONT, with Additions and Emendations ; the Political and Social Life by the Rev. G. R. GLEIG, M.A. With Maps, Plans of Battles, and Portraits. 4 vols. 8vo. £2. 14s.

Brodie. — Psychological Inquiries, in a Series of Essays intended to illustrate the Influence of the Physical Organisation on the Mental Faculties. By Sir BENJAMIN C. BRODIE, Bart. Third Edition. Fcp. 8vo. 5s.

Dr. Thomas Bull on the Maternal Management of Children in Health and Disease. New Edition. Fcp. 8vo. 5s.

Bunsen. — Christianity and Mankind, their Beginnings and Prospects. By Baron C.C.J. BUNSEN, D.D., D.C.L., D.Ph. Being a New Edition, corrected, remodelled, and extended, of *Hippolytus and his Age.* 7 vols. 8vo. £5. 5s.—Or in 3 Sections :

1. Hippolytus and his Age; or, the Beginnings and Prospects of Christianity. 2 vols. 8vo. price £1. 10s.
2. Outline of the Philosophy of Universal History applied to Language and Religion : Containing an Account of the Alphabetical Conferences. 2 vols. 8vo. price £1. 13s.
3. Analecta Ante-Nicæna. 3 vols. 8vo. price £2. 2s.

Bunsen. — Lyra Germanica. Translated from the German by CATHERINE WINK-WORTH. FIRST SERIES, Hymns for the Sundays and chief Festivals of the Christian Year. SECOND SERIES, the Christian Life. Fcp. 8vo. price 5s. each Series.

An Edition of the FIRST SERIES of *Lyra Germanica,* with Illustrations from Original Designs by JOHN LEIGHTON, F.S.A., engraved on Wood under his superintendence. Fcp. 4to. price 21s.

HYMNS from *Lyra Germanica* ......18mo. 1s.

* These selections of German Hymns have been made from collections published in Germany by Baron BUNSEN; and form companion volumes to

Theologia Germanica: Translated by Susanna WINKWORTH. With a Preface by the Rev. CHARLES KINGSLEY; and a Letter by Baron BUNSEN. Fcp. 8vo. 5s.

Bunsen. — Egypt's Place in Universal History : An Historical Investigation, in Five Books. By Baron C. C. J. BUNSEN, D.D., D.C.L., D.Ph. Translated from the German by C. H. COTTRELL, Esq., M.A. With many Illustrations. 4 vols. 8vo. price £5. 8s.

Bunting.—The Life of Jabez Bunting, D.D. : With Notices of contemporary Persons and Events. By his Son, THOMAS PERCIVAL BUNTING. VOL. I. *Third Thousand,* with Two Portraits and a Vignette, in post 8vo. price 7s. 6d. cloth; or (*large paper and Proof Engravings*) in square crown 8vo. 10s. 6d.

Bunyan's Pilgrim's Progress: With 126 Illustrations engraved on Steel and on Wood from Original Designs by Charles Bennett; and a Preface by the Rev. CHARLES KINGSLEY. Fcp. 4to. 21s. cloth; or 31s. 6d. bound in morocco.

Burton.—The Lake Regions of Central Africa: A Picture of Exploration. By RICHARD F. BURTON, Captain H.M. Indian Army; Fellow and Gold Medallist of the Royal Geographical Society. With Map and numerous Illustrations on Wood and in Chromo-xylography. 2 vols. 8vo. 31s. 6d.

Captain Burton's First Footsteps in East Africa; or, an Exploration of Harar. With Maps and coloured Plates. 8vo. 18s.

Captain Burton's Personal Narrative of a Pilgrimage to El Medinah and Meccah. *Second Edition,* revised; with coloured Plates and Woodcuts. 2 vols. crown 8vo. 24s.

Bishop Butler's General Atlas of Modern and Ancient Geography, enlarged to Fifty-four full-coloured Maps; with complete IN-DEXES. *New Edition,* re-engraved; with Corrections from the Government Surveys and the most recent authentic Geographical Researches. Edited by the Author's SON, the Rev. T. BUTLER, Rector of Langar. Royal 4to. 24s. half-bound.

Separately { Butler's Modern Atlas of 30 full-coloured Maps. Royal 8vo. price 12s. Butler's Ancient Atlas of 24 full-coloured Maps. Royal 8vo. price 12s.

Bishop Butler's Sketch of Modern and Ancient Geography. New Edition, thoroughly revised, with such Alterations introduced as continually progressive Discoveries and the latest Information have rendered necessary. Edited by the Author's SON. Post 8vo. price 7s. 6d.

The Cabinet Lawyer: A Popular Digest of the Laws of England, Civil and Criminal; with a Dictionary of Law Terms, Maxims, Statutes, and Judicial Antiquities; Correct Tables of Assessed Taxes, Stamp Duties, Excise Licenses, and Post-Horse Duties; Post-Office Regulations; and Prison Discipline. 18th Edition, comprising the Public Acts of the Session 1860. Fcp. 8vo. 10s. 6d.

The Cabinet Gazetteer: A Popular Geographical Dictionary of All the Countries of the World. By the Author of *The Cabinet Lawyer.* Fcp. 8vo. 10s. 6d. cloth.

Calvert. — The Wife's Manual; or, Prayers, Thoughts, and Songs on Several

Catlow.—Popular Conchology; or, the Shell Cabinet arranged according to the Modern System : With a detailed Account of the Animals, and a complete Descriptive List of the Families and Genera of Recent and Fossil Shells. By AGNES CATLOW. Second Edition, much improved ; with 405 Woodcut Illustrations. Post 8vo. price 14s.

Cats and Farlie's Book of Emblems.— Moral Emblems, with Aphorisms, Adages, and Proverbs of all Nations, from J. CATS and R. FARLIE : Comprising 60 circular Vignettes, 60 Tail-pieces, and a Frontispiece composed from their works by J. LEIGHTON, F.S.A., and engraved on Wood. The Text translated and edited with additions by RICHARD PIGOT. Imperial 8vo. price 31s. 6d. cloth ; or 52s. 6d. handsomely in morocco by Hayday.

Cecil.—The Stud Farm; or, Hints on Breeding Horses for the Turf, the Chase, and the Road. Addressed to Breeders of Race-Horses and Hunters, Landed Proprietors, and especially to Tenant Farmers. By CECIL. Fcp. 8vo. with Frontispiece, 5s.

Cecil's Stable Practice; or, Hints on Training for the Turf, the Chase, and the Road ; with Observations on Racing and Hunting, Wasting, Race-Riding, and Handicapping. *Second Edition.* Fcp. 8vo. with Plate, price 5s. half-bound.

Chapman.—History of Gustavus Adol- phus and of the Thirty Years' War up to the King's Death : With some Account of its Conclusion by the Peace of Westphalia, in 1648. By the Rev. B. CHAPMAN, M.A., Vicar of Leatherhead. 8vo. with Three Plans of Battles, 12s. 6d.

Clough.—Greek History from Themis- tocles to Alexander, in a Series of Lives from Plutarch. Revised and arranged by A. H. CLOUGH, sometime Fellow of Oriel College, Oxford. With 44 Woodcut Illustrations. Fcp. 8vo. 6s.

Conington. — Handbook of Chemical Analysis, adapted to the Unitary System of Notation. By F. T. CONINGTON, M.A., F.C.S. Post 8vo. 7s. 6d. Also *Tables of Qualitative Analysis,* designed as a Companion to the Handbook, price 2s. 6d.

Connolly's History of the Royal Sappers

Conybeare and Howson.—The Life and Epistles of Saint Paul : Comprising a complete Biography of the Apostle, and a Translation of his Epistles inserted in Chronological Order. By the Rev. W. J. CONYBEARE, M.A. ; and the Rev. J. S. HOWSON, M.A. *Third Edition,* revised and corrected ; with several Maps and Woodcuts, and 4 Plates. 2 vols. square crown 8vo. 31s. 6d. cloth.

⁎⁎⁎ The Original Edition, with more numerous Illustrations, in 2 vols. 4to. price 48s.—may also be had.

Dr. Copland's Dictionary of Practical Medicine : Comprising General Pathology, the Nature and Treatment of Diseases, Morbid Structures, and the Disorders especially incidental to Climates, to Sex, and to the different Epochs of Life ; with numerous approved Formulæ of the Medicines recommended. Now complete in 3 vols. 8vo. price £5. 11s. cloth.

Bishop Cotton's Instructions in the Doctrine and Practice of Christianity. Intended chiefly as an Introduction to Confirmation. *Fourth Edition.* 18mo. 2s. 6d.

Cresy's Encyclopædia of Civil Engi- neering, Historical, Theoretical, and Practical. Illustrated by upwards of 3,000 Woodcuts. *Second Edition,* revised and extended in a Supplement, comprising Metropolitan Water Supply, Drainage of Towns, Railways, Cubical Proportion, Brick and Iron Construction, Iron Screw Piles, Tubular Bridges, &c. 8vo. 63s.

Crosse.—Memorials, Scientific and Li- terary, of Andrew Crosse, the Electrician. Edited by Mrs. CROSSE. Post 8vo. 9s. 6d.

Crowe.—The History of France. By EYRE EVANS CROWE, Author of the *History of France* in the *Cabinet Cyclopædia.* An entirely new work, to be completed in Five Volumes. VOL. I. 8vo. price 14s. ; VOL. II. price 15s.

Cruikshank. — The Life of Sir John Falstaff, illustrated in a Series of Twenty-four original Etchings by George Cruikshank. Accompanied by an imaginary Biography by the late ROBERT B. BROUGH. Royal 8vo. price 12s. 6d.

Dale.—The Domestic Liturgy and Family
Chaplain, in Two Parts: PART I. Church
Services adapted for Domestic Use, with
Prayers for Every Day of the Week, selected
from the Book of Common Prayer; PART
II. an appropriate Sermon for Every Sunday
in the Year. By the Rev. THOMAS DALE,
M.A. Post 4to. 21s. cloth; 31s. 6d. calf;
or £2. 10s. morocco.

Separately { THE FAMILY CHAPLAIN, 12s.
{ THE DOMESTIC LITURGY, 10s. 6d.

The Dead Shot; or, Sportsman's Com-
plete Guide: Being a Treatise on the Use of
the Gun, with Rudimentary and Finishing
Lessons in the Art of Shooting Game of all
kinds; Dog-breaking, Pigeon-shooting; also
now and complete Rules for conducting
Pigeon Matches; and a variety of useful information. By MARKSMAN. With 6 Practical Illustrations. Fcp. 8vo. 5s.

De la Rive.—A Treatise on Electricity
in Theory and Practice. By A. DE LA RIVE,
Professor in the Academy of Geneva. Translated for the Author by C. V. WALKER,
F.R.S. With numerous Woodcut Illustrations. 3 vols. 8vo. price £3. 13s. cloth.

Domenech.—Seven Years' Residence in
the Great Deserts of North America. By
the ABBÉ DOMENECH. With a coloured
Map, and about 60 Illustrations. 2 vols.
8vo. £1. 16s.

The Abbé Domenech's Missionary Adventures
in Texas and Mexico: A Personal Narrative
of Six Years' Sojourn in those Regions.
8vo. with Map, 10s. 6d.

The Eclipse of Faith; or, a Visit to a
Religious Sceptic. 10th Edition. Fcp. 8vo. 5s.

Defence of The Eclipse of Faith, by its
Author; Being a Rejoinder to Professor
Newman's Reply. Third Edition, revised.
Fcp. 8vo. 3s. 6d.

Ephemera's Handbook of Angling;
teaching Fly-Fishing, Trolling, Bottom-

Fairbairn. — A Treatise on Mills and
Millwork. By WILLIAM FAIRBAIRN, F.R.S.,
F.G.S. With numerous Steel Plates and
Woodcut Illustrations. 2 vols. 8vo.
[In the press.

Fairbairn.—Useful Information for En-
gineers: A First Series of Lectures delivered
to the Working Engineers of Yorkshire and
Lancashire. With Appendices, containing
the Results of Experimental Inquiries into
the Strength of Materials, the Causes of
Boiler Explosions, &c. By WILLIAM
FAIRBAIRN, F.R.S., F.G.S. Third Edition;
with 8 Plates of Figures and many Woodcuts. Crown 8vo. price 10s. 6d.

Second Series of Fairbairn's Useful Informa-
tion for Engineers, just ready.

Falkener.—Dædalus; or, the Causes and
Principles of the Excellence of Greek Sculp-
ture. By EDWARD FALKENER, Member of
the Academy of Bologna, and of the Archæo-
logical Institutes of Rome and Berlin. With
numerous Illustrations. Royal 8vo. in covers
containing Two Medallions, price 42s.

Museum of Classical Antiquities: a Series of
Thirty-five Essays on Ancient Art, by va-
rious Writers, edited by EDWARD FALKENER.
With 25 Plates and numerous Woodcuts.
New Edition, Two Volumes in One. Impe-
rial 8vo. 42s.

Forester's Rambles in the Islands of
Corsica and Sardinia: With Notices of
their History, Antiquities, and present
Condition. With coloured Map; and numerous Illustrations from Drawings by
Lieut.-Col. M. A. BIDDULPH, R.A. Imperial 8vo. price 28s.

Letters of Sir A. S. Frazer, K.C.B.,
Commanding the Royal Horse Artillery
under the Duke of Wellington: Written
during the Peninsular and Waterloo Campaigns. Edited by Major-General SABINE,
R.A. With Portrait, 2 Maps, and Plan.
8vo. 18s.

Freeman and Salvin. — Falconry: Its

Gilbart's Logic of Banking : a Familiar Exposition of the Principles of Reasoning, and their application to the Art and the Science of Banking. 12mo. with Portrait, price 12s. 6d.

The Poetical Works of Oliver Goldsmith. Edited by BOLTON CORNEY, Esq. Illustrated by Wood Engravings, from Designs by Members of the Etching Club. Square crown 8vo. cloth, 21s.; morocco, £1. 16s.

Goodeve.—The Elements of Mechanism, designed for Students of Applied Mechanics. By T. M. GOODEVE, M.A., Professor of Natural Philosophy in King's College, London. With 206 Figures engraved on Wood. Post 8vo. 6s. 6d.

"PROFESSOR GOOD-EVE, in the *Elements of Mechanism*, supplies a want felt by those who require something more elementary than the more complete and elaborate treatise of Professor Willis. The principles upon which applied mechanics are based are here very clearly explained to those who have already some acquaintance with algebra and Euclid. The diagrams used for illustration are plentiful and well drawn." CRITIC.

Gosse. — A Naturalist's Sojourn in Jamaica. By P. H. GOSSE, Esq. With Plates. Post 8vo. price 14s.

Green.—Lives of the Princesses of Eng-land. By Mrs. MARY ANNE EVERETT GREEN, Editor of the *Letters of Royal and Illustrious Ladies*. With numerous Portraits. Complete in 6 vols. post 8vo. price 10s. 6d. each.

Greyson. — Selections from the Corre-spondence of R. E. H. GREYSON, Esq. Edited by the Author of *The Eclipse of Faith*. Second Edition. Crown 8vo. 7s. 6d.

Grove. — The Correlation of Physical Forces. By W. R. GROVE, Q.C., M.A., F.R.S., &c. *Third Edition.* 8vo. price 7s.

Gurney.—St. Louis and Henri IV. : Being a Second Series of Historical Sketches. By the Rev. JOHN H. GURNEY, M.A., Rector of St. Mary's, Marylebone. Fcp. 8vo. 6s.

Evening Recreations; or, Samples from the Lecture-Room. Edited by the Rev. J. H. GURNEY, M.A. Crown 8vo. 5s.

Gwilt's Encyclopædia of Architecture, Historical, Theoretical, and Practical. By JOSEPH GWILT. With more than 1,000 Wood Engravings, from Designs by J. S. GWILT. Fourth Edition. 8vo. 42s.

Hamilton. — Reminiscences of an Old Sportsman. By Colonel J. P. HAMILTON, K.H., Author of *Travels in the Interior of*

Hare (Archdeacon).—The Life of Luther, in Forty-eight Historical Engravings. By GUSTAV KÖNIG. With Explanations by Archdeacon HARE and SUSANNA WINKWORTH. Fcp. 4to. price 28s.

Harford.—Life of Michael Angelo Buon-arroti : With Translations of many of his Poems and Letters; also Memoirs of Savonarola, Raphael, and Vittoria Colonna. By JOHN S. HARFORD, Esq., D.C.L., F.R.S. *Second Edition*, thoroughly revised; with 20 copperplate Engravings. 2 vols. 8vo. 25s.

Illustrations, Architectural and Pictorial, of the Genius of Michael Angelo Buonarroti. With Descriptions of the Plates, by the Commendatore CANINA; C. R. COCKERELL, Esq., R.A.; and J. S. HARFORD, Esq., D.C.L., F.R.S. Folio, 73s. 6d. half-bound.

Harry Hieover.—Stable Talk and Table Talk; or, Spectacles for Young Sportsmen. By HARRY HIEOVER. 2 vols. 8vo. with Portrait, price 24s.

Harry Hieover.—The Hunting-Field. By Harry HIEOVER. *Second Edition;* with Two Plates. Fcp. 8vo. 5s. half-bound.

Harry Hieover. — Practical Horsemanship. By HARRY HIEOVER. *Second Edition*; with 2 Plates. Fcp. 8vo. 5s. half-bound.

Harry Hieover.—The Pocket and the Stud; or, Practical Hints on the Management of the Stable. By HARRY HIEOVER. Third Edition; with Portrait of the Author. Fcp. 8vo. price 5s. half-bound.

Harry Hieover.—The Stud, for Practical Pur-poses and Practical Men : Being a Guide to the Choice of a Horse for use more than for show. By HARRY HIEOVER. *Second Edition;* with 2 Plates. Fcp. 8vo. price 5s.

Hartwig. — The Sea and its Living Wonders. By Dr. GEORGE HARTWIG. Translated by the Author from the Fourth German Edition; and embellished with Wood Engravings, and an entirely new series of Illustrations in Chromo-xylography from Original Designs by Henry Noel Humphreys. 8vo. 18s.

Hassall.—Adulterations Detected; or, Plain Instructions for the Discovery of Frauds in Food and Medicine. By ARTHUR HILL HASSALL, M.D. Lond., Analyst of *The Lancet* Sanitary Commission; and Author of the Reports of that Commission published under the title of *Food and its Adulterations* (which may also be had, in 8vo. price 28s.)

Dr. Hassall's History of the British Fresh-water Algæ: Including Descriptions of the Desmideæ and Diatomaceæ. With upwards of One Hundred Plates of Figures, illustrating the various Species. 2 vols. 8vo. with 103 Plates, price £1. 15s.

Col. Hawker's Instructions to Young Sportsmen in all that relates to Guns and Shooting. 11th Edition, revised by the Author's Son; with Portrait and several Illustrations. Square crown 8vo. 18s.

Haydn's Book of Dignities: Containing Rolls of the Official Personages of the British Empire, Civil, Ecclesiastical, Judicial, Military, Naval, and Municipal, from the Earliest Periods to the Present Time. Together with the Sovereigns of Europe, from the Foundation of their respective States; the Peerage and Nobility of Great Britain; &c. Being a New Edition, improved and continued, of Beatson's Political Index. 8vo. price 25s. half-bound.

Hayward. — Biographical and Critical Essays, reprinted from Reviews, with Additions and Corrections. By A. Hayward, Esq., Q.C. 2 vols. 8vo. price 24s.

Hensman.—Handbook of the Constitu-tion: being a short Account of the Rise, Progress, and Present State of the Laws of England. By Alfred P. Hensman, Barrister-at-Law. Fcp. 8vo. 4s.

"MR. HENSMAN'S Handbook of the Constitution is exactly what it professes to be, namely, a short account of the rise, progress, and present state of the laws of England. How such an expansive and miscellaneous subject could be so ably condensed is a marvel; but Mr. Hensman has effected this, and the display | of the formation of English laws evinces no less clearness and historical research than the statement of its present condition manifests accuracy and succinctness. It differs from Lord St. Leonard's book in being a history, and not a guide for practice, but both ought decidedly to go together." JOHN BULL.

Sir John Herschel.—Outlines of Astro-nomy. By Sir John F. W. Herschel, Bart., K.H., M.A. *Fifth Edition*, revised and corrected to the existing state of Astronomical Knowledge; with Plates and Woodcuts. 8vo. price 18s.

Sir John Herschel's Essays from the Edin-

Hind. — Narrative of the Canadian Ex-ploring Expeditions through the Southern Part of Rupert's Land, from Lake Superior to near the foot of the Rocky Mountains, including the Region traversed by the proposed Overland Route from Canada to British Columbia; with a Description of the Physical Geography, Geology, and Climate of the Country. By Henry Youle Hind, M.A., F.R.G.S., Professor of Chemistry and Geology in Trinity College, Toronto; in Charge of the Assinniboine and Saskatchewan Exploring Expedition. With Maps of the Country Explored, Geographical and Geological; and numerous Illustrations, from Photographs, of Scenery, Native Races, Fossils new to Science, &c. 2 vols. 8vo. *[Just ready.*

Hints on Etiquette and the Usages of Society: With a Glance at Bad Habits. New Edition, revised (with Additions) by a Lady of Rank. Fcp. 8vo. price Half-a-Crown.

Hoare. — The Veracity of the Book of Genesis: with the Life and Character of the Inspired Historian. By the Rev. William H. Hoare, M.A., late Fellow of St. John's College, Cambridge. 8vo. 9s. 6d.

Sir Henry Holland's Medical Notes and Reflections. *Third Edition*, revised throughout and corrected; with some Additions 8vo. 18s.

Sir H. Holland's Chapters on Mental Physi-ology, founded chiefly on Chapters contained in *Medical Notes and Reflections*. Second Edition. Post 8vo. price 8s. 6d.

Horne's Introduction to the Critical Study and Knowledge of the Holy Scriptures. *Tenth Edition*, revised, corrected, and brought down to the present time. Edited by the Rev. T. Hartwell Horne, B.D. (the Author); the Rev. Samuel Davidson, D.D. of the University of Halle and LL.D.; S. Prideaux Tregelles, LL.D.; and the Rev. John Ayre, Domestic Chaplain to the Earl of Roden. With 4 Maps and 22 Vignettes and Facsimiles. 4 vols. 8vo. £3. 13s. 6d.

*** The Four Volumes may also be had *separately* as follows:—

Vol. I.—A Summary of the Evidence for the Genuineness.

Horne. — A Compendious Introduction to the Study of the Bible. By the Rev. T. HARTWELL HORNE, B.D. New Edition, with Maps and Illustrations. 12mo. 9s.

Hooker.—Kew Gardens; or, a Popular Guide to the Royal Botanic Gardens of Kew. By SIR WILLIAM JACKSON HOOKER, K.H.,&c., Director. 16mo. price Sixpence.

Hooker and Arnott.—The British Flora, comprising the Phænogamous or Flowering Plants, and the Ferns. Seventh Edition, with Additions and Corrections; and numerous Figures illustrative of the Umbelliferous Plants, the Composite Plants, the Grasses, and the Ferns. By SIR W. J. HOOKER, F.R.A. and L.S., &c.; and G. A. WALKER-ARNOTT, LL.D., F.L.S. 12mo. with 12 Plates, price 14s.; with the Plates coloured, price 21s.

Hoskyns.—Talpa; or, the Chronicles of a Clay Farm: An Agricultural Fragment. By CHANDOS WREN HOSKYNS, Esq. Fourth Edition. With 24 Woodcuts from the original Designs by GEORGE CRUIKSHANK. 16mo. price 5s. 6d.

Howard.—Athletic and Gymnastic Exercises: Comprising 114 Exercises and Feats of Agility performed with the Parallel Bars, the Horizontal Bar, the Suspended Bar, the Suspended Ropes, and the Indian Clubs; preceded by a Description of the requisite Apparatus. With 64 Woodcuts. By JOHN H. HOWARD. 16mo. 7s. 6d.

"THANKS to Mr. Kingsley and his followers, the importance of developing the physical powers, as well as cultivating the mental faculties, is now recognised by most of the instructors of youth; and since the rapid extension of the volunteer movement we are more likely to devote too much attention to athletic exercises than too little. The establishment of gymnasiums of great advantage to boys, who would be oftener kept out of mischief if they had some recreation on which to expend their redundant energies. To all such youthful Spartans this little volume will be of great assistance." SUN.

Howitt.—The Children's Year. By Mary HOWITT. With 4 Illustrations, from Designs by A. M. Howitt. Square 16mo. 5s.

Howitt.—Land, Labour, and Gold; or, Two Years in Victoria: With Visits to Sydney and Van Diemen's Land. *Second Edition.* Two volumes in One. Crown 8vo. 6s.

Howitt.—Visits to Remarkable Places: Old Halls, Battle-Fields, and Scenes illustrative of Striking Passages in English History and Poetry. By WILLIAM HOWITT. With about 80 Wood Engravings. *New Edition.*

William Howitt's Boy's Country Book: Being the Real Life of a Country Boy, written by himself; exhibiting all the Amusements, Pleasures, and Pursuits of Children in the Country. New Edition; with 40 Woodcuts. Fcp. 8vo. price 6s.

Howitt.—The Rural Life of England. By WILLIAM HOWITT. New Edition, corrected and revised; with Woodcuts by Bewick and Williams. Medium 8vo. 21s.

The Abbe' Huc's work on the Chinese Empire, founded on Fourteen Years' Travels and Residence in China. *New Edition,* with 2 Woodcut Illustrations. Crown 8vo. 5s.

Hudson's Executor's Guide. New and enlarged Edition, revised by the Author with reference to the latest reported Cases and Acts of Parliament. By J. C. HUDSON, late of the Legacy Duty Office, London. Fcp. 8vo. 6s.

Hudson's Plain Directions for Making Wills in conformity with the Law. New Edition, corrected and revised by the Author; and practically illustrated by Specimens of Wills containing many varieties of Bequests, also Notes of Cases judicially decided since the Wills Act came into operation. By J. C. HUDSON, late of the Legacy Duty Office, London. Fcp. 8vo. 2s. 6d.

Hudson and Kennedy.—Where there's a Will there's a Way: An Ascent of Mont Blanc by a New Route and Without Guides. By the Rev. C. HUDSON, M.A., and E. S. KENNEDY, B.A. *Second Edition,* with Plate and Map. Post 8vo. 5s. 6d.

Humboldt's Cosmos. Translated, with the Author's authority, by MRS. SABINE. VOLS. I. and II. 16mo. Half-a-Crown each, sewed; 3s. 6d. each, cloth: or in post 8vo. 12s. each, cloth. VOL. III. post 8vo. 12s. 6d. cloth: or in 16mo. PART I. 2s. 6d. sewed, 3s. 6d. cloth; and PART II. 3s. sewed, 4s. cloth. VOL. IV. PART I. post 8vo. 15s. cloth; and 16mo. price 7s. 6d. cloth, or 7s. sewed.

Humboldt's Aspects of Nature. Translated, with the Author's authority, by MRS. SABINE. 16mo. price 6s.: or in 2 vols. 3s. 6d. each, cloth; 2s. 6d. each, sewed.

Humphreys. — Parables of Our Lord, illuminated and ornamented in the style of the Missals of the Renaissance, by HENRY NOEL HUMPHREYS. Square fcp. 8vo. 21s. in massive carved covers; or 30s. bound in

Hunt. — Researches on Light in its Chemical Relations; embracing a Consideration of all the Photographic Processes. By ROBERT HUNT, F.R.S. Second Edition, with Plate and Woodcuts. 8vo. 10s. 6d.

Hunter's Art of Precis-Writing: An *Introduction to the Writing of Précis or Digests,* as applicable to Narratives of Facts or Historical Events, Correspondence, Evidence, Official Documents, and General Composition: With numerous Examples and Exercises. By the Rev. JOHN HUNTER, M.A., formerly Vice-Principal of the National Society's Training College, Battersea. 12mo. 2s.— KEY, *just ready.*

Hutchinson's Impressions of Western Africa: With a Report on the Peculiarities of Trade up the Rivers in the Bight of Biafra. Post 8vo. price 8s. 6d.

Idle's Hints on Shooting, Fishing, &c., both on Sea and Land, and in the Freshwater Lochs of Scotland. Fcp. 8vo. 5s.

Jacquemet's Chronology for Schools: Containing the most important Dates of General History, Political, Ecclesiastical, and Literary, from the Creation of the World to the end of the year 1857. Edited by the Rev. J. ALCORN, M.A. Fcp. 8vo. 3s. 6d.

Mrs. Jameson's Legends of the Saints and Martyrs, as represented in Christian Art. Third Edition, revised and improved; with 17 Etchings and upwards of 180 Woodcuts, many of which are new in this Edition. 2 vols. square crown 8vo. price 31s. 6d.

Mrs. Jameson's Legends of the Monastic Orders, as represented in Christian Art. Second Edition, enlarged; with 11 Etchings by the Author, and 88 Woodcuts. Square crown 8vo. price 28s.

Mrs. Jameson's Legends of the Madonna, as represented in Christian Art. Second Edition, corrected and enlarged; with 27 Etchings and 165 Wood Engravings. Square crown 8vo. price 28s.

Mrs. Jameson's Commonplace-Book of

Lord Jeffrey's Contributions to The Edinburgh Review. A New Edition, complete in One Volume, with a Portrait engraved by Henry Robinson, and a Vignette. Square crown 8vo. 21s. cloth; or 30s. calf.— Or in 3 vols. 8vo. price 42s.

Bishop Jeremy Taylor's Entire Works: With Life by BISHOP HEBER. Revised and corrected by the Rev. CHARLES PAGE EDEN, Fellow of Oriel College, Oxford. Now complete in 10 vols. 8vo. 10s. 6d. each.

Keith Johnston's New Dictionary of Geography, Descriptive, Physical, Statistical, and Historical: Forming a complete General Gazetteer of the World. *New Edition,* revised to April 1860. In One Volume of 1,360 pages, comprising about 50,000 Names of Places. 8vo. 30s. cloth; or 35s. half-bound in russia.

Kane.—Wanderings of an Artist among the Indians of North America; from Canada to Vancouver's Island and Oregon, through the Hudson's Bay Company's Territory, and back again. By PAUL KANE. With Map, Illustrations in Colours, and Wood Engravings. 8vo. 21s.

Kemble.—The Saxons in England: A History of the English Commonwealth till the Norman Conquest. By JOHN M. KEMBLE, M.A., &c. 2 vols. 8vo. 28s.

Kesteven.—A Manual of the Domestic Practice of Medicine. By W. B. KESTEVEN, Fellow of the Royal College of Surgeons of England, &c. Square post 8vo. 7s. 6d.

Kirby and Spence's Introduction to Entomology; or, Elements of the Natural History of Insects: Comprising an Account of Noxious and Useful Insects, of their Metamorphoses, Food, Stratagems, Habitations, Societies, Motions, Noises, Hybernation, Instinct, &c. *Seventh Edition.* Crown 8vo. 5s.

A Lady's Tour round Monte Rosa; With Visits to the Italian Valleys of Anzasca, Mastalone, Camasco, Sesia, Lys, Challaut, Aosta, and Cogne. With Map, 4 Illustrations from Sketches by Mr. G. Bar-

LARDNER'S CABINET CYCLOPÆDIA

Of History, Biography, Literature, the Arts and Sciences, Natural History, and Manufactures.

A Series of Original Works by

SIR JOHN HERSCHEL,	THOMAS KEIGHTLEY,	BISHOP THIRLWALL,
SIR JAMES MACKINTOSH,	JOHN FORSTER,	THE REV. G. R. GLEIG,
ROBERT SOUTHEY,	SIR WALTER SCOTT,	J. C. L. DE SISMONDI,
SIR DAVID BREWSTER,	THOMAS MOORE,	JOHN PHILLIPS, F.R.S., G.S.

AND OTHER EMINENT WRITERS.

Complete in 132 vols. fcp. 8vo. with Vignette Titles, price, in cloth, Nineteen Guineas.

The Works *separately*, in Sets or Series, price Three Shillings and Sixpence each Volume.

A List of the WORKS *composing the* CABINET CYCLOPÆDIA :—

1. Bell's History of Russia .... 3 vols. 10s. 6d.
2. Bell's Lives of British Poets .... 2 vols. 7s.
3. Brewster's Optics .... 1 vol. 3s. 6d.
4. Cooley's Maritime and Inland Discovery 3 vols. 10s. 6d.
5. Crowe's History of France .... 3 vols. 10s. 6d.
6. De Morgan on Probabilities .... 1 vol. 3s. 6d.
7. De Sismondi's History of the Italian
   Republics .... 1 vol. 3s. 6d.
8. De Sismondi's Fall of the Roman Empire 2 vols. 7s.
9. Donovan's Chemistry .... 1 vol. 3s. 6d.
10. Donovan's Domestic Economy .... 2 vols. 7s.
11. Dunham's Spain and Portugal......... 5 vols. 17s. 6d.
12. Dunham's History of Denmark, Sweden,
    and Norway .... 3 vols. 10s. 6d.
13. Dunham's History of Poland.......... 1 vol. 3s. 6d.
14. Dunham's Germanic Empire........... 3 vols. 10s. 6d.
15. Dunham's Europe during the Middle
    Ages................................. 4 vols. 14s.
16. Dunham's British Dramatists .... 2 vols. 7s.
17. Dunham's Lives of Early Writers of
    Great Britain .... 1 vol. 3s. 6d.
18. Fergus's History of the United States .. 2 vols. 7s.
19. Fosbroke's Grecian & Roman Antiquities 2 vols. 7s.
20. Forster's Lives of the Statesmen of the
    Commonwealth .... 5 vols. 17s. 6d.
21. Gleig's Lives of British Military Com-
    manders.............................. 3 vols. 10s. 6d.
22. Grattan's History of the Netherlands ... 1 vol. 3s. 6d.
23. Henslow's Botany .... 1 vol. 3s. 6d.
24. Herschel's Astronomy .... 1 vol. 3s. 6d.
25. Herschel's Discourse on Natural Philo-
    sophy .... 1 vol. 3s. 6d.
26. History of Rome........................ 2 vols. 7s.
27. History of Switzerland................. 1 vol. 3s. 6d.
28. Holland's Manufactures in Metal ...... 3 vols. 10s. 6d.
29. James's Lives of Foreign Statesmen ... 5 vols. 17s. 6d.
30. Kater and Lardner's Mechanics .... 1 vol. 3s. 6d.
31. Keightley's Outlines of History .... 1 vol. 3s. 6d.
32. Lardner's Arithmetic .... 1 vol. 3s. 6d.
33. Lardner's Geometry .... 1 vol. 3s. 6d.

34. Lardner on Heat....................... 1 vol. 3s. 6d.
35. Lardner's Hydrostatics and Pneumatics 1 vol. 3s. 6d.
36. Lardner and Walker's Electricity and
    Magnetism........................... 2 vols. 7s.
37. Mackintosh, Forster, and Courtenay's
    Lives of British Statesmen .... 7 vols. 24s. 6d.
38. Mackintosh, Wallace, and Bell's History
    of England.......................... 10 vols. 35s.
39. Montgomery and Shelley's eminent Ita-
    lian, Spanish, and Portuguese Authors 3 vols. 10s. 6d.
40. Moore's History of Ireland............. 4 vols. 14s.
41. Nicolas's Chronology of History .... 1 vol. 3s. 6d.
42. Phillips's Treatise on Geology .... 2 vols. 7s.
43. Powell's History of Natural Philosophy 1 vol. 3s. 6d.
44. Porter's Treatise on the Manufacture of
    Silk .... 1 vol. 3s. 6d.
45. Porter's Manufactures of Porcelain and
    Glass .... 1 vol. 3s. 6d.
46. Roscoe's British Lawyers.............. 1 vol. 3s. 6d.
47. Scott's History of Scotland .... 2 vols. 7s.
48. Shelley's Lives of eminent French
    Authors .... 2 vols. 7s.
49. Shuckard and Swainson's Insects .... 1 vol. 3s. 6d.
50. Southey's Lives of British Admirals .... 5 vols. 17s. 6d.
51. Stebbing's Church History............. 2 vols. 7s.
52. Stebbing's History of the Reformation.. 2 vols. 7s.
53. Swainson's Discourse on Natural History 1 vol. 3s. 6d.
54. Swainson's Natural History and Classi-
    fication of Animals .... 1 vol. 3s. 6d.
55. Swainson's Habits and Instincts of
    Animals.............................. 1 vol. 3s. 6d.
56. Swainson's Birds...................... 2 vols. 7s.
57. Swainson's Fish, Reptiles, &c. .... 2 vols. 7s.
58. Swainson's Quadrupeds .... 1 vol. 3s. 6d.
59. Swainson's Shells and Shell-Fish....... 1 vol. 3s. 6d.
60. Swainson's Animals in Menageries..... 1 vol. 3s. 6d.
61. Swainson's Taxidermy and Biography of
    Zoologists .... 1 vol. 3s. 6d.
62. Thirlwall's History of Greece.... .... 8 vols. 28s.

Mrs. R. Lee's Elements of Natural History ; or, First Principles of Zoology : Comprising the Principles of Classification, interspersed with amusing and instructive Accounts of the most remarkable Animals. New and revised Edition ....

Dr. John Lindley's Theory and Practice of Horticulture ; or, an Attempt to explain the principal Operations of Gardening upon Physiological Grounds. With 98 Woodcuts. 8vo. 21s.

Linwood.—Anthologia Oxoniensis, sive Florilegium e Lusibus poeticis diversorum Oxoniensium Græcis et Latinis decerptum. Curante GULIELMO LINWOOD, M.A., Ædis Christi Alumno. 8vo. price 14s.

Lorimer's (C.) Letters to a Young Master Mariner on some Subjects connected with his Calling. New Edition. Fcp. 8vo. 5s. 6d.

Loudon's Encyclopædia of Agriculture: Comprising the Theory and Practice of the Valuation, Transfer, Laying-out, Improvement, and Management of Landed Property, and of the Cultivation and Economy of the Animal and Vegetable Productions of Agriculture. New and cheaper Edition; with 1,100 Woodcuts. 8vo. 31s. 6d.

Loudon's Encyclopædia of Gardening: Comprising the Theory and Practice of Horticulture, Floriculture, Arboriculture, and Landscape-Gardening. With many hundred Woodcuts. Corrected and improved by MRS. LOUDON. New and cheaper Edition. 8vo. 31s. 6d.

THIS work, which is admitted to be the best work on Gardening, is now brought within the reach of Head Gardeners, Nurserymen, and of those gentlemen who wish to provide their Gardeners with a complete Work on the Theory and Practice of Gardening. The work comprises above 1300 closely printed pages, minutely classified in all the divisions of Floriculture, Arboriculture, Kitchen Garden, Landscape Gardening, &c. &c., and is illustrated with above One Thousand Engravings on Wood.

Loudon's Encyclopædia of Trees and Shrubs, or *Arboretum et Fruticetum Britannicum* abridged: Containing the Hardy Trees and Shrubs of Great Britain, Native and Foreign, Scientifically and Popularly Described. With about 2,000 Woodcuts. 8vo. price 50s.

Loudon's Encyclopædia of Plants: Comprising the Specific Character, Description, Culture, History, Application in the Arts, and every other desirable Particular respecting all the Plants found in Great Britain. New Edition, corrected by MRS. LOUDON. With upwards of 12,000 Woodcuts. 8vo. £3. 13s. 6d.—Second Supplement, 21s.

Loudon's Encyclopædia of Cottage, Farm, and Villa Architecture and Furniture. New Edition, edited by MRS. LOUDON; with more than 2,000 Woodcuts. 8vo. 63s.

Loudon's Hortus Britannicus; or, Cata- logue of all the Plants found in Great Britain. New Edition, corrected by MRS. LOUDON. 8vo. 31s. 6d.

Mrs. Loudon's Lady's Country Compa- nion; or, How to Enjoy a Country Life

Mrs. Loudon's Amateur Gardener's Calendar, or Monthly Guide to what should be avoided and done in a Garden. *New Edition*. Crown 8vo. with Woodcuts, 7s. 6d.

Love.—The Art of Cleaning, Dyeing, Scouring, and Finishing on the most approved English and French Methods: being Practical Instructions in Dyeing Silks, Woollens, and Cottons, Feathers, Chip, Straw, &c.; Scouring and Cleaning Bed and Window Curtains, Carpets, Rugs, &c.; French and English Cleaning any Colour or Fabric of Silk, Satin, or Damask. Followed by a List of Prices; and Abstracts of the Acts of Parliament relating to Apprentices, Workmen, and Jobbing by Journeymen Dyers. By THOMAS LOVE, Working Dyer and Scourer. Second Edition. Post 8vo. price 7s. 6d.

Lowe.—Central India during the Rebel- lion of 1857 and 1858: a Narrative of Operations of the British Forces from the Suppression of Mutiny in Aurungabad to the Capture of Gwalior under Major-General Sir Hugh Rose, G.C.B., &c., and Brigadier Sir C. Stuart, K.C.B. By THOMAS LOWE, M.R.C.S.E., Medical Officer to the Corps of Madras Sappers and Miners. Post 8vo. with Map, 9s. 6d.

Lowndes's Engineer's Handbook; ex- plaining the Principles which should guide the young Engineer in the Construction of Machinery, with the necessary Rules, Proportions, and Tables: Comprising amongst other matters the Rule for Calculating the Evaporation Power of Boilers, the comparative Economical effect of using Steam expansively, Principles which regulate the Speed of Steam Vessels, &c. Post 8vo. price 5s.

Lord Macaulay's Miscellaneous Writ- ings, comprising his Contributions to *Knight's Quarterly Magazine*, Articles contributed to the Edinburgh Review not included in his *Critical and Historical Essays*, Biographies written for the *Encyclopædia Britannica*, Miscellaneous Poems and Inscriptions. 2 vols. 8vo. with Portrait, 21s.

Macaulay. — The History of England from the Accession of James II. By the Right Hon. LORD MACAULAY. New Edition. VOLS. I. and II. 8vo. price 32s.; VOLS. III. and IV. price 36s.

Lord Macaulay's History of England from the Accession of James II. New Edition of the first Four Volumes of the

Lord Macaulay's Critical and Historical Essays contributed to The Edinburgh Review. Four Editions, as follows:—

1. A LIBRARY EDITION (the *Ninth*), in 3 vols. 8vo. price 36s.
2. Complete in ONE VOLUME, with Portrait and Vignette. Square crown 8vo. price 21s. cloth; or 30s. calf.
3. Another NEW EDITION, in 3 vols. fcp. 8vo. price 21s. cloth.
4. The PEOPLE'S EDITION, in 2 vols. crown 8vo. price 8s. cloth.

List of Fourteen of Lord Macaulay's Essays which may be had separately, in 16mo. in the TRAVELLER'S LIBRARY: —

Warren Hastings ....1s.	Lord Bacon ....1s.
Lord Clive ....1s.	Lord Byron; and the Comic
William Pitt; and the Earl	Dramatists of the Res-
of Chatham ....1s.	toration ....1s.
Ranke's History of the	Frederick the Great.........1s.
Popes; and Gladstone on	Hallam's Constitutional
Church and State ....1s.	History of England ...1s.
Life and Writings of Addi-	Croker's Edition of Bos-
son; and Horace Wal-	well's Life of Johnson...1s.
pole...............................1s.	

Lord Macaulay's Lays of Ancient Rome, with *Ivry* and the *Armada*. New Edition. 16mo. price 4s. 6d. cloth; or 10s. 6d. bound in morocco.

Lord Macaulay's Lays of Ancient Rome. With numerous Illustrations, Original and from the Antique, drawn on Wood by George Scharf, jun. Fcp. 4to. price 21s. boards; or 42s. bound in morocco.

Macaulay.—Speeches of the Right Hon. Lord Macaulay. Corrected by HIMSELF. 8vo. price 12s.—Lord Macaulay's Speeches on Parliamentary Reform, 16mo. price 1s.

Mac Donald. — Poems. By George MAC DONALD, Author of *Within and Without*. Fcp. 8vo. 7s.

Mac Donald.—Within and Without: A Dramatic Poem. By GEORGE MAC DONALD. *Second Edition*, revised. Fcp. 8vo. 4s. 6d.

MacDougall.—The Theory of War illustrated by numerous Examples from History. By Lieutenant-Colonel MACDOUGALL, Commandant of the Staff College. *Second Edition*, with 10 Plans. Post 8vo. 10s. 6d.

Colonel MacDougall's Campaigns of Hannibal, arranged and critically considered, expressly for the use of Students of Military History. Post 8vo. with Map, 7s. 6d.

Sir James Mackintosh's Miscellaneous Works: Including his Contributions to The Edinburgh Review. 1 vol. square crown 8vo. 21s. cloth; or 30s. bound in calf: or in 3 vols. fcp. 8vo. 21s.

Sir James Mackintosh's History of England from the Earliest Times to the final Esta-

M'Culloch's Dictionary, Practical, Theoretical, and Historical, of Commerce and Commercial Navigation. Illustrated with Maps and Plans. New Edition, containing much additional Information. 8vo. 50s. cloth; or 55s. half-bound in russia.

Supplement to the Edition of the Dictionary published in 1859; comprising the late Commercial Treaty with France, the New Tariff of the United Kingdom, the New Indian Tariff, with a variety of miscellaneous Information in regard to commercial matters. 8vo. 2s. 6d.

M'Culloch's Dictionary, Geographical, Statistical, and Historical, of the various Countries, Places, and principal Natural Objects in the World. Illustrated with Six large Maps. New Edition, revised; with a Supplement. 2 vols. 8vo. price 63s.

Maguire.—Rome; its Ruler and its Institutions. By JOHN FRANCIS MAGUIRE, M.P. *Second Edition*, revised and enlarged; with a new Portrait of Pope Pius IX. æt. 66. Post 8vo. 10s. 6d.

Mrs. Marcet's Conversations on Natural Philosophy, in which the Elements of that Science are familiarly explained. Thirteenth Edition, enlarged and corrected; with 34 Plates. Fcp. 8vo. price 10s. 6d.

Mrs. Marcet's Conversations on Chemistry, in which the Elements of that Science are familiarly explained and illustrated by Experiments. New Edition, enlarged and improved. 2 vols. fcp. 8vo. price 14s.

Martineau. — Studies of Christianity: A Series of Original Papers, now first collected or new. By JAMES MARTINEAU. Crown 8vo. 7s. 6d.

Martineau. — Endeavours after the Christian Life: Discourses. By JAMES MARTINEAU. 2 vols. post 8vo. 7s. 6d. each.

Martineau.—Miscellanies: Comprising Essays on Dr. Priestley, Arnold's *Life and Correspondence*, Church and State, Theodore Parker's *Discourse of Religion*, "Phases of Faith," the Church of England, and the Battle of the Churches. By JAMES MARTINEAU. Post 8vo. 9s.

Martineau.— Hymns for the Christian Church and Home. Collected and edited by JAMES MARTINEAU. *Eleventh Edition*, 12mo. 3s. 6d.

Marshman's Life of General Havelock.— Memoirs of Major-General Sir Henry Havelock, K.C.B. By JOHN CLARK MARSHMAN. With Portrait, Map, and 2 Plans. 8vo. 12s. 6d.

Marshman.— The Life and Times of Carey, Marshman, and Ward: Embracing the History of the Serampore Mission. By JOHN CLARK MARSHMAN. 2 vols. 8vo. price 25s.

Maunder's Scientific and Literary Trea- sury: A new and popular Encyclopædia of Science and the Belles-Lettres; including all branches of Science, and every subject connected with Literature and Art. New Edition. Fcp. 8vo. price 10s. cloth; bound in roan, 12s.; calf, 12s. 6d.

Maunder's Biographical Treasury; con- sisting of Memoirs, Sketches, and brief Notices of above 12,000 Eminent Persons of All Ages and Nations, from the Earliest Period of History: Forming a complete Popular Dictionary of Universal Biography. Eleventh Edition, revised, corrected, and extended in a Supplement. Fcp. 8vo. 10s. cloth; bound in roan, 12s.; calf, 12s. 6d.

Maunder's Treasury of Knowledge, and Library of Reference. Comprising an English Dictionary and Grammar, a Universal Gazetteer, a Classical Dictionary, a Chronology, a Law Dictionary, a Synopsis of the Peerage, numerous useful Tables, &c. New Edition, entirely reconstructed and reprinted; revised and improved by B. B. WOODWARD, B.A. F.S.A.: Assisted by J. MORRIS, Solicitor, London; and W. HUGHES, F.R.G.S. Fcp. 8vo. 10s. cloth; bound in roan, 12s.; calf, 12s. 6d.

Maunder's Treasury of Natural History; or, a Popular Dictionary of Animated Nature: In which the Zoological Characteristics that distinguish the different Classes, Genera, and Species, are combined with a variety of interesting Information illustrative of the Habits, Instincts, and General Economy of the Animal Kingdom. With 900 Woodcuts. New Edition. Fcp. 8vo. price 10s. cloth; roan, 12s.; calf, 12s. 6d.

Maunder's Historical Treasury; com- prising a General Introductory Outline of Universal History, Ancient and Modern, and a Series of separate Histories of every principal Nation that exists; their Rise, Progress, and Present Condition, the Moral and Social Character of their respective Inhabitants, their Religion, Manners and Customs, &c. New Edition; revised throughout with a new GENERAL INDEX. Fcp. 8vo.

Maunder's Geographical Treasury. — The Treasury of Geography, Physical, Historical, Descriptive, and Political; containing a succinct Account of Every Country in the World: Preceded by an Introductory Outline of the History of Geography; a Familiar Inquiry into the Varieties of Race and Language exhibited by different Nations; and a View of the Relations of Geography to Astronomy and Physical Science. Completed by WILLIAM HUGHES, F.R.G.S. New Edition, carefully revised throughout; with the Statistical Tables brought up to the latest date of information. With 7 Maps and 16 Steel Plates. Fcp. 8vo. 10s. cloth; roan, 12s.; calf, 12s. 6d.

Merivale. — A History of the Romans under the Empire. By the Rev. CHARLES MERIVALE, B.D., late Fellow of St. John's College, Cambridge. 8vo. with Maps.

VOLS. I. and II. comprising the History to the Fall of *Julius Cæsar.* Second Edition.............................28s.

VOL. III. to the establishment of the Monarchy by *Augustus.* Second Edition ....14s.

VOLS. IV. and V. from *Augustus* to *Claudius,* B.C. 27 to A.D. 54.............................32s.

VOL. VI. from the Reign of *Nero,* A.D. 54, to the *Fall of Jerusalem,* A.D. 70.............................16s.

Merivale.—The Fall of the Roman Republic: A Short History of the Last Century of the Commonwealth. By the Rev. C. MERIVALE, B.D. New Edition. 12mo. 7s. 6d.

Merivale (Miss).—Christian Records: A Short History of Apostolic Age. By LOUISA A. MERIVALE. Fcp. 8vo. 7s. 6d.

Miles.—The Horse's Foot, and How to Keep it Sound. *Eighth Edition;* with an Appendix on Shoeing in general, and Hunters in particular, 12 Plates and 12 Woodcuts. By W. MILES, Esq. Imperial 8vo. 12s. 6d.

. Two Casts or Models of Off Fore Feet, No. 1, *Shod for All Purposes,* No. 2, *Shod with Leather,* on Mr. Miles's plan, may be had, price 3s. each.

Miles.—A Plain Treatise on Horse-Shoeing. By WILLIAM MILES, Esq. With Plates and Woodcuts. *New Edition.* Post 8vo. 2s.

Minturn.—From New York to Delhi by way of Rio de Janeiro, Australia, and China. By ROBERT B. MINTURN, Jun. With Map of India. Post 8vo. price 7s. 6d.

Mollhausen. — Diary of a Journey from the Mississippi to the Coasts of the Pacific, with a United States Government Expedition. By B. MÖLLHAUSEN, Topographical Draughtsman and Naturalist to the Expedition. With an Introduction by Baron HUMBOLDT; a Map, coloured Illustrations,

James Montgomery's Poetical Works:
Collective Edition; with the Author's Autobiographical Prefaces, complete in One Volume; with Portrait and Vignette. Square crown 8vo. price 10s. 6d. cloth; morocco, 21s.—Or, in 4 vols. fcp. 8vo. with Portrait, and 7 other Plates, price 14s.

Thomas Moore's Memoirs, Journal, and Correspondence. New Edition for the People, with 8 Portraits and 2 Vignettes engraved on Steel. Edited and abridged from the First Edition by the Right Hon. LORD JOHN RUSSELL, M.P. Uniform with the *People's Edition of Moore's Poetical Works.* Square crown 8vo. 12s. 6d.

Thomas Moore's Poetical Works: Com-prising the Author's Autobiographical Prefaces, latest Corrections, and Notes. Various Editions of the separate Poems and complete Poetical Works, as follows:—

	s.	d.
LALLA ROOKH, with 66 Illustrations from original Drawings by JOHN TENNIEL and 5 Initial Pages of Persian Design by T. SULMAN, Jun., engraved on Wood; fcp. 4to. in ornamental covers	21	0
LALLA ROOKH, 32mo. ruby type, Frontispiece	1	0
LALLA ROOKH, 16mo. Vignette on Wood	2	6
LALLA ROOKH, square crown 8vo. Plates	15	0
IRISH MELODIES, 32mo. ruby type, Portrait	1	0
IRISH MELODIES, 16mo. Vignette on Wood	2	6
IRISH MELODIES, square crown 8vo. Plates	21	0
IRISH MELODIES, illustrated by MACLISE, super-royal 8vo.	31	6
SONGS, BALLADS, and SACRED SONGS, 32mo. ruby type, Frontispiece	2	6
SONGS, BALLADS, and SACRED SONGS, 16mo. Vignette on Wood	5	0
POETICAL WORKS, People's Edition, complete in One Volume, square crown 8vo. with Portrait	12	6
POETICAL WORKS, Cabinet Edition, 10 VOLS. ea.	3	6
POETICAL WORKS, Traveller's Edit., crown 8vo.	12	6
POETICAL WORKS, Library Edition, medium 8vo.	21	0
SELECTIONS, entitled "POETRY and PICTURES from THOMAS MOORE," fcp. 4to. with Woodcuts	21	0
MOORE'S EPICUREAN, 16mo. Vignette	5	0

Editions printed with the Music.

IRISH MELODIES, People's Edition, small 4to.	12	0
IRISH MELODIES, imperial 8vo. small music size	31	6

Moore.—The Power of the Soul over the Body, considered in relation to Health and Morals. By GEORGE MOORE, M.D. *Fifth Edition.* Fcp. 8vo. 6s.

Moore.—Man and his Motives. By George MOORE, M.D. *Third Edition.* Fcp. 8vo. 6s.

Moore.—The Use of the Body in relation to the Mind. By GEORGE MOORE, M.D. *Third Edition.* Fcp. 8vo. 6s.

Morell.—Elements of Psychology: Part I., containing the Analysis of the Intellectual Powers. By J. D. MORELL, M.A., One of Her Majesty's Inspectors of Schools. Post 8vo. 7s. 6d.

Morning Clouds. By the Author of *The Afternoon of Life.* Second and cheaper Edition, revised throughout. Fcp. 8vo. 5s.

Morton's Agricultural Handbooks. — Handbook of Dairy Husbandry: comprising Dairy Statistics; Food of the Cow; Milk; Butter; Cheese; General Management; Calendar of Daily Dairy Operations; Appendix on Cheese-making; and Index. By JOHN CHALMERS MORTON, Editor of the *Agricultural Gazette*, &c. 16mo. 1s. 6d.

Morton's Handbook of Farm Labour; Steam, Horse, and Water Power.
[*Nearly ready.*

Morton.—The Resources of Estates: A Treatise on the Agricultural Improvement and General Management of Landed Property. By JOHN LOCKHART MORTON. With 25 Illustrations in Lithography. Royal 8vo. 31s. 6d.

Moseley.—Astro-Theology. By the Rev. HENRY MOSELEY, M.A., F.R.S., Canon of Bristol, &c. *Third Edition.* Fcp. 8vo. price 4s. 6d.

Moseley.—The Mechanical Principles of Engineering and Architecture. By H. MOSELEY, M.A., F.R.S., Canon of Bristol, &c. Second Edition, enlarged; with numerous Corrections and Woodcuts. 8vo. 24s.

Murray's Encyclopædia of Geography;
comprising a complete Description of the
Earth: Exhibiting its Relation to the
Heavenly Bodies, its Physical Structure, the
Natural History of each Country, and the
Industry, Commerce, Political Institutions,
and Civil and Social State of All Nations.
Second Edition; with 82 Maps, and upwards
of 1,000 other Woodcuts. 8vo. price 60s.

Neale. — The Closing Scene; or, Chris-
tianity and Infidelity contrasted in the Last
Hours of Remarkable Persons. By the
Rev. ERSKINE NEALE, M.A. New Editions.
2 vols. fcp. 8vo. price 6s. each.

Works by the Rev. Dr. John Henry
Newman of the Oratory: —

The Scope and Nature of University Education.
Second Edition. Fcp. 8vo. 6s.

The Office and Work of Universities. Fcp. 8vo.
price 6s.

Lectures and Essays on University Subjects.
Fcp. 8vo. 6s.

The above three works form together a con-
nected work on University Teaching, considered
in its various aspects, viz.: —
In its abstract scope and nature;
In certain portions of its subject-matter;
And in a series of Historical Sketches.

Ogilvie. — The Master-Builder's Plan;
or, the Principles of Organic Architecture
as indicated in the Typical Forms of Animals.
By GEORGE OGILVIE, M.D. Post 8vo.
with 72 Woodcuts, price 6s. 6d.

" AMONG the numerous treatises on general zoology with which we are acquainted, we know not one from which the student can obtain an intelligible and satisfactory account of the leading principles of animal morphology, and of the higher generalisations of systematic zoology. The *Master-Builder's Plan* is intended to supply this defect in our literature. It has been the object of Dr. Ogilvie *not to advance new truths, but rather to gain additional currency for such as* | have a fair claim to be already established, and, in particular, to convey an idea of the laws of organisation to those who, without making natural history a special object of study, may wish to have a right comprehension of its general scope. In this we think he has succeeded. After a careful examination of its contents, we do not hesitate to recommend his work to all who are desirous of acquiring sound information on the important subject of which it treats." NATURAL HISTORY REVIEW.

Osborn.—The Discovery of the North-
West Passage by H.M.S. *Investigator*, Cap-
tain R. M'CLURE, 1850–1854. Edited by
Captain SHERARD OSBORN, C.B., from the
Logs and Journals of Captain R. M'Clure.
Third Edition, with Portrait, Chart, and
Illustrations. 8vo. 15s.

Professor Owen's Lectures on the Com-
parative Anatomy and Physiology of the
Invertebrate Animals, delivered at the Royal
College of Surgeons. Second Edition; with
235 Woodcuts. 8vo. 21s.

Professor Owen's Lectures on the Comparative

Palleske's Life of Schiller. — Schiller's
Life and Works. By EMIL PALLESKE.
Translated by LADY WALLACE. Dedicated
by permission to Her Majesty the Queen.
With 2 Portraits. 2 vols. post 8vo. 24s.

Memoirs of Admiral Parry, the Arctic
Navigator. By his Son, the Rev. E. PARRY,
M.A. of Balliol College, Oxford; Domestic
Chaplain to the Lord Bishop of London.
Seventh Edition; with a Portrait and
coloured Chart of the North-West Passage.
Fcp. 8vo. price 5s.

Peaks, Passes, and Glaciers: a Series of
Excursions by Members of the Alpine Club.
Edited by JOHN BALL, M.R.I.A., F.L.S.,
President. Traveller's Edition (being the
Fifth); comprising all the Mountain Ex-
peditions and the Maps, printed in a con-
densed form for the Traveller's knapsack or
pocket. 16mo. 5s. 6d.

⁎ The Fourth Edition of *Peaks, Passes,
and Glaciers*, with 8 coloured Illustrations and
numerous Woodcuts, may still be had, price
21s. Also the EIGHT SWISS MAPS, accompanied by a Table of the HEIGHTS of MOUN-
TAINS, price 3s. 6d.

The Late Sir Robert Peel, Bart. —
Sketch of the Life and Character of Sir
Robert Peel, Bart. By the Right Hon. Sir
LAWRENCE PEEL. Post 8vo. 8s. 6d.

Dr. Pereira's Elements of Materia
Medica and Therapeutics. *Third Edition*,
enlarged and improved from the Author's
Materials, by A. S. TAYLOR, M.D., and
G. O. REES, M.D.: With numerous Woodcuts. VOL. I. 8vo. 28s.; VOL. II. PART I.
21s.; VOL. II. PART II. 26s.

Dr. Pereira's Lectures on Polarised Light,
together with a Lecture on the Microscope.
2d Edition, enlarged from Materials left by
the Author, by the Rev. B. POWELL, M.A.,
&c. Fcp. 8vo. with Woodcuts, 7s.

Peschel's Elements of Physics. Translated from the German, with Notes, by
E. WEST. With Diagrams and Woodcuts.
3 vols. fcp. 8vo. 21s.

Phillips's Elementary Introduction to
Mineralogy. A New Edition, with extensive
Alterations and Additions, by H. J. BROOKE,
F.R.S., F.G.S.; and W. H. MILLER, M.A.,
F.G.S. With numerous Wood Engravings.
Post 8vo. 18s.

Phillips.—A Guide to Geology. By John
PHILLIPS, M.A., F.R.S., F.G.S., &c. Fourth

Piesse's Laboratory of Chymical Wonders : a Scientific Mélange intended for the Instruction and Entertainment of Young People. Fcp. 8vo. with Illustrations.
[*Just ready.*

Piesse's Chymical, Natural, and Physical Magic, for the Instruction and Entertainment of Juveniles during the Holiday Vacation. Second Edition; with 30 Woodcuts and an Invisible Portrait. Fcp. 8vo. price 3s. 6d.

Piesse's Art of Perfumery, and Methods of Obtaining the Odours of Plants : With Instructions for the Manufacture of Perfumes for the Handkerchief, Scented Powders, Odorous Vinegars, Dentifrices, Pomatums, Cosmétiques, Perfumed Soap, &c. ; and an Appendix on the Colours of Flowers, Artificial Fruit Essences, &c. *Second Edition*; with 46 Woodcuts. Crown 8vo. 8s. 6d.

Piozzi. — Autobiography, Letters, and Literary Remains of Mrs. Piozzi (Thrale), Author of *Anecdotes of Dr. Johnson*. Edited, with Notes and some account of her Life and Writings, by A. HAYWARD, Esq., Q.C. With a Portrait of Mrs. Piozzi, and an engraving from a picture by Hogarth, "*The Lady's Last Stake*," for the principal figure in which Mrs. Piozzi sat. 2 vols. post 8vo.

Pitt.—How to Brew good Beer : a complete Guide to the Art of Brewing Ale, Bitter Ale, Table Ale, Brown Stout, Porter, and Table Beer. To which are added, Practical Instructions for making Malt. By JOHN PITT, Butler to Sir William R. P. Geary, Bart. Fcp. 8vo. 4s. 6d.

Porter. — History of the Knights of Malta, or the Order of the Hospital of St. John of Jerusalem. By Major WHITWORTH PORTER, R.E. 2 vols. 8vo. 24s.

Powell.—Essays on the Spirit of the Inductive Philosophy, the Unity of Worlds, and the Philosophy of Creation. By the Rev. BADEN POWELL, M.A., &c., late Savilian Professor of Geometry in the University of Oxford. Second Edition, revised. Crown 8vo. with Woodcuts, 12s. 6d.

Christianity without Judaism: A Second Series

Pycroft. — The Collegian's Guide; or, Recollections of College Days : Setting forth the Advantages and Temptations of a University Education. By the Rev. J. PYCROFT, B.A. *Second Edition*. Fcp. 8vo.

Pycroft's Course of English Reading, adapted to every taste and capacity; or, How and What to Read : With Literary Anecdotes. New Edition. Fcp. 8vo. price 5s.

Pycroft's Cricket-Field; or, the Science and History of the Game of Cricket. Third Edition, greatly improved ; with Plates and Woodcuts. Fcp. 8vo. price 5s.

Quatrefages (A. De). — Rambles of a Naturalist on the Coasts of France, Spain, and Sicily. By A. De QUATREFAGES, Member of the Institute. Translated by E. C. OTTÉ. 2 vols. post 8vo. 15s.

Raikes (T.)—Portion of the Journal kept by THOMAS RAIKES, Esq., from 1831 to 1847: Comprising Reminiscences of Social and Political Life in London and Paris during that period. *New Edition*, complete in 2 vols. crown 8vo. price 12s.

Ramsay.—The Old Glaciers of North Wales and Switzerland. By A. C. RAMSAY, F.R.S. and G.S., Local Director of the Geological Survey of Great Britain, and Professor of Geology in the Government School of Mines. Reprinted from *Peaks, Passes, and Glaciers*; with Map and 14 Woodcuts. Fcp. 8vo. 4s. 6d.

"MR. RAMSAY has given us in this little volume 'a reprint of his contribution to *Peaks, Passes, and Glaciers*—thus reproducing in a very portable form pages which will constitute an invaluable companion to the tourist in North Wales, where the other experiences of the Alpine Club would not be necessary to his knapsack......The most unlearned tourist may take Mr. Ramsay's work and follow the tracks which he points out. For this book is not interesting alone to the scientific reader; it avoids as much as possible the technical vocabulary of the geologist and mineralogist, and renders its descriptions with a hearty and fluent freshness which only a genuine love of nature could inspire. And there are few travellers so unimaginative, so obdurate to the spell which the most poetic of mountains throws, as not to be set a-thinking more or less in a speculative way by Mr. Ramsay's observations." JOHN BULL.

Rich's Dictionary of Roman and Greek Antiquities ; with nearly 2,000 Woodcuts representing Objects from the Antique illustrative of the Industrial Arts and Social

Riddle.—Household Prayers for Four Weeks: with additional Prayers for Special Occasions. To which is appended a Course of Scripture Reading for Every Day in the Year. By the Rev. J. E. RIDDLE, M.A. *Second Edition.* Crown 8vo. 3s. 6d.

Riddle's Complete Latin-English and English-Latin Dictionary, for the use of Colleges and Schools. *New* and cheaper *Edition,* revised and corrected. 8vo. 21s.

Separately { The English-Latin Dictionary, 7s. { The Latin-English Dictionary, 15s.

Riddle's Young Scholar's Latin-English and English-Latin Dictionary. *New* and cheaper *Edition,* revised and corrected. Square 12mo. 10s. 6d.

Separately { The Latin-English Dictionary, 6s. { The English-Latin Dictionary, 5s.

Riddle's Diamond Latin-English Dictionary. A Guide to the Meaning, Quality, and right Accentuation of Latin Classical Words. Royal 32mo. price 4s.

Riddle's Copious and Critical Latin- English Lexicon, founded on the German-Latin Dictionaries of Dr. William Freund. New Edition. Post 4to. 31s. 6d.

Rivers's Rose-Amateur's Guide; contain- ing ample Descriptions of all the fine leading varieties of Roses, regularly classed in their respective Families; their History and Mode of Culture. Fcp. 8vo. 3s. 6d.

Dr. E. Robinson's Greek and English Lexicon to the Greek Testament. A New Edition, in great part re-written. 8vo. 18s.

Mr. Henry Rogers's Essays selected from Contributions to the *Edinburgh Review.* Second Edition. 3 vols. fcp. 8vo. price 21s.

Samuel Rogers's Recollections of Per- sonal and Conversational Intercourse with

CHARLES JAMES FOX, PRINCE TALLEYRAND,
EDMUND BURKE, LORD ERSKINE,
HENRY GRATTAN, SIR WALTER SCOTT,
RICHARD PORSON, LORD GRENVILLE, *and*
JOHN HORNE TOOKE, DUKE OF WELLINGTON.

Second Edition. Fcp. 8vo. 5s.

Dr. Roget's Thesaurus of English Words and Phrases classified and arranged so as to facilitate the Expression of Ideas and assist in Literary Composition. Ninth Edition, revised and improved. Crown 8vo. 10s. 6d.

Ronalds's Fly-Fisher's Entomology: With coloured Representations of the Natural and Artificial Insect, and a few Observations and Instructions on Trout and Grayling Fishing. *Fifth Edition,* thoroughly

Rowton's Debater: A Series of complete Debates, Outlines of Debates, and Questions for Discussion; with ample References to the best Sources of Information. New Edition. Fcp. 8vo. 6s.

Dr. Russell's Life of Cardinal Mezzofanti: With an Introductory Memoir of eminent Linguists, Ancient and Modern. With Portrait and Facsimiles. 8vo. 12s.

Mrs. SchimmelPenninck's Writings and Life, edited by her relation, CHRISTIANA C. HANKIN:—

Life of Mary Anne SchimmelPenninck. *Fourth* and cheaper *Edition,* with Corrections and Additions; complete in One Volume, with Portrait ....Post 8vo. 10s. 6d.

Select Memoirs of Port-Royal. To which are added Tour to Alet, Visit to Port-Royal, Gift of an Abbess, Biographical Notices, &c. from original Documents. *Fifth Edition,* revised.................3 vols. post 8vo. 21s.

The Principles of Beauty, as manifested in Nature, Art, and Human Character: with a Classification of Deformities; II. An Essay on the Temperaments (with Illustrations); III. Thoughts on Grecian and Gothic Architecture.......Post 8vo. 12s. 6d.

Sacred Musings on Manifestations of God to the Soul of Man; with Thoughts on the Destiny of Woman, and other subjects. With Preface by the Rev. Dr. BAYLEE, Principal of St. Aidan's Theological College, Birkenhead. Post 8vo. 10s. 6d.

Dr. L. Schmitz's School History of Greece, from the Earliest Times to the Taking of Corinth by the Romans, B.C. 146, mainly based on Bishop Thirlwall's History of Greece; and illustrated with a Map of Athens and 137 Woodcuts, designed from the Antique by G. Scharf, jun., F.S.A. *Fifth Edition,* with Nine new Supplementary Chapters on the Civilisation, Religion, Literature, and Arts of the Ancient Greeks, contributed by C. K. WATSON, M.A. 12mo. 7s. 6d.

Scoffern (Dr.) — Projectile Weapons of War and Explosive Compounds. By J. SCOFFERN, M.B. Lond., late Professor of Chemistry in the Aldersgate College of Medicine. *Fourth Edition.* Post 8vo. with Woodcuts, price 9s. 6d.

SUPPLEMENT, containing new resources of Warfare................................2s.

Senior.— Journal kept in Turkey and Greece in the Autumn of 1857 and the beginning of 1858. By NASSAU W. SENIOR,

Sewell (Miss).—New and cheaper Collected Edition of the Tales and Stories of the Author of *Amy Herbert*, in 9 vols. crown 8vo. price £1. 10s. cloth; or each work, complete in a single volume, may be had separately as follows :—

AMY HERBERT	2s. 6d.
GERTRUDE	2s. 6d.
The EARL'S DAUGHTER	2s. 6d.
The EXPERIENCE of LIFE	2s. 6d.
CLEVE HALL	3s. 6d.
IVORS; or, the TWO COUSINS	3s. 6d.
KATHARINE ASHTON	3s. 6d.
MARGARET PERCIVAL	5s. 0d.
LANETON PARSONAGE	4s. 6d.

Also by the Author of Amy Herbert,

Passing Thoughts on Religion. New *Edition.* Fcp. 8vo. 5s.

Ursula: A Tale of English Country Life. 2 vols. fcp. 8vo. price 12s. cloth.

History of the Early Church, from the First Preaching of the Gospel to the Council of Nicea. 18mo. 4s. 6d.

Self-Examination before Confirmation : With Devotions and Directions for Confirmation-Day. 32mo. 1s. 6d.

Readings for a Month preparatory to Confirmation : Compiled from the Works of Writers of the Early and of the English Church. Fcp. 8vo. price 4s.

Readings for Every Day in Lent: Compiled from the Writings of BISHOP JEREMY TAYLOR. Fcp. 8vo. price 5s.

Bowdler's Family Shakspeare : In which nothing is *added* to the Original Text; but those words and expressions are *omitted* which cannot with propriety be read aloud. Illustrated with Thirty-six Vignettes engraved on Wood. *New Edition,* printed in a more convenient form. 6 vols. fcp. 8vo. price 30s. cloth; separately, 5s. each. Each Play may be had separately, price 1s.

*** The LIBRARY EDITION, with the same Illustrations, in One Volume, medium 8vo. price 21s. cloth.

Shee.—Life of Sir Martin Archer Shee, President of the Royal Academy, F.R.S., D.C.L. By his Son, MARTIN ARCHER SHEE, of the Middle Temple, Esq., Barrister-at-Law. 2 vols. 8vo. 21s.

Short Whist; its Rise, Progress, and Laws : With Observations to make any one a Whist-Player. Containing also the Laws of Piquet, Cassino, Ecarté Cribbage, Backgammon. By Major A. New Edition; to which are added, Precepts for Tyros, by Mrs. B. Fcp. 8vo. 3s.

Simpkinson.—The Washingtons : a Tale of an English Country Parish in the Seventeenth Century. Based on Authentic Documents. By the Rev. J. N. SIMPKINSON, Rector of Brington. Post 8vo. 10s. 6d.

Simpson.—Handbook of Dining; or, How to Dine, theoretically, philosophically, and historically considered : Based chiefly upon the *Physiologie du Goût* of Brillat-Savarin. By LEONARD FRANCIS SIMPSON, M.R.S.L. Fcp. 8vo. 5s.

Sir Roger De Coverley. From the Spec- tator. With Notes and Illustrations, by W. HENRY WILLS; and 12 Wood Engravings from Designs by F. TAYLER. Second *and cheaper* Edition. Crown 8vo. 10s. 6d.; or 21s. in morocco by Hayday.—An Edition without Woodcuts, in 16mo. price 1s.

The Sketches: Three Tales. By the Authors of *Amy Herbert, The Old Man's Home,* and *Hawkstone. Third Edition ;* with 6 Illustrations. Fcp. 8vo. price 4s. 6d.

Sleigh.—Personal Wrongs and Legal Remedies. By W. CAMPBELL SLEIGH, of the Middle Temple, Esq., Barrister-at-Law. Fcp. 8vo. 2s. 6d.

Smee's Elements of Electro-Metallurgy. Third Edition, revised, corrected, and considerably enlarged; with Electrotypes and numerous Woodcuts. Post 8vo. 10s. 6d.

Smith (G.) — History of Wesleyan Me- thodism. By GEORGE SMITH, F.A.S., Member of the Royal Asiatic Society, &c. VOL. I. *Wesley and his Times;* and VOL. II. *The Middle Age of Methodism,* from the Death of Wesley in 1791 to the Conference of 1816. Crown 8vo. price 10s. 6d. each volume.

The Wit and Wisdom of the Rev. Sydney Smith: A Selection of the most memorable Passages in his Writings and Conversation. 16mo. 7s. 6d.

The Rev. Sydney Smith's Elementary Sketches of Moral Philosophy, delivered at the Royal Institution in the Years 1804, 1805, and 1806. Third Edition. Fcp. 8vo. 7s.

The Rev. Sydney Smith's Miscellaneous Works: Including his Contributions to The Edinburgh Review. Four Editions :—

1. A LIBRARY EDITION (the *Fourth*), in 3 vols. 8vo. with Portrait, 36s.

2. Complete in ONE VOLUME, with Portrait and Vignette. Square crown 8vo. price 21s. cloth ; or 30s. bound in calf.

3. Another NEW EDITION, in 3 vols. fcp. 8vo. price 21s.

4. The PEOPLE'S EDITION, in 2 vols. crown 8vo. price 8s. cloth.

A Memoir of the Rev. Sydney Smith. By his Daughter, LADY HOLLAND. With a Selection from his Letters, edited by MRS. AUSTIN. *New Edition.* 2 vols. 8vo. 28s.

Snow.— Two Years' Cruise off Tierra del Fuego, the Falkland Islands, Patagonia, and the River Plate : A Narrative of Life iu the Southern Seas. By W. PARKER SNOW. With Charts and tinted Illustrations. 2 vols. post 8vo. 24s.

Robert Southey's Complete Poetical Works; containing all the Author's last Introductions and Notes. The *Library Edition*, complete in One Volume, with Portrait and Vignette. Medium 8vo. price 21s. cloth ; 42s. bound in morocco. — Also, the *First collected Edition*, in 10 vols. fcp. 8vo. with Portrait and 19 Vignettes, price 35s.

Southey's Doctor, complete in One Volume. Edited by the Rev. J. W. WARTER, B.D. With Portrait, Vignette, Bust, and coloured Plate. Square crown 8vo. 21s.

Southey's Life of Wesley ; and Rise and Progress of Methodism. Fourth and cheaper Edition, with Notes and Additions. Edited by the Author's Son, the Rev. C. C. SOUTHEY, M.A. 2 vols. crown 8vo. 12s.

Spitta's German Household Hymns.— Lyra Domestica : Christian Songs for Domestic Edification. Translated from the *Psaltery and Harp* of C. J. P. SPITTA. By RICHARD MASSIE. Uniform with *Lyra Germanica*. Fcp. 8vo. with Portrait, 4s. 6d.

" A N attractive little book, pervaded by a spirit of quiet, loving, devout versification."   EVANGELICAL MAGAZINE.

Sir James Stephen's Essays in Ecclesiastical Biography. Fourth Edition, complete in One Volume ; with a Biographical Notice of the Author, by his SON. 8vo. 14s.

Sir James Stephen's Lectures on the History of France. Third Edition. 2 vols. 8vo. 24s.

Stonehenge.— The Dog in Health and Disease : Comprising the Natural History, Zoological Classification, and Varieties of the Dog, as well as the various Modes of Breaking and Using him for Hunting, Coursing, Shooting, &c. ; and including the Points or Characteristics of Toy Dogs. By STONEHENGE. With 70 Illustrations on Wood. Square crown 8vo. 15s. half-bound.

Stonehenge's Work on the Greyhound: Being a Treatise on the Art of Breeding, Rearing, and Training Greyhounds for Public Running ; their Diseases and Treatment : Containing also Rules for the Management of Coursing Meetings, and for the Decision of Courses. With Frontispiece and Woodcuts. Square crown 8vo. 21s.

Stow.—The Training System of Education; including Moral School Training for large Towns, and the Normal Seminary for Training Teachers to conduct the System. By DAVID STOW, Esq., Glasgow. Eleventh Edition, enlarged ; with Plates and Woodcuts. Post 8vo. price 6s. 6d.

Strickland. — Lives of the Queens of England. By AGNES STRICKLAND. Dedicated, by express permission, to Her Majesty. Embellished with Portraits of every Queen, engraved from the most authentic sources. Complete in 8 vols. post 8vo. price 7s. 6d. each.

Tate.—On the Strength of Materials ; containing various original and useful Formulæ, specially applied to Tubular Bridges, Wrought Iron and Cast Iron Beams, &c. By THOMAS TATE, F.R.A.S. 8vo. 5s. 6d.

THE TRAVELLER'S LIBRARY,

Complete in 102 Parts, *price One Shilling each, or in* 50 Volumes, *price 2s. 6d. each in cloth.—To be had also, in* complete Sets only, *at Five Guineas per Set, bound in cloth, lettered, in* 25 Volumes, *classified as follows :—*

VOYAGES AND TRAVELS.

IN EUROPE.

A Continental Tour, by J. Barrow.
Arctic Voyages and Discoveries, by Fanny Mayne.
Brittany and the Bible, by I. Hope.
Brittany and the Chase, by I. Hope.
Corsica, by F. Gregorovius.
Germany, &c., Notes of a Traveller, by S. Laing.
Iceland, by P. Miles.
Norway, a Residence in, by S. Laing.
Norway, Rambles in, by T. Forester.
Russia, by the Marquis De Custine.
Russia and Turkey, by J. R. M'Culloch.
St. Petersburg, by M. Jerrmann.
The Russians of the South, by S. Brooks.
Swiss Men and Swiss Mountains, by R. Ferguson.
Mont Blanc, Ascent of, by J. Auldjo.
Sketches of Nature in the Alps, by F. Von Tschudi.
Visit to the Vaudois of Piedmont, by E. Baines.

IN ASIA.

China and Thibet, by the Abbé Huc.
Syria and Palestine, by "Eothen."
The Philippine Islands, by P. Gironière.

IN AFRICA.

African Wanderings, by M. Werne.
Morocco, by X. Durrieu.
Niger Exploration, by T. J. Hutchinson.
The Zulus of Natal, by G. H. Mason.

IN AMERICA.

Brazil, by E. Wilberforce.
Canada, by A. M. Jameson.
Cuba, by W. H. Hurlbut.
North American Wilds, by C. Lanman.

IN AUSTRALIA.

Australian Colonies, by W. Hughes.

ROUND THE WORLD.

A Lady's Voyage, by Ida Pfeiffer.

HISTORY AND BIOGRAPHY.

Memoir of the Duke of Wellington.
The Life of Marshal Turenne, by the Rev. T. O. Cockayne.
Schamyl, by Bodenstedt and Wagner.
Ferdinand I. and Maximilian II. by Ranke.
Francis Arago's Autobiography.
Thomas Holcroft's Memoirs.
Chesterfield and Selwyn, by A. Hayward.

Swift and Richardson, by Lord Jeffrey.
Defoe and Churchill, by J. Forster.
Anecdotes of Dr. Johnson, by Mrs. Piozzi.
Turkey and Christendom.
Leipsic Campaign, by the Rev. G. R. Gleig.
An Essay on the Life and Genius of Thomas Fuller, by Henry Rogers.

ESSAYS BY LORD MACAULAY.

Warren Hastings.
Lord Clive.
William Pitt.
The Earl of Chatham.
Ranke's History of the Popes.
Gladstone on Church and State.
Addison's Life and Writings.
Horace Walpole.

Lord Bacon.
Lord Byron.
Comic Dramatist of the Restoration.
Frederic the Great.
Hallam's Constitutional History.
Croker's Edition of Boswell's Life of Johnson.

Lord Macaulay's Speeches on Parliamentary Reform.

WORKS OF FICTION.

The Love Story, from Southey's *Doctor*.
Sir Roger de Coverley, from the *Spectator*.
Memoirs of a Maitre-d'Armes, by Dumas.

Confessions of a Working Man, by E. Souvestre.
An Attic Philosopher in Paris, by E. Souvestre.
Sir Edward Seaward's Narrative of his Shipwreck.

NATURAL HISTORY, &c.

Natural History of Creation, by Dr. L. Kemp.
Indications of Instinct, by Dr. L. Kemp.
Electric Telegraph, &c., by Dr. G. Wilson.

Our Coal-Fields and our Coal-Pits.
Cornwall, its Mines, Miners, Scenery, &c.

MISCELLANEOUS WORKS.

Lectures and Addresses by the Earl of Carlisle.
Selections from Sydney Smith's Writings.
Printing, by A. Stark.

Railway Morals and Railway Policy, by H. Spencer.
Mormonism, by the Rev. W. J. Conybeare.
London, by J. R. M'Culloch.

Tennent. — Ceylon; an Account of the Island, Physical, Historical, and Topographical; with copious Notices of its Natural History, Antiquities, and Productions. Illustrated by 9 Maps, 17 Plans and Charts, and 90 Engravings on Wood. By Sir J. EMERSON TENNENT, K.C.S., LL.D., &c. Fifth Edition, thoroughly revised; with a new INDEX, and other Additions. 2 vols. 8vo. £2. 10s.

Thomson's Seasons. Edited by Bolton CORNEY, Esq. Illustrated with 77 fine Wood Engravings from Designs by Mem-

Thomson (the Rev. Dr.) — An Outline of the necessary Laws of Thought: A Treatise on Pure and Applied Logic. By WILLIAM THOMSON, D.D. Chaplain in Ordinary to the Queen; Provost of Queen's College, Oxford. *5th Edition,* improved. Post 8vo. 5s. 6d.

Thomson's Tables of Interest, at Three, Four, Four-and-a-Half, and Five per Cent., from One Pound to Ten Thousand, and from 1 to 365 Days, in a regular progression of single Days; with Interest at all the above Rates, from One to Twelve Months, and from One to Ten Years. Also, numerous

The Thumb Bible; or, Verbum Sempiternum. By J. TAYLOR. Being an Epitome of the Old and New Testaments in English Verse. 64mo. 1s. 6d.

Todd (Dr.)—The Cyclopædia of Anatomy and Physiology. Edited by ROBERT B. TODD, M.D.,F.R.S. Assisted in the various departments by nearly all the most eminent cultivators of physiological science of the present age. Now complete in 5 vols. 8vo. pp. 5,350, illustrated with 2,853 Woodcuts, price £6. 6s. cloth.

Tooke,—History of Prices, and of the State of the Circulation, during the Nine Years from 1848 to 1856 inclusive. Forming VOLS. V. and VI. of Tooke's *History of Prices from* 1792 *to the year* 1857; and comprising a copious Index to the Six Volumes. By THOMAS TOOKE, F.R.S. and WILLIAM NEWMARCH. 2 vols. 8vo. 52s. 6d.

Trevelyan (Sir C.) — Original Papers illustrating the History of the Application of the Roman Alphabet to the Languages of India. Edited by MONIER WILLIAMS, M.A., late Professor of Sanskrit in the East-India College, Haileybury. 8vo. 12s.

Trollope.—The Warden: a Novel. By ANTHONY TROLLOPE. New and cheaper Edition. Crown 8vo. price 3s. 6d. cloth.

Trollope's Barchester Towers, a Sequel to the *Warden*. New and cheaper Edition, complete in One Volume. Crown 8vo. 5s.

Sharon Turner's History of the Anglo-Saxons, from the Earliest Period to the Norman Conquest. Seventh Edition, revised by the Rev. S. TURNER. 3 vols. 8vo. 36s.

Dr. Turton's Manual of the Land and Fresh-Water Shells of Great Britain: With Figures of each of the kinds. New Edition, with Additions, by Dr. J. E. GRAY, F.R.S., &c., Keeper of the Zoological Collection in the British Museum. Crown 8vo. with 12 coloured Plates, price 15s. cloth.

Twisden. — Elementary Examples in Mechanics, comprising copious Explanations and Proofs of the Fundamental Propositions. By the Rev. JOHN F. TWISDEN, M.A., Professor of Mathematics in the Staff College. Crown 8vo. 12s.

"THIS excellent treatise is designed to be an introduction to the science of Applied Mechanics. It was originally intended as a supplement to other works of a similar kind already in existence, but the author found that by a few additional explanations are given in connexion with the more difficult examples, which, the author hopes, will be found sufficient to enable the reader to complete the solutions. So far as we are able to form an opinion, the work is well calculated to afford sound

Dr. Ure's Dictionary of Arts, Manufactures, and Mines; Containing a clear Exposition of their Principles and Practice. Fifth Edition, chiefly rewritten and greatly enlarged; illustrated with nearly 2,000 Engravings on Wood. Edited by ROBERT HUNT, F.R.S., F.S.S., Keeper of Mining Records, &c., assisted by numerous gentlemen eminent in Science and connected with the Arts and Manufactures. 3 vols. 8vo. price £4. cloth.

Walford.—The Handybook of the Civil Service. By EDWARD WALFORD, M.A., late Scholar of Balliol College, Oxford. Fcp. 8vo. 4s. 6d.

Warburton.—Hunting Songs and Miscellaneous Verses. By R. E. EGERTON WARBURTON. *Second Edition.* Fcp. 8vo. 5s.

Waterton.—Essays on Natural History, chiefly Ornithology. By C. WATERTON, Esq. With the Autobiography of the Author. THREE SERIES. 3 vols. fcp. 8vo. 16s.

"AS a writer of natural history, Waterton takes rank amongst the highest and best. He is second only to Gilbert White, the delightful historian of Selborne."
NEW MONTHLY MAG.

Webb. — Celestial Objects for Common Telescopes. By the Rev. T. W. WEBB, M.A., F.R.A.S. With Woodcuts, and a large Map of the Moon. 16mo. 7s.

"IN this small but practical volume Mr. Webb has furnished an interesting and compact book of reference and a guide for amateur astronomers, which will be doubly acceptable in directing their attention instructively to the various theoretical views of the most advanced science by a few brief but clearly expressed statements, and in teaching how to use so delicate an instrument as the telescope successfully and accurately — how to observe and how to record. There is no attempt to supply the place of each compendiums as the *Nautical Almanack* or the various catalogues of the stars; although a large portion of the book is occupied with the objects to be seen on the moon, and the multitude of stars, double stars, clusters and nebulæ; the positions and descriptions of which are very fully detailed."
DAILY NEWS.

Webster and Parkes's Encyclopædia of Domestic Economy; comprising such subjects as are most immediately connected with Housekeeping. With nearly 1,000 Woodcuts. 8vo. price 50s.

Weld.—Two Months in the Highlands, Orcadia, and Skye. By CHARLES RICHARD WELD, Barrister-at-Law. With 4 coloured Illustrations and 4 Woodcuts. Post 8vo. price 12s. 6d.

Weld's Pyrenees, West and East; a Summer Holiday in 1858. With Illustrations from Drawings by the Author. Post 8vo. 12s. 6d.

Weld's Vacation Tour in the United States and Canada. Post 8vo. with Map, 10s. 6d.

Dr. Charles West's Lectures on the Diseases of Infancy and Childhood. *Fourth Edition,* carefully revised throughout ; with numerous additional Cases, and a copious INDEX. 8vo. 14s.

Dr. Charles West's How to Nurse Sick Children : intended especially as a Help to the Nurses at the Hospital for Sick Children ; but containing Directions which may be found of service to all who have the charge of the Young. *Second Edition.* Fcp. 8vo. price 1s. 6d.

White and Riddle.— A Latin-English Dictionary. By the Rev. J. T. WHITE, M.A. of Corpus Christi College, Oxford ; and the Rev. J. E. RIDDLE, M.A. of St. Edmund Hall, Oxford. Founded on the larger Dictionary by Freund, revised by himself. Royal 8vo. [*Nearly ready.*

Whiteside. — Italy in the Nineteenth Century. By the Right Hon. JAMES WHITESIDE, M.P., LL.D. *Third Edition,* abridged and revised ; with a new Preface chiefly on the Events which have occurred in Italy since 1848. Post 8vo. 12s. 6d.

Wilkins.—Political Ballads of the Seven- teenth and Eighteenth Centuries, annotated. By W. WALKER WILKINS. 2 vols. post 8vo. [*Just ready.*

THE admirable use made of our satirical literature by Lord MACAULAY in his *History of England* has suggested the publication of this unique collection of Political Ballads. Mr. Wilkins's two volumes comprise several characteristic specimens of the ballads published originally as broadsides between the years 1641 and 1760, namely from the great Rebellion in the reign of Charles the First to the death of George the Second. Independently of their value as literary curiosities, these ballads constitute the best popular illustrations of the history of the period, inasmuch as they exhibit not only the idiosyncracies of rulers and statesmen, but also an eventful stage in the gradual development of our social and political system. In reproducing them in their present form, the Editor has aimed at supplying a volume acceptable to the general reader : admitting no pieces of an objectionable nature, he has appended a brief introduction and explanatory footnotes to each ballad, as well as determining its date, and in many instances the name of its Author.

Willich's Popular Tables for ascertain- ing the Value of Lifehold, Leasehold, and Church Property, Renewal Fines, &c. ; the Public Funds ; Annual Average Price and Interest on Consols from 1731 to 1858 ; Chemical, Geographical, Astronomical, Trigonometrical Tables ; Common and Hyperbolic Logarithms ; Constants, Squares, Cubes, Roots, Reciprocals ; Diameter, Circumference, and Area of Circles ; Length of Chords and Circular Arcs ; Area and Diagonal of Squares ; Diameter, Solidity, and Superficies of Spheres ; Bank Discounts ; Bullion and Notes, 1844 to 1859. *Fourth Edition,* enlarged. Post 8vo. price 10s.

Wills. — "The Eagle's Nest" in the Valley of Sixt ; a Summer Home among the Alps : Together with some Excursions among the Great Glaciers. By ALFRED WILLS, of the Middle Temple, Esq., Barrister-at-Law. *Second Edition* ; with 2 Maps and 12 Illustrations drawn on Stono by Hanhart. Post 8vo. 12s. 6d.

Wilmot. — Lord Brougham's Law Re- forms ; or, an Analytical Review of Lord Brougham's Acts and Bills from 1811 to the Present Time. By Sir JOHN E. EARDLEY-WILMOT, Bart., Recorder of Warwick. Fcp. 8vo. 4s. 6d.

Wilmot's Abridgment of Blackstone's Com- mentaries on the Laws of England, intended for the use of Young Persons, and comprised in a series of Letters from a Father to his Daughter. 12mo. price 6s. 6d.

Wilson's Bryologia Britannica : Con- taining the Mosses of Great Britain and Ireland systematically arranged and described according to the Method of *Bruch* and *Schimper* ; with 61 Illustrative Plates. Being a New Edition, enlarged and altered, of the *Muscologia Britannica* of Messrs. Hooker and Taylor. 8vo. 42s. ; or, with the Plates coloured, price £4. 4s. cloth.

Yonge.—A New English-Greek Lexicon : Containing all the Greek Words used by Writers of good authority. By C. D. YONGE, B.A. *Second Edition,* revised and corrected. Post 4to. price 21s.

Yonge's New Latin Gradus : Containing Every Word used by the Poets of good authority. For the use of Eton, Westminster, Winchester, Harrow, Charterhouse, and Rugby Schools ; King's College, London ; and Marlborough College. *Sixth Edition.* Post 8vo. price 9s. ; or with APPENDIX of *Epithets* classified, 12s.

Youatt's Work on the Horse, comprising also a Treatise on Draught. With numerous Woodcut Illustrations, chiefly from Designs by W. Harvey. New Edition, revised and enlarged by E. N. GABRIEL, M.R.C.S., C.V.S., Secretary to the Royal College of Veterinary Surgeons. 8vo. price 10s. 6d.

Youatt. — The Dog. By William Youatt. A New Edition ; with numerous Engravings, from Designs by W. Harvey. 8vo. 6s.

Zumpt's Grammar of the Latin Lan- guage. Translated and adapted for the use of English Students by DR. L. SCHMITZ, F.R.S.E. : With numerous Additions and Corrections by the Author and Translator. 5th Edition, thoroughly revised. 8vo. 14s.

[*October* 1860.

www.ingramcontent.com/pod-product-compliance
Lightning Source LLC
Chambersburg PA
CBHW052346110726
47901CB00005B/1380